Praise for Carolyne Aarsen and her novels

"Carolyne Aarsen writes with tender empathy and a true understanding of the struggles her characters endure in *A Family-Style Christmas*."
—*RT Book Reviews*

"In this heartfelt story, Aarsen reminds us that life's challenges can be met and overcome by trusting in one's faith."
—*RT Book Reviews* on *The Cowboy's Lady*

"A warmhearted story of great sorrow and the healing and hope for the future God can supply."
—*RT Book Reviews* on *The Rancher's Return*

"An emotional story with a heroine who is in danger of making bad decisions out of love and a hero who discovers God's plans are always best."
—*RT Book Reviews* on *The Baby Promise*

CAROLYNE AARSEN
A Family-Style Christmas

❦

Yuletide Homecoming

Love Inspired

Recycling programs for this product may not exist in your area.

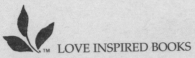 LOVE INSPIRED BOOKS

ISBN-13: 978-0-373-65157-3

A FAMILY-STYLE CHRISTMAS AND YULETIDE HOMECOMING
Copyright © 2012 by Harlequin Books S.A.

The publisher acknowledges the copyright holder of the individual works as follows:

A FAMILY-STYLE CHRISTMAS
Copyright © 2000 by Carolyne Aarsen

YULETIDE HOMECOMING
Copyright © 2007 by Carolyne Aarsen

www.LoveInspiredBooks.com

Printed in U.S.A.

CONTENTS

A FAMILY-STYLE CHRISTMAS   7

YULETIDE HOMECOMING   247

Books by Carolyne Aarsen

Love Inspired

†*A Family-Style Christmas*
 Yuletide Homecoming
 A Bride at Last
 The Cowboy's Bride
†*A Mother at Heart*
†*A Family at Last*
 A Hero for Kelsey
 Twin Blessings
 Toward Home
 Love Is Patient
 A Heart's Refuge
 Brought Together by Baby
 A Silence in the Heart
 Any Man of Mine
 Finally a Family
 A Family for Luke
 The Matchmaking Pact
 Close to Home
 Cattleman's Courtship
 Cowboy Daddy
 The Baby Promise
**The Rancher's Return*
 The Cowboy's Lady
*Daddy Lessons
**Healing the Doctor's Heart*
**Homecoming Reunion*

†Stealing Home
*Home to Hartley Creek

CAROLYNE AARSEN

and her husband, Richard, live on a small ranch in northern Alberta, where they have raised four children and numerous foster children, and are still raising cattle. Carolyne crafts her stories in an office with a large west-facing window through which she can watch the changing seasons while struggling to make her words obey.

A FAMILY-STYLE CHRISTMAS

As a mother comforts her child,
so I will comfort you.
—*Isaiah* 66:13

This book is dedicated to all foster parents,
official and unofficial. May God give you
the strength and love you need.

I owe a big thank-you to Anne Canadeo,
who has been an encouraging and inspiring editor
on my first four books. I also want to thank
my new editor, Ann Leslie Tuttle,
for her enthusiastic help on this series.

Besides the fact that my sister-in-law and good friend
are both nurses, I make no claim to being an expert
on nursing care. I had help in that department from
Corinne Aarsen, Diane Wierenga and Ruth McNulty.
Thank you as well to Steve Kondics, Hera Angelo
and Heather Toporowsky.

Prologue

"This is a fire-sale price, Simon, and you know it."

Simon Steele slipped his hands in the pockets of his leather jacket and lifted one shoulder in a shrug, negating the earnest comment from the real estate agent.

"Maybe," he drawled. "We both know the bank wants to dump this property, Blaine. Badly. The building needs major renovations to attract decent renters or owners." His quick glance took in the stained carpets and marked walls of the lobby before slanting the real estate agent a meaningful look and a smirk. "I'm prepared to offer thirty thousand less than the asking price. Firm." He ignored his partner, Oscar Delaney, who stood behind Blaine, shaking his head.

To his credit Blaine Nowicki never batted an eye. "Of course, I'll have to speak to my client on that and get back to you..."

"Phone them now and let's get this deal done," Simon interrupted, glancing at his watch. He didn't feel like playing out this fish any longer. He and Oscar had done their homework. They knew the situation at the bank and how long this particular apartment block had been on the market.

Long enough that Blaine's clients were willing to settle more quickly than he'd intimated.

"Simon, you're enough of a dealer to know that can't be done this quickly." Blaine fiddled with his tie as he favored Simon with an overly familiar smile that set Simon's teeth on edge. "This is a prime piece of property and worth far more than you're offering."

Simon held Blaine's determined gaze, his own features devoid of emotion. He lifted his hands, still in the pockets of his coat, signaling surrender. "Then, I'm history." He angled his chin in his partner's direction, "Let's go, Oscar. We've got a ferry to catch."

He turned and started walking away, measuring his tread so he looked like he was going quickly, yet giving Blaine enough time to protest before Simon hit the front doors of the lobby.

Oscar caught up to him, glancing sidelong at his partner with a frown. Simon gave him a warning shake of his head, then slowed fractionally as they approached the double doors.

For a moment he wondered if he had underestimated Blaine as he pulled his hand out of his pocket to grab the brass bar when…

"Wait," Blaine called out.

Simon allowed himself a moment of triumph, threw his partner an I-told-you-so glance, then forced the smirk off his face. When he turned to face Blaine, he was all business again.

"I'll call them right now," Blaine said, his cell phone in hand, his jacket flying open as he rushed over. "See what I can do for you." He punched in the numbers, frowning intently. Simon lifted his eyebrows at Oscar, who grinned back.

In ten minutes the papers were signed and Oscar and Simon were standing outside the building they had just purchased.

"I hope you know what you're doing," Oscar said as they stood outside on the pavement, shivering in the damp that had rolled in.

Simon looked back at the five-story apartment block behind them. The first-story walls were pitted and marked, covered with graffiti. A few of the sliding glass doors were boarded up, but the rest of the building was sound.

"When you get back from vacation, we'll get some quotes on renovations," Simon said, pulling his keys out of his pocket. "It's got a decent location. I'm sure once we get this thing fixed up, it will be full." He turned, squinting across the bay toward the hills of Vancouver Island now shrouded by the drizzle that had descended. He swung the keys around his finger. "It has a great view."

"When it's not raining," Oscar said, pulling his glasses off to clean them.

Simon grinned at his partner. "You sure you don't want to head south to the sun instead of camping with your wife's relatives? Why don't you come where I'm headed?"

"Right," Oscar said dryly, replacing his glasses. "I can see us already. Two overgrown teenagers on motorbikes heading down to the Baja." He pulled his coat closer, giving another shiver, moisture beading up on his dark blond hair. "Someone's got to be the mature, responsible one in this partnership."

Simon pulled a face. "Please, no bad language," he said with a laugh.

Oscar looked back at the apartment block. "You know, one of these days you should buy yourself a house instead of old apartment blocks and new businesses." He looked back at Simon, his expression serious.

"And start a family. Why not?" Simon flipped his keys once more, his tone sardonic. "One of those nice cozy groups of people you see on television commercials selling long-distance phone plans."

"Being on your own is no picnic," Oscar said as they headed toward a nearly deserted parking lot.

Simon stopped beside his bike and zipped up his leather coat with a decisive movement. "It's a whole lot easier than trying to work around other people's needs."

"Mr. Free Spirit personified," said Oscar with a rueful shake of his head. "One of these days you're going to get too old to keep running. Then you'll be panting and wheezing, wishing you had taken my advice and bought a nice house, found a nice girl and settled down."

"There is no such thing as a nice girl."

"Oh, c'mon. You just don't know where to look."

Simon pulled his helmet off his motorbike and dropped it on his head. "I suppose I could head out to your church. Scope out the girls there."

"Wouldn't hurt you to go once in a while anyhow." Oscar shivered again. "I gotta go. I've got a few things to do at the office before Angela and I leave town. She told her folks we'd be there before supper."

"See what I mean?" Simon said, buckling up his helmet. "Family means schedule, expectations. Watch the clock. Stifling routine."

Oscar just looked at him, and Simon felt a flicker of reproach in his partner's gaze.

"Family means people who care, too, Simon," Oscar said quietly. Simon looked away, snapping the top snap of his jacket, pulling on his gloves.

"Can't speak from personal experience on that," he said, forcing a light tone into his voice. He looked up at Oscar and shrugged the comment away. "I'll see you in a couple of weeks."

"Take care of yourself," Oscar said, hesitating as if he would have liked to say more. Then he got in his vehicle and left.

Simon watched him go, his shoulders lifting in a sigh. He and Oscar had been partners for three years now. Oscar was a discreet sort of guy. He didn't pry, didn't ask a lot of questions and didn't intrude on Simon's personal life. Which is just what Simon wanted in a partner.

Simon liked things to be businesslike and at an arm's length distance from him. It made things a lot easier that way. The less people knew about you, the less of a hold they had over you. Strict access to information, he reminded himself as he pulled his leather pants over his now-damp jeans. That's what made his and Oscar's partnership work so well. Oscar only knew what he needed to know about Simon that pertained to how their partnership worked and vice versa.

Starting his bike, Simon turned onto the Island Highway and settled into a safe speed. He still had lots of time and would probably beat Oscar to the ferry.

As he drove his mind went back to his conversation with Oscar. He wished Oscar would lay off the broad hints about settling down. It was like an obsession with him.

Four years ago he and Oscar had met in a bar, had formed their loosely based partnership on the basis of a shared interest in the stock market and real estate.

Then Oscar got married, got religion and was now the sickeningly proud father of a little girl. Like a reformed smoker he was on Simon's case to follow suit.

Something Simon had no intention of doing. Oscar might look happy now, but people always let you down. That much Simon knew from personal experience.

And the many foster homes he'd been in after his mother had given him and his brother up for adoption when he was four. As far as he knew he had no other family. For a brief while, they had a loving father, Tom Steele—a widower who adopted them. When he died, he and Jake were moved, then moved again and finally split up.

Now Simon had no one.

He cut in front of a car and wove through the traffic, pushing the memories back into the recesses of his mind where they belonged. Living in the past did nothing for the present. And for the present, he was doing quite well, thank you very much. He and Oscar had a good business going. They made enough money that they could both take vacations when it suited them. And he could do pretty much as he pleased.

Yes, Simon thought as he gave the throttle another twist, he was doing very well indeed.

Chapter One

Heartbreak must be a regular occurrence here, Caitlin Severn thought, ignoring the elegantly dressed people in the hotel lobby who were politely ignoring her. She would have liked to walk through the lobby with her head up, but she couldn't. Her eyes prickled with unshed tears, and her nose was starting to run. It always did when she cried. She gave her eyes a careful wipe, and walked down the few steps toward the entrance.

When she got there, she stopped.

Perfect, she thought, staring out at the moisture dripping down the glass door. Her life was becoming more like a bad movie script with each passing moment. This unexpected drizzle was a dramatic touch. All she was missing was a soaring soundtrack.

She hugged herself, glancing over her shoulder as if hoping that by doing so, Charles would come running up to her, pleading with her to change her mind. But he didn't.

The world carried on. Clichéd, but true. Nothing had stopped just because her own world had been rearranged.

Just ten minutes ago she had broken up with Charles Frost. Again. When Charles had made this date he'd said he had some special news. They'd been dating for three years, and she foolishly thought he was going to propose. Instead he told her about his promotion and subsequent move to Los Angeles.

In the moment when he lifted his glass of wine to her to toast his success, Caitlin was faced with something she knew she'd been avoiding.

Charles's career would always come before her.

Caitlin knew that this was not how she wanted to live her life.

So with a few succinct words, she broke up with him.

Caitlin took a step closer to the front doors and was grateful to see a row of cabs. With a last glance over her shoulder, she stepped out into the early evening drizzle.

She walked down the sidewalk, her high heels clicking on the wet pavement, moisture beading up on the fine fabric of the short, fitted dress she had chosen so carefully for this date and the "important news" Charles had to tell her.

Important to him, she thought with another sniff.

She hailed the first cab, then got in. She gave him

quick directions to her home, then sat back, shivering with a combination of cold and reaction, thankful she had an escape.

As the driver pulled away from the front of the restaurant, she felt the first sob climb up her throat. She covered her mouth with her fist, but the hoarse cry slipped past her clenched hand into the quiet confines of the cab. One more got past her guard before Caitlin regained control. The cabbie didn't even look back.

She wouldn't cry, she thought as she defiantly swiped at her cheeks.

But Caitlin knew it was more than her breakup with Charles she grieved.

She watched out the window vaguely noting the buildings flowing by. She had lived in Nanaimo in Vancouver Island all her life and had never moved. It seemed as if her life had flowed along the same lines for the past twenty-eight years.

Twenty-eight and single again. Tonight, after their supper, she and Charles were to have gone to stay with his parents at their cabin on Pender Island for ten days.

And now...

Caitlin sighed. She wished she could skip the next few days and head back to work right away. The comforting steadiness of her work at the hospital would have taken her through the week, would have helped her get over the pain she felt. Now she didn't even have that.

Thankfully the driver was silent. The tires of the cab hissed over the wet pavement as a lethargy came over her. Reaction, she thought remembering all too easily the sight of Charles's impassive face as she delivered her ultimatum.

He just didn't care.

The entire evening stretched ahead of her, and she didn't feel like going home. She knew what would be waiting there. Her dear parents sitting in their usual chairs, drinking tea. Her sister Rachel would be curled up with her husband, Jonathon, on the couch, reading while soft music played on the stereo. Rachel, who had just told their parents she was expecting.

Caitlin had been jealous.

Caitlin shook her head at that thought. She was unable to put her finger precisely on why. It had much to do with the malaise she felt before she broke up with Charles. That her life was following the same path without any variation. She had the job she had trained for. She loved her work. But she still wanted someone in her life. Someone who needed her. She wanted to start her own family.

A blast from a motorcycle passing them made her jump. It zoomed ahead then slowed as the cab caught up. Puzzled, she watched, wondering what the motorcycle driver was doing. She found out as soon as the cab came up beside him again. In the bright streetlights, she saw the driver look sideways and, with a cheeky grin, wink at her.

Caitlin only stared back as he kept pace, still looking at her. He didn't look like anyone she would know. His well-shaped mouth had an insolent twist to it, his eyes shaded by his helmet seemed to laugh at her. Not her type.

Then he tossed a wave in her direction and with a twist of his wrist and a flick of his foot, was off again.

Caitlin shook her head at his audacity, watching as he wove expertly around the cab and the vehicle slightly ahead of them. Then a car swerved unexpectedly.

She heard a sickening *thud* as the car hit the biker. The bike wove once, then dropped, spinning in one direction while the driver shot off in another.

The cab driver slammed on the brakes and swerved to miss the driver.

"Stop," yelled Caitlin, leaning over the seat. "I'm a nurse. Stop."

The cabbie screeched to a halt twenty feet away from the driver, who now lay in a crumpled heap on the side of the road.

The car that caused the accident slowed, then sped away.

Caitlin's breath left her in a swoosh, her hands shaking as she fumbled for the catch on the door. Finally she pushed it open and shot out of the cab. She ran to the driver who was moaning softly.

"Thank you, Lord," she breathed at the sound. He was still alive.

Ignoring the expensive hose bought for this, her special night, the drizzle dripping down her neck, she dropped onto the wet pavement.

The cabbie came up behind her. "I called an ambulance, and the police," he said.

"Get me something to cover him with," she called out, as she automatically did her own assessment of the situation, drawing on her limited experience with emergencies. The man had a pulse, was breathing, albeit shallowly, and blood from a head injury ran in an ugly rivulet down his forehead. His leg was twisted at a grotesque angle. His leather coat was ripped.

Possible broken femur and spine injury, Caitlin thought, noting the angle of his leg. He was in big trouble. She knelt close to keep him from moving, her finger on his pulse as she counted and prayed.

The cab driver came back with an overcoat. "This is the best I could do. I got a first-aid kit, too."

Caitlin opened the kit as he spread the coat over the prone man. Right about now she regretted not having had more emergency training. In her ward at the hospital, she only got the patients from the operating room or emergency. All the critical care had been done by either paramedics or emergency room nurses.

Caitlin willed the ambulance to come, praying as she dug through the kit for a bandage to stop the bleeding from the most serious cut on his head. Her sore knees trembled with tension, she almost shivered in the damp weather, but she was afraid to shift position.

The man at her feet moaned, tried to roll over but was stopped by Caitlin's knees. He cried out, and his eyes flew open, staring straight up at Caitlin. "Hey, angel, you found me," he murmured, then his face twisted in pain.

Caitlin felt relief sluice through her in an icy wave even as she steeled herself against the sounds of his pain. Thankfully he was conscious. That meant no major head injury other than the cut on his temple. She carefully laid the pad on his head wound, applying pressure. "Can you feel your hands, your feet?"

"Yeah." She could tell that even that one word was an effort. "Feel too much."

"What's your name?"

"Doesn't matter…" He bit his lip. "Please stay."

"Are you allergic to anything?"

"No." He blinked, looking up at her, then arched his back and cried out again, grabbing her hand.

Caitlin winced at his strength. "Can you tell me where it hurts the most?"

"Everywhere." His words were slurred, and Caitlin feared he would lose consciousness after all.

"What's your name?" she repeated.

"You're a pain," he mumbled, still clinging to her hand. "Everything's a pain." He squeezed her hand, hard, moaning. "Who are you, angel?"

"I'm Caitlin. Tell me your name. Stay with me."

But though his hand clung tightly, he wouldn't answer.

"Please, Lord, keep him with us," she prayed aloud. "Keep him safe, help him. Please send that ambulance, now."

She watched him as she prayed. His eyes were shut, his lashes lying in dark spikes against his high cheekbones. His hair hung over his forehead, some of the strands caught in the trickle of blood from the wound on his forehead, curling in the damp.

He looked to be in his late twenties, well built, she reasoned from the weight of his body against her legs, the breadth of his shoulders. It made his vulnerability all the more heart-wrenching. Caitlin wanted to check his pulse, but his hand still held hers in a death grip.

"Can I do anything?" The cab driver hovered over her.

Caitlin glanced over her shoulder, feeling utterly helpless.

"Pray the ambulance comes quickly," she said, shivering with reaction. The wind had picked up, chilling her.

In her peripheral vision she saw a few people coming out of their houses, some offering help. Someone even dropped a coat across her shoulders.

The victim's hand still clutched hers. Thankfully the flow of blood from his forehead eased, and Caitlin could put her finger on his pulse. It was weak, but then his grip loosened and his pulse slowed. Her prayers became more urgent as his eyes remained closed and beneath her trembling fingers she felt his life ebb away.

"Please, Lord, don't let him go. He's so young," she whispered, watching him. Nothing.

His breathing slowed.

Caitlin lifted his hand, clasped it against hers, her other hand still on his nonexistent pulse. *Please don't take him.*

Then, suddenly, his pulse returned, his hand tightened on hers.

His eyes fluttered open.

"You're still praying," he gasped.

"Yes, I am," Caitlin replied, relief turning her bones to rubber. He was still with her, he was still alive. "Thank you, Lord," she breathed.

She knew it wasn't over yet. His broken femur and the accompanying loss of blood were life threatening.

But she was reassured by the solid answer she received—a touch of God's hand on the situation.

"You're wasting your time praying," he said, his teeth clenched against the pain.

"No, I'm not," Caitlin whispered, shaky with reaction.

Then came the welcome wail of an ambulance's sirens and its blue and red lights, flashing through the gathering dusk.

"What happened?" A paramedic ran up to Caitlin

while the driver jumped out and pulled the stretcher out of the back.

"Motorcycle accident." As relief weakened her legs, she forced herself to stay calm, to be the professional nurse she was, relating what she had seen of the accident and how she'd treated his injuries. The police could deal with the driver of the car. She was more concerned about her patient. As the older of the paramedics immediately positioned himself at the victim's head, stabilizing it, she said, "I'm a nurse so tell me what to do."

"Just step back for now, ma'am."

She quickly got up and out of the way, her knees aching. She drew the stranger's coat around her, shivering against the chill wind.

The paramedic at the victim's head had his knees on either side, stabilizing him as he checked his breathing, the pulse at his throat. "Give me O2, ten liters, non-rebreather," he called out to his partner as he lifted the victim's eyelids.

"He's conscious. Superficial head injury," the young paramedic said as he started an IV.

"I need a C collar, large."

"Spine seems okay, no internal injuries so far. Fracture of right femur. Both arms, okay. Possible sprain."

"Got the fracture stabilized."

"Let's get him on the board."

The older paramedic at his head looked up at Caitlin. "We'll need your help, now, ma'am."

She nodded, and positioned herself. "Watch for that fracture," she couldn't help saying.

"On three." They rolled him onto the board, the paramedic still holding his head. With quick, efficient movements they had the victim strapped in, stabilizing him. Someone handed her her purse while she watched. The paramedics placed foam on either side of his head, taped the foam in, strapped the spine board on the stretcher and slid him into the ambulance, headfirst. It was all done with a calm efficiency that drew Caitlin along, comforting her. Routine she understood. What she didn't understand was her reluctance to let this man go.

"I'm coming," Caitlin decided suddenly. She handed the coat to someone and scooted into the ambulance before it sped away.

Caitlin's head ached in the overly bright lights of the ambulance's interior as she braced herself against the movement. She sat down on the long bench beside the stretcher. Vaguely she heard the driver on the radio, "Patch me into the hospital…"

Caitlin felt as if her breath still had to catch up to her.

The older paramedic switched the oxygen to a fixture in the wall of the ambulance.

"What can I do?" she asked, reaction setting in. She was a nurse, and she needed to be busy.

"Here's a blood pressure cuff and stethoscope. Get me a set of vitals." He smiled at her as he handed her the equipment. "I'm Stan."

"I'm Caitlin." She unrolled the cuff and stuck the stethoscope in her ears.

"Hey, guy, you with me?" Stan asked the victim while he did a head-to-toe check again, opening the patient's leather jacket and his shirt to check his chest and stomach. "What's his name?" he asked Caitlin, as he worked.

"I don't know." Caitlin looked up at Stan, then down at the patient. His face was hidden by the oxygen mask, his eyes shut. His skin had a waxy pallor that concerned her.

The driver called back, "Is he awake?"

"Yes, but poor response. He's a little shocky," said Stan, as he steadied himself in the moving ambulance.

"Vitals are b.p. 118 on 76, pulse 116, respirations 24," Caitlin told him, pulling the stethoscope out of her ears.

Stan nodded as he pressed on the patient's sternum. The ambulance swayed around a corner and then with a short wail of sirens, came to a stop.

"Let's go, Caitlin," Stan said as he pulled a blanket over the patient. The door swung open, and Caitlin grabbed the coat and purse, exiting with the stretcher into a murmur of voices.

She strode alongside the stretcher as they entered the warmth and light of the hospital, watching the unknown man. His eyes flickered open, looked wildly around.

Caitlin lightly touched his face and he homed in

on her. He blinked, and through the oxygen mask she saw his lips move. He lifted his hand toward her, then with a grimace of pain, faded away again.

Stan gave the triage nurse and doctor a quick run-down of what he knew and what they had done.

"Put him in the trauma room," she said and Caitlin stood back while they wheeled the stranger down the hall and away from her.

It was over, but she still couldn't walk away.

Caitlin felt the noise and heat press in on her aching head. For a brief moment, she felt all alone in a room full of people caught up in their own pains and sorrows.

She found an empty chair and sat on the edge, bunching her purse on her lap. Unbelievably the delicate shawl was still wound around her shoulder but her nylons sported a large hole in one knee, she noted with a disoriented feeling.

As an orthopedic nurse she rarely saw death. When she did, it was in a hospital setting where there was immediate help. Routine. What she had seen tonight was raw and powerful—a potent reminder of how fragile life was.

She heard a measured tread and looked up as the paramedic named Stan stood in front of her.

"Caitlin, you okay?"

"Yeah, I'm fine." She smiled weakly up at him, surprised he remembered her name. "How is he?"

"They've got him stabilized. They're going to get

him into O.R. right away. He's been asking for you by name. Do you know him?"

"No. I gave my name when I was trying to find out about him." Caitlin frowned, surprised this man who must be in a tremendous amount of pain would remember her. "Can I see him?"

"He's headed for the operation room. But if you wait, you might catch a glimpse of him as he's wheeled by."

Caitlin got up, her knees still trembling. She followed Stan down the hallway, her shoes clicking loudly on the floor. "Just wait here," he said. "I've got to go now. Take care, Caitlin."

Nodding, Caitlin waited until the curtain on the cubicle was pushed aside and the stretcher wheeled out.

Caitlin caught up to the stretcher, walking quickly alongside it.

"Are you Caitlin?" the nurse pushing the stretcher asked.

"Yes," Caitlin replied quietly, looking down at the stranger, his face still obscured by the oxygen mask. His eyes were open, focused intently on her, his hair still matted with blood. Caitlin couldn't stop staring at him. His high cheekbones and full mouth gave his features a fascinating appeal.

He reached out for her and once again, Caitlin caught his hand. "You'll be okay," she said as they hurried down the hallway. "I'll be praying for you. You're in good hands."

"I am now," he said, his voice muffled by the oxygen mask, his hand squeezing hers.

Chapter Two

This is ridiculous, Caitlin thought as she strode down the hallway to her own unit. You don't know anything about that motorcycle victim. He's not your concern. For the past two hours she had wandered around the emergency department then gone for coffee. It was now nine-thirty, and she'd decided to see this through to the end and go up to the ward where the unknown man would be taken after surgery.

It was the best way she knew of avoiding home and facing the questions of her family when she showed up there. It seemed the only logical thing to do.

Sort of logical, she thought, ignoring her self-doubts over this impulsive, un-Caitlin-like behavior.

She approached the desk of the ward she had been working at since she graduated from nursing school. It was as familiar to her as her own street.

And so was the face of the nurse at the desk.

"Hey, Caitlin, what are you doing here?" Danielle asked, leaning her elbows on the desk, fully prepared to chat. "Thought you and Charles had a date?"

"We did. I cut it short." She knew she had taken a chance coming up here instead of going home. Danielle Jones and Caitlin had been friends since nursing school. Danielle knew all Caitlin's secrets. But coming to her ward seemed the less painful of two evils. "You busy?"

"Steady. Got a guy coming up from O.R. in a while. Motorcycle accident."

Caitlin felt a guilty flush climb up her cheeks. "I know," she said. "I saw it happen."

Danielle frowned, shaking her head. "That must have been horrible. That why you cut your date with Charles short?" She glanced over Caitlin's dress. "By the way you look gorgeous, sweetie. That bronze dress sets off your blond hair just perfectly."

"Thanks," Caitlin said, ignoring her first question. She walked around the desk, glancing at the assignment board. "Mrs. Johnson's been discharged over the weekend?"

"She had a miraculous recovery when her reluctant daughter said she would come to the house to help." Danielle picked up a pen, made a few more notes on a chart then looked back up at Caitlin. "So, how is the very handsome Charles Frost?"

Caitlin felt a pain clutch her chest at the mention of her boyfriend's name. Ex-boyfriend she reminded herself. "He got a promotion," she murmured, flipping through some papers on the desk, deliberately avoiding the reality of what she had done.

"Wow, you must be pleased."

"As punch." Caitlin stopped her pointless fiddling.

"You don't sound pleased." Danielle tapped the pencil on the desk. "Sit down. I've got time."

Caitlin was just about to say no, but Danielle looked concerned and she needed a sympathetic ear. Who better than her best friend? So she sat down, unwinding her shawl from her neck.

Danielle reached over and laid a gentle hand on her friend's shoulder. "What's wrong, Caitlin?"

She opted for the direct approach and told her the day's events.

"I broke up with Charles tonight," she said, her tone deliberate.

"What?"

"He said he had good news." Caitlin plowed on, ignoring Danielle's expression of utter surprise. "Unfortunately like an optimistic idiot, I thought he meant…" Her voice trailed off as she took a quick breath, embarrassed.

"He was going to propose." Danielle finished off the sentence.

"I should have known," Caitlin said angrily, crushing the scarf on her lap. She loosed it, carefully smoothing it out again, glancing up at her friend. "The past few months we've been drifting apart, but I kept hoping things would change for both of us," she said with a wry laugh.

"Well, then, it's a good thing you broke up with him. If I find out in a couple of dates this isn't the kind of guy I want to spend the rest of my life with, *phwwt*..." Danielle made a dismissive gesture with one hand. "Out he goes. Companionship I can get from my friends and pets. Hanging on is a waste of time."

And how much time had she wasted, Caitlin thought, considering the three years of dating Charles.

"I thought Charles and I were headed in that direction, but I guessed wrong." Caitlin shook her head, winding the scarf around her hands. "Can you believe I was that dumb?" She clenched her fists, shaking her head.

"Well, at the risk of sounding like a cliché, I'm sure you'll get over it. I mean Charles is a nice guy, he's good-looking, he's ambitious, but..." Danielle lifted her hands as if in surrender. "I just don't sense a real spark between you two."

Caitlin said nothing at that, knowing that, as usual, her friend had put her finger directly on Caitlin's own malaise concerning the relationship.

Before she could formulate an answer, the recovery room called to say they were sending up the accident victim.

Caitlin glanced at the clock. There was no avoiding it, she had to go home sooner or later. "Well, I'm history," she said, winding the scarf around her shoulders and picking up her purse.

"I should make sure the room is ready for our new admission," Danielle conceded, getting up. "Will I see you before you fly down to visit your sister Evelyn and her new baby?"

Caitlin nodded, wondering how she'd fill the ten days before she left for Portland. "Yeah. I'll need something to do besides sit and watch my mother eagerly knitting baby booties. Rachel's expecting, too!"

Danielle touched her arm as if sensing Caitlin's yearning for her own family. "You want me to call a cab?"

"I'll get one myself. Thanks." Caitlin smiled at her friend. Danielle gave her a quick hug and then left.

Caitlin sighed lightly, and turned to go. But when the elevator door swooshed open, a stretcher was wheeled into the ward. The motorcyclist.

Caitlin stopped beside the stretcher, taking another look at the patient lying there. A fine net held his hair back, exposing his strong features. A dressing covered the gash on his forehead.

The patient moaned once, his eyes fluttered open and homed in on hers. He blinked, tried to lift his head and then closed his eyes again.

But once again his hand reached out toward her and once again, Caitlin took a step closer and took it in hers. He squeezed it lightly. "Angel," he whispered, the word coming out in a sigh. "Don't go."

And Caitlin knew she was staying.

Someone was talking to him. The words came slowly, echoing down a long, dark corridor. Simon tried to catch them but he couldn't move, couldn't focus on what the voice said.

More words and sounds coming closer, sharper. Then, finally, "He's coming around." The words pierced the haze of darkness holding him captive.

"Can you hear me?" the voice continued.

Why was it so much work to talk, to do something as simple as lift his eyelids?

He struggled and as awareness dawned so did the pain. It pressed down on him, heavy, overwhelming, taking over his slowly awakening senses.

He moaned, the sound forced out of him by the extent of an agony he couldn't pinpoint. Where was he?

He tried to focus, to comprehend. It was so much work. A face swam into his vision and he strained to see it better. He blinked hard, willing his eyes to function.

Finally the blurred edges coalesced. He recognized his angel of mercy, her soft green eyes like a refreshing drink.

He called out as he closed his eyes, fighting a fresh wave of pain. Cool fingers slipped through his. With another effort, he clung to her as if to a lifeline.

More movement as he felt himself being lifted, then a surge of pain.

He dug his head back into the pillow as he rode it out. It slowly eased, but he kept his eyes shut as he breathed through the last bit.

"Where are you?" he panted. "Angel."

"I'm here." She touched his face lightly. "Just try

to rest now," she said, fussing over the blanket, tucking it around his chest. She straightened, pulled up a chair and sat down beside him.

He felt himself drifting off again. He didn't want to go, didn't like the feeling but couldn't stop it.

Unaware of how much time had passed, he felt himself drifting, heard voices far away.

Then increasing agony pulled him up into awareness. He fought it, preferring the blessed relief of the darkness, the not knowing to the perception of deep aching overlaid with sharp pain.

"Hi, there." A soft voice beside him made him turn his head toward the gentle sound. "How are you doing?"

He forced his eyes open and there she was again. The face he'd been seeing since this all started. Every time he opened his eyes, she was there.

A name drifted out of another part of his memory, attaching itself to her serene beauty. Caitlin.

"It hurts," was all he could say when he wanted to say so much more. *Who are you? Why are you always here?*

"Do you want something for the pain?" she asked, leaning forward. Her hand was a light touch on his forehead, a connection with reality.

"Please," he gasped. Anything to escape this agony, he thought at the same time resenting his vulnerability. He closed his eyes, searching for some bit of memory to explain what had happened to him.

The only thing he could remember was seeing her again and again.

Then he felt that same gentling hand at the back of his neck. "Here," she said quietly. "Open your mouth." He obeyed and she placed something on his tongue. He opened his eyes again, seeking hers as she held a cup of tepid water to his lips. He swallowed, thankful for the moisture, then lay back, watching as she set the cup on the table and sat down again.

"What's your name?" she asked, leaning forward, taking his hand in hers.

"Why do you want to know?" he mumbled, pain pressing his eyes closed.

"So I know who I'm praying for," she said quietly, squeezing his hand lightly.

"Waste of time," he said.

"Please. I want to know who you are."

Light from the hallway, muted by the curtain around him shone on her delicate features. What was she doing here and why did she want to know his name?

The questions grew fuzzy, his need to find answers receding as the pill took effect.

She squeezed his hand again. "Don't drift off on me without telling me your name."

He sensed she wasn't going to stop. He didn't like the frustration that edged her voice and decided, reluctantly, to grant her request. "My name is Simon."

That made her smile and he was glad.

"Thanks for being here," he said, squeezing her

hand back. Then blessed unconsciousness brought him ease.

Again, he was unaware of the passage of time, aware only that each time he came up from the darkness, she was there, offering what comfort she could.

Once he woke to find her sleeping, her head pillowed on the bed, her face buried in her arms. The room was dark. He felt unaccountably bereft, alone. He didn't want to disturb her, but felt an urgent need to connect, to touch.

Her hair lay in tangled disarray close to his hand. He reached out and touched it, marveling at its softness, wondering again who she was and why she had stayed with him.

But his mind didn't have much room for wondering. It was taken up by a throbbing ache in his legs, arms, chest.

"Caitlin," he whispered, then he drifted off again.

Chapter Three

Caitlin didn't want to think what she was doing here. One o'clock in the morning was no time to figure out where else to go.

A moan from the bed made her turn. She'd only meant to catch a few winks when she laid her head on the bed, but had, instead, slept a couple of hours. She got up, the floor cool under her feet.

"Caitlin." Simon's voice was a harsh whisper. "My throat's sore."

It still gave her a start to hear him speak her name. She turned to see him looking at her, his eyes glinting in the refracted light coming from outside. For a moment she held his gaze, wondering again why she stayed, why he seemed to want her with him.

With a shake of her head she dismissed the thoughts. Walking to his side, she poured him some water, lifted his head and let him take a drink. He swallowed with difficulty and then laid his head back. "Your throat is sore from a tube that gets put down your throat during surgery," she explained. "Your chest will be sore, too."

"What happened to me?"

Caitlin relived the shock of the accident. She had been so close to it all.

"Caitlin?" he asked again. "Tell me."

"You were in a motorbike accident. You've sustained some very serious injuries."

"How serious?" he asked, closing his eyes and drawing in a breath.

"You've a fractured femur, a bruised pelvis and bruises that I'm sure you're beginning to feel."

"How did it happen?"

"I didn't see all of it. A car hit you, and your bike went down on top of you." She took a slow, deep breath, seeing the accident again. She'd explained what happened to other patients many times before, but never had the picture of the events been so indelibly printed in her mind. Never had she seen a cocky smile replaced by a grimace of pain, a man full of self-confidence in one moment, thrown like a rag doll across the pavement in the next. She wondered if she would ever forget it.

"You helped me."

Caitlin laughed a short laugh. "I did very little."

"You stopped." He turned his head, his hand reaching out to her. Caitlin wanted to pretend she didn't see it. Wanted to break the tenuous connection they had developed by her being by his side.

One look at his eyes narrowed with pain, the lines along his full mouth and she couldn't stop herself from placing her hand in his. "You're here now," he said, his voice hoarse as he tightly grasped her hand. "Why?"

Because I don't know where else to go right now? Because, unlike my ex-boyfriend, you needed me?

But as she looked at him, she knew it was more.

Caitlin kept her replies to herself and only squeezed his hand a little harder. "Doesn't matter. Just try to rest."

He took a slow breath, his eyes drifting shut. "Stay with me a little longer, Caitlin?"

"I'll be here," she said softly. "Now, don't talk anymore."

He lifted one corner of his mouth. A careful smile. Then she felt his fingers loosen their grip on hers but not enough to let go.

With a sigh, she pulled the chair up closer and tried to get some more sleep.

Caitlin woke a few hours later, blinking in the brightness of the room. The curtains behind her only muted the morning light pouring in over her shoulder.

Her one arm was asleep, her hand still anchored in Simon's. Carefully, she pulled it free. His fingers fluttered a moment as if seeking hers, and Caitlin thought he would waken.

But he slept on, his breathing heavy.

Caitlin stretched her hand in front of her, wincing at the harsh prickling. She yawned and pulled a face at the stale taste in her mouth.

She got up, grabbing the arm of the chair as her one leg gave way under her. She had slept in an awkward position, her arms on the bed.

Sometime in the night she had kicked off her shoes. She saw one beside the chair, the other had been pushed under the bed.

Her stomach was empty, a grim reminder of her missed supper last night. Her neck was stiff, her shoulders sore and her mouth felt fuzzy.

Last night she had been angry and her impetuous decision to come here wasn't made with a rational mind and now she was paying for it.

She bit back a sigh as the events of last night came back with the cold clarity that accompanies the sharp light of morning.

Charles and she had broken up, and this time she knew it was for good. She knew she didn't want to go back to the half limbo that had been their relationship the past while.

Caitlin glanced at Simon. His face was drawn, his hair was caked with blood at the temple. The sight of him reaching out to her, pleading for her to stay had struck the very spot Charles had wounded with his lack of caring. This man, this total stranger, made her feel needed, and after last night it was what drew her toward him.

But now, it was morning. The night was over and she had to get home and...

Caitlin bit her lip, thinking of telling her parents and her sister. Her family who all thought the world of Charles and who wanted so badly for Charles and Caitlin to come to a stronger commitment. Her family to whom finding someone and marrying was the natural progression of events. Her older sister was married and had just had her third child. Her younger sister was married and expecting her first. Even her unreliable brother was married, living off in the east who knew where.

But he's married, Caitlin thought wryly. *And I'm not.*

She glanced again at the man on the bed. He'd had a restless night and Danielle was thankful for Caitlin's presence. They had two more admissions and were running off their feet.

After her brief nap she'd given him his pain medication, adjusted his leg, keeping it elevated to avoid blood clots. She tried to talk to him when he was lucid, tried to ask him questions about his relatives, his family. They would need to be notified. But he'd said nothing.

There had to be someone who would need to know about him, she figured. Parents, brother, sister. Maybe a girlfriend?

"What do you care?" Caitlin admonished herself, reaching down and pulling her other shoe out from under the bed. "You won't be back here." She

slipped her shoes on, thinking of her much anticipated vacation.

"And what are you going to do about that?" she
asked herself, stretching once again.

She glanced at her watch, groaning at the time.
Six o'clock in the morning. Her parents would still
be sleeping, and she badly wanted to change.

"Hi there."

Caitlin turned at the sound of the sleep-rough-
ened voice. Simon was watching her, and she wondered how long he had been awake, listening to her
babble to herself.

"Hi, yourself," she said, crossing her arms across
her stomach as she walked to the side of the bed. He
looked pale, his eyes still dull with pain. "How are
you doing?"

"Horrible. I feel like I've been hit by a train." He
tried to lick his lips. "My mouth feels like I've been
on an all-nighter."

"In a way, you have," Caitlin replied. "Want some
ice water?"

"Sounds wonderful," his voice drifted off on the
last syllable and Caitlin guessed he was in pain again.

"Do you want some painkillers with that?"

"I don't know," he whispered, his teeth clenched.
"I hate the way they make me feel."

"I'm sure it can't be worse than the way that plate
in your leg makes you feel?"

"What?" Simon blinked, tried to raise his head

and then fell back with a grimace. "What are you talking about?"

"Drink first," she ordered, raising his head and placing the cup against his lips.

He took a long drink and then lay back. "Now tell me," he demanded.

"Do you remember what I told you about the accident?"

He nodded.

"They had to fix the fracture with a metal plate and screws. The surgeon will be doing his rounds later on and he can tell you exactly what he did to your leg."

"Where's my bike?"

"That I can't tell you. We'll be in contact with the police later on. They can let us know where it is and how badly it was damaged."

"What about the other guy?"

"The one who hit you?"

Simon only nodded, his eyes shut again.

"It was hit-and-run. Like I said, I saw it, but didn't get a clear view of the license plate. I'll have to tell the police what I know, and I'm sorry I can't tell you more."

Simon opened his eyes, zeroing in on her. "Why did you stay with me all night?"

Caitlin pulled her hand back, feeling the impact of his direct gaze. She still wasn't able to analyze why she had done it. "I saw the accident. I came with you in the ambulance. I stayed because the night staff was running off their feet...."

"Thanks," he whispered, his perfectly shaped mouth curving up in a smile. He closed his eyes again and was gone.

Caitlin drew in a shaky breath, trying to dispel the odd feeling his smile gave her. A feeling much different from any that Charles's smiles had created.

Rebound, she reminded herself with disgust. That and the ego-building feeling of being wanted by a man she knew had an earthy appeal most women would notice.

"So you can't leave earlier for Evelyn's place, what else are you going to do?" Rachel bent over and picked up a rock, angling her hand. With a flick of her wrist she tossed it out, and it skipped across the quiet water of Piper's Lagoon.

"I don't know. I sure don't feel like hanging around Nanaimo for ten days, but I don't have the energy to make other plans." Caitlin shoved her hands deeper into the pockets of her jean jacket, her feet scuffing through the shale and rock of the beach, retracing steps they had taken so often in their youth.

Caitlin needed to get out and away from her mother's sympathetic glances, her sorrowing looks. Her mother really liked Charles and had so hoped he would someday be her son-in-law.

Well, those hopes were dashed as surely as the shells she was even now crunching under her feet.

"Maybe you should go away. Take a trip with all that money you've got saved up."

"I don't know where I'd want to go. And I don't feel like traveling alone."

"Yeah, I know what you mean." Rachel slipped her arm around her sister's waist. "I just don't like seeing you like this, so lost and forlorn."

"I'm not forlorn," Caitlin said with a note of disgust in her voice. "I'm probably more ticked than anything. Going back to him and then breaking up with him." Caitlin stopped at a driftwood log and lowered herself to the sand, leaning against the log. The September air was quiet, unusually still. A white gull wheeled above them, sending out a shrill, haunting cry. The afternoon sun shimmered on the water. It was as if the entire world had slowed down.

"You look tired."

Caitlin shrugged. She had told her family about spending the night at the hospital, but not why. Sitting at Simon's bedside seemed quixotic in the harsh light of the day. She came home just before her family came back from church, giving her time to shower and change. It also gave her time for personal devotions, and a chance to question God about the events of the past twenty-four hours.

"What about going back to work?" Rachel sat down beside her, sifting her hands through the coarse sand, tilting her face to the sun.

"I would dearly love to, but unfortunately it's not an option." Caitlin settled farther down on the log, squinting against the sun to the mountains of the mainland beyond. Mountains as familiar as the wallpaper of her own bedroom. She and Rebecca spent hours here. It was a short bike ride from their parent's home. In the summer they swam here, on cooler days they walked along the beach, exploring, planning, dreaming. "All the shifts are planned out. Much as I'd love to get back to work, I'd throw a huge monkey wrench in the whole business if I tried to get back into it right now." She pushed her hand into the sun-warmed sand, reaching down to the cooler layer below.

"Well, you have to make some plans."

Caitlin wrinkled her nose and laid her head back against the log, letting the sun warm her face. "I don't have to make any plans. I've spent three years working around Charles's schedule, and I think the next week and a half will be a good opportunity for me to figure out my own life."

"Have you ever thought about moving out of Mom and Dad's house?"

Caitlin squinted across the bay again, looking but not seeing. Right now she didn't want to make any decision more strenuous than whether she should get up and keep walking or stay leaning against this log while her behind got slowly colder. "I should," she said. "It's just too easy at home. Mom takes care of me, and I don't have to think about anything."

"Well, someday you'll find somebody. Someone

you can care for." Rachel reached over and stroked her shoulder, trying to comfort Caitlin.

"I suppose I will," Caitlin said stifling a sigh. She didn't know if she wanted to invest her emotions in another relationship. It seemed a lot of work for little reward. She pushed herself up, brushing the cool, damp sand off her pants and giving her sister a hand, pulled her up. "I guess I'll just have to wait for someone to come and sweep me off my feet."

"Charles will regret this, you know."

Caitlin pursed her lips, nodding absently at her sister's confident proclamation.

"I think he was just taking you for granted. He's probably just afraid of commitment."

"He seems pretty committed to his job," Caitlin said dryly. "And if he can't give me that same kind of commitment, then I'm really wasting my time."

"Maybe breaking up with him will show him that you're serious. It will be a wake-up call for him." Rachel smiled at her sister in encouragement. "You just wait. He'll be calling you by the end of the week, begging you to come back."

"We've done this break-up-and-begging thing before. I wouldn't take him, Rachel," Caitlin said firmly, her hands bunched in the pockets of her jean jacket.

"What?" Rachel punched her sister on the shoulder. "Of course you would. Charles is such a great guy."

Caitlin looked down at some shells, kicking them

up and watching them fall. "He may be great, but I don't know if I've had any passionate feelings for him." She angled a questioning glance at her sister. "Surely that should be part of a relationship."

"I still can't believe you're saying this."

"I can. Amazing what a few different events can do to change your perspective on life."

"Like what?"

Caitlin stopped and turned to face her sister. "Yesterday you told me you were expecting. Yesterday I saw a man almost get killed. I realized how precious life is and how much of mine I've wasted waiting to see if Charles could squeeze me into his agenda."

"What?" Rachel said, frowning. "What do you mean about a man getting killed? You never said anything about that."

Caitlin held her sister's puzzled gaze and then turned away, walking a little quicker. "It happened after I broke up with Charles. Some guy on a motorbike." *His name is Simon,* her inner voice taunted her. *You stayed with him, all night. He's more than "some guy."* "It was pretty traumatic and it shook me up," she continued, ignoring the insidious thoughts. "He was afraid and wanted me to stay with him. So I did. That's why I was home so late."

"Wow, Caity. That was nice of you."

Caitlin was reassured by the tone of her sister's voice, by her use of an innocuous word like *nice.* It told her that what she had done was kindness, nothing more. It had nothing to do with emptiness and being needed. Nothing to do with eyes that demanded and a mouth that promised.

Chapter Four

"You didn't tell me Eva was working evenings." Caitlin pulled a face at the timesheet in front of her. Danielle had called her earlier in the day to offer her the shift for a nurse who'd wanted to take the week off but hadn't been able to because of Caitlin's pending vacation with Charles.

Danielle gave her friend a light punch on the shoulder. "Beggars can't be choosers, my dear. If it's any comfort, I'll be in the last two days of the rotation. We can gossip together." A light blinked on above the doorway across from the nurse's station and Danielle looked up with a frown. "There goes that Simon again," she grumbled. "Had that student nurse, Tina, all in a dither this morning."

"Do you want me to go?" Caitlin offered.

"Sure. Just don't let him get to you!" warned her friend.

Caitlin only smiled. "I think I'm okay in that

department," she said as she walked into his room. She knew she wouldn't be succumbing to any male charms for a while.

"Took you long enough," Simon grumbled as she walked to the foot of his bed. As he glanced at her he frowned, then his hazel eyes brightened. "Well, hi there, angel," he said, a slow smile curving his lips, his gravelly voice softening. "You came back to see me."

Caitlin could see how this man could get a young woman flustered. With just a smile, a shifting of his features, he changed from harsh to appealing. "I just came on the ward to see when I'm working again," she said, walking over to his side. "Danielle's busy. Did you want some water?" She poured him a cup.

"You work here?" He shifted as he reached for the cup, his smile disappearing in a grimace of pain.

"Yes, I do. I'm on vacation now though, but I'll be back tomorrow."

"Really?" He tried to smile again, but he squeezed his eyes shut and took a few slow breaths, fighting the agony Caitlin knew he must be suffering.

"Do you want a painkiller?" she asked quietly, taking the cup out of his trembling hands.

He shook his head once, quickly. "No," he gasped, "I'm okay."

Caitlin watched him battling the pain, his head pressed back against the pillow, his fists clenched at his sides.

"You don't have to suffer like this," she said,

touching his shoulder lightly. "You don't have to be so tough."

Simon took a few more quick breaths, then slowly exhaled, his eyes opening. "Maybe not," he said with a sigh. "I hate feeling out of control."

"Better than feeling like that motorbike landed on you all over again," Caitlin said dryly, setting the cup down on the table.

"Maybe," he whispered, beads of sweat glistening on his forehead.

"When's the last time you had something?" she asked, folding her arms across her chest.

"I don't know."

"I'm going to check."

He opened his eyes. "You coming back?"

Caitlin paused. His brusque question held a faint note of entreaty at odds with his character. Their eyes met, held, and for a heartbeat Caitlin felt the same emotion he had created in her the night of his accident.

He needed her.

Caitlin forced herself to look away, to break the tenuous connection.

Don't be ridiculous, she reprimanded herself as she walked out of the room and over to the desk. *He's just doing what comes naturally. Flirting.*

"So, what did the old bear want now?" Danielle asked, looking up from her paperwork.

"When was the last time he had a painkiller?"

Danielle reached over and pulled up Simon's

chart, shaking her head. "If you want to give him something, I wish you luck. He won't take anything unless he's just about dead from pain. I've been tempted to slip him something in his IV." She flipped through the papers. "Here. About five hours ago. He's got to be hurting now."

"He is."

Danielle nodded. "Dr. Hall changed the order this morning. He's got him on a stronger medication. I'll get him something. Maybe between the two of us we can get it in him." Danielle left and Caitlin walked back to the room.

Simon lay still, his arms at his sides, his eyes closed.

"Is that you, angel?" he asked, his voice quiet.

"It's Caitlin, not angel."

He carefully opened his eyes, zeroing in on her immediately. "When I first saw you, I thought you were an angel, then you saved my life."

"I didn't save your life, either," Caitlin said matter-of-factly.

"I felt myself slipping away, going down into darkness, I knew I was going…." He stopped, took a deep breath at the effort of talking. "But you pulled me back." He smiled wanly at her. "How did you do it?"

Caitlin held his gaze. "I prayed."

"Sure."

"Your heartbeat was weakening, almost nonexistent," she replied, ignoring the sarcasm in his voice.

"I was praying and then it came back. Simple as that."

Simon shook his head, closing his eyes again. "I don't believe you." He took another breath and Caitlin could tell from the lines around his mouth he was really hurting.

Danielle came in the room with a med cup. "Here we are," she said, handing it to Caitlin. "See if you can get that in him." She looked back at Simon. "I couldn't connect with Oscar, Simon. Do you want me to try again?"

"No," he replied tightly. "He's camping. I forgot."

"I'm going on a break now, Caitlin. I'll be back in about twenty minutes to check his dressings."

Danielle left and Caitlin set the small paper cup on the bedside table. "Are you going to take this?"

Simon opened his eyes again. "What are you going to do if I don't?" he said, forcing a wry smile. "Pray again?"

"That, and put something in your IV, or give you a needle. Either of those will really knock you out." Caitlin picked up the med cup and his glass of water. "This is a better alternative."

"Isn't that against my human rights?"

"Hospitals are not a democracy," she said shaking her head at his obtuseness.

"Total dictatorship," he said with a short laugh. He reached up and took the cup. He tipped the pill into his mouth and then grimaced. "This place sounds like my old foster home."

He handed Caitlin the paper cup and lay back again. His comment about foster homes piqued Caitlin's curiosity. "You know, I never did find out your last name," she said, pulling up a chair.

"Read my chart," he said obliquely. He glanced sidelong at Caitlin. "You settling in for a heart-to-heart chat?"

"Hardly," Caitlin said. "Just making sure you didn't put that pill under your tongue so you can spit it out later. If I sit here long enough it will dissolve."

"Do you want me to open my mouth so you can check?"

"That will be fine." She watched him a moment, knowing she should leave, but curiously unwilling to.

"So, where are you from?" she asked, leaning back in the chair, lightly tapping her fingers on the armrests.

Simon looked away, his hazel eyes narrowing. "Does it matter? Knowing that won't change anything." He sounded testy, angry.

Caitlin stopped tapping and tilted her head to one side, studying him. "It makes you more of an individual. Tells me something about you."

Simon curved his mouth into a smile but it lacked the warmth and appeal of the smile he favored her with a few moments. "I'm from nowhere, and I don't have a family." The statement was made without emotion, without any attempt to garner pity from the listener.

"What about Oscar Delaney?"

"He's my partner."

"You also said something about a foster home…."

Simon glanced sidelong at Caitlin, his eyes hard. "I think you better go now," he said firmly.

Caitlin held his gaze until he looked away. He was breathing quickly, fighting the agony she knew must be coursing through his body, confusing him and making him short-tempered. She got up and carefully pushed the chair back against the wall under the window, feeling slightly frustrated herself and wondering why she should care. "Do you want me to pull the curtains?" she asked, reverting to her role as a nurse and professional.

He shook his head, his eyes drifting shut again. Caitlin waited a moment, watching as his mouth relaxed, the frown eased from his forehead. The medication was kicking in, she thought. He looked more peaceful now, and Caitlin couldn't deny his appeal. Wavy hair that fell over his forehead, hiding the cut, high cheekbones, a mouth that could curl up in disdain and yet, now that he was asleep, show a softness she knew he wouldn't want to show.

She was still surprised that no one had come to see him, that no one missed him.

Then again, she wondered why she should care. In spite of his good looks, he was a patient. She was a nurse.

"But I need this information, Mr. Steele." The young nurse looked down at the clipboard she was carrying.

Simon looked up at the woman hovering at his bedside, wishing she would go. He hadn't slept much last night, his leg was throbbing, his arm and the top of his leg felt as if they were on fire and he was tired of feeling woozy from the medication he was on. And now he had an ambitious nurse standing by his bed pumping him for information. He still hadn't been able to connect with Oscar and he was feeling hemmed in and testy.

"I want you to leave me alone. You've got all the information you need to have. My insurance number, legal name, allergies and previous medical history, as far as I know."

"But we need an emergency contact number and…"

"Look, sweetheart, I already went through an emergency without a contact number. I think you'll do okay without it now." He glared at her and this time she took a step backward, her pen still hovering over the clipboard she was carrying.

"The police need to talk to you about pressing charges." She bit her lip, running her finger nervously along one side of the clipboard.

"I'm not pressing charges. I don't care about the bike. It can be replaced. If they say they want to talk to me, tell them that I'm in a coma, okay?" He stopped, as a fresh wave of pain washed over him.

"But, sir, that would be lying."

Simon took a breath, his anger too easily coming to the surface. "Just go," he snapped. He closed his eyes. For four days he had been in constant pain. Each time he thought it was getting better, the physiotherapist came and got him moving around and the agony would start all over again.

He felt the fuzziness of the painkiller slowly overtaking him and he fought it even as he welcomed it. *Out of control,* he thought, *I hate being out of control.* He drifted along for timeless moments. Then…

"Hello, Simon. How are you doing?"

That voice, he thought, forcing his eyes open.

Caitlin stood beside the bed, a stethoscope clipped around her neck. Her hair was pulled back away from her face, enhancing the delicate line of her chin, her narrow nose, eyebrows that winged upward from soft green eyes. He wished he didn't hurt so much. He wished he had the strength to reach up, pull her close to him and kiss that gently curving mouth.

But all he could do was lie immobile with metal and screws holding his leg together and some kind of wrap covering it. A cripple. It wasn't fair, he thought.

She unrolled a blood pressure cuff and gently raised his good arm, slipping it around. Her hands were cool, her touch careful.

"Hi, yourself, angel," he said slowly. "You working now?"

"Yes. I'll be taking care of you for the next twelve hours." She pressurized the cuff and she slipped the stethoscope in her ears.

"Sounds like a wonderful twelve hours."

She only set the stethoscope on his arm and listened. When she was done she pulled the cuff off, rolled it up and tucked it behind the fixture on the wall. She was all aloof efficiency and order and it bugged Simon more than he liked to admit.

When her soft hands lifted his wrist to take his pulse, he held his breath, knowing that the other nurses counted his respirations while they thought he wasn't looking. She dropped his wrist and pulled the stethoscope out of her ears.

Didn't even notice, he thought, feeling childishly disappointed.

She pulled a pen and pad out of her pocket and made a few quick notes. "Let's see, blood pressure normal, pulse strong, respirations—" Caitlin stopped and glanced sidelong at Simon "—normal, now."

He grinned back at her. "I guess you know all the tricks," he said.

"I'd say you need to get out more when someone your age needs to resort to tricks to get extra attention," she said, her voice dry.

"I got yours, didn't I?"

Caitlin looked up at him. "What you *got* was a nurse doing her job."

"And being so aloof is also part of your job?" Simon groused. He didn't like hearing that professional tone of voice. Not from a woman who looked like an angel with her wings clipped. "You weren't like that before."

"I wasn't working before," she said briskly. She picked up the machine that took his temperature and clipped a new earpiece on. "Turn your head to the side, please."

"Whatever happened to good old thermometers?" he asked as she inserted it in his ear.

It beeped and she took it out. "Good old thermometers aren't as quick or reliable." She marked something down and slipped the notepad in her pocket. "Of course, it was a great way to keep the patient quiet," she said with a quick lift of her eyebrows at him.

He smiled at that. She returned it with one of her own that made Simon catch his breath.

"How have you been feeling?" she said, her voice lowering, taking on a softer tone.

She had switched from efficient nurse to the caring woman who had stayed with him a whole night. He couldn't stop his response to her warmth and concern. "It's bad," he said simply.

"I know," she said softly. "But you fight the pain and the medication stops you from doing that. You may feel out of it, but you need to let your body rest so you can heal."

"I can't get out of here soon enough."

Caitlin shook her head. "I wouldn't rush it. You won't be walking when you do and you'll need therapy and home care. You'll probably be walking with the help of a walker, then crutches, then a cane. A broken femur is a huge injury and takes a long time to heal."

Simon nodded, not wanting to hear what she had to say or the vulnerability it represented.

"Where is home?" she asked suddenly.

"I've just got an apartment along the bay in Vancouver, on the mainland." Hardly home. More like a home base.

"You're going to need some help the first couple of weeks. Is there anyone who can come or will you have to hire a nurse?" She looked down at him, her one eyebrow lifted questioningly, but Simon didn't want to bite. She didn't need to know there was no one he could ask. He didn't want to be reminded of his lack of family—reminded that he had lost touch with anyone who had ever meant anything to him. It made his life less complicated. He had never needed anyone. Oscar's words came back to haunt him. They were frighteningly appropriate.

She waited a moment, then with a gentle sigh, turned his IV stand around and read some figures off it. He knew that once she was done recording all the numbers that nurses seemed so awfully fond of, she would be gone until later on this evening when she would check his dressings. Perversely, he didn't want her to go.

"Why do I need help?" he asked, reluctantly acknowledging her previous comment.

"Because you're not going to be able to move around very easily. You'll need help with bathing and moving around. You'll still be in pain…."

"I'll figure something out."

Caitlin looked down at him. "What about your work?"

"I work for myself. Have for years."

"Is that why you are so tough and independent?"

Simon heard the slight note of censure in her voice and bristled. "I've had to learn from early on to take care of myself, find my own way."

"Well, for now you're in our capable hands."

"And are you going to hold me in those capable hands?" he asked with a wink.

"See you later, Mr. Steele." And with that she turned and left.

Chapter Five

Caitlin pushed her chair back from the computer and stretched. She had trouble falling asleep yesterday after working her first night shift. It always happened. So she was feeling a little woozy. All the patients were asleep.

Except one. Simon.

She had to check his dressings. Now was as good a time as any. She had put it off for a while, hoping one of the other nurses on the team would, but they all seemed to avoid him.

Caitlin had avoided him, too. She was uncomfortable around him.

She walked into the room. The patient just recently admitted was asleep. His name was Shane. Football injury. Same temperament as Simon, just a little younger.

"Hey, company. Sit down, talk to me," Simon said

as she walked around the curtain dividing him and Shane.

"Sorry. Can't oblige." She checked his IV while she spoke, adjusting the flow. She turned back to him and lifted his bedsheet, folding it back to check his incision. Caitlin frowned as she rolled back the wrap that held the dressings in place. She bent over to take a closer look at the incision. It was redder than it should be.

"Does this hurt?"

"C'mon, Caitlin, it always hurts." He reached up and laid a warm hand on her arm, his finger moving up and down her arm in a caressing motion.

She felt her heart flutter at his touch and glanced sidelong at him. His eyes were crinkled up at the corners, and she didn't like the way he was smiling at her. It looked polished, purposeful, fake.

She took his hand and laid it back on the bed, angry at her own reaction. Simon was an accomplished flirt. She would do well to remember that.

"Does it hurt more than usual?" she asked, touching the skin lightly, forcing her mind back to her job. She frowned. His skin felt unusually warm.

"I don't know," he said. "Like I said, it always hurts." He placed his hand on his chest and sighed. "Just like my heart."

"Give it a rest, Mr. Steele," she said, now truly ticked with him. He was bored and she was overreacting.

She frowned and lowered the sheet, then walked

around the bed to his other side. "Let me see your arm, please."

"My goodness, aren't you all efficiency tonight?" he said, his voice suddenly testy.

Caitlin glanced at him, then away. He had been alternately flirtatious and cranky ever since she had come on duty this evening. Guys usually were ornery after a few days of being confined to bed, but Simon had been getting worse each hour she worked. It didn't help that his sleep had been interrupted when they brought the new admission into his room. Things were always busy the first hour after a patient came up from surgery, and Simon had been irritable at the constant comings and goings.

She carefully peeled back the tape, unable to avoid pulling the hairs sprinkled over his forearm.

He sucked in his breath at the pain. "That hurts, angel."

"Sorry," she murmured automatically, quickly pulling back the rest of the dressing.

He took a deep breath and then another, slowly relaxing. "That apology didn't sound too sincere, Caitlin," he said quietly.

"Probably not," she said evenly, determined not to let him get under her skin.

Simon laughed at that. Their eyes met and held, and Caitlin again felt her heart give a little kick. And again, she berated herself for her reaction. He was demanding and confusing, turning his charm on and off at will, yet she couldn't seem to reason her way past her reaction to him.

Because each time she saw him, what she remembered most was the feel of his hand clutching hers, the entreaty in his eyes, his vulnerability.

She looked down at what she was doing, forcing her mind back to the task at hand. She frowned. "Is your arm feeling itchy yet?"

"Do I have that to look forward to, as well?"

Caitlin shrugged. "If it's itchy, that's a sign that it's healing."

"Well, it's not."

"I'll change this for now."

"Why are you frowning?" Simon caught her hand in his, tugging on it.

"I'm a little concerned about infection," she said, pulling on her hand. But Simon was a lot stronger now than he was at first, and he wouldn't let go.

"You're a good nurse, Caitlin," he said with a wry grin.

"It's my job. Now let go of my hand so I can do it."

"Nurse means 'to take care of,'" he said, his voice lowering. He ran his thumb over the knuckles of her hand, his eyes on hers. "I want you to stay and talk to me, take care of me."

Caitlin wanted to be angry with him, wanted to dislike what he was doing. She wanted to pull away, but his hand was warm, his gaze compelling.

"Just talk," he said softly, tugging on her hand. "I'm lonely."

Caitlin forced herself to look away, reluctantly pulling her hand free. What was wrong with her? She knew virtually nothing about this man and here she was, at his bedside, holding on to his hand. Again.

"I've got to get some clean dressings," she said, turning away. "I'll be right back."

"I'll be waiting."

Caitlin grimaced at how that sounded. "I didn't mean it like that," she muttered to herself as she marched to the supply room. Once there she stopped a moment, frustrated. She, a professional nurse who prided herself on her objectivity, had let a patient get to her.

She shook her head as if to dispel the feelings she had experienced in the room a few moments ago. She straightened her shoulders, and wheeled the dressing cart back to his room.

He lay looking out the darkened window to the night outside. Most patients liked to have the curtains shut during the evening, but Simon always had his open. The light above his bed illuminated his reflection in the large sheet of glass.

But as Caitlin paused at the foot of his bed, she seemed to sense that he was looking beyond his reflection in the window, beyond the lights of Nanaimo that spread out below him. He seemed to be in another place and for a moment, she wanted to know where.

She sighed, exasperated with herself. Wasn't

it just twenty seconds ago that she prayed for detachment?

She walked between him and the window, pushing the cart to the side of his bed.

Caitlin usually liked to explain what she was doing to patients, just in case they had any concerns. This time, however, she worked in silence, careful not to hurt Simon any more than she had to.

When she was done, she tidied up and turned to leave.

"Do you have family, Caitlin?" Simon asked suddenly.

Caitlin paused, curious as to why he would ask. "Yes. I have two sisters and one brother."

"Do they live around here?"

"No. My brother lives in Toronto, my older sister in Portland, Oregon, and my younger sister and her husband live in Vancouver."

"They're all married and you're not?"

It was more of a statement than a question, but it still sounded mocking to her. And it sounded exactly like her mother.

"That happens sometimes," she said dryly.

Fortunately even he sensed that he had gone too far.

"What about parents?"

Caitlin smiled, wondering if he was joking. "Parents usually come with the package."

"No, they don't." His voice was quiet and when

Simon turned to look at her, his eyes were devoid of expression.

"I remember you said something about a foster home the first time I talked to you. Were you there all your life?"

Simon laughed shortly, then turned his head again, not answering her question. Caitlin waited a moment wondering if he would say anything more. When he didn't, she left, puzzled as to why he had even asked her the questions.

You're a fool, Simon Steele, or whoever you are. Don't get to know her, don't ask her questions. She's just a nurse, not an angel. When she stopped to help you she was just doing what she was trained to.

Including staying the whole night with you?

Simon closed his eyes, willing away the picture of Caitlin, her mouth relaxed, her hair spread out on her arms that night she slept at the foot of the hospital bed. So beautiful, so peaceful. He didn't want to wonder why she had stayed the night, why she wasn't married. He had almost asked her if she had a boyfriend. As if that should matter to him.

Forget her, Simon, he reminded himself, *she's not your type.*

Of course, he didn't know anymore what his type was. He used to be attracted to more obvious women—the ones who knew how to play the game. The ones he could date a few times then forget to call. The ones who didn't require commitment. The ones who didn't get close.

But the past few years he'd grown weary of the games, the empty talk. He was tired of the emptiness of the relationships in his life.

When the nurses asked about next of kin, he almost mentioned his older brother, Jake. Then he stopped himself. The last time he'd spoken with Jake was from a pay phone. Simon had run away from his last foster home and wanted Jake to join him in his search for their biological mother. Jake had refused. When Simon had told him that he had to choose between Jake's current foster parents or him, Jake had chosen the Prins family.

Simon told Jake that he'd never hear from him again. He didn't need Jake. He didn't need anybody. He would make it on his own.

And he had.

His fortunes went up and down, but he never cared. It was a game and one he was good at because it only required luck, some intuition and a lot of nerve.

And he'd done well. But as his bank account grew, his own dissatisfaction increased proportionately. He had indulged in the toys—a few fancy cars, a sailboat, his motorbike. He lived out of hotels, indulging and pampering himself. He bought what he wanted when he wanted, but as soon as he owned what he wanted he lost interest.

So he'd finally bought a condo in Vancouver, hoping that establishing some kind of home base would give him whatever it was that eluded him. Happiness, contentment. He wasn't sure. He only knew that the old restlessness that sent him out on the road as a young man had captured him again. He had promised himself once he'd settled down, once he'd made it, he'd contact Jake. But as each year passed it got harder. His pride kept him back. And his shame. For he knew that his life was still not what it should be and he didn't need to be reminded.

Now he lay in a hospital bed in a city that was supposed to be only a quick side trip, wishing he could get on with his life.

Tired of his own thoughts, he blew out his breath and pushed the Call button again. He didn't care if Caitlin got angry with him, he was hurting and bored. Not a good combination.

She came after a few minutes, appearing at his bedside to turn off his pager. She turned to him, her arms crossed over her stomach. "What can I do for you?"

Simon had to give her a lot of credit. He knew she was ticked but you couldn't tell from her voice. He didn't know exactly how he knew. He just did. "That's not really a nurse's uniform is it?" he asked, taking another look at her aqua pantsuit topped with a sweater in a paler shade.

"I'm sure you didn't summon me to discuss fashion," she said quietly. She glanced at his IV and walked to the foot of his bed. "Do you want me to lower the bed for you. You really should be sleeping."

"I'm tired of sleeping, of being drugged and lying here."

"Good. That means you're getting better." She flashed him a quick smile and bent over to crank the head of his bed down anyhow.

"Don't. Please." He didn't know where the "please" came from. It wasn't like him to beg.

She straightened. "You really need to sleep, Simon."

Her voice was no-nonsense and firm but hearing her say his name gave him a jolt. "I can't. I'm bored, and everything still hurts. I feel like a child."

"Do you want something to read?"

"I've read all the magazines already."

"What about books?"

Simon looked away, frowning, trying to remember the last book he read. "Maybe," he said with a shrug.

"We've got some Westerns, which might appeal to a modern-day cowboy like you, some science fiction, mysteries, thrillers—the usual cross section."

"I don't like fiction. Why don't you just sit and talk to me?"

Caitlin shook her head and walked over to the side of his bed, leaning against the metal radiator that ran along the wall below the window. "You are probably my most persistent patient. It's one o'clock in the morning, you really need to sleep."

"So you said." He smiled at her and folded his hands on his chest. She looked like she was willing to stay awhile, which suited him just fine. "How long have you been working here?"

"Five years."

He raised his eyebrows at that. "That long?"

"What do you mean?"

"I don't think I held a job down longer than a year."

"What did you do?"

Simon hesitated, lifting his thumbs and inspecting them. "This and that."

"Sounds fishy," Caitlin said, dropping her head to one side, as if inspecting him.

"Not really." He frowned at her. "Did you grow up here?"

She nodded, her head still angled slightly sideways. "My parents own a house close to the ferry terminal. I've lived there all my life."

"Tire swing, tree house, big porch?"

"Yes, actually." She smiled and once again Simon felt a peculiar tightness in his chest and once again he wondered why she had this effect on him. "My dad built us a tree house and Mom helped us furnish it."

"Us being the brother and sisters?" He couldn't help the sardonic tone in his voice. "Sounds very cozy and small-town America."

Caitlin shrugged. "It was, until I pushed Tony off the ladder because he and his friends were chasing me. He ended up with a broken leg, and I ended up being banished from the tree house for a month."

"But you nursed him back to health, and that's how you discovered you wanted to be a nurse?"

"Right," Caitlin said with a short laugh. "Tony wouldn't let me within five feet of him, then or now. We weren't close then. Unfortunately we still aren't."

Simon heard the plaintive note in her voice and couldn't stop himself from asking, "Why not?"

"My brother has made some pretty poor choices in his life that we've had a hard time living with."

"That sounds 'Caitlinese' for he messed up."

Caitlin tilted her shoulder up in a light shrug. "I guess that was full of euphemisms." She held his gaze as if weighing his reaction. "Tony got involved with a gang when he was young. They ran wild, and he ran with them. He married one of the girls, moved to Toronto and we haven't heard from him since."

"The black sheep of the cozy family."

"Why do you say that with such sarcasm?"

Simon didn't reply, not sure himself. He had spent most of his life disdaining family, so it just came naturally. No one had challenged him on that before.

"Our family is close, but we're not an unusual group of people," Caitlin continued, pushing herself away from the radiator. "Stable American families are more common than television, newspapers and movies would have us believe."

"And you probably pray before every meal, too."

Caitlin drew in a slow breath, as if weighing her

answer. "As a matter of fact we do. We read the Bible regularly, and we struggle each day to live out our faith in all the things we do and say. Tony gets mentioned in just about every prayer that gets uttered either aloud or in quiet."

Caitlin spoke quietly, but Simon easily heard the sincerity in her words. They intruded upon a part of his life he thought he had safely pushed aside. He tried to hold her steady gaze, to keep his eyes on her soft green ones, reaching for the sarcasm he knew would push her away from the place she had ventured too close to.

"Nice to know I'm in such good company."

"What do you mean?"

He winked at her, but it lacked conviction on his part. "You prayed for me, too," he said sarcastically. "Do you still pray for me?"

She held his eyes captive, her expression serious. "Yes I do, Simon." Her voice was quiet, her words simple, yet what she said shook him to the core. "Do you need anything else?"

He watched her a moment, noting the change in her expression at his tone and suddenly disliking it more than he thought he would, but knowing he had to take this through to the end. "I still need something to read."

She reached behind her and pulled open the drawer of his bedside table. She pulled out a Bible and laid it gently beside his hand. "You said you didn't like reading fiction, this might be just the thing."

And with that she left.

Chapter Six

"Cup of tea, honey?"

"That sounds wonderful." Caitlin yawned, shooed the cat off the wooden chair and sat down at the kitchen table. She finger-combed her hair, still damp from her shower, as she looked around the brightly lit room, smiling.

Watching her mother move unhurriedly around the kitchen gave her a sense of order and continuity. As long as she could remember, her mother made her tea when she woke up whether it was in the morning for a regular day of school or work or in midafternoon when she started working shifts.

Her mother set a steaming mug in front of her. Caitlin wrapped her hands around it, stifling another yawn.

"And how was work?" her mother asked, sitting down at the table close to Caitlin, holding her own cup.

"Busy." She spooned sugar into her tea. "Where's Rachel?"

"She and Jonathon packed a picnic and headed up to Denman Island. They were hoping to check out the market there." Her mother took a careful sip of tea and brushed a lock of graying hair out of her face. "You could have gone with them if you hadn't decided to work."

Caitlin shrugged, ignoring her mother's heavy hint and the guilt that came with it. Spending time with her sister should be more important than working but it wasn't.

Her mother had tried to convince her she needed time at home to catch her breath. She didn't understand Caitlin's desire to get busy, to work in an effort to push aside what had happened, to get on with her life.

"I got a phone call last night." Her mother's soft voice broke the silence.

"From…" Caitlin prompted, her heart fluttering at the intensity of her mother's gaze.

"Charles."

I knew she was going to say that, Caitlin thought. "What did he want?" she asked, putting down her cup.

"He said he still had your suitcase and was hoping to drop it off."

Caitlin had forgotten about the arrangements she and Charles had made for their holiday. A day before their fateful date she had brought her clothes to his parents' place. They were to bring it to the cabin so that Caitlin and Charles could leave directly for Pender Island after supper.

"What did you tell him?"

Jean Severn pulled in her lips, looking down at her cup of tea. "I told him when you would be awake, but he said he would bring it to the hospital once he was done work."

"Why didn't you tell him to just bring it here?" Caitlin didn't want to see him again.

Jean looked up with an encouraging smile. "I thought he might want to talk to you. Maybe he wants to get back together...."

"Don't even say it, Mother," Caitlin said, raising her hand in warning. "He's moving to L.A. He doesn't want to commit himself. We've been through this before."

Caitlin knew her mother had loved Charles and had such high hopes for the two of them. That those hopes had been dashed was more of a disappointment to her than it had been to Caitlin.

"How many evening shifts are you going to be working?" her mother asked, wisely changing the subject.

"I've already done three, so I'll be working two more."

"Too bad your tickets to Portland are booked already, otherwise you could leave earlier."

Caitlin shrugged. "Doesn't matter. Maybe I'll

head up-island myself. Hit Hornby Island for a while, go up to Miracle Beach."

"You don't sound very enthusiastic about that," her mother said intuitively.

"You're right. I'm just thinking aloud." Caitlin pulled one leg up on the chair, hugging it. "I'm just feeling a little mixed-up right now. Maybe I kept dating Charles because I thought if I let him go, who else would I have?" Caitlin rubbed her chin on her worn jeans, feeling distinctly melancholy. "I think we were just a convenience to each other."

"You and Charles were never a passionate couple, Caity, but you were never a passionate person. You've always liked things orderly and neat. I never had to nag you to clean up your room like I did your siblings."

"You make me sound boring."

Jean leaned over and ran her hand over Caitlin's cheek. "You are anything but boring, Caitlin. You have a caring, steady nature and a solid faith I know many people envy."

I still sound boring, Caitlin thought. *Nice, but boring.* But she smiled at her mother, secure in the love that surrounded her. "And you're a good mom." She leaned her head against her mother's shoulder. "I feel like I'm still in high school, coming home and dumping on you."

Jean stroked Caitlin's hair, rubbing her chin over Caitlin's head. "I am glad you can. I pray you will find some direction in your life. I know that God isn't…"

"…through with me yet," Caitlin interrupted, finishing the familiar saying with a smile. She straightened and gave her mother a quick kiss. "Let's see, what else could you tell me. I'm still young and there's lots of other fish in the sea. There's not a pot so crooked that a lid doesn't fit on it." There were many more homilies her mother often used and all had to do with finding someone in her life. Marriage, the ultimate goal.

Jean shook her head and tousled her daughter's hair. "That's enough, you pest. You had better head upstairs and get dressed if you want to get to work on time."

Caitlin stood up, looking down on her mother. Much as she teased her mother about her truisms, she also knew that there was a lot of truth in those simple phrases. Truth and love dispensed in equal measure.

She smiled, and bending over, dropped a kiss on her mother's forehead. "I love you, Mom. I hope you know that."

"Yes, I do." Jean Severn smiled up at her daughter. "You're a wonderful daughter and a wonderful person. That hasn't changed."

"And how have our model patients been doing?" Caitlin walked into the hospital room and stopped by Shane's table. Schoolbooks, papers and cards covered it. He was hunched over a handheld computer game, ignoring her.

"Hey, you little twerp," Simon said from the bed beside him, "Caitlin asked you a question."

Shane looked up at that, his eyes opening wide when he saw Caitlin. He laid down the game, the frown on his face fading away to be replaced by a sheepish grin. "Sorry," he said, pushing himself to a sitting position. "I didn't know it was you." He looked up at her again, smiling.

"That's okay," Caitlin said, puzzled at the change.

Yesterday he had been snappy. Now he seemed eager to please.

"You working tonight?" he asked pulling the table closer. He laughed shortly. "Of course you are," he said without giving her a chance to reply. "That's why you're here. Sorry."

Caitlin could see he was embarrassed and resisted the urge to smile. "I'm just checking up on everyone. Usual beginning-of-the-shift stuff."

"Well, thanks."

"I noticed you had a bunch of visitors today."

Shane nodded, relaxing enough to sit back. "Friends from school, some of the teammates."

"The day nurse told me your girlfriend came," Caitlin prompted, smiling now.

"Well, she's just a friend. We're sort of seeing each other, but not really."

"I wish my girlfriends treated me like that," Simon interjected from his side of the room. Caitlin turned to him with a frown, and he only winked at her. "She was hanging on him like a bad suit."

Shane looked down at his computer game. "Well, she'll dump me quick enough, when she finds out I can't play football anymore," he muttered.

"Oh, she'll stick around for a while," Simon disagreed, his voice holding that world-weary tone that set Caitlin's teeth on edge. "As long as you've got money, you'll be okay."

"Thanks for your input, Simon." Caitlin's voice took on a fake sweetness as she turned to him. "I'll talk to you later." And with that she pulled the curtain between them. It was a flimsy barrier, he could still hear everything she said to Shane, but it gave the idea of privacy. Hopefully Simon would take the hint.

"Do you think she went out with you just because you are a football player?" Caitlin asked, lowering her voice.

"Maybe." Shane lifted one shoulder in a negligent shrug. "But that doesn't matter anymore." He looked up and tried out a smile that aimed for the same casual familiarity that Simon had mastered to perfection. But Shane's missed the mark. Obviously not as experienced, Caitlin thought.

"I'm sure the fact that you won't play football doesn't matter as much to her as it does to you," she said, her voice taking on a brisk, reassuring tone. "And who knows. Once you get mobile, you might be surprised what you can do yet." She left, fighting the urge to smile.

"You're looking mighty cheerful," Simon said as she came around the curtain.

Caitlin shook her head as she glanced at him. "And you seem pretty good compared to what your chart says. Your temperature is up a bit, and you look flushed."

"I'm fine." Simon winked at her then tried to push himself up with his hands. He sucked in a quick breath through clenched teeth, his eyes shut. He lay still for a moment then was about to try again.

"Don't, Simon." Caitlin laid a warning hand on his shoulder. "Here, I'll put another pillow behind your back, then you don't have to move."

He nodded weakly, showing to Caitlin how deep his agony really was. She got a pillow from the foot of his bed and carefully inserted it behind him. He was breathing with slow, controlled breaths, riding out the pain. He lay back against the pillow, which allowed him to sit up a little higher. "Thanks, angel," he said, pulling in another slow, deep breath as he smiled up at her.

Her heart softened as their eyes met. While she had thankfully never had to endure what many of her patients had, experience had given her an idea of how they felt. Seeing a man of Simon's age and strength made so weak and helpless always wounded her deeply.

He slowly settled back, relaxing now. "Are you going to stick around awhile? My girlfriend didn't come today."

Caitlin felt a slight jolt of disappointment. So, he had a girlfriend after all. "Does she know you're here?" she asked, trying to sound nonchalant.

Simon angled a grin up at her. "She doesn't even know I exist. I don't have a girlfriend."

"Oh. I see." Caitlin didn't see, though. She didn't see why that should matter to her. She didn't see why she should care. But she did.

"But Shane over there does have a girlfriend, even though he doesn't want you to think so." He waggled a finger. "Come here," he whispered. "I've got to tell you something."

Puzzled, she stepped closer to the bed, bending down slightly.

"You're too far away," he whispered.

Caitlin bent nearer, disconcerted to feel Simon's hand on her neck, pulling her down.

"I think that boy likes you."

Caitlin heard his words, but even more than that, she felt his warm breath feather her hair, felt her own breath slow at his touch. She pulled abruptly away, her heart pushing against her chest. "Don't be absurd," she said, quickly trying to cover up her reaction to him. What was wrong with her?

"I'm not absurd." Simon smiled up at her, his mouth curved in a mischievous smile that showed her quite clearly what kind of a man he really was. "And you know what? I have a crush on you, too." He cocked his head, raising his eyebrows suggestively and Caitlin turned away, disgusted with him and even more, herself. In spite of what she knew about him, his smile still gave her a slight jolt.

"I'll check on you later" was all she said.

She made the rest of her rounds. The next two patients she saw were a good balance to Simon and his innuendos and leading comments. He was a study in frustration. It seemed each time he showed his vulnerability, he had to counteract that with some ridiculous behavior.

Caitlin continued her rounds, checking her patients' vitals. When she stopped to check on Shane again, his parents had him laughing so she left him alone for now. The curtain was drawn between his and Simon's beds and when she stopped on Simon's side, it was to find him with the head of his bed elevated as he stared at the curtain dividing the room. He seemed to be listening to the chatter going on beside him. If Caitlin didn't know him better, she would say his expression was almost wistful.

Her earlier pique with him had dissipated in the routine of her work. Once again she found herself watching him, wondering who he really was and where he really came from, why no one visited him or phoned. Not even the elusive Oscar.

He turned his head and caught her looking. He gave her a bold wink and sly grin, which completely broke the very temporary mood.

"You still love me, angel?"

I give up on this man, Caitlin thought. She walked to his side, clipping the stethoscope in her ears. "How are you feeling?" she asked as she put on the blood pressure cuff.

He held her gaze a moment, then looked away. "Not great," he said succinctly.

His face was still flushed, and she laid her hand on his forehead. It was warm.

"Have you been feeling shaky, or trembly at all?"

"Not really." He picked up the book he had been reading and closed it. "Can you put this back on the table?"

Caitlin took the book, surprised to see that it was the Bible. She glanced at Simon, but he was looking sidelong at the curtain again, listening to the voices beyond, so she laid it beside the bed.

He laid his head back and sighed, his eyes squeezed shut. Caitlin was concerned. By now she knew Simon well enough to realize he wouldn't tell her if he was dying.

She took his temperature.

"Still good. Only .04 above normal. Must be something else," she murmured, making a note on his chart.

"How often do you hear from your brother in Toronto?" Simon asked. "The black sheep."

Caitlin felt taken aback, surprised that he remembered, wondering why he brought it up. "My parents haven't heard from him in four years. We don't know where he lives anymore."

"And what would you do if he showed up on your

doorstep?" Simon opened his eyes, holding hers with a steady gaze.

"Let him in. Feed him and then give him a smack for making us worry about him."

"Would you forgive him for making you worry?"

"Of course."

Simon quirked an eyebrow up at her, his expression slightly cynical. "You say that so easily. C'mon," he urged. "Try to imagine him coming back, then tell me you'd just let him in."

Caitlin looked past Simon, lost herself for a moment in memories and wishes. "You're right. I said that quite easily. I think it would be hard. But in spite of never being close, he's still my brother." Caitlin looked back at Simon. "That will never change no matter how I wish it. My mother and father love him dearly. For their sake as much as my own I would probably forgive him. I believe God has forgiven me a whole lot more."

"Sort of like the parable of the debtors."

"Which one do you mean?"

"You know. The one where the king forgave a man a huge debt and then the man turns around and sends one of his debtors to prison for an even smaller debt."

"That would be the one," she said, surprised that he knew it. "How did you know that?"

"My adoptive father used to read the Bible to us pretty regularly." Simon shrugged as if uncomfortable admitting even that much.

"I'm glad to hear that." She smiled, pleased to

find out that he'd had some faith training in his life. It made him more approachable somehow. "I'll be back in half an hour, and I'll check your temperature again. I'm a little concerned about how you're feeling."

She looked down at him, still holding the thermometer. His hazel eyes held hers and she couldn't look away. She felt as if she were drifting toward him, falling, losing herself in his mesmerizing gaze.

"Caitlin." His voice was quiet, barely above a whisper, and the sound of it speaking her name created a subtle intimacy.

She couldn't look away, didn't want to.

She was standing close to him, and when he reached up to touch her, to gently run his fingers along her elbow, she couldn't stop him.

"What are you doing to me?" he murmured, stroking her upper arm with light movements of his fingers, his eyes warm, soft, holding hers. "You save my life, you stay with me, you take care of me, you've even got me reading the Bible, something I haven't done in years." He laughed lightly, his fingers encircling her arm with a warmth that quickened her pulse. He gave her a light shake, as if in reprimand. "What are you really, Caitlin? An angel?"

Caitlin swallowed, trying to find her breath. "I'm just a nurse," she replied, her own voice tense with suppressed emotion.

The words, spoken aloud, were a palpable reminder of where she was and who she was. "Just a nurse," she repeated again. Shaken, she pulled away and without looking back, left.

She managed to make it to the desk, sat down behind its high wall and dropped her face into her hands. What was happening to her? She, who prided herself on her professionalism, her detachment, her ability to calmly assess a situation, was getting drawn into something that was moving out of her control.

She was falling for a patient.

All through her training warnings against precisely that had been drilled into each nurse. The dangers of the enforced intimacy of the patient-nurse relationship. The helplessness of a patient creating a false romanticism. Bored patients who whiled away their time trying to get nurses to pay attention to them.

Simon was all the warnings she had ever heard, all the warnings she had ever given other student nurses, wrapped up in one dangerous package. And she was falling for him.

Blowing out a sigh, she pulled her hands over her face, resting her fingers against her mouth. She had been crazy to come back to work so soon after breaking up with Charles. She thought it would help. But she was emotionally vulnerable and Simon was bored and carelessly handsome.

A bad combination all the way around.

Chapter Seven

Simon closed his eyes, wishing sleep would drift over his mind, pulling with it the thoughts that wouldn't stop. But sleep was the one thing he couldn't accomplish through force of will.

At the bed beside him, Shane's parents were saying goodbye. The quiet sound of their voices created an unexpected sorrow he disliked.

All evening people had come and gone through this room, and the only people who stopped by his bed were Caitlin and the cleaning lady. He wasn't a maudlin sort. Ever since he and his brother Jake had been split up he knew that to need people was to give them an edge over you. And once they had an edge over you, they were in charge.

The solution was easy. Keep relationships light and superficial and don't let anyone get close. He had accomplished both quite well.

But that meant Simon now lay, alone, in a hospital bed and no one knew or cared.

Snap out of it, Simon, he reprimanded himself. *You want it this way. You don't want anyone intruding on your life with their expectations, telling you what to do.*

He heard the scrape of chairs beside him, heard Shane's mother murmur, "Make sure you get enough rest, honey."

"Don't go racing down the hall," his sister added with an attempt at humor.

"Like I could," Shane replied but his voice didn't have the petulant whine of a few days ago.

"We'll come by again tomorrow," Shane's father said. Simon didn't want to look, but did anyhow. He saw the faint shadow of someone bending over the head of the bed, then another and another.

"Love you, Shane," the mother whispered.

"Love you, too, Mom," he whispered back.

Simon turned his head back to the window. Wasn't that cute, he thought. Mom and Dad and sister kissing Shane goodbye. He didn't think anyone did that anymore. He didn't think anyone did that, ever.

He closed his eyes, but he couldn't erase the image. He wondered what it would have been like, at Shane's age, to have lived with adults who touched in kindness instead of in anger. Parents who cared, who loved, who surrounded you in times of need.

Once in his life he had been surrounded with love. The love of his adoptive father, Tom Steele.

Once he had been tucked in and kissed good-night by his adoptive father. But that was in another age, another life.

"Do you want me to turn off your light?"

Caitlin's soft voice gave him a start. He opened his eyes, to see her standing beside his bed.

"No," he replied, unable to keep his eyes off her. "I can't sleep."

"You have to. You haven't been able to sleep for a couple of nights now." Caitlin frowned, looking concerned as she stepped closer. She fussed with his sheet, folded his blanket back—little maternal things that touched on a hidden sorrow, reinforcing the mood brought on by Shane's family.

Her hair was loose this evening, framing her delicate features. Her eyes looked brighter, her cheeks pinker and her lips shone.

"You really are beautiful," he couldn't help but say.

Caitlin's cheeks grew even pinker. She was blushing, he thought with a measure of wonder. Without thinking, he reached out and took her hand.

Maybe it was the loneliness, maybe it was the sappy mood he had worked himself into, but when he felt her delicate fingers in his, he couldn't stop himself. He lifted her hand to his face and pressed a kiss in her palm.

And what was even more amazing, she let him. He felt her fingers curve around his cheek, brushing it lightly, then she slowly pulled her hand back.

"How are you feeling?" she asked, sounding breathless.

Like I should be standing up, with my arms around you, kissing you, he thought, sucking in a deep breath. "I'll be okay," was all he could say. He really had to get out of here. This woman was starting to get to him.

Caitlin laid the back of her hand on his forehead and frowned. "You're not feverish, thank the Lord."

"Why thank Him?' he said, trying for his usual flippant attitude, the one he knew she hated. Anything to avert his reaction to her gentle touch. "He didn't have anything to do with this."

Caitlin only smiled. "I think He did."

"You been praying again?"

"Yes."

"I told you not to do that." Her talk of prayer always made him uncomfortable. Just like reading the Bible had. It reminded him of living with Tom Steele and Jake.

"Well, I did it anyhow."

"Like I said before, you're wasting your time. I'm just a blip in your life, sweet Caitlin." Simon could tell from the look on her face he had hurt her, which was what he intended to do.

Then why did it bother him? he wondered. "So what do you want from me now?"

She was supposed to say "Nothing" and then leave. She was supposed to stop tormenting him with her sincerity, her concern, her talk of prayers.

Instead she pulled a chair close and sat down beside him in spite of how he had just talked to her.

"Simon, isn't there anyone we can call, anyone who we should tell about your accident?"

"There's no one else."

"You had said something about a foster home…."

"I've been in a bunch of them, Caitlin." Simon turned to face her, unable to keep the bitterness out of his voice. "I ran away from just about every one of them. They don't care. The very nature of foster homes is temporary."

"Why did you run away?"

Simon held her soft gaze, a gentle pain building in his chest and warnings ringing in his head. But he was lonely and in pain, and Caitlin was here. She'd be out of his life in a week anyhow so he took a chance and told her the truth. "Because it was easier than letting someone get close," he said finally. "At least that's what the counselors always said."

"You've been to counseling?"

"Seeing a counselor doesn't make me crazy, you know."

"Don't be so defensive," she chided, lightly shaking her head. "Seeing a counselor is a sign of strength, not weakness."

Simon felt himself relax at what she said, felt that peculiar tension that always gripped him when she was around, loosen. "I saw some when I was in foster care, and I went a bunch of times in the past few years."

"So how old were you when you ended up on your own?"

"Sixteen."

"Wouldn't you have been in care until you were eighteen?"

Simon shrugged. "If I had followed the rules, yes. But I took off from the treatment foster home they put me."

"Where did you go from there?"

"I ended up hitching a ride with a bunch of tree planters. They told me about the good money they made and I joined them."

"And then…" she prompted, smiling in encouragement.

"Then I moved from one job to another. I made good money tree planting, worked on the rigs offshore, saved my money and invested it."

"So what do you do now?"

"This and that. I play the stock market, own some property. Oscar takes care of the details." He caught her gaze and smiled. "I've done well for myself. I've got a lot of money. I can do pretty much what I please." Simon stopped himself. He sounded as if he were trying to impress her and maybe in a way he was. He had gotten where he was by virtue of his own hard work, his own luck and making his own choices. "I've been luckier in the second part of my life than the first."

"Until now," she said, her mouth curving up.

He swallowed, her smile winding around his

heart, warming and softening it as he held her eyes with his own. She didn't look away and slowly all else drifted away, meaningless, unknown. His past, his need for independence all seemed to disappear. There was only him and Caitlin. It seemed too right to reach out, to feather his fingers against her soft cheek. She turned her face oh-so-slightly, her eyes drifting shut as her hand came up to hold his hand close to her face.

They stayed thus, the tenuous connection holding them, creating a fragile bond. Then a cart rattled past the door and Caitlin abruptly dropped her hand. Simon could see her stiffening, straightening, pulling back.

"I have to go," she said quietly, getting up. She pressed her hand to her cheeks, as if to cool them. She looked away, biting her lip, then turned to him. "I'm sorry, Simon, this shouldn't have happened."

How could she say such a thing? That was traditionally his line. "Why not?"

She faced him, her eyes now clouded with sorrow. "I'm a nurse, that's why not. This was a mistake. It's unethical and wrong."

Her words were like repeated douses of cold water. His feelings for her had been confusing ever since the first moment he saw her, but he would never have called them unethical and wrong.

Because for him, for the first time in his life, what he felt for a woman was pure and decent.

"You better go, then," he said, his voice tight.
She did.

Stop it, Caitlin rebuked herself. *Stop thinking about him.* She bent over the sink in the ladies' room, splashing cold water on her face, the shock of it clearing her mind. She did it again, and again and again until her cheeks were numb and her fingers stiff.

She dried her face and hands, pausing a moment to look at herself in the mirror again. A wide-eyed, frightened face stared back at her. Her lips looked as if they had been kissed. Puzzled, she lifted a finger to her mouth, wondering what it would be like to have Simon's lips on hers, to feel his strong arms hold her close.

Please help me, Lord, she prayed. *I can't have this happen. It's wrong and it doesn't make sense. Please help me stay objective. Help me remember I'm a nurse, a professional who doesn't fall in love with her patients.*

She closed her eyes, took a breath as she felt a peace come over her. *I want to take care of Simon, Lord, but I want to do it the right way. Help me keep my focus. Show me what I should do.* And as she laid it in God's hands she was reminded that she didn't go through life on her own strength. She waited a minute, regaining her composure, then, when she felt her control return, she left.

The ward was quiet when she returned to her desk. It was only nine o'clock, and she had an hour of charting ahead of her. Danielle was on her break and Valerie, one of the other nurses, was just returning to the desk when Caitlin sat down. Thankfully she didn't indulge in any chitchat and Caitlin could get to her work.

Routine, that's what she needed, she thought, pulling out Shane's chart. She clicked the pen when the *ping* of the elevator made her look up. Who would be coming on the ward this time of the night?

The doors of the elevator slid open, and Charles stepped out.

Caitlin felt as if the cold water she had recently splashed on her face shot through her veins. Her throat went dry, and her hands went still.

He stopped just outside the elevator, looking around, his expression puzzled. He saw her then and with a hesitant smile, walked over to where she sat.

"Hello, Caitlin," he said, his deep voice familiar. He came to a stop in front of the high desk, his face and shoulders visible above it. He wore a black topcoat over a navy suit, setting off his blond hair and blue eyes. He was handsome in a clean-cut way.

She only nodded at him, fully aware of the curious stares of Valerie beside her.

"Do you have a few minutes?" he asked quietly.

"I'm kind of busy right now," she replied. She didn't want to spend any more time with him and she was afraid to leave the familiar territory of her desk.

"I brought back your suitcase," he said, lifting it

slightly so she could see it above the high wall she sat behind.

"Just set it down where you're standing. Thanks." She was surprised how easy it was to keep her tone impersonal.

Charles disappeared as he set it down. When he straightened, he rested his elbows on the desk, leaning closer to her. He glanced sidelong at the nurse sitting beside Caitlin then back. "How have you been?" he asked, his voice lowering.

"I'll just be in the supply room, Caitlin." Valerie pushed her chair back.

Caitlin wanted her to stay. She didn't want to be alone with Charles, not after what just happened in Simon's room. She felt as if her life were spiraling out of control, and the last thing she needed was to face Charles, the man who had started it.

But she said nothing. Charles smiled his thanks then when Valerie was gone, turned back to Caitlin.

"Can we go for coffee, or something?"

"No. I just got off my break." *Which I spent beside the bed of a patient, with Simon,* she thought guiltily busying herself with some papers.

"I need to talk to you." Charles's voice held an intensity she had never heard before. She looked up to see his eyes staring down at her, his mouth unsmiling. For the first time she noticed how drawn and tired he looked. Very un-Charles-like.

"What do we have to talk about?" she asked, pulling back from the force of his gaze, unable to stop the touch of sympathy she felt.

"Us. What happened last week. What's going to happen in the future."

"We don't have a future, Charles. I don't know now if we ever did." Caitlin felt intimidated by him towering over her and stood up.

"I made a huge mistake that night. You caught me by surprise."

Caitlin couldn't believe how obtuse he could be. "We've been dating, Charles. Wondering where our relationship is going is hardly a surprise. Moving to Los Angeles, now, *that* was a surprise."

Charles pulled his hand over his face, looking away from her. "I know that, Caitlin. I know all that. It's just that…"

"You've been busy with your career, and I've been busy with mine," she finished for him, crossing her arms over her waist as if in defense. Charles was still attractive, familiar in a comfortable way. But she also knew she never cared for him the way she should have. "We've broken up before for the same reasons."

"That's true, Caitlin, but you know—" he looked back at her, leaning even closer "—I got the promotion I had been wanting for years. Now I have it and I don't have you. I don't know if I came out ahead."

"Are you saying you miss me?"

He sighed as he rubbed his forehead with one finger. "I'm saying I want to try again. I know I haven't always been as attentive as I should and I'm hoping we could find a new footing for our relationship."

Caitlin heard him and knew that beneath the vague words, he still cared for her. He looked up, his expression pained, and it hurt her to see him like this.

"I'd like to try again, Caitlin. I know we have a good relationship, we share a common faith, we have the same interests. Please."

"And what about Los Angeles?"

Charles bit his lip. "I'm still going."

Caitlin nodded. "Come, I'll walk with you to the elevator." They were silent until they came to the shining doors. Caitlin turned to him, unable to prevent herself from comparing him to Simon.

"I know it won't work, Charles," she said softly, lifting one shoulder in a negligent shrug. "This isn't the first time we've had to analyze the relationship. Nor is it the first time we've broken up." She softened her words with a smile. "But this time it's for good. Goodbye, Charles" was all she said.

He stared at her a moment, then turned and left.

Caitlin pressed her hand against her chest, but her heart beat steady and sure, her breathing was regular, pulse moderate. Her old boyfriend had stopped by to see her, had asked her for another chance and she didn't really feel any different.

No passion here, she thought with a vague disappointment, remembering what both her mother and sister had said about her. Maybe it was a genetic disorder. Maybe rapture and thrills were not part and parcel of her relationships.

"That your boyfriend?" Valerie asked, finally daring to make an appearance. "He's a honey."

Caitlin sat down, staring sightlessly at the notes pinned on the board in front of her, easily recalling Charles's blue eyes, blond hair styled to perfection. "I suppose," she said vaguely, picking up her pen again.

"What do you mean, you suppose? He's got the good looks of a male model."

Caitlin only shrugged. She knew that when she and Charles first went out, she was attracted to his looks, but over time his face simply became familiar, as did his personality.

Now, he wanted her back and she knew she couldn't be with a man whose touch did nothing to her.

Nothing compared to what happened when Simon had placed his hand on her cheek just minutes ago.

Caitlin bit her lip at the memory. Tried to eradicate pictures of Simon's face, his eyes, the memory of how he had made her feel with that simple touch, wondering why only thoughts of him could do more to her heart than actually seeing Charles did.

Simon stared ahead, listening to voices outside his room. Sound carried so well in this hospital. He often heard the nurses chatting, not realizing how well he could often understand what they were saying.

He had heard the nurses talking about what a difficult patient he was, usually in exasperated tones. He heard them talk about what they were going to be doing when they got off work. He could recognize Danielle's rough voice, Tina's shrill one. Knew that a nurse named Valerie was working tonight and that she thought Caitlin's boyfriend was attractive.

You're a fool, Simon, he berated himself. *You should have known that someone like her would have a boyfriend.*

He remembered the sound of the guy's voice as he talked with Caitlin. Simon only heard snatches of the conversation but enough to know they had planned a date.

He didn't know why he should care. Caitlin was merely a distraction. He was bored and out of sorts and what he felt toward her was gratitude, nothing more.

He shifted his weight, riding out the pain that accompanied the movement. This morning the physiotherapist had him up on crutches, putting what he called "feather" weight on his leg. He had felt dizzy, but it passed. When Caitlin had said he would be discharged in a couple of weeks, he hadn't believed her, but each day he progressed a little further and he knew it would come.

He was looking forward to leaving. He needed to get out of this room, away from this hospital. In the past few days he had spent too much time thinking about things he had managed to avoid.

Jake, his mother, the lack of family in his life.

Caitlin.

He remembered too vividly the softness of her cheek, how her fingers felt against his. He liked the sound of her voice and too often, when he was bored and lonely, yearned to hear her talking to him.

He found himself wishing she worked the day shift so he could see her more, then thankful she worked the night shift when it was quieter and she could spend some time with him.

He had spent half of today trying to reason his way past how he felt about her, wondering what he meant to her.

He pushed himself over with his elbow, ignoring the pain that accompanied the movement and wishing he could forget Caitlin Severn.

Tonight he had touched her, she had touched him. He had discovered feelings he never knew he possessed. A tenderness of emotion, a caring that passed beyond a physical attraction.

He needed her and even as the thought had bothered him, it gave him a peculiar ache that wasn't unwelcome.

Then after being told that the pure and tender emotions he felt for her were unethical, he found out she had a boyfriend.

He had to quit thinking, that's what he had to do. He never spent this much time sitting around. He was far more accustomed to spending his day on the phone, reading reports, investigating hot leads, analyzing data, running around until it was time to either find a date, or go to bed.

One of the day nurses had brought him a book, an action-adventure thriller. He figured he may as well read it now. It would be just what he needed to get his mind off a nurse who prayed, for goodness' sake.

He heard Shane snoring quietly and, without thinking, rolled over to turn on his light. The quick movement sent shattering pain down his leg. He waited until it eased then reached farther to take the book he had been reading off his night table.

He opened it, turned a few pages to find his spot. The words flowed past his eyes, black lines and circles on paper that were supposed to take him away from this hospital, push aside the thoughts that circled in his mind, tormenting him and teasing him.

His mind returned back to his brother, wondering once again where he was, what he was doing. Wondering if Jake regretted not leaving with him that day Simon had called him from a pay phone.

Simon wondered about his mother and where she was, if she was even still alive.

He turned back a page, trying again to read words he had just finished. Concentrating, he managed to pull himself into the story; then he heard Caitlin's voice, and his heart missed its next beat.

He glared past the curtain to the open door.

"Simon, do you need anything?" Caitlin stopped at the foot of his bed, her hands resting on the rail. Her smile was hesitant, appealing, and Simon reminded himself of what she had said only a few moments ago. He reminded himself of the boyfriend. Time to retreat.

He forced himself to look back down at the book. "Nothing you can give me, sweetie."

"I'll be in later to check your dressings. The day nurse was concerned about some discharge."

"Can't someone else do it?" he asked, forcing a disinterested tone into his voice. He looked up and curled his lip into a smile. "I wouldn't mind seeing that Valerie again. She's kind of cute."

"I'll tell her you said so," she said, her voice quiet, her face registering no emotion.

"You do that, Caity honey." He winked at her and, setting his book down, leaned back, clasping his hands behind his head in what he hoped was a nonchalant pose. Lifting his arm like that made it throb but he refused to let that show. "Or is thinking she's cute *unethical?*" He put a hard emphasis on the last word, hoping it would create some kind of reaction.

"You can think whatever you want, Mr. Steele." Caitlin showed neither by action nor expression that what he said struck home, but as she turned and left, Simon instinctively knew he had hurt her.

It was what he had wanted to do, wasn't it?

Then why did it bother him so much?

Chapter Eight

"Rachel, when you first met Jonathon, what did you feel?" Caitlin asked as she sat on the couch, sipping the hot chocolate her sister had brought her. Caitlin had come home from work, tired and confused. She needed to talk. Thankfully Rachel had been waiting for her.

Rachel smiled, her expression turning dreamy. "Like all the air had been squeezed out of my chest."

Caitlin felt a twinge of jealousy at the emotion in her sister's voice, the breathy sigh at the end. "And when you see him now," she continued, "what do you feel?"

"You know, we can be sitting together in a room and he can look up at me and I can still feel the same thrill."

"Well, I never felt that way with Charles." *And I have with Simon.*

"Never?"

Caitlin slowly shook her head, setting her cup down on the table in front of her. "Nope. Never."

"A relationship is more than thrills, you know," Rachel said, leaning forward to lay a consoling hand on her sister's arm. "And like I said before, this sure doesn't sound like the Caitlin I know."

"I don't know, Rachel." She pulled her legs under her, laying her head along the back of the couch. "Sometimes when I'm praying, I feel a thrill. When I feel especially close to God, it makes my heart beat faster. I don't think it's unrealistic to expect the same feelings from a relationship with a man."

Rachel held her gaze, then nodded knowingly. "I see what you mean."

Caitlin looked past her sister, remembering another man's touch, the glow of his eyes.

His swaggering attitude.

The clock's resonant *bong* chimed off the hour and Caitlin reluctantly got up, yawning. "I've got to go to bed."

"How many more shifts are you working?"

Caitlin stretched her shoulders back, working a kink out of her neck. "One more night and then I'll be around for a few days. After that it's off to Portland to spend time with Evelyn and Scott."

"Jonathon and I will be here until Monday. We can do something together then."

"Sure." Caitlin bent over and dropped a kiss on her younger sister's head. "I'll see you tomorrow."

She trudged upstairs to the bathroom and had

a shower, indulging in a long soak, hoping the hot water would chase away thoughts of mocking eyes, a cocky grin.

A man who could set her heart beating with just a lift of his mouth, the angle of his head. Something her boyfriend of three years couldn't quite manage.

Caitlin closed the door to her bedroom, walked over to the bed and fell backward on it with a *twang* of the bedsprings. She pressed her hands against her face, trying to find equilibrium, a place where she didn't have to do all this thinking and wondering.

Simon.

How easily his face slipped into her mind. *His deep-set eyes, the way his hair falls over his forehead, framing his face, the curve of his lips. He has a beautiful mouth.*

Too bad he misuses it so often.

Ah, the sharp voice of her own reason, pulling her back to reality. Simon was, as he had said, a blip. He was confusion and frustration and mixed-up emotions all tied in with the reordering of Caitlin's own life. He was a textbook case of the problems encountered with the enforced intimacy between patient and nurse. He was totally out of her league. She knew precious little about him. He didn't share her faith, in fact he often mocked it. He was overbearing and...

And vulnerable and handsome and fascinating in a deep, heart-clenching way that Charles never was.

She knew so little about Simon, his past. The little bits and pieces he threw her were just vague hints.

He spoke of a brother, foster parents, an adoptive father, but no mother, no other family. So casually he spoke of his inability to let people get close, as if it were merely a fact of life, not something to deal with.

She got up and slipped into bed. Yawning, she reached over and picked up her Bible from the nightstand and opened it to the passage she'd been reading. Ecclesiastes. She'd started reading it a few weeks ago, taking comfort in what she saw as a basic realism, an almost world-weary take on life that suited her own mood.

It put her own problems in perspective and reading it reminded her of something she'd known since she was young. She had one basic mandate in life. To love and serve God. Everything else, as the writer said, "was meaningless, chasing after the wind."

But when she got to verse eight of chapter four, she stopped.

Her finger traced the words and as she reread them, they filled her with an eerie sadness. "There was a man all alone; he had neither son nor brother. There was no end to his toil, yet his eyes were not content with his wealth. 'For whom am I toiling,' he asked, 'and why am I depriving myself of enjoyment?'"

She placed her fingers on the words, thinking immediately of Simon. How proud he was of his success, that he had done it all on his own. Yet she sensed a sorrow and a loneliness that his money hadn't been able to assuage.

He had no one who missed him, no one who cared enough to visit, to phone or call or send a card or letter.

He was all alone. Like the writer of Ecclesiastes said, "he had neither son nor brother." He had money, but no one who mattered to him.

She closed her eyes, laying her head back as she lifted her heart in prayer for him. It was the one time she could think of him and not feel guilty, when she prayed for him.

"Just go slowly now," the physiotherapist urged Simon, "and we'll do this once more."

He nodded, easing his weight to his injured leg. He breathed through the pain.

"Good, you're doing just great," he encouraged, standing close to Simon to support him.

"I'm doing nothing, Trevor," Simon grunted, gripping the crutches.

"Considering you had major surgery to the largest bone in your body almost a week ago, you're doing a lot." Trevor Walton nodded, watching Simon's leg. "Okay, back onto the bed and we'll work on your other exercises. Tomorrow we'll get you down to the gym for some mat work. Arm over my shoulder now," he instructed as he easily got Simon onto the bed.

Simon allowed Trevor to help him, much as it galled him. Helplessness was a foreign concept to him. It was something he had fought his whole life.

The helplessness of being moved around, of being shifted from home to home. He had vowed he would never be in a situation where he wasn't in control again.

And here he was. In many ways more reliant than he had been as a child. He was completely dependent on people bringing him his food, on helping him in and out of bed. He hadn't been outside for days now and in order to accomplish that, he would have to ask someone.

All day people came in, did something, then left. His bedding got changed, his dressings checked. The day shift was always busy, though some of the nurses would take time out to chat with him.

He laughed with them, told them jokes, talked about inane things, but none of them caught his fancy enough that it mattered whether they stopped and visited or not.

But it seemed he spent his entire day waiting for the night shift to come on. Waiting for Caitlin to stop by, hoping she had time to talk.

You're nuts, he chastised himself, trying to get comfortable again. *Tonight is her last night and then she's finished.*

The thought stopped him momentarily. He didn't want to think he might never see her again.

Nor did he want to acknowledge how important she had become to him. He made it a rule with the women he met to keep things at a superficial level. Once he sensed they wanted more, he would leave.

But Caitlin had worked herself into his consciousness, into his very being. He wanted to find out more about her, to spend more time with her.

It was her eyes, he figured. Eyes that watched him, watched over him during that first night, eyes that could soften with caring. His heart fluttered as he remembered touching her face yesterday, how she had turned her head into his hand.

When she had called what was building between them unethical, it made him angry. It was the first time in his life he recalled wishing he was a better person. It was the first time in his life that a woman challenged him to do just that.

She's got a boyfriend, idiot. He forced himself to remember that, to recall the date he heard them arrange last night. Caitlin belonged to someone else.

Yet if she did, why did she allow Simon to touch her? Why did he feel so right with her? Why had she stayed?

Well, after your little performance last night she won't be spending much time with you tonight, he reminded himself, recalling how he had made that ridiculous comment about wanting Valerie to check his dressings.

Simon picked up the action-adventure book he'd begun, forcing his mind back to the story and away from a woman who made him more confused than anyone before.

He read the same page about four times before putting the book down.

Still bored. Bored and confused and his head was busy with thoughts he couldn't seem to still.

Glancing sidelong, he saw the Bible again.

Why not? he thought, reaching for it. He had read it a couple of times since he came here. This time he flipped past the first books of the Old Testament and stopped at Isaiah, not really sure why. He skipped the first part with its woes and imprecations of doom for Israel.

Then he saw it. "Comfort, comfort ye my people." Isaiah 40. The words spoke to a part of him he hadn't wanted to bring out in a long time. Comfort. Who had ever offered him that before? Counselors spoke of owning the problem, of acknowledging his part in what happened in his life, of taking charge and being in control. Foster parents spoke of letting down his guard and allowing people to care.

But other than his adoptive father none of them had offered the comfort he had just read about.

The words were familiar in an old way, he thought, tracing them with his finger. "The voice of one crying in the desert, prepare the way for the Lord." He vaguely remembered hearing them at a church service with candles.

Christmas, he realized as the memory returned. Christmas with Jake and Tom Steele, the widower who'd adopted them. The picture of the three of them sitting in a church pew slipped unbidden into his mind, the soft glow of candlelight as the minister spoke the words of Isaiah 40. The words of promise, of peace, of rest.

Allowing even that small memory to come back created a sharp surge of pain. Simon swallowed, closing his eyes. Weakness, he thought. Dependence. Loss.

He almost threw the book aside, but forced his eyes open, forced himself to get past the pain. He was alone out of choice. Simon pushed his memories aside and read on, determined to get past this.

He got to verse 28 and read, "Do you not know? Have you not heard? The Lord is the everlasting God, the Creator of the ends of the earth. He will not grow tired or weary, and His understanding no one can fathom. He gives strength to the weary and increases the power of the weak. Even youths grow tired and weary, and young men stumble and fall, but those who hope in the Lord will renew their strength. They will soar on wings like eagles; they will run and not grow weary, they will walk and not be faint."

Simon read the words, his heart constricting. He had stumbled and fallen in so many ways. Reading the verses vaguely familiar to him made him look backward to memories he thought he had safely stored away, and by doing so, he compared them to his current life. The decisions he'd made that were so far from the ones he'd been raised to make.

I had no choice, he reiterated to himself. *I had to learn to take care of myself. No one else would.*

He willed the memories away, laying down the

Bible. Mentally he cursed the disability that kept him here in this hospital. He needed to get out, to leave, to keep himself busy.

He needed to outrun the thoughts that plagued him, reminded him of a different life and values.

He didn't want to look at himself anymore. Because when he did, he saw himself through Caitlin's eyes and he didn't like what he saw.

As Caitlin walked up the steps to the ward, she wished she could suppress the sense of expectation that lifted her steps. Much as she liked to deny it, deep within her she knew it was because of Simon.

His behavior yesterday should have put her off, should have made her realize what kind of guy he was. So why did thoughts of him still make her heart flip?

I'm really going nuts, she thought pushing open the door to the ward. Thank goodness she would be leaving in a few days. She needed to get away, see other places. Balance out the strangeness of her attraction to a patient compared to the lack of emotion she felt around Charles.

Thank goodness it was her last day of work here. Once today was over, Simon would be part of her history.

"Hi, girl." Danielle already sat at the desk. "How was yesterday?"

Val piped up from behind the desk, "Her boyfriend stopped by. What a babe."

Danielle gave Caitlin an appraising look. "What did Mr. Frost want?"

Caitlin shrugged, pulling her purse off her shoulder. "To take me out."

"And…" Danielle said.

Thankfully the charge nurse from the previous shift had come to the desk, ending the conversation.

Caitlin checked on a new admission. Vitals had just been done so she would be okay for a while. With a flutter of trepidation, she stepped into Shane and Simon's room. The crowd around Shane's bed was noisy and boisterous. She only recognized Shane's older brother, Matthew, out of the group of mostly teenagers.

"You'll have to keep it down a bit, I'm afraid," Caitlin warned the group with a smile. "There are other patients in this room."

"We can do that," Matthew said with a wink. The girl beside him noticed and turned to give Caitlin an appraising stare that wasn't really friendly. He added, "If there's anything else I can do for you…" He was cut off by an elbow planted in his midsection.

"Give it up, Matt," Shane joked, glancing quickly at Caitlin. "She's got a boyfriend."

Caitlin didn't bother to correct him.

She gave them an inane smile and then stepped around the curtain to face Simon, suppressing a silly schoolgirl flutter at the thought of facing him again.

The light was off above his empty bed, the sheets thrown back.

Her heart stopped, then started again as she noticed a figure by the window, leaning on a pair of crutches.

I never realized he was so tall, she thought. He stood sideways to her. Even in the subdued light from Shane's bed, it wasn't hard to make out his broad shoulders, long legs. He had thrown a hospital-issue dressing gown over his pajamas but even hunched over the crutches, he had a commanding presence.

"Hi, there," she said unable to think of anything else to say. "How did you get out of bed?"

"Determination," he said, still looking out the window. "What can I do for you?" His voice held the same mocking indifference she had come to associate with him.

"I just came by to see how you're doing. The usual shift-change stuff." She clasped her hands in front of her and lifted them in his direction. "According to Trevor's report, you've been working quite hard today. You should have waited until someone could help you out of bed," she said carefully, striving to keep her voice neutral.

"I had to try myself. I figure the further I progress, the sooner I'm out of here."

It was what she had thought as well, but hearing him articulate it gave it a sense of finality.

"I'll be by later to check on you and help you back into bed. Don't overdo it, okay?"

"You don't have to worry about me, Caitlin," he

said quietly, still looking out the window. "I'm sure you don't when you're out of this building."

If only you knew, Caitlin thought. But she wisely said nothing and left.

The evening moved along with painful slowness. Once visiting hours were over a quiet settled onto the ward. Danielle managed to convince Simon to sit in a chair.

Caitlin had checked on the patients after all the visitors had left. Some were sleeping, some were reading.

Simon now sat in his chair, reading, as well.

Caitlin walked closer, her pulse quickening as he looked up at her.

"You should let me help you back into bed," she said, trying to keep her voice steady.

"I've spent too much time in that bed already," he said, looking down again at the book on his lap. With a start Caitlin recognized the Bible from his bedside table.

She wanted to say something, to acknowledge what he read, but she felt suddenly tongue-tied and self-conscious.

But he didn't seem to be so afflicted. "So what is it about this book?" he asked, turning a page and looking up at her. "Why am I reading it so much?"

Caitlin took a casual step nearer, encouraged by his questions, the change in his attitude. She wished she could figure him out. "What are you reading?"

Simon looked up with a wry grin. "Isaiah."

"Why did you choose that book?" she asked, surprised. Most people looking for encouragement chose the Psalms.

Simon gave a careful shrug. "I've been going through a bunch of them. Did some of the Psalms, but this fit."

"Fit what?"

"My life." He ran one finger along the gilt edge of the pages, a frown pulling his dark eyebrows together in a scowl. "You know, the wayward, stubborn people."

"But Isaiah holds out hope, as well," Caitlin said. "That was the whole purpose of all of the prophets. To point toward the hope of the Messiah, the hope of reconciliation with God."

"The only reconciliation I do is at year end." Simon tilted his head up to her, still frowning. "Did you learn everything you know from Sunday school?"

"Amongst other things." Caitlin recalled the different Bible studies and classes she had attended. "I didn't always enjoy them, but now that I'm older I appreciate the tremendous heritage and wealth of Bible knowledge I've been given by my parents and teachers."

"I went when I was younger," Simon said. "Used to like it."

"Used to..." Caitlin prompted. Simon gave out so little of his past, every bit he handed out made him more real, more accessible.

"Just used to," he said with finality, closing the Bible. Caitlin heard the weariness in his voice.

She knew he would say nothing more tonight so she reverted back to her own job. "According to the physiotherapist, you spent the requisite amount of time sitting. You don't want to overdo it."

"I'll be okay." He shifted his weight and grimaced. "If you don't mind, I'd really like to be alone," he said without looking up. He was pushing her away again, she realized with dismay. He had shown her too much.

"Buzz someone when you want to get back into bed," she said softly, hesitating a moment yet. But Simon said nothing and she left.

Chapter Nine

As Caitlin looked over the inventory in the supply room, she couldn't keep the picture of Simon as he sat in his chair reading the Bible out of her mind. She wondered if he gained any comfort from it, if it made him think. What was he seeking there?

She knew he wouldn't ask. She knew Simon well enough by now to know that, to him, asking was a sign of weakness.

When she was done she glanced at her watch. This was crazy. It didn't matter anymore what he wanted to prove, she had to get him back into bed.

As she passed the desk, she dropped the inventory sheet off and kept walking to Simon's room.

His light was still on and as she came around the curtain dividing the two beds it was to see him staring out the window. The Bible no longer lay on his lap.

He turned his head when she came in and this time, instead of indifference, she saw sorrow.

"How are you doing, Simon?" she asked, her voice quiet.

"I'd like to get back into bed now."

"I'll call Danielle to help."

"No. I got out by myself. I could probably get back in by myself..." His words drifted off and Caitlin wondered what he was going to say. But he kept silent.

"But you're tired now."

He simply nodded and Caitlin took it for acquiescence. "Just put your arm around my shoulder and lean on me when you stand up." Caitlin approached the chair, bending at her knees to take up a position right beside him. Simon laid his arm across her shoulder. "Lean on me and on three we'll stand up." She counted and Simon slowly got up as she straightened. She put her other arm around him, trying to ignore the strength of his muscles and the warmth of his torso through his pajamas, the thin hospital gown. "Now take a few short steps backward to your bed."

Simon didn't move and Caitlin looked up at him, puzzled.

His dark eyes glittered down at her and as she watched, he shifted his weight to his good leg, turning to face her.

"What are you doing?" she asked, her voice suddenly breathless as, for the first time since she met him, she looked up at him. She had to tilt her head back to do so.

"Something I've been wondering about for too long." His other arm came around her waist to hold her close to him and then, as Caitlin watched, mesmerized, he lowered his head. In a last, futile effort to keep her sanity, she kept her eyes open when his mouth touched hers. Then as his lips moved softly, gently, she felt her eyes drift closed, all coherent thought fled. There was only him, and the strength and warmth of his arms, his mouth on hers.

He was the first to draw away, resting his forehead against hers as he drew in a ragged breath. "What are you doing to me, angel?"

Caitlin felt as if all her breath had slowly been pressed out of her chest. She tried to take a breath, tried to force herself to move, but all she wanted was to be held by Simon, to stay in this place where time had ceased to exist, where she was no longer a nurse and he no longer a patient.

"I used to know what I wanted," he said, his breath teasing her hair as he touched his lips to her temple. "I thought I didn't need anything. Now you've got me all mixed up, reading the Bible, finding out what a scoundrel I really am…." He kissed her hair, a light touch of his mouth.

Caitlin heard his words, felt a surge of hope at his doubts. But her practical nature took over and she carefully drew back. "You have to let me go, Simon," she whispered.

His chest lifted in a sigh and he pressed her head in the lee of his neck. "No. I don't want to."

"Please, Simon." She didn't dare shift her weight for fear he'd fall. She wished she had asked Danielle to help.

He raised his head, as he let one arm drop to his side. The other still lay heavily across her shoulder. For a moment they stood, facing each other, unasked questions keeping her from taking that small step closer to him to lessen the distance.

Why did you do that? What do I mean to you? What am I doing? The questions tripped over themselves with no answer coming.

He was all wrong for her. He was a dangerous unknown, a lost, lonely soul.

"Caitlin, what's wrong?"

"Nothing's wrong," she lied, ignoring the tripping of her heart, the breath that refused to return to her lungs. She resisted the urge to run away, to flee.

He shook his head as he reached for her, sliding one rough finger down her cheek. "How do you manage to turn your emotions off so quickly?" he asked, tilting his head to one side to look at her.

"Simon, please. It's late, and you need to get back into bed."

"I'm safer there, aren't I, Caitlin? I can't reach you there."

She didn't want to listen, to know he was partially right. She didn't want to admit that he frightened her.

"Once I'm lying down you're in charge," he continued. "You can keep me at a distance. You can fool yourself into thinking just like I've tried to do that what's happening between us will simply go away once you leave this hospital and you can go back to Charles." As he took a step nearer he swayed slightly and Caitlin instinctively reached out to catch him.

Once again his arms were around her. Once again his mouth sought hers. As they met, he stifled her cry of protest. He held her tight against him, his arms strong, protective, his mouth insistent. He pulled away, a grin lifting the corner of his mouth. His expression was triumphant.

She didn't like the look on his face and forced his arms down. "Stop it, now. I don't care what you think, I don't care how you see me. This is wrong, and you can't make it right just by force of your will." She didn't want to look at him, didn't want to acknowledge the emotional hold he had over her. "What's happening between us is nothing new. Once you're gone, you'll forget all about me and the same will happen to me."

"And you can go back to Charles?" he said with a sneer.

Caitlin's heart flipped but she forced herself to concentrate, to remind herself that he was her patient, that she had a job to do. "My personal life is none of your concern." She drew in a slow breath as she prayed for equilibrium, for strength, for wisdom. "And now, I'm going to ask you once again to let me help you back into bed."

Simon stayed where he was, as if measuring her strength, then with a shrug, turned.

"Wait a minute, Simon," she warned.

But he moved too quickly. He didn't get his injured leg around soon enough to bear the weight. He threw out his arms just as Caitlin rushed forward.

Simon let out a harsh, loud cry as his leg twisted. She caught him, but his momentum combined with his weight was too much for her to hold up.

Caitlin managed to turn him so that he fell on top of her instead of the floor. She felt her breath leave her as they landed with a crash.

Stars and electrical impulses shot through her head, followed by a jolt of pain. Above her, Simon cried out again and she could do nothing. He was a dead weight.

She heard the squeak of rubber-soled shoes as thankfully, someone rushed into the room.

"What happened?" Caitlin heard Danielle's voice and then Simon was carefully rolled off of her.

"He moved too quickly," Caitlin said, her voice groggy with pain. "Then he fell. I couldn't stop him."

"Simon, Simon can you hear me?" Danielle was crouched over Simon's inert body, checking him over.

"Where's Caitlin?" he called out, his eyes shut against the agony Caitlin knew must be coursing through his body. "Is she okay?"

"I'm okay," she said. She could get up, but her

head was spinning and she couldn't seem to focus on what was happening.

"What about you, Simon? How's your leg?"

"Hurts," he whispered tightly.

Another nurse, Eva, came running into the room as Caitlin slowly got to her feet.

"Page the resident, Dr. Foth. Get him down here stat." Danielle said.

Eva ran out of the room leaving Caitlin and Danielle with Simon.

Simon's cries cut through Caitlin. Sweat broke out on his forehead, and he was clenching his teeth.

"He's going to need an X-ray," Danielle said, holding Simon's head. Caitlin only nodded, her head spinning.

Thankfully they didn't have long to wait. Dr. Foth came immediately, Eva right behind him pushing a gurney. Dr. Foth checked him over and ordered him to be taken immediately to X-ray.

"We need to make sure there's been no damage to that plate." He shook his head as he got up.

Hating her ineffectiveness, Caitlin managed to work her way around to the other side of the gurney, pushing it closer to Danielle, Dr. Foth and Eva. As they carefully lifted Simon on it, he cried out again, a harsh sound in the usual quiet of the night.

He lay panting, his eyes closed, his hands clenching the sheets at his sides. Each breath came out on a whimper that tore at her heart. Head spinning, Caitlin had to force herself to focus, to concentrate as she stepped closer to him. She had to touch him, to let him know she was there.

"Angel," he breathed, when he opened his eyes and saw her. "I hurt you."

"No. Just relax now." Talking was an effort but she needed to reassure him, to ease his own suffering. *Please Lord, let his leg be all right. Please don't let anything serious have happened to him,* she prayed, touching his arm, connecting with him.

She felt Eva take her arm and resisted. She didn't want to leave until she knew he was okay.

"Danielle and the doctor will take him down," Eva said, gently drawing her away from Simon's side. "You should get checked over, too. You don't look too good."

"I'm okay," she lied, straightening and walking slowly out of the room.

I hope they take good care of him, Caitlin thought as she watched the elevator doors slide behind them.

She blinked slowly, swaying as the lights above her seemed to dim. Then the desk in front of her tilted, spun then receded down a long black corridor.

"Are you sure you should be up and about?" Rachel asked from the bottom of the stairs.

"I'm okay," Caitlin protested, her head pounding ferociously with each step. "I'm sick of lying around."

"Here, let me help you." Rachel held out her arm.

"I'll be okay," Caitlin said, ignoring her sister's

help. She misjudged the last step, and the jolt of hitting the floor too hard sent pain slicing behind her eyes.

"Don't be so stubborn, Caitlin. What if all your patients acted like you do?"

I already have one who does, Caitlin thought. She realized her folly and leaned on her sister's arm, grateful for the help.

"We're just going to start lunch." Rachel brought her down the hallway to the kitchen.

Caitlin's mother got up. "Oh, honey. You should still be in bed."

"I'm fine Mom. It's just a concussion."

It wasn't "just" a concussion and Caitlin knew that. She had experienced a loss of consciousness. After being checked over by a neurologist she was ordered home to bed. After lying around for a day, she knew exactly why Simon had been so irritable. In fact, she gave him a lot of credit for not being even worse than he was.

Her mother pulled out a chair for her. "Sit down then and have something to eat. You're so pale."

Caitlin obediently sat down, allowed her mother a moment of fussing as she met her father's eyes. He smiled at her over his glasses, but his expression was concerned.

"Let's have a moment of prayer," he said as they all bowed their heads.

Caitlin heard her father's familiar voice as he prayed, his tone familiar, as if he were addressing a well-respected friend. She heard the words of his prayer as he asked for a blessing on the food, a blessing on each of their children, healing for Caitlin, strength for Jonathon and Rachel, and Evelyn and Scott in Portland. He didn't mention Tony by name this time, but each family member present echoed his unspoken words. Before raising her head at the end of his prayer, Caitlin sent up her own prayer for Simon, that he didn't suffer any major injury from his fall.

Her own head still throbbed, but it was a bearable pain. She knew that by tomorrow it would be gone.

"I made some chicken soup, Caitlin. I know it's your favorite." Jean handed her a bowl of steaming broth, with thick egg noodles and chunks of chicken floating in it.

"Smells and looks delicious." Caitlin smiled her thanks up at her mother as she took the bowl.

Soon everyone was eating, the conversation desultory.

"So, what exactly happened to you, Caitlin?" Rachel asked, turning to her sister.

"I was helping a patient into bed and we fell," Caitlin said simply.

"And how's the patient?"

"I don't know. I was hoping to phone the hospital once I felt a little better."

"I always told you, one day you'd fall for a patient," her father teased.

Caitlin couldn't stop the blush that warmed her neck and crept up her cheeks.

After lunch, the rest of the day slipped by. Caitlin napped, tried to watch television and tried not to think about Simon.

She and Rachel sat out in the backyard for a while, but the rain and wind soon sent them back inside again. They ended up in Caitlin's room, sorting through old pictures. Rachel wanted to make up a photo album for her future child.

"Oh, look. This is a cute one of the two of us." Rachel leaned sideways, tilting a photograph of Caitlin and Rachel dressed in identical bathing suits. "This was taken at Long Beach, over twenty years ago."

Caitlin obediently looked and smiled. She couldn't get excited about pictures from the past when her future seemed to loom ahead of her uncertain and vague.

She didn't know in which neat compartment of her life to put Simon. He was unsuitable in so many ways. His past was a question, and he didn't care about the future. He seemed to be searching, yet wouldn't admit that to anyone.

He didn't profess to believe in or hold the same values she did, yet she sensed that he had been raised with them. He read the Bible, yet didn't want to talk about it.

She recalled the look of confusion and yearning on his face yesterday as he sat in the chair, the Bible on his lap. He looked defenseless and once again she was drawn to him.

"...one of the only times I saw you really angry."

Caitlin blinked, pulling herself back to the here and now. She glanced sidelong at Rachel, wondering if her sister had noticed her lapse.

Rachel was looking directly at her. "I don't think it's the concussion that put that dreamy look on your face, Caitlin." She set the box of old pictures aside and turned to sit cross-legged on the bed, facing Caitlin. "What's been happening at work, Caitlin? You didn't say much the other night when I waited up for you, but I could tell something's been going on."

Caitlin frowned, pretending not to understand. She had spoken to Danielle about Simon, but only in the vaguest terms. She wouldn't get away with that with her sister, but at the same time she wasn't sure she wanted to pull out and examine such new and fresh feelings. Feelings that were confusing and frightening.

"You've met someone, haven't you?" Rachel said quietly, leaning her elbows on her knees.

Caitlin leaned back against the headboard. "Yes," she replied softly. "Yes, I have."

"And…" Rachel prompted.

"And what?"

"Does he make your heart do those painfully slow flips when you see him? When your eyes meet, does it feel like you might never breathe again? Does he give you that thrill you've been looking for?"

Caitlin could only nod, feeling that very sensation right now. "Yes, he does," she said, thinking of Simon's dark hazel eyes that could tease and challenge at one time and yet show glimpses of vulnerability and need.

"Who is he? Do I know him?" Rachel leaned forward, grabbing her sister's hands. "How come you never mentioned him before? Is he the reason you broke up with Charles?"

Caitlin met her sister's excited gaze and debated the wisdom of telling her. It would make something that she thought of as nebulous, real and the thought frightened her.

"No, you don't know him," Caitlin said, adding with a short laugh, "I barely know him."

"What do you mean?"

Caitlin pulled her hands free from her sister's, folding her arms across her chest. "He's a patient in the hospital."

Rachel's eyebrow shot up and she tilted her head sideways as if inspecting a person who had mysteriously taken the place of her sister. "A patient?" she asked, incredulous.

"You don't have to act as if it's evil, for goodness' sakes. Happens often," Caitlin replied, a defensive tone creeping into her voice.

"I know that. But I remember how you used to talk about the nurses it happened to…." Rachel's voice trailed off. "You used to get so angry at them."

"Well, maybe the Lord figured I needed some humbling," Caitlin said, her shoulders lifting in a sigh. "Believe me, I've fought it myself. I don't even know if what I'm feeling is really what I'm feeling, or if it's just rebound. The circumstances are a little extenuating. I was at the scene of the accident where he was injured."

"The one that you talked about? The motorcycle accident?"

Caitlin nodded. "He was in really rough shape. Broke his femur, a very major and life-threatening injury. I was at the scene, my hand on his pulse. I could feel him slowly drifting away. I'm sure he was dying, Rachel. Right in front of my eyes. I started praying and then his pulse came back. I still get the shivers when I think about it. He claims I saved his life. He wouldn't let me go, kept asking for me in spite of the pain he was in." Caitlin drew in a steadying breath, holding her sister's surprised gaze.

Rachel puffed up her cheeks and slowly released her breath. "Wow, Caity. That's quite dramatic."

"I know. I'm wondering if that's part of the problem."

"What's his name?"

Caitlin let out a short laugh. "It's Simon. From the precious little he's told me, he was raised in a variety of foster homes. He ran away from the last one at age sixteen."

"If I didn't know you as well as I do, I would say that what you feel for him is a type of misplaced mothering syndrome. But you're not the type, Caity." Rachel traced the pattern on the quilt, looking down. "It sounds like he's had a pretty rough life…." Rachel's voice trailed off and Caitlin could hear the un-spoken question in it.

"I'm not going to marry him, for goodness' sakes." Caitlin said. "I don't know what's happening between us, if anything." She lifted her hands in a helpless gesture. "I have to admit he's very appealing and he makes me feel…"

"Weak in the knees."

Caitlin laughed shortly. "Yeah. Pretty much. I suppose it's just a physical thing, yet sometimes there's more. I've caught him reading the Bible, but one of the first things he told me was that praying was a waste of time."

"Cynical, then."

"Big time." Caitlin frowned. "Yet, I see in him a searching. He as much as said he won't let people close."

"How does he feel about you?"

"I wish I knew. He claims something is happening between us and at the same time he pushes me away."

"Defense mechanism." Rachel rested her elbows on her knees, her chin on her hands. "He sounds the complete opposite of Charles, maybe it's like you said—a type of rebound thing."

Caitlin shook her head, then winced. "But you know what? When I saw Charles again, I realized there was something missing. More than just how Simon makes me feel…" She paused, thinking of Simon, remembering her last evening with him, how his arms felt around her, his mouth on hers, remembering him reading the Bible, his questions. She and Charles had always made assumptions about their faith. They never spoke much of it. But Simon's questions showed her a man who, in spite of his own bravado, still wasn't afraid to show his own weakness.

She didn't know Charles's weaknesses, she thought.

"You're going dreamy again, sis," Rachel waved a hand in front of Caitlin's face. "Suitable or not suitable, you've got it bad."

Caitlin blinked. "Maybe I do," she said, sighing lightly. "I just know that for the first time in my life, I *don't* know what to do." Caitlin closed her eyes, her head throbbing. "Maybe it's just this concussion that's got me all confused." But even as she said that, Caitlin knew it wasn't true. Simon had her befuddled long before this.

"Caitlin, you have never known any other boyfriend but Charles. This Simon guy sounds like trouble, yet when you talk about him I see a hint of that passion you were talking about. I think you care for him and I don't think that's so wrong. Don't worry about it Caitlin. Pray about it. God will work His perfect and pleasing will, whatever that may be." Rachel gave her sister a hug.

Caitlin returned the hug, comforted by what her sister said, realizing that no matter how many times she heard the phrase, it was true.

"And I'll expect a progress report when we come back for Mom's birthday," Rachel said with a wink.

Chapter Ten

It was just like before. Dim sounds. Snatches of conversation. Unknown. Unable to understand.

Simon struggled to open his eyes, his head pounding but he couldn't focus.

"Caitlin," he called out involuntarily, then stopped himself. Why did he always want her? What made him call out for her?

"It's okay, Simon," he heard. But it wasn't Caitlin. He tried to turn his head in the direction of the voice, tried to focus.

"Who are you?" he croaked. "What's wrong with me?"

"Danielle. I'm the evening nurse. You've got a bad case of the flu. Do you want a drink?"

"No. Where's Caitlin?" he couldn't help asking.

"She's not working."

As her words registered, a sudden panic pressed down on him. "She's supposed to come. She said she'd stay."

"Lie still or you'll be in trouble again."

"No, I can't...." Part of his mind registered his incoherence, yet he couldn't stop the agitation that gripped him. His thoughts spun around his head. He couldn't pin them down, couldn't catch them. All he knew was that he wanted Caitlin beside him. He wanted to tell her...to tell her...

He closed his eyes as a wave of vertigo washed away the words. He drifted away, his eyes burning, his leg on fire.

Time was nothing. There was no way to measure what was happening. Nothing made any sense.

He thought he saw Jake standing beside the bed but Jake didn't know he was here, did he? He tried to reach out for him, but his brother slowly disappeared. He heard voices, laughing, mocking. Sounds amplified and confusion reigned.

He was afraid, alone, wandering through darkness, pushing aside hands that held, that pulled on him, trying to find a brother who was always out of his reach. How could Jake turn his back on him? How could he so easily forget him? Everyone had forgotten him. Everyone.

My son, pay attention.... You are my son.... This is my beloved son...my son, give me your heart....

Words slipped through his delirium. Words from a father to a son. Words he realized came from the Bible.

He didn't want to remember them. He wasn't anyone's son, but the words echoed, words of love.

Such a weak word, *love.* So overused and over-rated.

He didn't want to think about love. Didn't want to think about being a son, having a father, a brother. He wished he could stop his thoughts, he wished he could control them. Hearing voices happened to crazy people.

"He's been like this for most of today."

More voices, but these came from outside. Real voices.

"He's really spiked a temp." Caitlin's voice. He was sure of it. He tried to open his eyes but the light was too harsh. "Infection?" he heard her ask.

"No. Blood work shows nothing. It's that flu that's been going around."

"I'll stay with him. You can go back to work."

Then through the heat and confusion he felt a cool touch on his forehead, a click as the light above his bed was turned down a notch. He didn't know if he imagined the gentle touch of lips on his cheek.

"Simon, I'm here."

He felt a soft peace drift over him at the sound of her voice. "Angel," he whispered, thankfully. He could finally open his eyes without a sharp pain from the light hitting him behind his eyes.

And there she was. Leaning above him, her hair framing her face, as she gently smoothed his own hair back from his forehead. "You came," he said.

She nodded, as she let her hand linger on his

cheek. He smiled back at her and tried to lick his lips. They were dry and cracked.

"I'll get you a drink," she said, straightening. He heard the clatter of ice and water being poured into a plastic cup, then her hand was behind his head again and she was helping him to drink.

The water was cool, soothing. When he was done he looked up at her, remembering with a sudden clarity what he had done the last time they saw each other. He remembered that he had hurt her then.

"Caitlin, I'm sorry." He forced the words past his own resistance. He wanted to touch her, to connect with her but it seemed each time he did it wrong. "I'm sorry I hurt you. I'm sorry I kissed you…." He tried to find the right words to do something he wasn't very good at. Apologizing.

"No, Simon, don't say that." She sat down beside him, the chair pulled up close.

"Are you going to stay with me?"

She nodded, laughing shortly. "Yes, it seems that is to be my fate. Holding your hand through your various crises."

He smiled weakly, then closed his eyes again. Unorganized thoughts were coming back, spinning around, sucking him down.

"Caitlin," he whispered.

"What, Simon?"

"Pray for me."

"I always do," she replied. "Now just rest. I'm here."

And that knowledge made it easier for him to sleep.

The dreams came anyhow. Unbidden and unorganized—a jumble of memories and people from his past and present melding, accusing. Verses from Bible passages he read condemned him, his lifestyle. In his dreams he tried to run away, to leave the voices behind him, but they always found him, circling, attacking. He tried to beat them off but couldn't. There were too many—old girlfriends that he walked away from without a second glance, foster parents he left with a shrug, people he had ignored. Jake. His brother, his only brother.

They all hovered and tormented...

"Comfort, comfort my people, says your God."

There were those words again. Simon strained toward them, reaching out. Caitlin was reading, her voice an anchor, the words soothing. "Speak tenderly to Jerusalem, and proclaim to her that her hard service has been completed, that her sin has been paid for, that she has received from the Lord's hand double for all her sins."

Simon heard the words of assurance, the same words he had read only a few days ago. They gently brushed away the confusion.

Paid for, Caitlin had read. Hard service completed, sin paid for. It sounded too easy.

Simon opened his eyes. The first thing he saw was Caitlin's bent head. She was still reading aloud, her voice resonant with conviction. She glanced up as she turned a page and met his gaze with her own.

"Hi," she said with a hesitant smile. "You were so restless, I thought I would read for you." She held up the Bible. "You had a bookmark in this section. Isaiah 55."

Simon felt a blessed moment of coherence. "Yeah," he said with a short laugh. "Thought it was appropriate, considering where I've been."

Caitlin lowered the Bible to her lap. "And where was that?"

Simon heard the concern in her voice and once again wondered at this woman. Wondered why she willingly spent time with him in spite of what he had said and done to her.

"If you don't want to talk about it I understand."

He shook his head and smiled. "No. I want to." He drew in a slow breath. "I've been all over and nowhere."

"Where did you start from?"

"Foster home."

"What about before that?"

Simon was quiet, remembering Tom Steele, his adoptive home and the vague memories he had of a mother before that. He had tried to keep the memories alive but over time they had faded into the dim picture of a smile, dark hair and the faint smell of bread baking. It was all he had left of her, and it was all he had left of Tom Steele, the only father he ever knew. Memories.

"My mother gave me and my brother up when I was four years old. I don't remember much of her."

Caitlin leaned closer. "Do you know why she gave you up?"

"No." His head ached again and he felt a burning pain in his leg. "I wanted to go looking for her but Jake didn't."

"Jake is your brother?"

Simon nodded, turning his head to look back at the ceiling. "We used to visit each other after we got split up. He ended up in a great place."

"And you got split because of your running away?" Caitlin sounded surprised.

"Well, I was the bad boy and Jake was the good boy. Special Services wanted to give him a chance separate from me." He felt the ache behind his eyes and a peculiar pressure building in his chest. "But Jake didn't want to leave. Didn't want to come with me. He made the right choice, I think."

"Where is he now?"

"I don't know." Simon drew in a long breath, surprised at the emotions those few words brought out. Sorrow, regret, pain. In his weakened state he couldn't fight them. Had no defenses to draw from. "When he wouldn't leave with me," he continued, "I told him he'd never hear from me again. And he hasn't."

"Would you want to see him again?"

Simon shrugged, but the movement sent a wave of dizziness over him. "I don't know," he said, suddenly weary. "It's been so long. I don't feel I have the right." He closed his eyes and felt Caitlin lightly lay her cool hand on his forehead.

"You're burning up," she murmured. "I'll see if I can get you something."

She walked out of the room, a shadow in the half light and Simon felt bereft.

How had she done it? he wondered. How had this woman managed to so completely take hold of him, invade his thoughts and dreams, make him talk about things he had long buried and tried to forget? Remind him of where he had come from and make him wonder where he was going?

He needed her and didn't want to need her.

Simon forced that thought aside. He couldn't allow those emotions to take over his life, determining what he would do. He had been too long on his own, too long independent. He couldn't afford to lean on anyone, to be weak. Caitlin had the potential to destroy everything he had worked so hard to build. He reminded himself that she was a temporary part of his life. She told him over and over again. She was a Christian, far removed from him. She had a boyfriend. A family—something he knew nothing about.

So why did he feel this way about her? Confused, frustrated. Seeking.

Comfort, comfort my people. Those words again, he thought, clinging to them, remembering that God promised that sins would be paid for. He remembered vague snatches of Sunday school songs, words of promise and hope, but also of responsibility.

He had to confess, to show his need to God, to recognize his part in what had been happening in his life. He had to open himself up, look at what he had done.

He didn't know if he could.

His thoughts circled again and when Caitlin returned he was tired and confused.

"Here," she said, lifting his head again. "Take this."

He obediently swallowed the pill she gave him and laid back. She placed a damp cloth on his forehead and he felt immediate relief.

"That feels good," he murmured. "Thanks."

"You want to sleep?"

"No. Just talk to me." He was tired, but he feared the confusion of his dreams. He wanted to hear her voice, to keep the connection between them, however fragile.

"About…" she prompted.

"Tell me about you."

"I already have," she replied quietly. "You know most everything about me."

Simon turned his head, his eyes blinking slowly. "No, I don't. I don't know your favorite color, what you like to do when you're not holding my hand, what you order in a restaurant?"

"I like the color blue, I read books in my spare time and I always order chicken." She fussed with his sheets, her fingers lingering on his shoulder. "Now rest."

Simon laughed shortly. "That was supposed to be the start of a longer conversation." His head ached and his body felt as if it were slowly being pulled in different directions. He should be sleeping, but he had Caitlin all to himself. She wasn't going to rush off to be with another patient, she wasn't here as a nurse, but as a visitor.

He didn't want to speculate on the reasons she was at his side. He was thankful for her presence and for the moment he just wanted to enjoy having her undivided attention.

"I could ask you a few questions," she said.

"You already have."

"These will be simpler. Your favorite color."

"Brown."

"Favorite food."

"French fries."

"Hobbies?"

Simon paused. "I don't know. I keep pretty busy with my work."

"Which is?"

"Work. Just work."

"Sounds fishy, Simon." Caitlin leaned back, crossing her arms, her I-mean-business pose.

"I don't know what else to say," he replied defensively. "I'm self-employed. I buy and sell stocks and businesses and real estate. I have a couple of fast-food franchises, a soft-drink franchise. I manage my own funds…." He stopped, looking at her, trying to read her expression, feeling as if he had to justify what he did. "It's not your usual nine-to-five, pack-a-lunch job. I worked enough for other people, spent enough of my life trying to rise up to other people's expectations and failing…." He stopped again, realizing he had said more than he had wanted to.

"Do you mean the foster homes you lived in?"

Simon said nothing, as a band of sorrow squeezed his heart into a tight knot.

"You said your mother gave you up when you were four," Caitlin persisted.

"You said easy questions," Simon said, trying to smile.

"Sorry." She leaned forward. "I can't help it. I want to know more about you. More than you're telling me."

Simon met her eyes and once again felt as if he were falling. He closed his eyes and took a few deep breaths. "When my mom gave us up we were brought to a foster home. The man was an older man. A widower. We were only supposed to be there temporarily, while we waited for an adoptive home. It took a little longer than Social Services thought it would. He got attached and adopted us. He took care of us until we turned twelve. Then we were moved."

"How come?"

Simon clutched the bedsheet as he stared sightlessly up at the ceiling tiles. "It wasn't because of our father. Tom Steele was a good man. He took us to church, taught us about God. He took us to hockey games, came to parent-teacher interviews. Did all the right things." Simon stopped, untangled his hand from the sheet and closed his eyes.

"What happened?"

Caitlin wouldn't let up, he thought. Her soft-spoken questions slowly kept him going back to places he had thought he had long abandoned.

He drew in a deep breath, swallowing. Sixteen years had passed and dredging up this memory still hurt.

"He died." He ignored Caitlin's cry of dismay. "And Jake and I were moved." He waited a moment, letting the pain pass. "Jake seemed to take it better than me. I couldn't take it at all. So I ran away. I said it was to find my mother. The home they moved us to couldn't handle it so Social Services moved us again. I kept running. And we were moved again." He stopped.

"What happened at that time?" she said, her voice quietly persistent.

"Jake went to stay on a farm in the country and I ended up in a treatment foster home. But I kept running."

"Why?"

The question was simple enough but it required so much. He didn't want to analyze his past. It was over. There was nothing he could do about it. But against his rational judgment, he wanted her to know all about him. Wanted her to see what his life was like. That way, if she stayed then it meant…it meant…

"I'm sorry," she said quietly. "I'm getting nosy."

"No," he replied, looking back up at the ceiling. "That's okay." He went back through his memories, digging up old emotions, realizing he was laying himself bare for her. But he didn't want to analyze, to defend, to hold back. He wanted her to know. "I hated everyone for a long time. I hated my mother for giving us up. I hated Tom Steele for dying and leaving us. I never knew what to do with the emotions. The first home we were moved to was a good place, but I never gave it a chance. I didn't want to. I figured the only way I would be in charge was if I was the first one to leave. The family kept coming after me and finally they couldn't handle it anymore. So Jake and I got moved. And the same thing happened. Finally we were split up. Jake hated me for a while. I hated him. He ended up in a good place, and I ended up in a sterner home. So I kept running. I suppose by that time it was just a habit, a way of avoiding life."

"And where is Jake now?"

Simon shrugged. "I don't know. Once kids in foster care turn eighteen, they're on their own. I figured he left there, too!"

"Have you ever tried to contact him?"

"No."

"Why not?"

Simon felt it again. Regret, hurt, pride. "I don't know if he'd want to hear from me."

"But he's your brother."

Simon shook his head slowly. "Family doesn't work the same for me as it does for you. We've been apart longer than we've been together. He's got his own life. He doesn't need me."

Simon stopped, reaching up to touch his forehead.

Caitlin got up right away, took the now warm cloth off his forehead and replaced it with another. She gently smoothed it against his head, her fingers lingering at his temple, stroking his damp hair back. He saw pity on her face.

He caught her hand, squeezing it hard. "Don't do that, Caitlin," he said, his voice low. "Don't feel sorry for me."

She only smiled, turning her hand in his to curve around his fingers.

"That's not what I want from you."

"That's not what I feel for you," she whispered.

Caitlin's eyes met his, held, and Simon felt his breath leave his chest.

Then she bent forward, touching her lips to his cheek. Her mouth lingered a moment, then she raised her head, clutching his hand.

"What am I going to do with you, Simon?" she asked.

He didn't answer, only held her gaze with his own, yearning and fighting at the same time. He felt a fear grip him at the feelings she evoked in him, the vulnerability she was creating. But he knew that for now, he needed her. "Just stay here, okay?"

She nodded and gently touched his eyelids. "Go to sleep now," she said, her voice quiet, weary.

He kept his eyes closed and clutched her hand as he slowly slipped away into a dreamless sleep.

Caitlin yawned and stretched her arms in front of her.

The light above Simon's bed reflected off the ceiling, creating a soft glow, a soft intimacy.

Beyond the drawn curtain, the bed was empty. Shane had left this morning.

Déjà vu all over again, Caitlin thought remembering another evening, sitting at Simon's bedside. Except this time she was dressed more for the part with sensible shoes and pants. This time she came out of choice.

And this time she couldn't keep her eyes off Simon's face, couldn't keep herself from touching him, connecting with him however she could. In sleep he looked defenseless, his features relaxed, the parenthetical frown between his eyebrows eased. His mouth lost its cynical twist, softened and curved into a gentle smile.

Caitlin tried to reason out her attraction to him, hoping that by doing so she could deal with it and maybe, understand it.

Simon wasn't as handsome as Charles, she thought, her eyes traveling over his face. He didn't have the classical profile or the even features. If she was to be honest, his nose was a little large, his eyes deep set, yet as she looked at him she felt a yearning, a need to touch him, to comfort him. Thinking of his eyes made her heart give a silly jump. Thinking of his kiss made her jittery.

All the things Charles had never made her feel.

Caitlin knew it wasn't enough to build a relationship on. As Rachel had said, maybe it was merely rebound. Maybe once she was in Portland she would discover that it was Charles she really wanted.

If dating for the rest of your life is what you want, she thought wryly. And that was the harsh reality of going out with Charles. That and moving to L.A.

What kind of relationship did we have? she wondered, leaning back in the chair. *We dated for three years. I'm apart from him a couple of weeks and I easily forget him.*

She slouched down in the chair, opening the Bible. As she flipped through the pages she stopped to read a few Psalms, then turned to Isaiah, still puzzled as to why Simon had chosen this particular book. She turned to the passage she had read to him just a few moments ago remembering how it had settled him.

He was seeking, she knew that. How close he was, well, that appeared to be another question. Simon didn't answer them very readily.

Help me to understand what I should be feeling, Lord, she prayed. *I want to serve You, I want to do what is pleasing in Your sight. I want to be a faith-*

*ful child of Yours and I know that any future part-
ner must also be Your child. Otherwise it just doesn't
work.*

She knew what happened to relationships where
one was a Christian and the other not. She had seen
evidence of it over and over again. Even in her own
family. She wasn't going to make the same mistake
her brother had.

Simon moaned softly and laying the Bible down,
Caitlin got up. The cloth she removed from his forehead was warm, attesting to the fever that racked
him. She took it to the bathroom sink, soaked it in
cold water and when she came back, he was awake.
Barely.

He smiled at her, his eyes blinking slowly. "Dear
Caitlin," he whispered as she laid the cool cloth carefully on his forehead again.

He watched her as she carefully wiped away the
excess water that ran in a rivulet down the side of
his head. She tried to ignore him, tried not to answer
the gentle summons of his gaze.

But she couldn't. As their eyes met, she felt her
heart lift. Then he smiled once again, and drifted
back off to sleep.

Caitlin watched him a moment, then shaking her
head, sat down in the chair again.

Chapter Eleven

"Simon." The soft voice slowly pierced his sleep, a warm hand held his shoulder. *Caitlin,* Simon thought.

"Hi," he said, focusing on her face. "You're here."

Caitlin nodded, pulling her hand away from him. "How are you feeling?"

"Much better." He blinked, and looked around testing his vision. "A lot better."

"Your fever is down." She straightened his blankets, her hand lingering on his arm. "You slept pretty deep."

"Sorry, I would have preferred to talk to you." He didn't know how long he slept, but even if it was only an hour, he felt as if it was too long. "What's on the agenda for the rest of the day?"

Caitlin looked away, pulling her bottom lip between her teeth. "Not a whole lot."

Simon grinned. "Then I have you to myself."

"Not really. I have to leave this afternoon."

"For home?"

"No." She straightened, turning away from him. "I've got to catch a plane in three hours. I'm going to Portland to stay with my sister for a week. She had a baby by Caesarean a couple of weeks ago, and I promised her a long time ago I would come and help her. By the time I'm back you'll be discharged."

"You're leaving," he said flatly.

Caitlin turned to him, but didn't look at him. "I already have the ticket."

"Of course. Of course you have to go. I understand." And he did. He knew the rules. Never let anyone get close, never share anything with someone. He had made them his mantra. And in the past few weeks he had broken each one of them, on his own. If his heart hurt, if he felt a roiling anger beginning, it was his own fault. Well, that was how it went. But now he had one more thing to do.

"Help me sit up," he said shortly.

"But you've been sick."

"I said, help me up, Caitlin."

He could see hurt on her face at the anger in his voice, but he ignored it. He had to start relearning the lessons life had taught him.

She raised the bed slowly and an attack of vertigo gripped him. He rode it out, focusing on the wall above Caitlin's head, forcing himself not to look at her, not to meet her puzzled gaze.

He carefully pivoted himself, swinging his legs

over the edge of the bed until he was sitting up without support.

"Simon, what are you doing?" She hurried to his side, her hand automatically catching his shoulder.

"I want to stand up."

"No. You can't."

"The doctor said the plate was fine, didn't he?"

"Yes."

"Well, then. I was standing before I got sick. Help me stand up now." She only stared. "Now," he barked.

She jumped, then he could see her straighten, could almost hear each vertebra snap into place. Now she was angry, as well.

All the better, he thought. It would make everything much easier.

She helped him up and he was surprised to find that his leg didn't hurt nearly as much as it had before. He was healing, just as everyone had promised him.

Caitlin supported him with her arm. His lay across her shoulder. It was just a matter of turning slightly, slipping his other arm around her waist and he had her.

"If you're leaving me, I can't let you go without saying goodbye, can I?" He looked down at her soft green eyes, the delicate line of her cheekbone sweeping down to a narrow jaw. He memorized the curve of her mouth, the faint hollow of her cheeks, each detail of her beautiful, beautiful face. He didn't want to forget her.

She wanted to fight him, he could feel her tense in his arms, but he also knew she didn't dare. Not after what happened the last time. Ignoring the flare of panic in her eyes, he lowered his head, capturing her mouth with his.

She resisted at first, her arms stiffly at her sides, then, as he murmured her name against her lips, as he drew her closer to him, he could feel her soften, feel her arms slip around him, then hold him close.

His heart tripped, his breath felt trapped in a chest that grew tighter the longer their kiss went on. What he had started in anger, changed with her soft response. When she whispered his name, when her hand reached up to caress his cheek, to hold his head, he felt a melting around his heart and a pain that pierced with a gentle sweetness. Almost he spoke the words, almost he bared his soul.

But he couldn't.

She was leaving and so was he. It wasn't meant to be.

Caitlin sat on the edge of her bed, staring down at the phone in her hand. Jonathon, her brother-in-law had just called her here at Evelyn and Scott's house in Portland. By using his connections in the Royal Canadian Mounted Police, Jonathon had found Jake Steele.

Now Caitlin had the number she had to call and she didn't know if she dared.

It was the best time. The house was quiet. Evelyn and Scott were already in bed, as were the children.

With the time difference, it would only be nine o'clock where Jake lived.

She couldn't stop the restless pounding of her heart, the trembling of her fingers. Was she doing the right thing? Did she have a right to intrude on Simon's life? Simon—who didn't need anyone?

But she thought of her own brother and knew that if something had happened to him, she would want to know. She thought of Simon lying on his hospital bed, staring with longing at Shane's family. She knew in spite of what he had done to her, she had to make this call for him.

Caitlin took another breath, sent up a prayer for wisdom, courage and the right words, and punched in the numbers. The phone rang in her ear, and she felt her heart skip. Another ring. A third.

Disappointment and relief vied for attention. She was going to let it ring one more, no, maybe two more times then she would hang up.

And then what?

Caitlin rubbed her hand over her jeans, waited and was just about to lower the phone to push the button to end the call when...

"Hello?"

Her heart jumped and she was momentarily speechless.

"Hello?" the voice repeated.

"Hello, Mr. Steele," Caitlin replied breathlessly, frantically searching for the right words. What if Jonathon was wrong? What if this wasn't who he thought it was?

Well, then you make a fool of yourself in front of a stranger you will probably never talk to again, she reassured herself. "My name is Caitlin Severn," she continued struggling to catch her breath. This was ridiculous. She was acting as if she had never made a phone call to a complete stranger before. *A complete stranger who happens to be the brother of a man who you are fascinated and possibly in love with.* "I'm a nurse at Nanaimo General Hospital. I'm calling about a patient I took care of, who I believe is your brother. Simon Steele."

Silence. Utter, heavy and complete silence.

Wrong number, Caitlin thought, stifling a hysterical laugh.

"What happened to him?"

Well, it was the right number after all, she thought. "Before you get too concerned," she continued, forcing herself to breathe, to remain calm, "I want to tell you that he's fine now, Mr. Steele. He was in a bad motorcycle accident. Broke his right femur. I was at the accident when it happened and I worked in the ward he was on." She forced herself to stop, to keep from babbling nervously on.

"How do you know he's my brother?"

Because right now, you sound exactly like him,

thought Caitlin, hearing the defensive tone enter Jake Steele's voice. This was harder than she thought. "He gave me your first and last name and told me you were his twin. I didn't think there were more than one Jake Steele born on February 16."

"Did he ask you to call me?"

Caitlin bit her lip. "Actually, no."

"Then why are you calling?"

Caitlin fiddled with the edge of her sweatshirt, folding it back and forth as she tried to find the right way to explain her reasoning. From the sounds of things, Jake didn't appear to be any happier to hear about Simon than she presumed Simon would be to hear about his brother.

It disturbed her. "I'm calling because I care for your brother...." The words sounded lame and she knew it. She had been gone from Nanaimo for only four days, and each morning she woke up with a heaviness pressing down on her heart. She had resisted the urge to phone the hospital every day to see how Simon was, reasoning it was better this way. Better for who became less clear each day she was away. She had hoped and prayed that being with her sister and her family would bring clarity to her thoughts. Instead, she felt more confused than before.

She didn't just care for Simon. She loved him.

Caitlin forced her thoughts back to the present, to the phone in her hands and the muted anger of the man on the other end of the line. "Simon sustained very serious injuries and is currently in the hospital in Nanaimo. He's been there for about two weeks. He talked about you and the homes you've been in."

Jake was silent and Caitlin could almost feel the antagonism over the phone. Whatever it was she had expected from this phone call, it wasn't these clipped questions and curt replies.

Somehow she had foolishly thought he would be eager and happy to hear from his long-lost brother. She thought he would be thankful that she took the time to track him down.

"So, why did you think I needed to know this?"

Caitlin straightened, her own anger coming to the fore. "Your brother has been through a lot of pain and has been struggling in many ways, physically as well as spiritually. I called you because in the entire time he was in the hospital, your brother never received one visitor, or one phone call. He is all alone...."

"The fact that my brother doesn't have anyone doesn't surprise me," Jake said, his voice even, almost harsh. "Simon has never needed anyone, never cared for anyone except himself."

Caitlin almost gasped at the coldness of Jake's reply. "I can't believe you're talking like this," Caitlin replied, now thoroughly angry. "He's your brother. Doesn't that relationship mean anything to you?"

"Simon hasn't been a part of my life for a long time now, out of his own choice. If he wants to talk to me I would imagine he could get hold of me."

Caitlin knew the truth of that, but also knew that Simon, for whatever reason, wouldn't do that. "I don't know Simon as well as I would like to," she said, "but I do know that he is seeking and that he is unsure of what he's looking for."

Jake was quiet and Caitlin knew she had touched something in him.

Please Lord, help me find the right words, she prayed as she spoke. "He is your family. I have a brother who I haven't seen for a long time, out of his choice. I know that if something happened to him, I would want to know and I would want to see him again, to be a family again."

"I don't think it's your place to lecture me on family reunions, Miss..." He paused and for a moment Caitlin was tempted to simply hang up and put the Steeles and their brokenness behind her. But she thought of Simon clutching her hand, his eyes full of sorrow and pain he couldn't express and she knew she had to fight for him.

"Severn. Caitlin Severn," she reminded him, clutching the phone, forcing herself to stay calm.

"Well, Miss Severn. I suppose it would be incumbent on me to ask where he is right now."

Incumbent? Oh, brother, Caitlin thought, he sounded just like Charles. *Please Lord, if ever I needed to keep a clear head and a soft tongue it's now. Help me. Help this coldhearted man who I don't even know to understand how important this is.*

"Right now he's in the orthopedic ward of the Nanaimo General Hospital," Caitlin said, forcing her voice to a more even tone. "He's due to be discharged in less than a week, so if you want to see him, I would suggest you go as soon as possible."

"Well, I thank you for your time and persistence, Miss Severn. Unfortunately I'm in the middle of my busiest season. It's been a late harvest and I won't be able to get away for at least another month."

"Please, Jake. I'm not asking for myself. I'm asking for you and Simon. I don't know if you're married…."

"Not currently," he replied curtly and Caitlin sensed there was a whole other story behind those two clipped words, but she kept on.

"Then you and Simon are all each of you have. I would like you to see this as a gift from the Lord. A gift not given lightly." *There was a man all alone. He had neither friend nor brother.* The words from Ecclesiastes came back to her and in that moment she realized they might just as easily apply to Jake. "I believe that you and Simon are meant to find each other. You're his brother. You can't change that."

Silence again. But Caitlin waited, forcing herself not to try to fill it, to let what she said sink in as she prayed and prayed.

"Like I said, I won't be able to get away for a while, but I will make the effort. I'd like to thank you for your call…."

Which was a neat way of sounding thankful without really being thankful, Caitlin thought. She didn't know if she liked him.

"Are you currently working on the ward?"

"No. I'm staying with my sister in Portland. If you want more information, you can call the hospital. But you are more than welcome to call me, as well." Without waiting for him to ask, she gave him her sister's number as well as the number of the hospital. More silence as she prayed that he wrote them down.

She took a breath and forced herself to continue. "I don't know exactly what happened to you after you and Simon were split," she said. "Simon said that you went to a good home. However, I do know that you and he were raised together in a Christian home. I believe the Lord has brought me to you, and I want you to know that I'll be praying for both of you."

She could almost feel a melting, a relenting coming across the line.

"Thanks," he said, his voice quiet. "And thanks for taking the time to call." Then a *click* sounded in her ear and she knew he had hung up.

Caitlin laid the phone on the bedside table then dropped backward on the bed, her hands trembling, her heart racing. She covered her face with her hands as she prayed.

Please Lord, let Jake go. Let them become brothers again. Reconcile them to each other.

Because it didn't sound as if either of them was too eager to meet again.

"Has Simon Steele been discharged yet?"

Caitlin looked up from her desk with a start at the mention of Simon's name.

"I'm pretty sure this is his coat," the orderly in front of her said, holding up a leather jacket. "It's been hanging around emerg for a while now. One of the nurses who was on duty when he came in just came back from vacation. Said he was up here."

"He was discharged over a week ago. But we can see that it gets to him."

"There were some keys in the pocket and a few other things," the orderly said, handing her a plastic bag holding the personal effects that must have come out of the jacket. "There were a pair of leather chaps, but they got cut to ribbons and had been tossed."

"I'll see that this gets to him," Caitlin said, taking the jacket with a smile.

As the orderly left, Caitlin walked into the office behind the front desk, setting the coat on an empty table. She couldn't stop a foolish trill of her heart at the sight of Simon's coat. She reached out, touching it with a forefinger, tracing the rip in one arm of the coat, the marks left behind when he had gone skidding across the pavement.

She closed her eyes at the memory of him, lying so helpless on the side of the road. His life had been completely rearranged by that one event.

Unfortunately, so had hers.

Caitlin thought her visit to her sister in Portland would have given her back a sense of equilibrium. Instead she'd spent most of her days wondering how Simon was and if Jake had contacted him.

She wondered if he even gave her a second

thought. She knew she should forget him, but couldn't. Now, seeing his jacket seemed to bring all the memories she had slowly filed away, flooding back.

She lifted up the bag and, ignoring the voice of caution, opened it up. Inside were a set of keys, as the orderly had said, a folded-up piece of paper, a receipt for a restaurant in Vancouver and some change. Curious, she unfolded the piece of paper.

But it told her no more about Simon than did the other impersonal effects. It was merely a listing of numbers, some scratched out and a few calculations. On the other side was an address and the name of an apartment block with a phone number underneath it.

Frustrated, Caitlin put the things back in the bag and the bag in the pocket of the coat. It shouldn't matter to her what happened to it, but she knew it did.

"What've you got there?" Eva, one of the other floor nurses walked into the office and laid a folder on the desk.

"It's Simon Steele's jacket," Caitlin said, forcing an impersonal tone in her voice.

"I imagine that will have to get sent back to him."

"Probably." Caitlin shrugged, leaving the room. For a foolish moment she had thought of bringing it back to him herself, of testing the newness of her emotions away from the hospital.

She was crazy, she thought, forcing her mind back to her job. But it was difficult. While she was in

Portland her sister commented on how listless she seemed.

She *had* been listless and she had tried to pray and reason her way out of it. But ever since Simon had kissed her, she had felt as if her entire world had been flipped end over end. She, who so dearly liked order and control.

Before Charles she had dated precious few men. Too busy getting her degree. Then she wanted to work and then she started dating Charles.

But not even Charles had managed to get her in such a dither, she thought, doodling on the calendar in front of her. She wanted to see Simon again, she didn't want to see him again. All too well she remembered their last time together, the touch of his mouth on hers, his arms around her. She remembered the sorrow in his eyes.

She was sick and tired of her own dithering. In her own lectures to student nurses she talked about patient-nurse intimacy and how it seldom lasted beyond the walls of the hospital. She just didn't know if she wanted to test it out.

Chapter Twelve

"Here are figures on those funds we were talking about before I left on vacation." Oscar dropped a file folder on the desk beside Simon. "I don't know why you're in such a rush on them."

"I want to catch them before they go up," Simon said, clicking on the save icon. He leaned back in his chair, wincing as a twinge of pain shot through his leg.

"How's the leg?" Oscar asked, sitting down in an office chair beside the desk Simon had set up in one empty corner of his condo.

Oscar had balked at moving their office to Simon's home. Simon had merely stated that it worked easier for both of them. He liked being able to work out of his living quarters. Besides, it gave him another tax write-off. Now he was glad they had done it.

"Some days are better than others."

Oscar shook his head. "I still can't believe you didn't try a little harder to get ahold of me. I would have cut my vacation short, you know that."

"You were camping. How in the world was I supposed to find you?"

"The Mounties could have found me."

"It wasn't important." Simon dismissed his comment by grabbing the file folder. "Tell me a little more about these funds."

Oscar's sigh told him Oscar wasn't pleased, but they knew each other well enough to know that he would go along with whatever Simon chose to tell him.

"I've checked out the funds, and it looks like they've bottomed out and should pick up in the next couple of days. European funds are a better bet than Asian these days." Oscar tipped back his chair, his hands locked behind his head.

"Sounds okay. Hear anymore from the contractor on that apartment block in Nanaimo?"

"He gave me a quote. I'm shopping around for a better one yet, but it comes in where it should."

Simon pulled a face. "Don't get too picky. We'll do okay, even with the higher quote."

"We'll do more than okay. The cash flow looks pretty healthy." Oscar glanced around the bare apartment. "I bet we make enough money you could even buy some decent furniture," he said, his tone heavily sarcastic.

Simon looked around and shrugged. "I don't know if I feel like furnishing an apartment. I might sell it."

The condo was large, spacious and sunny. Everything the real-estate agent said it would be. But Simon had little inclination to make it a home. It was just like the boat, the trips, all the other toys. Once he had it, it didn't do what he had hoped it would.

He had bought a large leather couch and matching chair at the same time he'd bought the condo. A wall unit stood holding only a stereo and some of the books Simon had collected over the years. He hadn't collected enough possessions over the years to fill such a large space.

Oscar leaned ahead, his elbows resting on his knees. "Would you feel more like fixing up, say—" he hesitated, his hands spreading out "—a Victorian house on five acres, north of Nanaimo, facing the mainland?"

Simon leaned back, making a steeple of his hands. "And why would I want to do that?"

"Because it's a good deal." Oscar held up his hand, ticking off the virtues. "The buyer needs to sell it, and because I think you're ready to buy a house instead of sharing halls and elevators with complete strangers. You need a place to bring a girlfriend."

"I don't know about the last," Simon said, forcing aside thoughts of an angel with soft blond hair and sea-green eyes. Caitlin was out of the question, out of the picture, and he was out of his mind to be even thinking about her. She represented obligations and commitment.

Family.

He got up, pushing aside his own thoughts.

"It's a great deal even from a business standpoint," Oscar continued, leaning back with a creak in the old office chair Simon had bought for his apartment. "And since your accident, I sense you've gone through some soul-searching, some change-of-heart-type stuff. You might even be ready to, dare I say it—" Oscar lowered his voice, his eyes wide, and did a quick drumroll on his knees "—settle down."

"Wishful thinking on your part, Oscar," Simon said shortly. Oscar was too intuitive by half.

"After I met Angela, I would walk around with this dazed look on my face, just like you are now. Someone would be talking to me, and I wouldn't even hear them. Just like you were a few moments ago."

"You won't quit, will you?" Simon said irritably.

"Nope." Oscar rocked back and forth, and Simon resisted the urge to snap at him to sit still.

He was like that more often these days. Irritable and easily angered. Peace eluded him. Before his accident, life had flowed along quite well, but not anymore.

Now all he could think of was Caitlin and the words she had read to him out of the Bible. The passage that offered comfort and at the same time required more of him than he was prepared to give.

All he could think of was how he'd destroyed the fragile bond building between them with a kiss born out of anger.

A kiss that had changed to need and want and a desire to protect and nurture.

"I've got the information you wanted on that company that's going public," Simon said, forcing his mind back to business, back to the safe and predictable. "They're in my bedroom, if you want to get them."

"Okay. Change the subject. I can do this," Oscar said with a laugh, getting up.

The sudden chime of the doorbell broke the quiet.

"Shall I get it?" Oscar asked.

"No. That's okay. The papers are in a folder beside the bed," Simon replied over his shoulder as he walked to the door, wondering who it could be. The home-care nurse stopped by only weekly now and she had come yesterday. He wasn't expecting anyone else to come.

He worked his way slowly across the living room and then to the hallway. This condo was way too big, he thought, trying not to hurry.

Finally he reached the door and opened it.

"Delivery for Simon Steele." A ponytailed delivery boy held out a form for Simon, who signed it. "Do you want me to bring it in for you?" the boy asked, noticing Simon's cane.

"Sure. Just set it on the table there."

Whistling, the boy brought in a package, then

sauntered out, closing the door on a very curious Simon.

It was from the Nanaimo General Hospital.

For a weird and wonderful moment he thought it might be something from Caitlin but when he opened it, surprised to see his fingers trembling, he pulled out his jacket.

"What was that?" Oscar walked into the room, frowning at the box on the table.

"My jacket. From the hospital."

"You dropped something." Oscar bent over and picked up a piece of paper, handing it to Simon.

Simon took it, read it and swallowed. It was a note from Caitlin, asking how he was, hoping that all was well with him. Signed with her name. Underneath that, in smaller letters she wrote that she was praying for him.

"What's up, Simon? You look like you've been told your biggest stocks just tanked." Oscar tilted his head, as if to get a better look at his partner. "You okay?"

"Yeah." Simon took a deep breath, rereading the note as if trying to find something else, some hint of her feelings in it.

"Who's it from?"

"Caitlin," he said without thinking.

"Newest girlfriend?" Oscar asked with a grin. "Is that how she got your coat?"

"No. She works at the hospital. She was my nurse."

"Is she why my tough wheeler-dealer partner is looking as mushy as a cooked marshmallow?"

"Never mind, Oscar," Simon snapped, dropping the letter in the box.

"Ooh. Touchy, too."

"I wasn't mushy."

"Maybe *mushy* was the wrong word. Maybe *wistful* would be better." Oscar sighed dramatically, placing a hand over his heart.

Simon ignored him, putting the coat back on the table. "Can we get back to work?"

"Sure." Oscar grinned as he walked back to the desk. He dropped into a chair. "Caitlin," he said with a tinge of sarcasm and a wink. "I like that name. She's obviously a very organized and caring person. Sending you your coat like that."

"Drop it, Oscar."

Oscar held his partner's gaze, his expression suddenly serious. "I don't know if I will. I've never seen you this flustered, ever. You're cranky on the one hand and on the other, you seem to take things easier. Like I said, I catch you staring off into space. Definitely twitter-pated."

Simon sighed, realizing Oscar wasn't going to let this one go. "Okay. I like Caitlin. You happy now?"

"Nope. Not until I know what you're going to do about it."

"Nothing. Zilch. Nada."

"Which begs the question, why not?"

"Beg all you want. She's off-limits." Simon got

up, rubbing his leg. It ached again, which meant he should probably lie down. But he didn't want to do that, either. "Did you want to go over those funds?"

"No. I want to check out that Victorian house on the Island for you, and I want to see you phone the lady who has you all tied up in knots and ask her out."

Simon sighed, plowing his hand through his hair in frustration. "By all means, check out the house. Maybe you can move there yourself," he said, thoroughly exasperated with his partner.

"Nah. Angela always gets sick on the ferry. You're more flexible than I am, anyhow. Doesn't matter where you live. But I'll check it out for you." Oscar pointed at Simon, winking at him.

"Then do it now. Anything to get you off my back."

"You know, I think I will." Oscar bounded off the couch with a grin and shoved the papers into his briefcase. "Catch ya later, pardner," he said with a smile as he headed out the door.

Simon glared at it as his partner left, feeling pushed and hemmed in by the people in his life. Oscar would never have dared talk to him as he did a few weeks ago. Simon wouldn't have let him.

But as Oscar had said, things had changed. Simon was tired of the loneliness and emptiness of his life. He had allowed Oscar to get closer.

Had allowed Caitlin to get closer still. The downside was the vulnerability, the obligations.

Obligations and the promise of a pair of green eyes that haunted him at every turn.

And the sooner he got that out of his system, the better.

Simon pockcted his car keys, moved the flowers over to his other arm and sighed deeply. A quick glance at his watch showed him that he could figure on the shift change to be happening in about fifteen minutes.

He gave the arrangement a critical once-over. Looked innocuous enough. Carnations and lilies and a few roses.

A very proper thank-you-type bouquet, he figured, no strings attached. It was the least he could do after being such a miserable patient.

He sucked in another deep, cleansing breath, blew it out again, straightened his new lcather jacket and then forced himself to move. The December air was chilly, even for the Island, and hc hoped the flowers would be protected enough until he got to the hospital.

Once inside, he felt a slight moment of panic. What if Caitlin wasn't working at all?

Well, then, so be it, he thought, sauntering down the hallway toward the ward, trying to recapture the laissez-faire attitude that had taken him through other situations with other women. The kind of attitude that gave him a measure of protection.

But his cavalier attitude seemed to dissipate as

quickly as frost in the sun when he rounded the corner to the ward and came near the desk. He wiped one palm on his jeans, the other hand still holding the flowers. No one was there.

He looked hopefully around, wondering where everyone was, resisting the urge to just drop off the flowers and go. Then he heard the sound of voices in the room opposite. *My old room,* he thought, turning.

Danielle walked out, laughing. She turned her head and stopped dead in her tracks.

"What are you doing?" Another nurse came up behind her, gave Danielle a light shove and then stopped herself.

"Hi," Simon said, shifting the flowers uselessly to the other hand. He couldn't stop the thrum of his heart at the sight of Caitlin. She wore her hair up today, emphasizing the delicate line of her jaw. Her face was flushed, her eyes bright. She licked her lips once, her hands clasped in front of her, and gave him a curt nod.

"Thought I'd drop these off for you ladies," he said, holding up the flowers. "A thank-you for all you did."

Danielle gave Caitlin a nudge, who stepped slowly forward. "Nice to see you again, Simon," Caitlin said softly, taking the flowers. She walked around the desk and set the basket on the ledge, pulling the plastic off. With her eyes still on the flowers, she bent over, sniffing them. "They're beautiful. I'm sure everyone will appreciate them. Thank you."

Her voice was quiet, well modulated, unemotional. Simon wondered if he had done this all wrong.

He shoved his hands in his back pockets and shifted his weight to his good leg. "You're welcome," he said, casting about for something witty and urbane to say. It would have been easy a couple of months ago, but much had happened to him since then.

"How's the leg?" Danielle asked, breaking the silence.

"Good," Simon replied, glancing at her, his eyes returning to Caitlin who still fussed with the flowers. "It hurts once in a while, but even that's getting better."

"And work? How's that going? Still dabbling in the stock market? Got any good tips for some poor lowly nurses? Any inside information?"

Simon forced his attention back to Danielle. "All I can tell you is that helium is up," he said, grasping for something, anything that would make Caitlin look up from those infernal flowers and at him.

Caitlin's head came up at his poor attempt at humor, a grin teasing the corner of her mouth. "I suppose diapers remain unchanged," she returned quickly.

Simon felt the tension that held him slowly release and he smiled back at her. "How are you doing, Caitlin?" he asked quietly.

"I think I should get the report ready for the new shift," Danielle said to anyone who cared to listen, then left, leaving Caitlin and Simon looking at each other.

"I'm fine," she said, looking away again. "Been busy on the ward."

"You'll be done in a few minutes?" He asked it as a question even though he knew what the answer would be.

She nodded, glancing sidelong at the clock on the wall. "Ten minutes to be precise."

"You want to go for a cup of coffee?"

She looked up at that, smiling again. "Sure. Sounds good. I have to do a report for the new shift coming on and then I'm done."

"I'll wait for you by the entrance," he said. She nodded her assent and he turned and left, unable to stop his grin.

Pacing around the entrance took up about five minutes. Synchronizing his watch so that it was on time with the clock in the entryway took another sixty seconds. Running his hands over his hair filled fifteen seconds.

Shaking his head at his own behavior, he found an empty chair, picked up a magazine and tried to read about landscaping a summer home. He turned the page to an article about the advantages of shrubs in a backyard.

He thought again about the Victorian that Oscar said he was going to look at. A home. Was he nuts? What did he know about homes and families? Nothing. He had never given himself enough time to figure out how they worked.

Then what are you doing waiting for Caitlin Severn to show up?

He threw the magazine down and instead kept himself busy watching the people, his legs stretched out in front of him, feet crossed at the ankles. *You're not proposing to the woman. You're just asking her out for a cup of coffee,* he told himself. *You've done it hundreds of times before with dozens of other women.*

But none of the other women had shown him what Caitlin had shown him. None of them had encouraged him to return to his faith in God, had nurtured a sense of shame and need.

Chapter Thirteen

Caitlin walked down the hall, her steps brisk, efficient. She caught sight of him, then slowed, one hand coming up to smooth her hair.

Simon got up slowly, ignoring the slight pain in his leg.

She wore a yellow anorak and blue jeans. Her hair was loose and at the sight, he smiled. She looked more approachable now. Less a nurse, more a woman.

"Hi," she said, stopping in front of him.

Did he imagine that breathless note in her voice? Was it wishful thinking on his part?

"Hi, yourself." He pulled his car keys out of his pocket, jingling them a minute, just looking at her. "Any place special you want to go to?"

"There's a nice spot past the mall heading up-island," she said, fiddling with her purse straps.

"I've got my car in the parking lot. Do you want a ride with me?"

"Sure."

"Then let's go." They walked in silence out of the hospital, to his car. He unlocked the door for her, watching as Caitlin ducked her head and got in. He walked around the front of the car, his eyes still on her and got in on his side.

He drew in a steady breath as he buckled up and turned the key in the ignition. Caitlin sat back against the headrest, watching him as he backed out of the hospital parking lot and turned onto the road.

"This is a lot different than your motorbike," she said, looking around the interior. "Are you turning over a new leaf?"

"More like starting another book," he said quietly. "The motorbike had to go."

"That sounds profound. How is your leg?"

"Good." Simon drew in a deep breath, smiling. "Really good." He glanced sidelong at her. "And how was your visit with your sister, the one in Portland?"

"Nice. Evelyn and her husband have a lovely little baby girl."

Silence.

Well, that exhausted those topics of conversation, he thought.

They drove on for a while, both quiet. Simon never had trouble talking to a woman before, but Caitlin made him uneasy, nervous.

Caitlin glanced at Simon while he gave the waitress their order. His hair was longer than before, hiding the small scar she knew was on his forehead. His eyes held the same glint, his mouth curved up in the same impudent grin. He looked far more at ease than she felt.

His street clothes emphasized his masculinity and at the same time created a distance. This was a Simon unfamiliar to her. Strong, in charge and independent. When she had seen him standing by the desk, she felt as if all the breath had been squeezed out of her chest.

She fiddled with her spoon and, just for something to do, put some sugar in her coffee, stirring it slowly. She could feel Simon's eyes on her but didn't know what to say.

"Isn't this where we are supposed to make intelligent conversation?" he asked suddenly. "You ask me a question, I ask you a question…." He let the comment fade as he smiled at her.

"And the purpose is?"

"Getting to know each other in a neutral setting." Simon set his cup down. "The hospital was definitely your territory. This is just a restaurant. Neutral ground."

Caitlin looked down at her own cup, hardly daring to hope that he wanted the same thing she did. Something had started between them, something she didn't know if she dared explore.

He was right about territory. They had met on the unequal footing of patient and nurse. She had seen his vulnerability. However, he had also voluntarily opened himself up to her in a way no other man had. She had seen him searching for God and that, in itself, touched her deeply.

"I'll start with a question for you, seein's how you're not saying anything," Simon said, pushing his cup and saucer around on the table, a hint of a smile teasing the corner of his mouth. "What new and exciting things have happened in your life? How's the boyfriend?"

Caitlin frowned. "Boyfriend?"

"Yeah. The guy who came to the ward that night. Charles." Simon spun his cup in the saucer, holding her gaze.

"He's not my boyfriend. I broke up with him a while ago."

Simon stopped the spinning, his hand resting on the rim of the cup. "What did you say?"

"I said Charles is not my boyfriend."

Simon sat back, a smile curving his beautiful mouth. "Really."

"I broke up with him the night you had your accident." Caitlin swallowed as she saw the glint in his eyes and knew that in that moment something had shifted, changed. "He came to the ward hoping to get back together with me. I told him again that it was over." She looked down, remembering all too vividly the reasons she knew she would never go back to Charles Frost. Remembering Simon's gentle touch and the not-so-gentle kisses of a mouth that now curved up in a smile.

She felt her cheeks warm at the memory and quickly took a sip of coffee to cover up her embarrassment.

"I see," Simon said quietly.

Silence slipped over them as they sat opposite each other. A silence broken by the murmur of the other patrons of the restaurant. She searched desperately for something to say. "And how is your work going?"

Simon lifted a hand and waggled it back and forth. "Good. Making money in some places, losing it in others."

She nodded, and that topic was exhausted.

Simon pushed his cup and saucer aside and took her hand in his. "This isn't working really well, is it?" he asked, his deep voice low. "I was hoping we could exchange some idle chitchat, get to know each other better. Start over on a more equal footing." He lifted his eyebrows quickly at that. "If you'll pardon the pun."

Caitlin smiled, her heart thrumming at his contact, her hand nestled in the protective warmth of his. She raised her eyes to his and once again was lost. She had never felt this way about any man before, this sense of belonging, a feeling that with Simon all in her life that was annoying and frustrating became meaningless. "So, how do we do this?"

"I don't know." Simon looked down at her hand, stroking her thumb with his. "I already know that your favorite color is blue, your favorite food is chicken. That you are a great nurse and a sincere Christian." He looked up at that, his head tilted to one side. "I know that much about you."

Caitlin swallowed at the intensity of his gaze. "And I know that your favorite color is brown. You like French fries, and you don't like taking painkillers."

His slow, lazy smile wound its way around her heart, tightening it with bands of yearning.

"I know that you have a brother," she continued, striving for an even tone, determined to do this right, to confront all the issues of his life. "That you were raised in foster homes and that deep within you is a need for something more that only God can give. What I don't know is, if you've found it."

"Well, that was quite an exposé," he said, his tone dry.

"It's the truth. And if you want us to get to know each other better, then we had better start on that footing." Caitlin looked down at their joined hands, hoping and praying that she hadn't said too much, yet knowing that she was right.

"Do you want to get to know me better?" Simon asked. Caitlin saw the smirk on his face, but heard in his voice a faint note of yearning, of wanting.

"Yes, I do, Simon."

"You might not like what you discover."

"I know what I'm in for," she said quietly.

Now he sat across from her, one hand cradling hers, the other tracing her knuckles. He laughed softly, then looked up at her again. "I don't think you know what you've done to me, Caitlin. For years I've been on my own. I've done what I've wanted to do. I've made money and lost money and none of it mattered. I've never been a responsible kind of guy because I've never wanted to have something that I couldn't afford to lose. But you've made me take another look at myself." He shook his head, as if trying to understand it himself. "I didn't like what I saw. I was angry that you made me vulnerable. I've been trying all my life to be tough and strong. To be independent." He squeezed her hand, hard. "Now I've been reading the Bible, struggling with what God wants me to be. Trying to accept obligations. I don't know if I can do it."

His words alternately warmed and chilled her. "What are you trying to say, Simon?"

Simon lifted her hand up to his mouth and touched his lips to it. "I don't know," he whispered. "I just know that I care about you and that your opinion is important to me." He blew out his breath in a sigh that caressed her hand. "When I was sick, that last night you were with me in the hospital, you were reading that passage from Isaiah, something about comfort. I know what I have to do, but I'm not sure I'm ready to do it yet." He shrugged and gently lowered her hand to the table.

Caitlin smiled. "Well, then, I guess I have to keep praying for you, Simon."

He smiled back and gave her hand a quick squeeze. "You do that, Caitlin Severn."

The talk had gotten heavy, yet Caitlin felt a lightness pervade the atmosphere. As if a foundation had been laid. But she could see from Simon's frown that it was time to change the subject.

"So, tell me about Oscar. How in the world did you two ever meet up?"

Simon lifted his head, smiling. "That's a long story."

Caitlin shrugged, glancing at her watch. "I've got tomorrow off, so I've got time."

So he told her. The talk moved from Oscar to books they had read, places they'd been. Simon was well traveled, she discovered. He'd been to places she had only dreamed of seeing, done things she had only imagined. Scuba diving off the Tasmanian coast, trekking in Nepal, taking his chances on the Trans-Siberian railway. She shook her head with every new adventure.

"My life sounds horribly dull," she said after he'd recounted a harrowing trip on a bus through Africa.

Simon shrugged her comment away. "Traveling can be dull, too. Planes and hotels and rented cars. It's all the same after a while, if you're on your own." He caught her eye and smiled a lazy smile. "It's more fun with someone."

Caitlin's breath caught in her throat at the suggestion in his eyes, his smile.

"Aren't there places you would love to go, Caitlin?" he asked, his voice lowering almost intimately.

"Lots. I've always wanted to see Paris and Greece. The usual tourist travel destinations. I'm not much for adventure, I guess."

"I liked Paris. But it's not a city you should visit on your own," Simon said, leaning slightly forward, one corner of his mouth curved up in a smile. "Paris needs to be seen walking arm in arm with someone you care about." He took her hand again, playing with her fingers.

Caitlin felt her breath catch in her throat, felt her heart slow, miss a beat, then race as she understood the suggestion in his voice, his posture.

What am I going to do with this man, Lord? He confuses me, makes me afraid, makes me want to care for him. She swallowed, her hand still in his as he ran his index finger over hers again and again.

He looked up at her, his eyes intent, and Caitlin knew that if the table hadn't separated them, he would have kissed her.

And she would have let him.

The drive to Caitlin's home was done in silence, an awareness humming between them. Each time Simon glanced sidelong at Caitlin, he could see her eyes glowing in the reflected light of his car's dashboard.

He couldn't suppress the feelings of unworthiness that her gentle smile gave him. But he also knew that in spite of his feelings, he had to see her again. It was like a hollow need that only she could fill. He didn't like the hold she had over him, but he liked even less the notion of not seeing her again.

They pulled up to her house, the front window shedding light in the gathering darkness.

"Thanks for the ride," she said, reaching for the door handle. "And the coffee."

Simon watched her turn, watched as she pulled her purse close to her in readiness to get out. "Wait," he said softly, catching her arm.

She turned to face him, her eyes wide. "What?"

Simon let his eyes drift over her face, come to rest on her softly parted mouth. Ignoring the cold voice of reason, he bent over and fitted his mouth to hers. The kiss started out so gentle, so plain, but then she murmured his name, slipped her arms around him, pulled him closer.

And he was undone. He caught her close, almost crushing her, his mouth slanting over hers.

Simon was the first to draw away, his eyes seeking hers, his hand reaching up to touch her mouth in wonder.

"What are you doing to me?" he murmured, remembering his own response the last time he had kissed her. The absolute rightness of having her in his arms, the sweetness that pierced him when she spoke his name.

"Kissing you, I thought," she replied, her voice trembling.

Simon drew in a careful breath, unable to suppress the smile that threatened to crack his jaw. He stroked her hair back from her face, just because he wanted to. He didn't want to think about what was happening to him, didn't want to think that he was running the risk of making himself vulnerable to another person. This was Caitlin. She wasn't just anybody, he reasoned.

"Are you busy tomorrow?" he asked, looking down into her soft green eyes, losing himself in their warmth.

She shook her head. "Not until the evening," she whispered.

"How would you like to take a trip up-island? I have a place I want to have a look at." Not the most romantic date he had ever taken a woman on, but he sensed with Caitlin he needed to take things slow. For his own protection as much as anything. Maybe spending some more time with her would ease the ache thinking about her created in him.

Maybe pigs could fly, he thought.

"I'd like that," she said with a soft murmur. She touched his cheek, stroking it lightly with warm fingers.

"Good," he replied, turning his head to kiss her fingertips. "I'll pick you up at three."

She traced his mouth, smiling up at him. "Then I'll see you tomorrow," she said, leaning closer to press a light kiss on his lips.

Then she opened the car door, letting a blast of

cold air in, jumped out and was striding up the walk to her parents' house before he had a chance to open his own door.

He got out and called to her over the hood. "You're supposed to let me walk you to the door."

She turned, walking backward, laughing at him. "Next time," she said. Then tossing a wave at him, she turned and jogged up the steps and went into the house.

Bemused, Simon got back in his car, put it in gear and drove away. He felt bamboozled by what had happened. He had gone to the hospital simply to deliver flowers and ended up with a date with Caitlin Severn tomorrow. He wondered if he knew what he was getting himself into.

Chapter Fourteen

"What do you plan to do with it?" Caitlin asked, as Simon unlocked the front door of the old Victorian house.

"It's an investment," Simon replied, standing aside to allow Caitlin to walk into the main foyer. Their footsteps echoed in the large open hallway. To one side was a set of doors, now boarded up. The other set of doors led to a large open room and a hallway flanked the large, wide stairs directly in front of them.

"Oh, look at that." Caitlin ran up the first flight of stairs, stopping at the landing. A stained-glass window shed a colored pattern of diffused light on the landing. "This doesn't look Victorian."

"I suspect one of the hippies that lived here made it." Simon came up beside her, his hands in his pockets.

They walked upstairs, inspecting each room. The

heavy odor of incense hung in one of the rooms and in the other, dark paper covered a broken window. Water stains on the ceilings attested to the need for a new roof.

"It's going to be a pile of work, Simon. Are you sure you want to even bother?" Caitlin shook her head as they walked down the hall.

Simon shrugged, reaching around her to open the door of the last room. "A person could always bulldoze it and build a new one." He had to push to open the door and when they stepped inside the room, Caitlin had to stop her surprised gasp. Windows from floor to ceiling ran along one wall and flowed in a three-quarter circle instead of a corner to the other wall. "This is beautiful," she breathed, walking farther into the room, straight to the semicircle of windows. "Wouldn't a set of chairs be just perfect here?" She stepped closer to the window, resting her fingertips lightly against it as if to touch the view.

Beyond the shoreline below them, beyond the water, she could see the mountains of the mainland with their variegated colors of blue, mauve and gray. A few gulls wheeled past them, celebrating their utter freedom punctuated by their piercing cries.

"This is just incredible." She glanced over her shoulder, disconcerted to see Simon directly behind her. His hands were safely in the pockets of his khaki pants, holding back his leather jacket, but the way he looked down at her left her with no illusions as to what was on his mind.

"It is incredible," he agreed, his hazel eyes twinkling down at her.

"I meant the view, Simon," she said breathlessly.

His lazy smile crawled across his beautiful mouth. "So did I," he replied.

Caitlin looked away, fully aware of Simon behind her, aware of the fact they stood in what was probably the master bedroom of this large, rambling house. For a brief moment she allowed herself a fantasy. Simon and her, standing together, looking out over a view they saw day after day.

It would be early morning. They would each be getting ready for work, but taking time to just be together, sharing a quiet moment before the busyness of the day separated them.

She let her eyes close as she hugged herself, unaware of the fact that she was slowly leaning back toward Simon until barely a breath separated them. Then his arms surrounded her, held her against him, his face buried in the hair that lay on her neck.

"Caitlin," he breathed, holding her closer, rocking her slightly.

It was a small movement, a mere twisting of her head, a shifting of her weight, and her cheek touched his forehead. He lifted his head and once again, their lips met in a kiss as soft as a baby's sigh.

He was the first to draw back, and Caitlin murmured her disappointment. He dropped a light kiss on her forehead and then stepped back.

Caitlin felt bereft and frustrated at the same time.

She knew something important was building between them, but at the same time she didn't know if she should trust her own feelings. She cared for Simon deeply and if she were to truly examine her feelings, she would be able to say she loved him.

But she didn't dare say so, and so far he hadn't expressed how he truly felt about her. Once before she had made a mistake and wasn't eager to spend another few years of her life wondering about another relationship.

If she were to face the truth, she would realize that she was afraid to push Simon too hard. She knew enough about his life to know that Simon was afraid to tie himself down. Buying this house could be a signal that he was ready to do so, but then again, Simon was a consummate businessman. It could just be another investment.

Caitlin turned back to the view, frustrated with herself, frustrated with emotions she couldn't control. *Please Lord,* she prayed, wrapping her arms around herself, *show me what I should do. I'm confused. I'm afraid I love him, and I'm afraid that love will go nowhere. Help me to trust You, help me to be satisfied with Your love first and foremost.*

"We should be getting back."

Simon's voice broke into her prayer, and she turned to face him, forcing a smile to her face. He only stared at her, his own expression slightly dazed. Then he abruptly turned around, the sound of his booted heels echoing in the silence of the house.

Caitlin followed him more slowly, glancing over her shoulder once more at the remarkable room with the wonderful windowed nook.

Then she relegated her own wisp of a daydream back where it belonged. Reality.

"So, what's the verdict?" Simon asked as they drove away from the property.

Caitlin craned her neck for one last look then turned to Simon. "I think you should buy it. If nothing else, you could turn it into a bed-and-breakfast."

Simon pursed his lips, nodding at her suggestion. "Could do that." He glanced sidelong at her, then quickly away again. "I'd have to find someone to run it for me, though."

Their conversation seemed to carefully pick its way through dangerous territory, Caitlin thought. Simon hardly dared say that he might want the house for himself and she didn't dare suggest it. To do so would give a wrong signal, create a misunderstanding.

How she hated this stage of the relationship, she thought. She had gone through it enough times with Charles, she should be good at it. The hesitation, the uncertainty. Wondering if you were presuming too much. Wondering if it was going to go beyond a few kisses, a few casual dates.

In spite of all the gains women said they had made in terms of equality over the past few years, they hadn't made many strides when it came to women being able to read men, or vice versa.

He pulled up in front of her house and Caitlin turned to him, deciding to stick her neck out a bit. "Would you like to come in? It's my mother's birthday party."

Simon shrugged, biting his lip as he looked past her to the house.

"I can't intrude on that."

"You don't intrude on families, Simon," she said quietly. "Just come in for a quick cup of coffee. Say hi to my parents, wish my mom a happy birthday."

Simon blew out his breath in a sigh, still contemplating.

Please, Lord, let him say yes, she thought. She wanted him in her home. She wanted him to meet her family. In some foolish way she felt it would show her whether she was wasting her time or not.

She didn't want to feel that way about Simon because in spite of her doubts, she knew she was falling in love with him.

"Okay," he said quietly, giving her a quick grin. "I'll do that."

Caitlin let out her breath, not even aware she was holding it. Then with a grin she couldn't suppress, she got out of the car, waiting for him to catch up to her and together they walked up the path to her home.

As soon as they opened the door, Caitlin wondered if she had made a grave mistake. She heard the unmistakeable tones of Rachel's laughing voice, Jonathon's deep one and those of her grandparents'.

"Got extra company," she said with forced brightness as they walked in the door. Caitlin took his coat and hung it up in the cupboard in the entrance. Then taking a breath for courage, walked through the arched entryway into the living room.

"Oh, hi, Caity," her mother said from the couch directly facing the opening. "I'm so glad you made it back. I…"

But whatever she was about to say died on her lips when she saw Simon. She glanced back at Caitlin with a puzzled look, then back at Simon.

Caitlin almost groaned. She just knew her mother was mentally comparing Simon to Charles.

"Everybody," she said encompassing the entire room with a casual wave of her hand, forcing an overly bright smile. "I'd like you to meet Simon."

The introductions were made. Simon was gracious. He wished Caitlin's mother a happy birthday. He was witty and made Rachel laugh. Rachel tossed Caitlin a bemused look but thankfully was politeness personified when introduced.

Caitlin kissed her grandparents and listened to her grandfather's usual doctor joke. Grandma gave her a kiss and asked when she was coming over again. Her mother couldn't hide her surprise. Thankfully her father covered up by clearing the newspapers off a love seat, indicating they should sit there.

A moment of silence followed as Caitlin and Simon sat down, then…

"Do you want some birthday cake and coffee?" her mother offered both of them.

"How is work going?" Rachel asked Caitlin with a knowing smirk.

"So what do you do?" Jonathon asked Simon at the same time.

"Where did that dog go now?" her father muttered to no one in particular.

The dog was retrieved from under the couch and sent downstairs to sulk. Her mother left to get Simon and Caitlin each a cup of coffee but not before she threw Caitlin a slightly puzzled look.

Soon the usual ebb and flow of family conversation filled the room again as Caitlin answered the "duty" questions about her work from her grandparents and asked after Rachel's health. From that the topics ranged from the traffic coming off the ferry to politics to the best way to get rid of fleas on dogs. Caitlin laughed with her sister, answered her grandparents' frequent questions and occasionally glanced sideways at Simon. He was talking to Jonathon, but would, from time to time, look at her. His expression was unreadable, and Caitlin felt a stirring of disquiet. When he smiled it was forced. As he sat drinking his coffee, he sat on the edge of the couch, as if ready to bolt.

Simon finally finished his coffee, set down the cup and then stood up. "Mr. and Mrs. Severn, it was nice to meet you and best wishes again on your birthday," he said, his voice achingly polite. He said his farewells to the rest of the family and with a quick look at Caitlin left.

She followed him, her discomfort growing.

"What's wrong, Simon?" she asked as he pulled his jacket off the hanger in the entrance. He glanced over her shoulder at the group who she knew was watching them. She lowered her voice. "Did someone say something wrong?"

He snapped up his coat, the sounds echoing in the quiet. "Come say goodbye to me outside," he said, turning to open the door.

Caitlin hugged herself against a sudden chill as they stepped outside, closing the door quietly behind her. "What's the matter?"

He shoved his hands in his coat pocket, the overhead porch light casting his face in shadows. She couldn't read his expression, couldn't understand what precisely was happening, but her inner sense told her it wasn't good.

"Nothing's the matter. Your family didn't say anything wrong. They seem like wonderful people."

She relaxed at that, her shoulders losing their tension. "I'm glad you like them."

"I do. You're a lucky woman, Caitlin." She could see his careful smile. "No, not lucky. Blessed." He leaned closer and touched his lips to hers. A brief kiss, gentle and soft.

Then he turned and sauntered down the walk to his car, got in and drove away.

Caitlin watched his rear lights until he turned, then she leaned back against the door.

He had denied it, but she knew, deep inside, something had happened. Something very wrong.

It had been seventeen days, Caitlin figured, glancing at the calendar hanging on the wall in her parents' kitchen. Seventeen days since Simon had walked away from her standing on her parents' porch.

And he hadn't called.

How could she have been so stupid? she thought. Simon had dangled her along from the first time she met him. Back and forth, back and forth. Like she was some kind of fish on a hook. A kiss here and there, a serious conversation and then he pulled back again.

A sucker, she thought angrily, pushing her chair back and getting up, that's what she was. First Charles, now Simon. It seemed it was her fate to end up with guys who were afraid to commit.

She glanced at her watch. In an hour Danielle was going to pick her up to go Christmas shopping. And she dreaded it.

The season had sneaked up on her, she thought with a rueful shake of her head. Usually she was in the thick of preparations, helping her mother bake and putting up decorations long before it was time.

But not this year. This year it was a chore, a burden to get even the most simple of tasks done. The Christmas spirit was decidedly missing in her life.

And she knew exactly why.

She had prayed, had read her Bible, had talked to

her sisters, but she couldn't seem to get around the problem of her love for Simon. Because much as she didn't like to face it, she did love him.

She wasn't able to analyze exactly why. He was exasperating, complicated, troubled.

But each time she thought of him, it was with a trembling heart and a yearning to be with him again. He made her complete, whole.

She wandered around the house, from the kitchen to the living room. A Christmas tree sat in one corner, a few presents under it already. Her mother had made up arrangements of cedar and candles and laid boughs of cedar on the mantel of the fireplace. Clusters of cedar bound with bright red ribbon hung on the wall bracketing an embroidered nativity scene her mother had done years ago.

The aroma of cedar and fir filled the house. Her sisters were on the phone every other day, making plans, gearing up for another Severn family get-together. Tony had even called, much to her parents' delight and surprise.

Caitlin wondered if anything had ever come of her phone call to Simon's brother.

And then she thought of Simon. Again.

She was tired of feeling this confused and frustrated. She walked back to the kitchen and taking a steadying breath, sat down by the phone. She knew his number by heart. Sad, really.

It rang once, then again and she wondered if he was on the road, wheeling and dealing again.

On the fourth ring, someone picked up.

Even over the sterile medium of the phone line, his deep voice could give her shivers, she thought fatuously.

"Hello, Simon. Caitlin here."

Silence hung heavy over the line.

"Hello, Caitlin."

She wished she could see his face, wished she could see his expression. But all she had to go on was his voice. And that didn't sound too welcoming.

She decided to forge ahead. "I hadn't heard from you in a while," she said. "You must be busy," she added hopefully.

"Yeah." Silence again.

"I was wondering if that was the reason I haven't heard from you."

"Well, things have been hectic with that new apartment block."

"What about the house?"

"I've decided to give it a miss. Didn't seem like a good investment."

"I see." And she did. Silly as it sounded, the house seemed to represent settling down, a desire on his part for more than a sterile apartment. Her silly fantasy had been just that. She would have gladly shared that home with him. But Simon only saw opportunities.

"Look, Caitlin. I've got to go. Oscar is coming pretty soon…."

"Am I going to see you again?"

A hesitation, then Simon cleared his throat. "Caitlin, I'm sorry." He paused, and in that moment Caitlin felt her throat thickening, choking her. She swallowed and swallowed, afraid of the next words, willing them out of him, yet at the same time wanting to slam the phone on the hook so she wouldn't hear them.

"Caitlin, it just isn't going to work between us," he continued.

"Explain that, please," she said abruptly. How could he say that? They had shared so much. She remembered reading Isaiah to him, talking to him, sharing. She felt more complete with him than she had with Charles, with any man she had met.

"You're a great person and you've got a lot going for you...."

"Spare me the platitudes, just give me the truth." She forced the words out, clutching the phone so hard she was surprised it was still intact.

"I have nothing to give you Caitlin."

She forced a laugh. "Whatever do you mean, Simon? I thought you had quite a bit of money."

"I know money isn't important to you, Caitlin. But I know family is. And I can't give you that." He paused. "I'm sorry."

"Don't you dare hang up yet, you coward," she blurted, hardly believing she actually spoke the words out loud. "I don't know where you come off thinking that family is like a dowry, an endowment you bring to a relationship. I know where you come from. I know where you've been...."

"No, you don't Caitlin." Simon's voice was hard now. "You don't know and don't presume to think you do."

"Do I need to experience precisely the same thing to be able to understand you?" She got up, pacing back and forth, trying to find some outlet for her anger, her frustration. "I have agonized over our relationship. I have wondered what I really feel for you. I've lain awake nights over you, I've watched over you. I've prayed for you and loved you. And now you so casually tell me 'it won't work' just because I have a family and you don't. I've been told by one ex-boyfriend that 'it won't work' because I don't want to move, but never because I happen to come from a loving home."

"You really don't understand, do you?" he growled. "It's over, Caitlin." He hesitated while Caitlin drew in another breath to give him another blast. "It's over." Then unbelievably, she heard a click of the phone in her ear. She looked at it, dumbfounded, then slowly hung up.

She turned around, walked upstairs to her bedroom, sank down on her bed. Then she buried her face in her hands and wept.

She cried for herself, for Simon and his confusion and for the pain she heard in his voice. She cried for all the brokenness in this cold lonely world that created people without families, without a parent's love.

When the worst of her heartache had flowed over her and dissipated, she lay back on the bed, her eyes sore from the sorrow, staring sightlessly up at the ceiling. In spite of her own sorrow, she couldn't help her prayer. *Please be with Simon,* she whispered. *Please show him Your love and Your comfort. Help me to understand. Show me what to do.* Somehow, she knew she and Simon weren't finished yet.

Simon laid the phone down and pressed his fingers against his eyes. He sucked in a deep breath.

I've prayed for you, loved you.

Caitlin's words were spoken in anger, but he heard the absolute sincerity behind them.

He knew he had done the right thing by breaking up with her. He knew any relationship with Caitlin would go beyond casual. All the way to marriage and what kind of father would he be? What did he know of parenting, of how families worked? He came from nowhere and had nothing.

Sitting in Caitlin's house with her family had reminded Simon far too vividly of each time he was moved into a new home. Those first few weeks of uncertainty, of trying to figure out how this family worked, of wondering if this was going to be a good home or bad home. The feeling of not belonging, of being on the outside of a family that had been together long before him and would still be together after he left.

He had spent half his life outrunning responsibilities, the ties that a family like Caitlin's entailed would bind around him. He hadn't given himself time to maintain close friendships, hadn't bothered to get to know anyone other than Oscar on the most casual basis.

Somewhere in Alberta he had a brother he hadn't talked to in so long, he wouldn't even know how to begin reestablishing their long-lost relationship. There was no forgiveness for that long a silence and he knew it.

The end result of all that was he had nothing to give Caitlin.

I've prayed for you, loved you.

Her words echoed through his mind. Blowing out a sigh, he dragged his hands over his face then looked up.

He needed to get some work done, that's what. He never spent this much time contemplating his own life before. Never gave himself enough time to do it.

He flipped on the computer and as he waited for it to boot up, picked up the estimate a contractor had sent him on renovating the apartment block in Nanaimo. Under the file folder lay a Bible.

Simon glanced at it.

He remembered a quiet voice reading to him through the delirium of his fever. *Comfort, comfort ye my people.* Words that soothed, filled, smoothed the rough places of his life. Caitlin had stayed at his side then, as well.

Simon didn't deserve her, he knew that. But he

also knew that he couldn't put her out of his mind. It was sheer cowardice on his part that kept him away from her. He hadn't been able to run, but he had retreated.

But oh, how he had missed her. He knew he cared for her more deeply than he had for anyone. He knew that every time he thought of her, his heart ached. Love shouldn't hurt, he thought. Love was supposed to be a soft, gentle emotion, not these hooks that dug into his heart.

Frustrated with his own thoughts, he picked up the Bible, leaned back in his chair, crossed his legs at the ankle and started leafing through it.

He turned to Isaiah 40. "Comfort, comfort my people, says your God." Caitlin had certainly followed that command, he thought with a sad smile. He read on until he came to Isaiah 41. "I took you from the ends of the earth, from its farthest corners I called you. I said, 'You are my servant;' I have chosen you and have not rejected you. So do not fear, for I am with you; do not be dismayed, for I am your God. I will strengthen you and help you; I will uphold you with my righteous right hand."

He laid his head on the high back of his computer chair, letting the words become a part of him. *Called, chosen. Not rejected.*

He had been here before, he thought. In the hospital. That last night he had been with Caitlin. He remembered his broken dreams. Words and snatches came back to him now. *My son, give me your heart,* he remembered.

He had hesitated then. To give one's heart was to open oneself up to weakness, to give someone something to hold over you.

But what was the alternative? he thought, opening his eyes and looking around his stark apartment. *Keeping to yourself, making more money? Eating your heart out over a beautiful woman with a gentle smile?*

His life seemed rather pathetic right now. Empty and purposeless. He closed his eyes. The Bible was still open on his lap. He knew what he had to do. He just wasn't sure exactly how to go about it. *Show me, Lord. Help me through this,* he prayed. *I can't go on like this. I love her. I know I do. I know what You want of me. I don't like being weak. I don't like letting others be in charge, but I'm hereby putting You in charge of my life.* He stopped, as if analyzing the data, then shook his head. *I'm letting go. I surrender.*

And at that moment, as he mentally pried his fingers from all the events of his life that he clung to so tightly, he felt a lightness, a peace pervade him.

He spent the next half hour paging through the Bible, remembering passages that Tom Steele used to read. He reacquainted himself with a book that had once been a part of every meal, every evening before bed.

And he slowly felt the tension leave his shoulders. He laid the Bible aside with a rueful grin. Salvation or no, he still had some work to do. And he still had to figure out how he was going to reconcile himself with Caitlin, praying he hadn't blown it.

The harsh peal of the doorbell broke his concentration on the computer. With a dazed glance he looked up. Darkness had fallen while he had worked. He wondered who it could be. For a brief moment the thought pierced him that it might be Caitlin. But common sense told him to forget that idea.

Simon got up, walked to the door, opened it and frowned.

A tall figure stood backlit by the light from the hallway. He wore a red plaid jacket over a denim shirt tucked into denim jeans. Cowboy boots completed the picture.

"Simon Steele?" the man asked.

Simon nodded, then, as the voice filtered through his memories he felt the blood drain from his face, felt his heart slow.

"Jake?"

Chapter Fifteen

"Hello, Simon," Jake replied, his hands hanging at his sides, not making a move in his brother's direction.

Simon couldn't help but stare. It was Jake all right. Same dark hair with a tendency to wave, same brown eyes that looked steadily at the world from beneath level brows. Same uncompromising mouth. Same Jake, only older.

Simon forced his gaze away. "Come in," he said, stepping aside, shock making him almost incoherent.

He flicked on some lights as Jake walked into the room.

Jake stopped halfway, not sitting down, just looking at his brother. But what do you say after all those quiet years? Their last phone call had been full of anger and accusations and they hadn't spoken to each other since.

Now two grown men stared across the room at each other as the silence stretched out.

Finally Simon asked, "How did you find me?"

Jake sat down then, his elbows resting on his knees. "I got a phone call," he said slowly, clasping his hands. "From a woman named Caitlin. She called when you were still in the hospital. I would have come to visit you then, but she called in the middle of fieldwork. We were way behind so I couldn't come."

Simon sat down at that. Caitlin again. Dear, sweet, wonderful, beautiful, organizing Caitlin. "How did she find you?"

Jake lifted one shoulder, shaking his head. "Don't have a clue." He looked up at Simon. "I thought you might have told her."

"I haven't talked to you in over twelve years." Simon blew out his breath as the reality of the words settled in for both of them. He looked at his brother as he struggled to find something that would bridge the gap of time and space between him and one of the few people in his life that he had ever truly loved.

Jake looked up and for a moment their eyes held. Jake was the first to look down, pressing his thumbs together and apart. "So, what kind of work have you been doing these past years?"

Chitchat, thought Simon. A warming up, a way of circling and checking each other out from the safe distance of work and occupation. "I own a few franchises, dabble in stocks and bonds." Simon laughed shortly as he heard his job through his brother's ears. "What about you?"

Jake pursed his lips, tilted his head to one side. "I'm farming with Fred Prins. My foster father."

"So you stayed there?"

Jake nodded. "I was fortunate there."

Simon clasped his hands over his stomach, letting a silence drift up between them, full of memories. "So, you ever get married?" he asked finally.

Jake laughed shortly. "Yes. I have a little girl. My wife is dead, though."

Simon sensed a history there, but didn't pursue it, recognizing the need to keep things light for now. "Well I didn't. Always been restless, I guess."

More silence. They both knew what the end result of that restlessness had been.

"So, how long can you stay?" Simon asked.

"I've got a couple of days off. I thought I would stay around for a while tomorrow. I have to be back the next day, though. Christmas is coming."

Simon nodded, feeling a clutch of sorrow at the mention of Christmas. He was usually gone this time of the year. However, for now his sorrow was alleviated by the reality of his brother, here. A brother who wanted to reconnect the broken thread of their mutual past. Family.

"Did you have supper?" Simon asked.

"I grabbed a burger at Blue River," Jake said.

"Then you're probably ready for something else.

We could go out, but you're probably tired. I'll order in."

Half an hour later they sat across from each other at the table—a steaming pizza in a box between them. Bachelor food, thought Simon wryly. Jake paused a moment, bowing his head, and Simon realized he was asking a blessing.

Simon did the same. *I'm a little rusty at this, God,* he prayed, *I'm not exactly sure what I should be saying, but thanks.* He paused then added, *Thanks for Jake.* He lifted his head and caught Jake's surprised look. He ignored it and started eating. When they were done, they moved to the living room, settling into an awkward silence.

"Why don't you ask me the questions you want to, Jake," Simon said after a few minutes, knowing he wanted to get things out in the open. "We can get all of this stuff from our past out of the way."

"We'll never get it *all* out of the way," Jake said, standing up and turning to face his brother. "Things don't just go away because you've decided they will."

Simon held his brother's steady gaze. "You came a long way to see me, Jake. I think you're allowed a few questions."

"Okay." Jake plowed his hand through his hair, rearranging the neat waves. "May as well get to it. Did you ever find Mom?"

"No. I would have called you if I did."

"Would you have?" Jake asked, his short laugh sounding harsh. "It would have been nice if you had, anyhow. Because I didn't have the first clue where you were, Simon. In over ten years not a letter, a phone call, not even a postcard or a message sent via someone else. I thought you were dead, man. I really thought you were dead."

And as Simon listened to the pain in his brother's voice, he was forced to face the consequences of his own actions.

"I remember asking why you always ran, and you'd say you were looking for Mom. Were you really?" Jake's voice was quiet now.

Simon shrugged. "At first I was. After Dad Steele died, I hated the idea that we got moved and had no say. I missed Dad and I didn't know how to show it. So I would take off."

"The social workers would get so ticked off at you for running away all the time. I remember how flustered our foster parents would get," Jake said.

"The one, Mary Arnold, would always cry and her husband would yell."

"I think they liked us but couldn't handle the stress. So we got moved again."

"For what it's worth, Jake, I'm sorry," Simon said quietly.

"Well, we only went through one more. Then we were split up...."

"And you landed on your feet at the Prins's home," Simon said wistfully. "I was always jealous of you, you know that?"

"You didn't like it at your last foster home, did you?"

Simon shook his head. "The Stinsons were decent people but hard. I used to hate it when she would punish me by taking away visits with you." Simon smiled. "I always enjoyed our visits together. I remember coming to visit you at the Prins's, and Mrs. Prins would always give me a big hug. It was about the only time I got one."

"Really?"

Simon held his brother's gaze. "Yeah, Jake. Really."

"You never said."

"C'mon. We were fifteen. What guy of that age is going to admit that he still likes to get a hug?" Simon shrugged off the memory. "Like I said, the Stinsons did what they were supposed to, but I didn't get a lot of affection there."

"That why you ran away?"

"Partly. I was sick of getting told what to do. I was a cocky, mixed-up sixteen-year-old who had some weird notion of finding our mother so that you and I could get back together again. You were so happy at the Prins's home, I knew you wouldn't run away unless I gave you a good reason to."

"Tilly and Fred Prins treated me like a son. Running away to find our mother was a dead end."

"I didn't look that hard, Jake," Simon conceded. "I didn't have the time, money or resources. And after a while, I didn't even have much of a reason."

"Do you think we might find her yet?"

"I'd like to think we might."

"If we both put our energy behind it, we could find out if she's still alive or not."

Simon had always lived under the impression that Jake wasn't interested in looking into their past. "Sounds good to me. I'd like to connect with her, be a family again. When I was in the hospital, the kid next to me would get visits from his family. And I would get jealous...."

"If I had known..."

"Doesn't matter, Jake. You're here now and for that I thank God."

They spent the rest of the evening catching up, exchanging idle chitchat, reconnecting.

The next morning Simon and Jake went to a restaurant for breakfast and Jake asked him who Caitlin was.

"A nurse at the hospital."

"But she didn't call from the hospital."

"No?" Simon was surprised. "Where did she call from?"

"Said it was her sister's place. She seems like a great person, Simon," Jake continued. "When she phoned I wasn't exactly hospitable, but she kept at me."

"She does that well," conceded Simon with a wry grin.

"She told me that she believed God had brought her to me and told me she would be praying for us."

He laughed lightly, pouring syrup over his pancakes. "Told me that you and I needed to be a family again."

"Family's pretty important to her. As is her faith." Simon fiddled with his eggs.

"I get the feeling that she's special?"

Special? The word was totally inadequate to describe the hunger that clutched him when he thought of her. The regret that he felt just now. "I think I love her, Jake," he said, unable to keep the words down, needing to talk to someone about it. Who better than his own brother?

"That's great."

Simon sighed. "I guess."

"So, what's the problem?" Jake continued.

"She's a wonderful person, just like you guessed. Her faith is so strong and so much a part of her," Simon continued, staring into the middle distance, thinking about her. "She comes from a secure, happy family. I don't know if I can give her the same. I've run away from every family I've been a part of."

"Don't underestimate what you have to offer." Jake forked up a piece of pancake. "She must care for you. Why else would she call?"

Simon hardly dared believe what his brother said. He knew he and Caitlin shared something. He knew that he loved her dearly. But for the rest of their time together, Caitlin wasn't mentioned again.

They walked back to Simon's apartment, talking, catching up. "You want to come to the farm for

Christmas?" Jake asked after a moment. "I know you'll be more than welcome."

Simon shrugged, his hands in his pockets, his shoulders hunched against the cold. "I don't know. I usually spend Christmas in warmer places. I wouldn't know what to do."

"What's to do? You show up, eat, laugh. Come to church. You could meet my little girl."

Simon smiled as he opened the door of his condo for his brother. "A niece. Imagine that."

"She's a cutie, 'Uncle Simon.'" Jake nudged him. "You'd love her."

"Uncle Simon. That has a nice ring to it." Simon tried to imagine Jake with a little girl, tried to see himself as an uncle. Family.

"So are you going to come?"

Simon pulled in a deep breath and blew it out again. He had missed Caitlin more each day, wanted to be with her. *I've loved you, prayed for you.* Her words haunted him. He had told her it was over, yet he knew he would never forget her.

"No," he said suddenly, shrugging off his coat. "I think I should finish off some unfinished business first."

"Caitlin?"

Simon caught his lip between his teeth and nodded.

"I think that's wise. She sounds like a sincere, warm person. I didn't come across real well when I talked to her, but she didn't hang up on me. Thanks to her, I'm here. I'd like you to go and thank her for me."

"I haven't had to contend with so much advice since last time I saw you."

"It's good advice you know." Jake glanced down at his watch and got up. His grin softened into a wistful smile as he took a step closer to Simon. He held out his hand. "I'm sorry, but I've got to go. It was so good to see you again."

Simon took his brother's hand and then, grasping it tightly, pulled him closer. Their arms came around each other and Simon swallowed down a knot of emotion. His brother. His family.

Thank You Lord, he prayed, squeezing his eyes shut.

When he pulled away he could see Jake was as moved as he was.

"I'll walk you to your vehicle."

"That's okay. Let's just say goodbye now. I don't like goodbyes."

Simon held his brother's dark eyes as the unspoken words whispered between them as each remembered other separations, other goodbyes. "I promise this one won't be as long," Simon said, his voice thick with emotion.

Jake smiled back, and then they were hugging again, their arms tight. "Thanks for everything," Jake said, pulling back. "You make sure you come."

"I will. I just have some things to do yet. But I'll be there." He hardly dared think past the current moment, that things might work out. He only knew regardless of how Caitlin took it, he had to tell her how he felt.

"Keep me posted," Jake said picking up the overnight bag he'd left by the front door.

"I will." Simon watched as Jake left, closing the door behind him. The visit had come and gone so quickly, but he knew he would see his brother again.

Thank You, Lord, he prayed, closing his eyes in thankfulness. *Now if You could only help me out with this next thing.*

Caitlin leaned against the wall, wrapping her arms around herself as she listened to the carolers coming down the hallway of the hospital, fighting down the emotions that were so close to the surface. She blinked, staring ahead at the bright lights that someone had strung along the ward. They swam, sparkled, danced. She blinked again, and her vision cleared.

It was the season, she figured, wiping the tears from her face. Christmas was a time rife with emotions. For Caitlin it was a reminder of how alone she was this Christmas. She smiled at that thought, thinking of all the people swarming through her parents' home, filling it with laughter and noise. Hardly alone.

Her mother had been busy for weeks beforehand, cooking, baking and cleaning in preparation for the holidays. It had been a few Christmases since the three girls were together. Tony and his wife never came.

Where are you, Simon, she wondered, closing her eyes as she dropped her head against the hard wall behind her. Another tear slid down her cheek but she let it go. Are you alone this Christmas? She swallowed a lump that filled her throat. She let herself think of him, pray for him, yearn for him.

Just a few more minutes, she thought, a few more minutes of remembering what he looked like, how his voice could lower and send shivers down her spine, what his mouth felt like on hers.

She bit her lip, clutched her waist harder, knowing she was playing a dangerous game. She was alone and in an hour she had to face her family. She wouldn't have the defenses if she kept this up.

Sucking in another steadying breath she opened her eyes, pushed herself away from the wall and blinked.

Then again.

A tall figure stood five feet away from her, his shoulders hunched beneath a leather jacket, hands in the pockets of blue jeans. Softly waving hair the color of sand touched the collar of his jacket, piercing hazel eyes beneath level brows eyed her intently. His mouth was unsmiling.

Simon.

He's so tall, she thought. She closed her eyes and opened them again. He looks tired. Her thoughts made no sense as she stared, unable to form another coherent thought. Then he started coming nearer and she took a step backward. Immediately she hit the wall behind her, but he kept coming. Finally he was directly in front of her, his deep-set eyes pinning her against the wall.

"Hi, there," he said, his voice quiet. His lips were parted and Caitlin had to clench her fists to keep from reaching up to trace their line, to touch his cheek, to make sure he was real.

"Hi, yourself," she said past dry lips, her heart beating so hard against her chest she thought it would fly out. She had missed him so much, had prayed, had wondered. Now he stood in front of her and she didn't know what to say.

"Caitlin, I need to tell you something," he said with a short laugh.

She looked up at that and saw uncertainty in his eyes, saw two small frown lines between his eyebrows. "Okay."

"I love you," he said, his deep voice surrounding her with its reality, warming her with its sound. "I was wrong. I thought I didn't have anything to give you, but that doesn't matter, does it?"

She shook her head as sorrow and pain and loneliness were washed away by his first three words. "I love you, too," she couldn't help but say.

He closed his eyes, resting his forehead against hers, his fingers lying on her neck. "Oh, Caitlin. I can hardly believe this." His breath came out in a sigh, caressing her mouth, her cheek.

Then his arms were around her, crushing her, pressing her close, his mouth molding and shaping hers. He murmured her name again and again, kissing her cheeks, her eyes, her forehead, her mouth.

Then, he pressed his face against her neck, as he drew out a shuddering sigh.

Caitlin couldn't hold him tight enough, couldn't stop herself from repeating his words back to him. "I love you, Simon. I love you with all my heart." It seemed a weak expression of the fullness in her chest that threatened to turn into tears of happiness.

Simon was the first to draw away, his eyes traveling hungrily over her face. "I can't believe this," he whispered, shaking his head lightly. "I can't believe you said that."

She smiled so hard, she felt as if her face were going to split. She wanted to kiss him again, to throw her arms out and shout it out to the world. I love Simon. Instead she reached up and did what she had longed to do from the first time she had realized her changing feelings for him. She traced the line of his mouth, his beautiful, expressive mouth. Then she pressed her fingers against his lips as if accepting a kiss, then touched her own.

"Okay you two, break it up." A loud voice behind Simon made him whirl around, his arms still holding Caitlin.

Danielle faced them, her head tipped to one side, grinning a crooked grin. "Just because it's Christmas doesn't mean you can flirt with the nurses, Simon."

He looked back at Caitlin, who felt her face redden in response. "I'm not flirting," he said quietly. He dropped a quick kiss on her forehead. "This is serious business." He looked down at Caitlin. "I need to talk to you later," he said, his voice full of meaning.

Caitlin looked up at him, her eyes wide at first, then as she understood, spilling over with tears. "Talk to me now," she said softly.

He glanced around the hospital ward. "No. I have a better place in mind."

"Okay, I know what you're talking about," Danielle said with a laugh. "Why don't you head home, Caitlin, and you can put this poor man out of his misery. But first, let me be the first to congratulate you." She gave her friend a quick, hard hug. "Good on you, girl," she said in her ear.

Danielle pulled away and sniffed, wiping her eyes surreptitiously. She gave Simon a quick hug, as well, smiling at him as she pulled away. "You take good care of her," she said, a warning note in her voice.

"With God's help, I will," he said, his voice solemn as a vow.

Danielle nodded then turned to Caitlin. "You're not going to be any good to me for the next half hour, Caitlin. You may as well go home."

Caitlin looked up at Simon. "You have to come with me, you know." She waited, almost holding her breath while he seemed to consider.

"I was hoping you'd ask."

Caitlin smiled up at him, her heart full.

Danielle gave her a push. "Just go already."

"Thanks, Danielle," Caitlin said to her friend. "I hope you have a blessed Christmas."

"I will and I know you will, too."

Caitlin nodded, slipped her arm around Simon and together they walked out of the hospital.

The drive back to her parents' place was quiet. Caitlin sat with her head on the headrest of the car, facing him. Simon felt the same way he had that evening sitting by his computer desk. A lightness, a lifting of burdens that had been weighing him down. He drew in a careful breath, trying to find the right words, a place to start.

"I want to thank you for Jake," he said, glancing at her quickly, then back at the road. "He came a few days back. For a visit."

"Thank the Lord," Caitlin breathed, laying a gentle hand on his arm. She squeezed lightly and it was as if her hand held his heart.

"I thank Him, too." Simon shook his head at the memory. "It was so good to see him again." He bit his lip, knowing that his next words were even more important to her. "I also want you to know that I've done a lot of discovering in the past few weeks. I've discovered a need for redemption in my life, for reconciliation with God." He laughed lightly. "It's been a long road, but I've found the way back. I know I've got a long way to go yet, but for the first time in my life I feel like I'm running toward something, instead of away." He gave her another sidelong glance. "Even though I didn't dare come any sooner than this."

"I'm glad you finally dared." Her fingers touched his cheek, lingering a moment, teasing him, and Simon made a sudden decision. They were on a quiet street and he pulled over.

He put the car into neutral, unbuckled his seat belt and turned to face Caitlin. She sat up straight, her eyes gleaming in the reflected light of the dashboard. Outside, lightly falling snow ticked against the windshield, but inside they were warm, secure. Alone.

He wanted to talk to her but was unable to articulate the feelings that welled up in him. He reached out and almost reverently traced the line of her eyebrows, her cheeks. She turned her face to meet his hand.

"I need to tell you something else."

She opened her eyes, her hand coming up to meet his. "So you said. You're not nervous are you?"

"Yes, I am." He stroked her face, his fingers rough against her soft skin. Did he dare? Was he presuming too much? Maybe, but he also knew for the first time in his life he didn't want to leave, run away. He wanted to stay. Stay with Caitlin.

With shaking hands, he reached into his pocket and pulled out a small velvet box. He took a slow, deep breath and flipped it open.

The solitaire diamond nestled in the box caught the nebulous glow of the streetlights and magnified them, winking out rays of color like a promise.

"I know this is kind of sudden, but I'm scared to wait too much longer. Caitlin Severn, will you marry me?"

Caitlin bit her lip, her eyes suspiciously bright. She looked up from admiring the diamond and let her hands linger down his face, catching him around the neck. "I told you I love you, Simon. I don't know if I can say it enough. I will marry you."

He felt the tension surrounding his lungs loosen at her words. Then he leaned closer, his lips lightly touching hers, their breaths mingling in a sigh. "I want to get to know all about you," he said softly. "I want to laugh with you, to pray with you. Have children. Maybe move into that rambling house we looked at." He slipped the ring on her finger. Then he pulled her close, and then there was no more need for words.

Caitlin was the first to draw away. "We should go. My family is waiting. I want so bad for them to get to know you better."

Simon nodded, nervous again. But he started the engine and drove through the city to her home.

He came to a stop in front of the brightly lit house, festooned with Christmas lights. Caitlin was out of the car and waiting for him as he locked the doors. He came around the front of the car and took her outstretched hand, lifting it to look once more at the ring on her finger. A symbol of commitment. He raised her hand to his mouth, pressing it to his lips.

"Are you sure it'll be okay with your family?"

Simon asked as Caitlin tugged on his hand, signalling her desire to go into the house.

"Of course it will be." She opened the door, glancing up at him. "Hurry up. I want my family to share this."

Simon looked past her through the large bay window, its bright light streaming out onto the lawn. Inside, by a colorfully lit tree, Rachel and her husband stood with their arms around each other. Beside them a man he didn't know slept in a recliner, his head tilted to one side, a baby resting in the crook of his arm. A child played at the feet of the embracing couple and as Simon watched, Caitlin's mother walked into the room with a tray of steaming mugs. He could faintly hear Christmas music playing and then the sound of laughter. It looked too good to be true.

"C'mon Simon, what are you staring at?"

He watched yet another moment, wondering again what they would say when he came in with Caitlin as someone who wanted to marry her.

He felt his stomach tighten as it used to all those years ago each time he was introduced to another family, a new place.

But this was Caitlin's family and that made it even more difficult. Now, even more than then, he longed to be accepted, to be a part of that family.

"Did your leg seize up, mister?" Caitlin called out from the porch. "My family is waiting."

Simon gave himself a mental shake, drew in a deep breath and sent up a heartfelt prayer. Then he slowly walked up the steps, through the door and into light and noise and the sounds of an excited family.

"Caitlin, you're here…Caitlin's here…."

"Oh, good… Finally…what took you?" Then a moment's silence descended as the people crowding into the entranceway saw Simon and then the ring on Caitlin's hand.

Then more noise and hugs and cries of congratulation.

He greeted Caitlin's parents as Mr. and Mrs. Just like in all the foster homes, wondering what they would think of him now that Caitlin wore his ring.

"You didn't meet my sister Evelyn and her husband Scott from Portland." Caitlin indicated a couple he hadn't met before. He struggled to commit their names to memory.

Simon drew a deep breath, unconsciously wiping his damp palms down the sides of his blue jeans. He was hugged by Evelyn, shook hands with Scott.

Caitlin caught Simon by the arm as the family moved ahead of them into the living room. "Do you mind if I leave you for a bit? I'd like to change into other clothes."

"You look great just the way you are, Caitlin."

She glanced down at her uniform with a pained look. "Thanks, but I prefer not to look like a nurse at home."

"Go then, but hurry up."

"You'll be okay?"

Simon cupped her face in his hands and brushed

a kiss over her lips. "You've got a great family, Caitlin. I think I can manage."

Caitlin pressed her hand to his. "I'll be right back."

Simon watched her run up the stairs, stop at the top, then turn and smile down at him.

He couldn't help but return her smile. Even so, as he entered the living room, he felt a slight touch of panic. This was one family he badly wanted to feel a part of.

"Sit down, Simon. If I know Caitlin, she'll be a while yet." Caitlin's father indicated the couch and Simon sat down, looking around at the family who were trying not to look too hard at him. The first time he'd met them it was only as a friend. Now, he entered their home as a future in-law.

They made small talk. Caitlin's father asked him how his work was going. Simon supposed it was a subtle way of measuring how he would be able to support Caitlin. The talk was stilted for a while and Simon could hardly wait for Caitlin to return.

"Wow, sis. That looks good."

All eyes turned to the doorway as Caitlin walked into the room.

She looks like a ray of light, Simon thought, his heart swelling with pride as she came to his side. She wore a simple red dress made of velvet, short and fitted, accented by a plain gold chain around her neck. Her hair shone, backlit by the light coming from the hallway, framing a face that radiated happiness. He stood up as she approached.

"Sorry I took so long," she said as she came to Simon's side. She brushed her hair back from her face with a casual gesture, the diamond on her finger catching the light from the Christmas tree.

"Long?" Jonathon snorted. "I've seen you take more time to change your mind."

General laughter followed that comment. Caitlin answered in kind and as Simon and Caitlin sat down again, the talk became general.

Caitlin's nephew, Scott and Evelyn's child, came and sat on her lap, her mother passed around the warm cider and noisy talk roiled around the two of them.

Simon felt the tightness in his stomach relax as family business carried on, as if it were the most normal thing in the world for a stranger to come into their Christmas celebration. Scott ended up beside him. Simon found out he had also spent time tree planting and soon they were exchanging hardship stories.

The other family members flowed around them. Evelyn interrupted them to hand Scott the baby. She rested her hand lightly on Simon's shoulder and only smiled at him. Simon felt her acceptance. Rachel gave him a quick hug from behind, Jonathon gave him a curious thumbs-up while Mr. and Mrs. Severn smiled benignly at him and Caitlin.

The Severns were a warm, loving family. The

very people he had once derided. He knew he had done it out of self-protection, but now he dared accept what was freely given him.

As he looked around the pleased faces of Caitlin Severn's parents, sisters and brothers-in-law, he knew that with God's help he had discovered a family's love.

He thought of his own brother and his brother's daughter. Another family he was a part of. His heart felt full.

But the best of all was Caitlin tucked into his side, his arm around her, her fingers playing with the solitaire on her hand. He glanced down at her and as their eyes met, he felt as much as saw her slow smile.

She pulled his head closer to hers. "I love you," she whispered in his ear.

Simon felt his heart lift. Would he ever tire of hearing her say that, he wondered? He pressed a kiss to her forehead and drew her even closer.

Someday, he thought, with God's blessing, they would be a family, as well.

Epilogue

"I figured I'd find you here."

Simon's voice from the doorway made Caitlin turn her head. She still wore her nurse's uniform and had meant to change as soon as she got home from work, but she had made a cup of tea and taken it up to their bedroom.

She had paused at the bow window on her way to the cupboard and as she often did, she stopped to look out over the Strait of Georgia, to the hazy blue mountains of the mainland.

"Don't you ever get tired of that view?" Simon teased as he walked up behind her. He slipped his arms around her waist and pressed a kiss to her neck, then nuzzled her ear.

"Nope," Caitlin said, setting her tea cup on the small table beside her. She wrapped her arms over his, leaning back into his embrace. With a shiver of satisfaction she laid her head back against his chest, reveling in his strength, his warmth.

"Why not," he murmured against her hair. "It doesn't change much."

"Of course it does. The morning light makes the water and the mountains look fresh and new. When it rains or storms and the water has whitecaps on it, I feel all safe and cozy in here. In the evening, like now, everything looks so soft and peaceful."

Simon looked up, rocking her lightly. "Every time I see it I think, 'oceanfront property.'"

"Oh, you do not," Caitlin chided, hugging his arms even tighter. "You just say that to get a rise out of me. I know you love this place."

Simon sighed, his chest lifting behind her, his breath teasing her hair. "You see right through me, my dear," he confessed. "I do love this place." He turned Caitlin to face him and she looped her arms around his neck. "But to me the best part of coming to this house is seeing my own dear wife standing at our bedroom window, waiting for her prince to come."

"And he always does." She brushed a kiss over his mouth and laid her head on his shoulder. "But you know the real reason I like to stand at this window and stare out of it?"

"Tell me."

"Because every time I do, you come up behind me, and put your arms around me and my day gets better."

Simon laughed, a gentle rumble beneath her cheek. "You truly are a gift from God, Caitlin Steele."

Would she ever get tired of this, she wondered, holding Simon more tightly. She knew they would have their difficulties. Any relationship came with ups and downs. They'd had their differences already, but worked through them.

But she also knew that their love was founded on God's love. And with His help, their home would be a place of refuge and comfort.

"Let's go have supper," Simon said, drawing away from her.

Caitlin smiled and hooked her arm in his. But as they left, she glanced back over her shoulder, out of the windows to the mountains beyond, praying they might be able to show the same view to their children and, Lord willing, children's children.

Their family.

* * * * *

Dear Reader,

Our family has fostered for a number of years. Throughout that time we've seen the brokenness that can happen to children and their siblings when they are separated. We've seen some happy endings and some sad endings. Some children have stayed in touch, others we never hear from again. As foster parents, we've had to learn to truly let go of "our" children and pray that what we've shown them of God's unfailing love will someday take root.

This book, the first of a series of three, was a way of saying "what if" with some of the stories we've been a witness to in both our and other foster parents' homes. I've portrayed some "good" homes and, in Simon's case, one that wasn't quite as good as the norm. Most of the people we have met, however, are strong, faithful stewards of what God has blessed them with. This book is for them.

P.S. I love to hear from my readers! Send your letters to Carolyne Aarsen, P.O. Box 114, Neerlandia, Alberta T0G 1R0, Canada.

Carolyne Aarsen

YULETIDE HOMECOMING

Bear with each other and forgive whatever grievances you may have against one another. Forgive as the Lord forgave you.
—*Colossians* 3:13

To those who struggle with the hurts of the past.

Chapter One

Thirty-six minutes to go. And though Sarah Westerveld had been driving west for five days to get to her old hometown of Riverbend, she needed every second of those thirty-six minutes to compose herself before meeting her father.

She tapped her fingers on the steering wheel in time to the song blasting from the radio and waited at the town's single stoplight. Not much had changed in the six years she had been gone. The bakery, the bank, the drugstore and the flower shop still anchored the four corners of the main street. Just down from the bakery was her cousin's coffee shop, a rare new addition to Riverbend.

And the place she had arranged to meet her father.

Since she had moved away, she had received an envelope from him on the first of every month, his decisive handwriting on the outside, a check inside.

And nothing else. No letter. No note. Nothing to show that this came from her father.

A few weeks ago, however, instead of the check, inserted in the envelope was a single piece of paper with the words "Come Home. I need to talk to you" written on it.

When she phoned to find out what he wanted, he kept the call short, as he always did, and business-like, as he always did. He said he wanted to tell her what he had to, face-to-face.

Her father wanted to meet her at home, but after all this time, she had no desire to visit with him in that large empty house echoing with memories. So they had arranged to meet at her cousin Janie's cof-fee shop. Neutral ground, and not far from his office.

A horn honked behind her and Sarah jumped. The light had turned green. She gunned her car through the intersection and slid over the snow and into the lone parking spot down the block from her cousin's coffee shop. Obviously Mr. Kennerman, the street maintenance man, was still around, and still not on the job.

She wound her scarf around her throat and pulled out a toque, jamming it over her long, blond hair be-fore stepping from the warm confines of her car into the crisp winter weather.

I missed this, Sarah thought, tugging on a pair of gloves. Missed the bite of the cold, the invigorat-ing freshness of the chilly air. Sarah pulled back the cuff of her glove.

Thirty-five minutes to go.

She had planned to stay at her cousin's. Her father hadn't objected when she told him. Still, she wasn't sure if it was because he understood why, or because he simply didn't want her in the family house, either.

Sarah locked her car and glanced down the road. The trees, now bare, reached farther over the street than she remembered. One of the older buildings in town had been renovated to its original glory. Flags, hanging from new streetlights, drifted in the cool breeze that scuttled rivulets of snow across the street.

The town was busy this early in the day. Busy for Riverbend, which meant most of the parking spots on Main Street were taken. A few people wandered down the sidewalks, their conversation punctuated by puffs of steam. Sarah shivered as she hurried along the path toward the coffee shop, anticipation fluttering through her at the thought of seeing her cousin after all this time.

The door of the coffee shop swung open and a man stepped out.

Dark was the first thought that came to mind. Dark eyebrows. Dark hair. A lean jaw shadowed by whiskers. Angular features molded in a look that both challenged and engaged all comers. His coffee-brown hair brushed the collar of a faded canvas coat open to reveal a denim jacket and sweatshirt. Brown eyes swept over her and Sarah's heart did a slow turn in her chest.

Logan Carleton.

Logan of the scribbles in her notebook, the long, slow looks across the gymnasium and stolen kisses that still haunted her.

Logan of the Across the River Carletons of whom her father couldn't speak without risking a coronary. Which, in turn, had given the broodingly handsome Logan an additional forbidden appeal.

An appeal that only grew when they secretly started dating.

He still had it, she thought as she met the eyes she thought held no sway over her anymore. But old emotions flickered deep within her and the six years she'd been gone slipped away as easily as a young girl's tears.

Six years ago all he'd had to do was send her that crooked smile across the cab of his truck and her heart would do the same slow turn it just had.

Sarah put the brakes on those silly, schoolgirl thoughts. She was older now. Wiser. Harder. She had left Riverbend with tears in her eyes because of this man. Now, after all this time, just seeing him could bring forth feelings she thought she had reconciled into her past.

And then, thankfully, his mouth lifted in a faintly cynical smile negating the connection.

"Sarah Westerveld. So you've come back west." The tone in his voice was cooler than the freezing air.

"Hello, Logan," she said quietly. In a town as small as Riverbend, this first meeting was inevitable. She just hadn't counted on it being five minutes after her arrival.

"You remembered who I am." He lifted one eyebrow in a mocking gesture. "I'm surprised."

His tone cut. But life and time away from Riverbend had changed her. She wasn't the girl who longed for his approval. Needed his smile.

"I was sorry to hear about your father's death." She had stayed in touch with her friends and family here, so she knew.

Logan's eyes narrowed and for a moment she thought she had crossed an unseen line.

"Me, too," he growled. "He had a hard life."

"That he did." And Sarah knew part of the blame for that difficulty could be laid at her father's door.

Nine years ago, Jack Carleton had been falsely accused of murdering his business partner. The lengthy trial had scandalized the community and, even though Jack had been exonerated, the verdict hadn't stopped Frank, Sarah's father, from canceling his gravel-crushing contract with Jack. This in turn created the animosity between Frank and Jack that Sarah grew up with but couldn't completely understand.

"I heard you took over your father's gravel business," Sarah continued, determined to act as if meeting Logan was no different than meeting any other high school acquaintance. She had a hard time looking at him, so she focused on the top button of his jacket. "How is that going for you?"

Logan gave a short laugh. "It's going to be better."

Sarah couldn't stop her attention from flying upward at the harsh tone of his voice.

"So how long are you around for this time?" he continued.

"I'm here to visit my father. That's all."

"That's all? I shouldn't be surprised, should I?" He held her gaze a heartbeat longer, then stepped past her and walked away.

Just as she had walked away from him six years ago.

As Sarah watched him, his hands tucked in the pocket of his canvas coat, his whole demeanor one of a man in charge of his world, she felt her heart twist with pain. Logan had always had a strong self-confidence, which had served him well amid the whispers and innuendos during his father's trial.

It was that self-assurance to which Sarah had been drawn. Unfortunately, Sarah had not possessed the same confidence while they were dating; she had insisted they keep their relationship secret. And they had. For the entire eight months. And then her father, who had never disguised his active dislike for the Carleton family, found out.

Sarah pushed open the door to the shop, shivering in the warmth and letting the welcoming scent of ground coffee beans draw her back to the present. She wasn't here to reminisce over old flames. She had a job to do, plain and simple.

As the door sighed closed behind her, she drew

in a slow breath, willing her heart to stop its erratic beating.

"Sarah. You're here!" A high-pitched squeal pierced the low murmur of the customers in the coffee bar.

Janie Corbett threaded her way through the people perched at high stools and tables, her arms outstretched, her Westerveld blue eyes wide with excitement. With great relief, Sarah walked into her cousin's embrace, letting Janie's arms pull her tightly close.

Janie patted Sarah's cheeks, her smile threatening to split her face. "Look at you. All grown-up and even skinnier than ever. And I love the longer hairstyle," Janie said, flicking her fingers through Sarah's shoulder-length curls. "Looks elegant. Refined."

"Well, I'm not. Refined or elegant, that is."

"Not the way you play basketball." Janie adjusted the bandanna holding her own pale blond hair back from her face. "I heard that Uncle Morris and Ethan saw you in action in Calgary, at some university competition."

Sarah remembered and smiled. Seeing her uncle and cousin's familiar faces after the game had been a bright spot in her life. "That wasn't my best game."

Sarah followed Janie to the counter, glancing around the shop as she did. She saw a few familiar faces but could tell from the slightly puzzled frowns sent her way that her own face wasn't ringing any bells.

"They were still pretty impressed," Janie said,

pulling out a large mug. She gave Sarah a quick smile. "I'm so glad you're here."

"I am, too." Sarah released a gentle sigh as she perched on an empty stool. She folded her arms on the granite countertop as she took in the bright and cheery decor. "This looks great, Janie. You did a fantastic job."

"Well, Aunty Dot helped me with the design and Uncle Dan and Uncle Morris rounded up all the cousins to do the heavy work."

Sarah glanced up above the coffee machines to the chalkboard filled with pink-and-green swirling script describing the menu for the day. "And the good people of Riverbend are really ready for espressos, cappuccinos and flavored macchiatos?"

"Honey, they are lapping it up."

"From cups I would hope."

Janie gave her a blank look, then laughed. "Very funny."

"You walked right into it." Sarah smiled and glanced at her watch while her stomach did another flip. Twenty-nine minutes left.

"You want something now, or do you want to wait for your dad?"

"I'll have a hot chocolate."

"And when are you coming over?"

"When I'm done here."

"Your dad wasn't really impressed with the fact that you're staying with me, but I told him that I wasn't going to get involved." With a hiss of compressed air and quick, practiced movements, Janie layered thick whipping cream on top of the steaming cup of hot chocolate and carried it around the counter. "Let's sit by the window."

She waved away the cash Sarah pulled out of her purse. "On the house. Consider it a temptation to stay longer."

"I hope you don't do this for all the Westervelds," Sarah said as she settled in at the table Janie led her to.

"I'd be broke if I did that."

Sarah angled her cousin a quick smile then scooped up a dollop of whipped cream and popped it into her mouth with a sigh of satisfaction. Fat. The main ingredient in all good comfort food. Bring it on.

"So. Three weeks." Janie leaned her elbows on the table. "What ever made you decide on that puny length of time?"

"It's longer than the two weeks I had originally planned." Sarah knew this conversation was a trial run for the many she suspected she would have with other family.

"I guess we were hoping we could convince you to stay longer, but my mom said you've got your escape ticket booked." Janie gave her a penetrating look, as if trying to push past the defenses Sarah hastily erected.

"What? A girl can't go traveling?"

"You've definitely got the family in a dither. We're all trying to figure out why, after being gone so long after finishing school and graduating, you're only here awhile." The hurt in Janie's voice teased out memories. Sarah had grown up with cousins and aunts and uncles all of whom had staked the claim of heredity on her life. Though she owed them collectively more than she could ever repay, she had hoped her current stay would cover some of the emotional debt. But to the Westervelds, if you didn't live within twenty minutes of Riverbend, you were "away" and if you were "away" you had better make sure that you made the pilgrimage at least for Easter, Christmas or Thanksgiving.

But in spite of the pull of some family's heredity and expectations, Sarah had stayed away, and her father had never extended any kind of invitation.

Until now.

"And what's with this, not sticking around until Christmas?" Janie pressed.

"Christmas is not my favorite season." This was her catchall comment when people back at the college would ask every year if she was going home for the holidays. Most people accepted that at face value and didn't pry. But here in Riverbend, people didn't have to pry. Most of them knew.

"I'm sorry." Janie's teasing look slipped off her face to be replaced by sorrow. "It's been six years since Marilee died, hasn't it?"

"Six years on the twenty-third of December." Sarah swallowed down an unexpected knot of pain she thought had eased away.

"You know we all lost something that day," Janie said, reaching over and covering Sarah's hand with her own. "I just wish you could have let us help you through it all. You left so soon afterward. I'm sure your father missed you."

And Sarah was sure he didn't. Other than a terse phone call once a year on her birthday, she had instigated every connection between them. Every phone call, every letter. She had spent her whole life trying to please her father and in the end, her slavish devotion had turned out to be like pouring light into a black hole. She could never give enough to fill it.

Because Sarah was not Marilee, and Marilee was not here.

"Well, I'm here now."

"I guess we were all hoping you'd want to spend some time here. I mean, it's like you've wiped away all our years of family and visiting and holidays." Janie waved her hand, the casual gesture underlining the hurt in her words. "And then you only come back for three weeks."

"C'mon Janie," Sarah protested. "I wrote you every week, posted on your blog, checked out the cousins' MySpace sites, phoned…"

"A face-to-face visit would have been nice."

"I know." But a face-to-face visit would have meant seeing her father again, something she had avoided ever since that horrible confrontation after Marilee's funeral.

Even coming here had been fraught with second

thoughts and fears that she was simply slipping back into the role of the good daughter.

She had worked so hard to get where she was. After a couple of lost years of dithering, she had settled on an education degree. Now that she had graduated, she had a job waiting for her in Toronto, teaching at an all-girl's school, a prestigious coup. She looked forward to applying all the things she had learned. But first, this trip she and her friends had planned since they first met two years ago—six months backpacking through Europe.

"I don't suppose you could change the ticket?"

Sarah was spared yet another explanation when Janie glanced sideways and straightened, her one hand drifting up to her hair in a preening gesture. "I wondered when Logan would remember his work gloves."

Sarah wasn't going to look, the very sound of his name sending a shiver of apprehension chasing down her spine but as Janie got up to get the gloves her head moved of its own accord. And she saw Logan pause in the process of opening the frost-encrusted glass door to the coffee shop. He was looking back over his shoulder. An older man coming out of the bank across the street had caught his attention.

Her father. Frank Westerveld.

And he was coming here. From the tight look on her father's face, Sarah could tell he was not one bit happy to see Logan Carleton.

Her father's tailored wool coat, crisp white shirt

and silk tie were an elegant contrast to the canvas coat, stained jean jacket and faded blue jeans of the younger man who had turned to face him.

Sarah found herself clenching her fists as she watched Logan, the man she had once dated, face down her father, the man who had demanded they stop. Her father was talking… Logan replying. But while her father stabbed the air with his finger as if punctuating his words, Logan kept his hands in his pockets when he spoke; the picture of nonchalance.

"Oh, boy," Janie murmured, returning. "This will not turn out well."

"Some things haven't changed," Sarah said with a sigh, watching her father, remembering his fury when he found out that she had been seeing the rugged young man. It would seem her father's latent anger with her old boyfriend hadn't abated one jot in spite of Sarah having fallen in with her father's wishes.

"I didn't expect to be facing both my dad and Logan as soon as I got here."

"Looks like Logan doesn't want his gloves after all," Janie said.

Sarah turned in time to see Logan salute her father, then turn away, his coat still open.

Her father stood with his back to the shop, his hands clenched into fists at his side.

"Doesn't look as if Logan's gained any more points with your dad," Janie said.

"Logan has never been concerned with points, or

my father's opinion," Sarah murmured. "Or anyone else's for that matter."

"Oh c'mon. I know there was a time he cared what *you* thought," Janie said, giving Sarah a playful poke.

"Not for very long." Sarah pulled her attention away from Logan's retreating figure.

The door jangled, heralding some new customers, but still her father stood outside.

"You'd better see to your customers. I should go say hi to my dad, let him know I'm here." Sarah got up and, before she knew what was happening, Janie caught her in a quick, hard hug. "I'm so glad you're back."

Sarah felt a flood of sentiment for her brusque and straightforward cousin.

The hug felt better than she remembered.

Janie drew back and patted her awkwardly on her shoulder. "I'll see you on Sunday? At church?"

She felt it again. The gentle tug of expectations. She knew the drill. If you were a Westerveld and you were in town on Sunday, showing up at church was mandatory. But Sarah, who used to love church, hadn't been since she left Riverbend. However, though she had let the faith of her childhood slip, she couldn't completely eradicate the notion that God did still have some small hold on her life.

And there was the guilt. Always a good motivator.

"Yeah. I'll be there."

"You'll have to be or you'll have all the aunties calling you up demanding to know if you're sick. Or dead." Janie stopped, her eyes growing wide, then pressed her hand to her mouth. "I'm sorry," she said behind her fingers. "Wasn't thinking."

"Don't worry about it." Sarah stroked her cousin's arm to reassure her.

But Janie wasn't looking at her. "What…something's wrong."

The frightened note in Janie's voice made Sarah look up in time to see her father's head drop, his gloved hand pressed against the window, his other hanging by his side.

She moved, her chair clattering to the floor behind her. Her feet wouldn't move fast enough. She burst out of the coffee shop in time to keep her father from falling to the sidewalk.

When she regained her senses, she realized Logan had also seen what had happened and returned.

"Here. I got him," he said, catching Sarah's father under his arms.

But Frank pushed Logan's hand away, his face growing red. "Go away, Carleton."

"Call nine-one-one," Logan said, ignoring Frank's warning. "Use my cell phone," Logan ordered. "Coat pocket. Right side."

Sarah hesitated only a moment, then dug into Logan's jacket and pulled out the small phone.

Her father pushed at Logan, his breath coming in short gasps of distress. "I asked you." He glanced at Sarah. "I asked him…"

"I'll hold him. You call," Sarah said, holding out

the phone to Logan while her father pushed at him with increasing clumsiness.

"Why? Logan. Why?" Her father's speech grew slurred, his eyes unfocused.

What was going on?

Whatever it was, her father seemed more distressed about Logan's presence than about what was happening to him.

"Dad. I'm here." Sarah pushed Logan's hand away, slipping her arm under her father.

She put her finger on her father's neck, not knowing what she should be doing but knowing that she had to keep Logan away from her father because his presence wasn't helping him calm down at all. "Dad. Look at me. What is happening? Does your chest hurt? Is the pain going down your arm?"

He shook his head, his eyes growing wide.

Oh, dear Lord, not now, she thought, helplessness washing over her in a wave. Not after all these years. *He had to tell me something. Had to say something. Don't take that away from me.*

Sarah's prayer was instinctive, a hearkening back to a time when she thought God listened.

But her father's angry focus was on Logan, who was barking directions into his cell phone.

"Logan…" Frank tried to lift his arm, but it fell back to his side.

His speech grew increasingly slurred.

"Never mind him, Dad. Talk to me. Look at me,"

she called, trying desperately to get him to even glance her way.

He took a breath and Sarah caught his head as it slumped to the side, turning his face to her. But even as Sarah tried to catch his attention, Frank Westerveld's entire focus was on Logan Carleton.

And then his eyes fell shut.

"Dad. *Talk to me,*" she found herself screaming.

Chapter Two

The unconscious man lying on the bed wasn't her father. Frank Westerveld would never have allowed anyone to invade his body this way.

Tubes and drains and electrodes and monitors indicated changes in his breathing and his pulse. An oxygen line hooked over his ears, tiny tubes inserted in his nose.

Ischemic stroke the doctor had called it. Prognosis? Time would tell whether he would gain control of his body, whether he would be able to speak again, walk again.

The hospital in Riverbend wasn't equipped to deal with her father's condition. As soon as he had come into the emergency room there, he had been stabilized and rushed off to Edmonton.

Janie had called the family and by the time Frank had arrived, the uncles and aunts had gathered at the city hospital.

"You're looking at a long, slow recovery," Dr. Williamson said, his hands hanging in the pockets of his lab coat. "The CT scan showed a clot as the cause of stroke, which means that the injury sustained did some irreversible damage, the extent of which we can only discover in time."

"Will he be able to speak at all?" Dot, Sarah's aunt, asked.

Sarah was thankful for Dot Westerveld's presence. Other than "why," Sarah didn't know what questions to ask.

Her emotions were thrown into turmoil. Too well she remembered another panicked drive to the hospital, her sister's broken and battered body laying on a bed in the emergency room.

But Marilee was already gone by the time she and her father got to the hospital. Her sister's vital and fragile spark of life had been extinguished sometime between Sarah telling Marilee that she wasn't going to break curfew to pick her up and the police showing up on her father's doorstep, two hours later.

They never even got to say goodbye.

She wrapped her hands around the rail of her father's bed, desperately trying to blank the memory from her mind, turning her focus instead to her father now lying helpless but alive.

Marilee was gone and father needed her now.

"He'll have some type of speech ability, but as to how much, that depends on how he responds to therapy." Dr. Williamson lifted his shoulder in a vague shrug. "Each stroke patient is different, so I can only give you a vague prognosis."

The words *long* and *slow* resonated in Sarah's brain.

"How long? Can you tell us anything?" Sarah finally asked.

Dr. Williamson shook his head slowly. "I'd say you're looking at at least three months of therapy, and even then…"

Three months.

In twenty-two days her friends were meeting her in Toronto to begin the first leg of a European trip Sarah had been saving toward for the past year.

But she was here now. Her father lay silent in the hospital and Sarah had to make a decision. Could she really leave her father here?

"And what do you need me to do?" she asked, fighting a mixture of exhausted tears and frustration.

The doctor spoke of the need for stability, the importance of having family close by, reinforcing her vague decision. "Right now your father just needs your presence," the doctor said.

How odd that now, when he couldn't speak or act, he needed her. For most of Sarah's life, he hadn't seemed to need anything from her.

Questions and self-recrimination beat at her like ravens around a carcass, just as they had the last time she'd stood by the hospital bed of someone she loved.

Why hadn't she gone out and talked to her father before Logan had made him angry? Why had she avoided him? Would this have happened if she had greeted him right away?

And had Logan said something to cause her father such distress?

"The stroke…could something stressful have caused it?" Sarah asked.

The doctor shrugged. "There's a study that has shown that a sudden change in behavior can trigger the stroke. Anger does seem to be a potent trigger for ischemic strokes."

Anger. Arguing. What if she had gone out before, as she should have, what if Logan hadn't come back for his gloves, what if…

The words were too familiar. Six years ago she had spent months going over "what if" scenarios about Marilee. What if she had gone and picked her up? What if she hadn't tried to do what her father wanted? What if she and Marilee hadn't had that fight before she left the house? What if Marilee hadn't gone out with Logan?

"You look exhausted, Sarah."

Sarah jumped as her aunt's voice penetrated the memories and regrets burying her.

"Do you want me to take you home?" Aunt Dot continued.

Sarah wanted nothing more than to go home and rest. But concern mixed with guilt kept her standing beside her father in ICU. If she'd gone outside, stopped him from talking to Logan, he might not be lying here.

"I should have gone out," Sarah whispered to her aunt, still looking at her father, who lay so silent on the bed. "I was waiting for him, so why couldn't I go out and talk to him? Why did this happen?"

Dot clutched her niece's arm. "We don't know why things happen, but you know, I believe it was our heavenly Father's will that brought you here. He knew that you needed to be right here, right now."

If this was God's will, then Sarah was ready to give up on Him completely. Six years ago, after Marilee's death, Sarah's faith in God had taken a severe beating. Nothing she had seen since had reinforced the impression that she needed to spend any time with Him anymore.

Sarah glanced around the ICU ward. Nurses moved about, monitors beeped and oxygen sighed. The buzzing in her head told her it must be late, but she had no idea of the time. Frank's brothers, Morris, Dan and Sam, had come and stood vigil and were now waiting outside of the ICU, waiting to take their turns to stay by his side.

"He's okay for now. We'll come back tomorrow," Dot assured her. "Uncle Sam is waiting. He'll watch while you're gone."

As the others left the room, Sarah looked down at her father, so helpless now.

Then, miraculously, Sarah saw her father's head move and his eyes open.

And he was looking directly at her. His one eye widened and one corner of his mouth moved just a fraction. She caught sight of a small movement of his opposite hand, his fingers curling ever so slightly.

She waited but then his face relaxed again and his eyes closed.

Was he trying to talk to her? Trying to tell her something?

Whatever it was, it was again locked behind that immobile face.

Sarah reached out and touched her father's hand, willing the response to return. But nothing happened.

Finally, after another twenty minutes of waiting, she allowed her aunt to usher her past the nurse's desk to the waiting room. Uncle Morris, Dot's husband, Dan and Sam stood up from the bench and each took a turn giving her a hug.

"We'll be praying," Sam whispered into her ear. "You go rest."

Sarah nodded and slowly walked down the hallway, her aunt's arm around her, holding her up.

"Janie said you were staying with her. Shall I take you there?"

Sarah shook her head. Right now, she just wanted to be alone with her thoughts. Alone with her regrets.

"I'll call her and tell her to meet us at the house with your car."

"That would be nice," Sarah said as they stepped out of the warmth of the hospital into the chill air outside.

An hour and fifteen minutes later, she and her aunt pulled up in front of her father's house, her car indicating Janie had already arrived. A light from the living room glowed, sending a falsely comforting image of a family at home, doing family things.

Janie came to the door and, as Sarah came in, her cousin reached out to take her coat. "I brought your suitcases. They're up in your old room."

Sarah thought of the airline tickets tucked deep in her coat pockets.

Thought of her father's prognosis.

Three months.

Tomorrow, she thought, repressing a shiver. *Time enough to deal with that tomorrow.*

"It might take a few minutes for the house to warm up. Your dad keeps the thermostat turned way low," Janie continued.

"I'll wait outside, Janie," Aunt Dot said. "I'll be back tomorrow if you want, Sarah. Tilly said she would be willing to drive, too. Just say the word."

"Thanks, Aunt Dot. Thanks for everything you did today."

Dot just smiled at her. "That's what family is for." Then she leaned over and dropped a light kiss on Sarah's head. "It's good to have you here, again, Kitten." And then she left.

"Are you sure you're okay?" Janie asked as the door closed behind their aunt. "Do you want me to stay with you?"

"Thanks for the offer. I really need some alone time."

"Don't blame you. Your wish to get eased into

family life didn't exactly happen, did it?" Janie stroked Sarah's hair back from her face in a motherly gesture. "Do you want me to take you to the hospital tomorrow?"

Sarah just shook her head, stifling a yawn. "I'll drive myself."

"I'm sure Mom and Dad and Uncle Morris and Aunty Dot are going."

And Sarah was sure she didn't want to depend on someone else's schedule. "I like to have my own transportation."

"I hear you," Janie said. "I hope you can sleep."

"Thanks." Sarah followed Janie out the door and stood on the step, waving as Aunt Dot and Janie drove down the driveway, then closed the door on the outside world.

Silence, heavy and dark, fell on her.

As Sarah dragged her feet up the stairs, exhaustion fuzzed her mind and blurred her eyes. Driving overnight to get here had been a very bad idea to start with. Had Sarah known what lay ahead she would have taken more time. Started earlier. Had Sarah known what would happen, she would have gotten up off the chair at Janie's coffee shop and gone outside to talk to her father.

Unfortunately, no one knew what the repercussions of their decisions would be. Not until events played out.

Just as they had those many years ago.

Sarah's steps slowed as she came to the door to

her sister's bedroom. A door that had stayed closed and locked for the last few months she had lived here.

On impulse, Sarah grabbed the cold metal handle but froze as she saw, etched into the frame, lines marking out Marilee's height, her age and the year behind each one. The last one was dated six years ago. Four days before the accident. Four days before Sarah found out that her sister had sneaked out to meet the boy Sarah had just broken up with.

Logan Carleton.

Sarah swallowed down the unexpected pain.

The wrong daughter had died...

Sarah twisted the knob. To her surprise, it wasn't locked. Slowly she nudged the door open. The light of the hallway fell into the room and Sarah's heart leaped into her throat.

It was as if she had stepped back in time.

Marilee's favorite pink shirt was draped over the back of the chair, her blue jeans bunched up in a crumpled heap on the floor. A schoolbook lay open on the desk, a notebook beside it, Marilee's scrawling handwriting was visible even from where Sarah stood just inside the room.

A portable stereo still sat on an unmade bed, CDs scattered on the blanket.

Gooseflesh rippled down Sarah's arms as she looked from the bed to the desk to the assorted clothes scattered on the floor. She half expected her sister to stick her head out of the closet and bark at her for not knocking.

Sarah rubbed her arms again, an old, familiar sorrow pressing down on her chest, and, following that, guilt. If only...

Sarah pushed the thought aside and in a fit of anger at the resurrected feelings, snatched her sister's shirt from the back of the chair. She didn't know her father had done this. When they came home after the funeral, he had locked himself away in his study downstairs. Sarah couldn't go into the room and her father had told her that one of his sisters would take care of cleaning it out. Obviously, no one had ever been here.

This felt wrong, twisted, to not have her sister's things attended to.

But as she folded the shirt and hung it back over the chair, a puff of dust and the faintest hint of Marilee's perfume were released and her heart stuttered. Sarah clutched the shirt and allowed, just for a moment, the scent to surround her, eking out memories of her younger sister.

Marilee helping Sarah with her hair as she got ready for a date. Marilee screaming with abandon from the stands whenever Sarah played. Marilee bouncing down the hallway of the school, trailing admiring people in her wake. Marilee—sunshine and laughter and open, unabashed rebellion. Her father's favorite.

For years, Sarah had tried to emulate her bubbly, fun-loving sister, but she could never come close to bringing a smile to her father's face the way Marilee could. Sarah could never catch her father's attention the way Marilee had so effortlessly.

As they grew, Sarah tried to find her own place in Riverbend, in the family. She thought she had when she started playing basketball, but her father was always more interested in Marilee's dance recitals, Marilee's plays, Marilee's anything.

The favoritism wasn't lost on the family and often her uncles and aunts would try to compensate by showing up at her games en masse, cheering her on.

Frank Westerveld had never seen her play.

Sarah closed the door on her sister's room and strode down the hall, past the door to her father's room to her own bedroom. As she opened the door, nostalgia assailed her.

The same posters hung on the wall. The same flowered bedspread still covered the bed. But, while Marilee's had the curious stopped-in-time feeling, Sarah's had the tidy order of an occupant that had moved on.

And as Sarah dropped her suitcase on the floor, it was as if she had stepped back in time.

Once again she was a young girl, waiting to hear if Marilee was going to sneak home in time or if her father would catch her this time.

Somehow Frank never did.

As she crawled into bed, she saw her old Bible lying on the bedside table. She used to read it regularly and take comfort and encouragement from the words between the worn covers.

She could use some comfort tonight. Some answers.

But she had learned the hard way that God's voice didn't always resound or give answers.

As she pulled her blankets around her, the glow from the streetlight outside shone onto the same patch of floor it always had, and with the familiar sight came the memories.

Sarah spun over onto her other side only to face the wall on which Marilee had written Sarah's name in calligraphy.

She should have gone to Janie's after all, she thought, closing her eyes. But even as she blocked out images from the past, more recent pictures swam into her exhausted mind. Her father, angry with Logan, her father collapsing.

And Logan, watching her.

Chapter Three

Sarah looked up from the bulletin and glanced around the building that had been her church home since her first memory. Other than a colorful banner hanging in the front of the church, nothing had changed here, either. Sarah glanced up at the ceiling with its 1,578 ceiling tiles, and then over at the thirteen small stained-glass windows with their simple colored panes, for a total of 104 panes of blue, green, gold and brown.

She had grown up in this church, as had her parents and grandparents. Her great-grandfather and -grandmother were buried in the graveyard beside the church alongside assorted aunts and uncles.

And Marilee.

"There you are." A tall body dropped into the pew beside Sarah and gave her a good-natured shove with her hips. "Janie said you were going to come."

"Hey, Dodie." Pure pleasure leaped through Sarah

at the sight of Janie's outspoken and irreverent sister. And before she knew what was happening, Dodie had grabbed Sarah in a tight hug.

"So Sarah," Dodie said pulling back and giving Sarah a sad look. "Sorry about your dad. Mom told me while I was gone. I just got back last night. How's he doing?"

"We won't know for a couple of weeks yet."

"That's too bad. So how long are you around for?"

Sarah pleated the bulletin once, then again. That was the question of the week. "I'll stay as long as he needs me," she said quietly.

"I'm guessing this interferes with your trip?"

"I think I'm going to call it off."

"Maybe you can go when this is all over."

The words "long slow recovery" hung in the back of Sarah's mind. "Maybe."

"So, what's up for the week ahead?" Dodie asked, plucking the bulletin from Sarah's unresisting fingers. She ran one blue-painted fingernail down the paper, moving her lips as she read. "A Soup Supper. Ladies are singing in the homes again. Did you read this?" Dodie angled the bulletin to Sarah, who shook her head. "Your old basketball coach, Dick DeHaan, ended up in the local hospital. Looks like he had a heart attack. I'm not surprised the way he was putting on weight. The Kippers family is leaving for Nigeria again, I'm sure her mom is going to miss those kids…"

Sarah knew no response was required so she kept quiet as Dodie continued to narrate the events of the church community, maintaining her own running commentary on the various people, condensing Sarah's six-year gap in six minutes. The *Reader's Digest* version of Riverbend.

When Dodie finished her speed gossiping, she handed the bulletin back to Sarah and glanced around the church, then elbowed her cousin.

Sarah turned in the direction Dodie was angling her head and her heart did a slow flip as Logan walked down the center aisle of the church, his tall, dark figure looming over his mother.

"I didn't know Logan came to church." Sarah willed her heart to resume its normal beat.

Dodie gave Sarah a knowing look. "He just started coming the past few months. And now he's bringing his mom, though I know she's not too hot on the residents of Riverbend or us Westervelds. She still blames your dad for her husband's death. Although I don't know how she figures that."

Logan stood aside to let his mother into a space two pews ahead of them. The brown wool blazer and tan-colored shirt gave him a more civilized look than the jean jacket he had worn the other day, though he still had on blue jeans and cowboy boots.

At that moment Logan glanced back at Sarah. A faint frown flickered between his dark brows, as if he was surprised to see her here.

But why should he be? When they were dating, she was the one who went faithfully to church while he stayed away, claiming that church was simply a collection of hypocrites.

So what had made him come now?

The praise team started singing and there was no more opportunity for puzzled glances or speculation. Logan turned to his mother again.

As the congregation was swept along, Sarah felt left behind. Despite her previous time in the church, none of the songs were familiar and she felt like a bystander. Logan seemed to know most of them.

When they were done singing, the minister greeted the congregation in the name of the Lord then gave the people an opportunity to greet each other, which offered Sarah another glimpse of Logan as he turned to shake the hands of several people.

Again their eyes met, and again Sarah felt a troubling frisson of awareness, an echo of younger, more immature feelings.

You are crazy, she thought as she broke the connection, anger coming hot on the heels of her schoolgirl reaction to his good looks. He was part of her past. Those times were gone.

"Before we begin, I want to ask our congregation to remember Frank Westerveld in prayer," the minister said when everyone had settled. "He suffered a stroke yesterday afternoon. We don't know any more, but we will continue to remember him and his family in our prayers."

The minister paused a moment, as if to let the news settle in. A quiet murmur began in the congregation.

Logan glanced back, frowning.

She shouldn't have been looking at him and quickly averted her eyes.

But then the minister began to speak again, bringing them through the liturgy, and Sarah, determined to focus, forced all her attention back to him.

Yet his words, once so familiar, did not touch her. Once upon a time church had meant something to her, but Marilee's death had robbed her of a vital spark—had stolen a gentle innocence that equated good fortune with God's blessing.

When her father had dropped into the dark pit of grief and mourning, he had left Sarah behind to muddle through the hard, eternal question always put to a purportedly loving God: Why?

And with each day that Frank kept himself apart from her, each week that Sarah slipped quietly through a house heavy with sorrow, alone and grieving, Sarah had pulled further and further into herself.

When Frank finally did emerge from his grief long enough to notice Sarah, it was to cry out that the wrong daughter had died.

That phrase had reverberated through the following years and had kept Sarah at arm's length from Frank. Until now.

Sarah glanced down at the bulletin she held, pretending to read it as she shut out the present and the past, thinking about her future and the job waiting for her.

A poke in her ribs threw her abruptly back into the present. She blinked, looking around. Dodie got up, taking Sarah by the arm and pulling her up as well. The service was over.

One down, who knows how many more to go?

She glanced around at the congregation then froze as she saw Logan coming down the aisle toward them. She couldn't face him again. She had to get out.

"Sarah. Sarah Westerveld. How are you?" A hand caught her from behind, and, as Sarah turned, she smiled. In spite of the toddler clinging to one hand and the baby on her hip, Alicia Mays looked as cute and put together as she had in high school. Her curly hair was pinned up. Her eyes shimmered with subdued eye shadow and her trim figure was enhanced by a narrow blue dress.

"Hey, Alicia. How are you?" Though her words were automatic, Sarah's heart trembled at the sight of the young mother. Marilee's one-time best friend.

Alicia bounced the baby. "Busy, as you can see." She just giggled. "God's been good." She flashed

Sarah another smile. "I've got another one on the way."

Sarah glanced at her trim stomach and pulled in her own.

"Mommy, I want to go," Alicia's little boy said, tugging on her hand.

"And you? How are you doing?" Alicia asked. "Haven't seen you around in ages."

"I've been in school. In Halifax and working there over the summer. I've graduated and have a job starting next September in Toronto."

Alicia gave a slow nod, as if filing away this information. "And, any special person in your life since Logan?"

The question was pure Alicia. Direct and to the point. She and Marilee were two of a kind.

"I've been busy with school." Sarah didn't want to talk about the precious few boyfriends in her life. It would make her look like some loser who had been pining after her high school love, when, in fact, she had simply been too busy for any kind of meaningful relationship. She had been determined to excel in her schoolwork, determined to make her own way, and she had.

"He's still single, you know." Alicia gave Sarah a knowing look, which puzzled Sarah. Surely she knew of Marilee's tryst with Logan that horrible night? And if she did, why was she dropping hints like rocks at Sarah's feet?

Though her curiosity was piqued, she didn't want to delve into that now. Not with Alicia's little boy tugging on her hand and people milling about them.

"Mommy. I have to go. Now." The toddler tugged on Alicia's hand, dragging her sideways.

And Sarah was rescued from the wink-wink, nudge-nudge that Alicia excelled at.

"We'll catch up some time," Alicia called out as she left.

"Sure. You take care." Sarah gave Marilee's old friend a smile and, with a sigh of relief, turned.

And came out into the aisle right beside Logan's mother.

Sarah caught a quick sidelong glance from Donna, received a curt nod and a mumbled "Hello."

But when Sarah responded, Donna glanced away, her mouth pursed. Behind, she felt Logan's looming presence like a storm cloud waiting to let loose.

It didn't take a mind reader to realize that at that moment, she was as welcome as a gravy stain on a tablecloth.

But even as her discomfort grew, so did her anger.

What did Donna know about Sarah? Nothing. She and Logan had been discreet when they were dating and thus Donna and Sarah had never met face-to-face.

She had to get away. Her emotions were too fragile to deal with the animosity she could feel surrounding her.

"Excuse me," she murmured to anyone who would care. She ducked into the first open pew and walked over to the next aisle.

"Oh, Sarah, honey. There you are." Aunt Dot caught her unaware and, before Sarah could step aside, her aunt had enveloped her in a smothering hug. Behind her, Auntie Tilly looked at Sarah with a pitying look.

From the fire into the frying pan, thought Sarah, gently extricating herself from her aunt's buxom bosom and giving her other aunt a quick smile. But at least this way it looked as if she had deliberately chosen to go to her aunts, instead of trying to give herself some space.

"Hey, Auntie." She gave her Aunt Dot a feeble smile. She was stuck here now.

"Oh, my dear girl." Dot stroked Sarah's face, then was about to hug her again, but Sarah neatly avoided the hug.

"How is your father?" Aunt Tilly asked. "Have you heard anything this morning?"

Sarah dutifully reported back what the doctor had told her this morning on the phone.

"Don't you worry, dear," Aunt Dot said. "Don't you worry about a thing. Uncle Morris and I will take you there right after church."

Sarah gave her aunt a smile, allowed Auntie Dot

to tuck her arm through hers and pull her back into the bosom of the family.

He shouldn't have been surprised.

Logan watched Sarah scramble between the pews, headed away from him and his mother and diving headlong into a Westerveld refuge. Running away again. Sarah's specialty.

Six years ago, after breaking up with him over the phone, she had scurried off to Nova Scotia without another word.

Now she was showing him her back again.

The momentary peace he had felt from the church service was effectively wiped away with that one simple action by Sarah.

He had started coming to church in the past six months, trying to find answers to the myriad of questions he'd had since his father died. Questions that had only increased when he overheard a conversation between Dan and Frank Westerveld.

For weeks after that, Logan wished he had walked away when he'd heard his parents' names mentioned, because that information had only reignited the anger that had burned white-hot against Frank Westerveld since Frank had cut off his father's livelihood. Anger that had only increased when Frank pushed Sarah to break up with him a couple years later.

Logan had hoped that the church, which had once given his father such comfort, could help him deal with some of that anger, old and new.

Logan gave himself a mental shake and laid his hand on his mother's shoulder in a tacit gesture of comfort.

But his mother had her stern gaze fixed firmly on Sarah, and Logan could see that she stared like a mother bear protecting her cub.

He chanced another look across the empty pews at Sarah. She wore her blond hair longer and she was thinner. Her soft blue eyes held a haunted sadness that he understood a little too well.

But she was as beautiful as the first time he had seen her running across the gym playing basketball, that blond hair pulled back in a ponytail, her eyes bright, her lips parted in a smile that showed anyone watching how much she loved the game.

He'd fallen half in love with her then and there. Even when he found out she was Frank Westerveld's daughter, the man who owned half of Riverbend, the man his father spoke of with a mixture of fear and contempt, he wasn't fazed.

And when she stopped, turned and looked back at him, still holding on to the basketball like a trophy, he fell the rest of the way in love.

Logan willed his wayward thoughts to the back of his mind. That infatuation and those rampant emotions were a thing of the past. Too much had come between them now.

Sarah was just back to visit her father, that much he had understood from the bits and pieces of gossip he'd picked up since the ambulance took the man away. She wasn't back to take a stroll with him down memory lane.

He and his mother came to the open foyer and people spread out, moving faster now.

From the corner of his eye, Logan could see that in spite of her quick escape Sarah was going to meet up with him after all.

If he slowed his steps just a fraction…

"I've got to give something to Angie Flikkema," his mother said, stopping and pulling an envelope out of her purse. "I'll meet you at the car."

And when she left, Sarah's aunts were heading toward them, Sarah in their wake. Dot had her head turned toward Tilly, who was digging through her purse. As they swept past, neither of them saw him.

Sarah, however, lagging a few steps behind, had him with a vigilant eye.

Her wariness gave him a curious reluctance to confront her, but by the time his second thoughts had caught up with the situation, she was directly in front of him.

"Hello again."

Her only reply was a curt nod and a clipped "Hi."

Great conversation starter. "How is your father doing?" He fell into step with her.

She didn't reply, winding her scarf around her neck with jerky movements, but he waited, letting the bubble of silence between them grow.

"I'm surprised you want to know," she said, coming to a stop and glaring up at him. "Especially when…"

He frowned at her anger, as unexpected as it was uncharacteristic. "What do you mean?"

Sarah pressed her lips together, then shook her head. "Doesn't matter."

But it did. "You were going to say something else."

She sucked in a quick breath. "He didn't want you there. You were making him upset." Her words popped out of her mouth like single-syllable darts.

Her animosity resurrected the niggling sense of remorse that his conversation with Frank might have had something to do with the man's collapse. Except that it had been Frank who had initiated the conversation. "And what was I supposed to have done? Left you alone with a man who was stumbling on the street?"

"He wanted you gone," Sarah said in a choked voice. "He wouldn't even look at me."

Was that hurt in her voice?

Then Sarah looked up at him, her eyes snapping with anger and he realized he had read her wrong again. Their last words before her departure had been ones of anger, as well. They had argued about her father, as well.

Six years, and nothing had changed. Nothing at all.

As for her father? Well, Frank Westerveld had other actions to answer for.

As Sarah watched Logan leave, the bitterness that had held her in its hungry grip loosened its jaws. And once again, she felt as if everything she had said had come out all wrong, twisted in the space between thinking and saying. Sarah pressed her fingers to her temples, massaging away a low-level headache that threatened to take over.

She had driven across the country on the strength of a rare request by her father, to see what he had to say. Yet, when she finally connected with him, the last intelligible words he had uttered were directed toward Logan. And she, Sarah Westerveld, dutiful daughter, had been sidelined once again.

She thought she had grown up and away from her life here.

Obviously not.

She counted to fifteen, took a calming breath, then walked toward the door. She needed to get out, get into her car and drive her frustration away.

"Sarah. Hey, Sarah," Uncle Morris, her father's brother, called out. She waited a beat, then turned to face her uncle, drawn away from her tottering emotions by the obligation of family.

"Are you going to the hospital? Do you need a ride?" Her uncle wiped his hand over his balding head, shiny with perspiration from his exertion.

"No. I've got my own car, I'll drive myself."

"Good…good." He tugged on his crooked tie and straightened his suit coat. Sarah sensed a lecture coming. "I noticed you were talking to Logan Carleton."

"He was talking to me," Sarah corrected, preparing to defend her actions.

"Well, it's good to see him and Donna here." Uncle Morris's words surprised her. Then he slipped his arm around Sarah's shoulder, just as he used to when, as the principal of her high school, he would meet her in the hallway. "Dan tells me you are going to be sticking around for a while. To help take care of your father."

"Well, as much care as I can give him."

"That wouldn't take up all of your time, I'm sure."

"Probably not."

"I imagine you read about Mr. DeHaan's heart attack?"

"Yes. That's too bad. Does he still coach?" Sarah asked, wondering about her uncle's leap in topics.

"He coaches the boys team now. Or did."

"So you'll need a new coach."

Morris nodded, looking at Sarah with an expectant look. "Would you be interested?"

So this was where he was headed. "I don't know anything about coaching a basketball team," she protested. "Especially not a boys' team."

"Sarah, you were a star basketball player when

you played here. I've been following your career in college basketball. I know how well you've done there. I won't find anyone of your caliber locally. The team we've got is one of the best ones we've had in years. They have a real shot at the provincial title. It's not going to happen if I don't get a good coach for these boys. You could do the job."

"Uncle Morris, coaching and playing are two different disciplines and they require two different approaches."

"They're a real good team and you know what that can do for some of these boys," he said, as if she hadn't voiced her protest. "Getting to the provincials could be their ticket to an education. A chance to expand their horizons."

Sarah knew exactly what basketball could do. It was thanks to her own scholarship her second year of college that she had been able to put herself through school without depending on her father's help anymore. And the thought of being involved in a game she loved and had poured so much energy and emotion into did tantalize her. She tested the picture, trying it on for size, and for the first time since she came to Riverbend, she felt a trickle of excitement. "I might be interested."

"Great, I can arrange for you to come later on next week."

Her uncle's earnest gaze made her smile. Uncle Morris was a curious combination of Uncle Dan's gentleness and her father's hard-nosed intensity. If he wanted her to coach the basketball team, he wasn't going to stop until she said yes.

But the old Sarah, who would have agreed immediately, was buried under six years of independent decision making and away from her father's influence.

"I said *might,*" she reprimanded gently, surprised at her own temerity. "Give me some time to think about it."

Uncle Morris looked momentarily taken aback, as if surprised at this new attribute of his niece, but then he smiled and patted her on the shoulder. "I don't want to pressure you, but the season starts in a couple of weeks. The boys' coach would have started practices and tryouts already. I want to make sure these very talented boys can get started as soon as possible."

No pressure at all, thought Sarah. "I'll let you know."

She said goodbye and, as she was leaving, her cousin Dodie appeared and grabbed her by the arm. "You're coming to our place for lunch before you go to the hospital. Mom told me to make sure I drag you, pull you, whatever it takes." Dodie gave Sarah's arm a tug as if to underline her threat.

"It won't take dragging," Sarah said. "I love your mom's cooking." It would be no hardship to spend some time at Uncle Dan and Aunt Tilly's beautiful home.

"I noticed Logan talking to you. What did he want? What did he say?" Dodie demanded as they walked toward the door of the church.

Sarah dismissed her questions and all six foot two of Logan with an abrupt wave of her hand. She did not want to talk. She still had to process the moment herself.

Chapter Four

She was prettier. Older. And in the six years since he had seen her, she'd gained an edge she didn't have when they were dating.

Logan ran water over his grimy hands, wishing he could as easily remove Sarah from his mind.

When he had first seen her on the sidewalk in town, he thought he had imagined her. But when she spoke, she sounded as distant as she had the last time they had talked.

He hated hearing that tone and he hated that it could still elicit such a strong reaction. Sarah Westerveld had dropped out of his life and moved on. He had moved on. He had other Westervelds to deal with.

His hands stopped their ceaseless lathering as his mind flitted back to that truncated conversation in front of the coffee shop. He knew he should have been more diplomatic. He probably should have walked away instead of showing his hand by telling Frank to his face that he was going to buy Crane's contract with Frank's business. Whether Frank liked it or not.

Sarah's veiled accusation that he had caused her father's stroke still stung—partly because he felt guilty about it himself, but mostly because it came from her.

He shook the water from his hands. Enough. He had enough things on his mind right now. Sarah was just a blip on the radar. And she would be gone in a matter of days.

"Are you coming?" his mother called out from the kitchen.

He shook his head, dried his hands off on the towel, closed his mind to the memories, then joined his mother and brother just as Donna spooned some potatoes on her plate and handed the bowl to his younger brother, Billy.

Logan breathed deeply. When his father came back from that last day in court, acquitted but broken, his mother had put the Bible away and they had never again prayed before meals.

But after his father died, emptiness had overtaken Logan's life. And when he found out that Frank Westerveld had stopped going to church, Logan started attending again. Occasionally his mother and Billy would come along; more recently, Donna had been attending more regularly. He'd slowly been making room for faith and God, though he wasn't sure how to put it all together in his life.

"So we found out who our new basketball coach is going to be," Billy said as he pulled the plate of hamburger patties toward him.

"And let me guess, you're not impressed." Logan gave his mother a quick wink. Billy hadn't been impressed with the previous coach, either. Logan guessed that even Kareem Abdul-Jabbar would not have completely met with Billy's approval.

"At least Mr. DeHaan was a guy."

Logan frowned. "What you mean?"

"You heard me. Our new coach is a female. A woman. A lady. What am I supposed to call a woman coach?"

"'Coach' would probably work," Donna said.

Logan felt a trickle of premonition. "Sarah Westerveld?"

Billy shot him an irritated look. "Yeah. It is. How do you know?"

Logan put his fork down. "When did you find this out?"

"At tryouts today. Mr. Westerveld came to the gym to introduce her. His niece." Billy rolled his eyes. "Can you say *nepotism?*"

"I'm surprised *you* can, the way you've been studying." Donna turned to Logan. "Can they do that? Can that Morris Westerveld just give his niece the job?"

"I don't know how much say parents have in the

process," Logan said, trying to process this new and unwelcome piece of information. He thought Sarah was going to be leaving.

"The guys aren't happy about a woman coach," Billy grumbled.

"Can't say I'm so happy about it, either," Logan said. Basketball was Billy's potential ticket out of Riverbend, a way to leave all its petty politics and dirty little secrets. Billy stood a good chance of getting a scholarship, but, in order for that to happen, his team needed to stand out. Needed to win.

Billy was a gifted player and needed the right kind of coach to bring his talents out. Someone who would push him. Get him motivated.

There was no way Sarah Westerveld, the girl who couldn't even stand up to her own dad, could do that.

"Is she going to be coaching the entire season?" Logan asked.

Billy's only reply was a shrug.

Logan dug into his supper. He had to do something. It seemed the Westervelds would always cast a long shadow over the lives of his entire family. But he wasn't going to sit back and let his brother lose his chance because of another Westerveld.

Not without a fight.

Déjà vu all over again, thought Logan as he lounged in the doorway of the high school gym, the heat produced by fifteen players filling all available space and passing out the door around him.

He used to stand in this same place and watch Sarah play. She had always relied more on strategy than aggression, which made any game she played more fun to watch.

He slipped his hands into the pockets of his worn jean jacket as his narrowed eyes followed the group of boys, sweat darkening their hair, T-shirts with the sleeves ripped off flapping around tall, rangy forms as they ran up and down the wooden floor. The thumping of the basketball kept time with the pounding of sneaker-clad feet. His brother, Billy, was carrying the ball. He pivoted, dipped and then launched himself into the air. It was as if he kept going up and up—and at the apex of his jump, he even had time to pause, eye the basket, aim and shoot with perfect execution. As he came down, heads pivoted to follow the ball.

A "clang" resounded through the gym as the ball bounced off the rim, followed by a mixed chorus of exaltation and disappointed anger. A miss. Billy caught his rebound in his large hands, then slammed the ball against the wall in a fit of frustrated anger.

Logan shook his head at the testosterone-laden display. Obviously a brother-to-brother chat about self-discipline was coming up.

The sharp bleat of a whistle broke into the moment, then a young woman's voice called out to the boys to hit the showers.

And Logan's narrowed eyes found a new focus.

Sarah kept her focus on the boys as they paused.

Billy dribbled the ball a few more times, a show of defiance. The other boys glanced from Billy to Sarah, as if gauging whom they would follow.

Sarah kept the faint smile on her face, holding her clipboard close to her chest as she stared the boys down. One by one, they slunk off, leaving Billy behind.

Billy bounced the ball a few more times, then pushed it away with a look of disgust as he followed his teammates out of the gym.

The ball bounced across the gym, then rolled past Sarah.

"Billy, put this away, please," she said, her voice pleasant, her pretty face angled to one side as she stopped it with her foot.

Just like the other boys had only moments ago, Logan looked from Billy to Sarah to see what would happen.

"You're the last one to touch it, *you* put it away," he said with a sneer. Then he sauntered out of the gym full of his own self-importance.

Logan shook his head at the familiar scene. Though he was disappointed in his brother's behavior, it was nice to see someone else on the receiving end of his brother's sass for a change. He certainly had put up with enough of it over the past few years.

Sarah's sigh drifted past Logan as he pushed himself away from the doorway and walked toward her.

The movement caught her attention and she turned. She tucked a hank of hair behind her ear, a welcoming smile on her face that quickly faded. Her lips pressed together and she clutched the clipboard even closer.

A flicker of something indefinable crossed her features. "Logan Carleton. Stalking me again?"

"You played basketball the same way," he said, stopping within a few feet of her.

"Pardon me?" Her frown deepened.

"You were never much with the defense, were you? You always liked to lead the attack."

Sarah rocked back on her heels, still holding her clipboard like a shield. "Sounds to me like your strategy right about now," she returned with a cynical half smile.

She surprised him. Cynicism was his specialty, not hers. In high school Sarah had always been a positive, upbeat girl with an open smile and pleasant demeanor. That attribute had drawn him to her.

"I'm not stalking you," he said, returning to her original comment. "Just watching the practice."

"Just like you used to." Sarah pulled in a long, slow breath and released it quickly, as if pushing the past away, as well. "What can I do for you, Logan?" She bent over and scooped up the basketball with one hand, tossing it into the container beside her.

"I've actually come to talk to Morris but wanted to watch Billy's practice."

"What do you need to talk to my uncle about?" Sarah pulled the whistle from around her neck, still headed toward the bench.

Logan wondered what she would say if he told her the truth, then figured he may as well. She was going to find out sooner or later.

"I want to ask him to get someone else to coach the team."

Sarah spun around, almost losing her clipboard in the process. "What did you say?"

"This team has a real good shot at the provincial title and I want to make sure that nothing stands in their way."

"And you think I will?"

"I think these boys need a firm hand. They're used to Mr. DeHaan. He took no nonsense from these boys. He knew exactly how to handle them. And they responded."

"Unfortunately Mr. DeHaan is in the hospital right now." Sarah tapped her clipboard against her chest, facing him down.

"That is unfortunate. But, as I said, these boys need guidance. They need someone tough. Someone who won't back down."

"And you think I will."

"I think you have in the past. I think it can happen again."

Sarah glanced away and Logan knew he'd scored a direct hit. He felt a moment's regret but couldn't allow himself to give in to that. He had come here with one purpose in mind. Right now, his focus had to be his little brother and his chance to get out of this narrow-minded and petty community. A chance he'd never had.

Unlike Sarah.

Yet, as he looked down at her bent head, a resurrection of old attractions, old feelings rushed through him. Feelings of protectiveness, of yearning for the moments of peace he had felt when he was with her. The gentle balm of her giving and caring nature that stilled the anger that could still consume him.

She was the first person who had shown him how faith worked. It didn't matter to her that her sister was more popular, more vivacious and, generally, more fun. It didn't even matter to Sarah that her sister had more boyfriends.

Sarah loved her sister unconditionally.

She had told Logan while they were dating that it didn't matter to her what Marilee had, she had him. Sarah's simple statement had given him more confidence, more hope, more joy than anything he'd heard since.

He closed his eyes a moment, shutting out those memories. The girl in front of him wasn't that girl anymore. The girl in front of him hadn't even had the guts to break up with him in person or to explain why.

Though they had only dated for eight months, and in secret at that, she was the first girl he had ever truly cared for.

And then she had left.

She looked him straight in the eye now, her own

eyes snapping with a surprising anger. "I don't think you'll have much luck with Uncle Morris in getting rid of me, Carleton."

Her use of his last name set off something in him. It was as if she was deliberately underlining the differences between them, bringing up her family connections to show him where he stood in the Riverbend hierarchy.

"Of course not." He laughed, but it was without humor. "I forgot about how this family sticks together." He pointed to a scar on his forehead. "I believe it was your cousin Ethan who did this to me when I told him that his uncle should have stuck by my dad and believed him when he was falsely accused."

He held back the rest of his sentence, bitterness roiling in his gut.

"And that uncle would be my father," she said quietly.

And he could tell from the cool tone of her voice that he had not only stepped over her sacred line, he had obliterated it. Sarah's loyalty to her father was legendary. He should know. She had chosen her father over him.

But he didn't take back anything he said. He meant it then and he meant it now. For seven years, Logan's father, Jack, had supplied Westerveld Construction with the gravel they needed. When Logan's father was accused of murder, Frank canceled the contract. In the past few weeks Logan had discovered that Frank had his own secrets, and, possibly, his own misbegotten reasons for taking away the contract his father had depended on for his livelihood.

This was the man Sarah had always acquiesced to. Always defended.

Sarah held his gaze, her eyes slightly narrowed as if she was trying to see him differently than with the wide-eyed innocence she'd once had.

"I'm not going anywhere," she said quietly. "I can coach this team as well as anyone else you might suggest. Better maybe."

Her icy tone was something he would never have imagined from her before. That he had caused it created a flicker of regret.

Stay on task, he reminded himself.

"I guess we'll see," he said. Then, without another glance her way, he turned on his booted heel and left.

"I wish I knew what my father was trying to say," Sarah said as her uncle Morris pushed the button for the hospital elevator. "It's so hard to watch him struggling to talk."

This was the first time Sarah had come to see her father with one of her uncles. Her previous visits had all been solo. She had hoped that what he wanted to say to her would manage to come out despite his unresponsive lips. But each visit he labored to get out even the most basic of sounds.

When Uncle Morris had found out that her car

was in the garage and she couldn't make the trip to the city, he had offered her a ride.

Morris stood back, his hands clasped in front of him as he watched the numbers above the elevator flash. "I can imagine, Sarah, but you have to believe that your visits are making a big difference for your father. The doctors and nurses all say he is much happier after you come."

"Thanks, Uncle Morris. That makes me feel a bit better."

She wished she could be sincere about what she said, but the reality was her visits always felt forced. Fake. She and her father had never had a close relationship. They had never laughed or traded jokes and stories. Marilee was the one who could make him smile even in spite of her antics. Marilee could cuddle up to him when he was busy working and tease away his faint frown of displeasure at being distracted from whatever he was doing.

She knew basketball bored him. Aunt Dot and Aunt Tilly kept him abreast of the happenings in and around the town. So most of her visits with him were spent reading out loud to him from an old *Reader's Digest* or any book she found lying around.

"He missed you when you were gone, you know."

Had Sarah imagined the faint reprimand in Morris's comment?

"Funny, I didn't pick up on that in the lack of letters he sent me," Sarah said, glancing sidelong at her uncle.

Morris laid his hand on her shoulder. "I think he feels guilty."

"What do you mean?"

"Sarah, the whole family knows that Marilee was your father's favorite and that you were your mother's. We all thought Frank would change after your mother died, and he did, but not for the better. And showing such obvious preference for Marilee? He should never have treated Marilee the way he did. He didn't do that girl any favors."

Sarah tried to shrug away the well-meant sentiment. Truth was, it was embarrassing to discover that Frank's favoritism was so blatant that the entire family had seen it. Had the community, as well? Wouldn't that make her look like the loser of the decade.

The elevator doors opened and Sarah hoped this was the end of the discussion.

"Then, a few years after you left, your father changed," Morris continued as they exited the elevator. "I don't know what happened, but he grew softer. He talked about what you were doing. We were all glad he was finally showing interest in you. He missed you."

"He had a funny way of showing it. In all the time I was gone, he never sent me a personal note."

"But he said he wrote you every month." Morris frowned.

"He wrote a check every month, Uncle Morris. Nothing else was ever in the envelope."

"You know your father is not a chatty man. He doesn't know how to display affection."

"Maybe not, but would it have been so hard to even put one small note in the envelope? Just *once?*" Sarah felt frustrated that the old pain returned so easily.

The first few months she got her checks, she had eagerly ripped open the envelopes, hoping for some personal note. But every month the only paper was the money. Her second year of school, she ripped up his monthly checks, determined to make her own way.

But her father kept sending them. She had gotten used to it, but each month the lack of a letter stung.

And now her uncle was saying that her father missed her? Was that what his succinct note was about?

The elevator doors opened and they walked to her father's room.

They caught the doctor making his rounds, and while Sarah spoke to him, her uncle wheeled Frank down the hall to the visitor's section at the end of the hallway.

When Sarah joined them a few minutes later, Uncle Morris was relating a play-by-play of the basketball game.

"You should have seen those boys, Frank," Morris said, leaning forward, resting his elbows on his knees. "Sarah is really whipping the team into shape."

Frank glanced from his brother to his daughter. Her own frustration had left, as it always did when she actually saw her father. Anger was always easier in the abstract. When she saw Frank sitting hunched in his wheelchair, his body a mockery of his former strength, his face loose and slack jawed, sympathy easily erased any negative emotion she could have felt.

She thought of what Uncle Morris had said. Clung to it, in fact. She knew her father wasn't demonstrative. Even Marilee, his favorite, had complained about it.

Maybe Uncle Morris was right. Maybe her father did miss her. Maybe he simply didn't know how to show it.

She gave her father the benefit of the doubt and a careful smile.

Had Sarah imagined his eyes lighting up? Did the lift of one side of his mouth represent a smile? Then he raised his hand a fraction and moved it toward Sarah.

The joy she felt at that simple movement was almost out of proportion to the action.

She took his hand and held it in her own. He nodded and Sarah felt, for the first time, that her visit was worthwhile.

"I…I…for…" He struggled to formulate the words and Sarah leaned forward, almost willing the sounds past his immobile lips. Then his fingers tightened on hers.

Sarah squeezed back. "It's okay, Dad. It will come. The doctor is really pleased with your progress." And so was she. This was the most personal response she had gotten from him since his stroke. "Once you're transferred to Riverbend, I can visit you more often."

Frank nodded, his eyes on Sarah.

All the tension of the past six years seemed to loosen. Would she and her father get a second chance at some kind of relationship? The thought settled, and for the first time since she had run away from Riverbend, tears in her eyes, angry and hurt with her father, missing her beloved Logan, she felt as if maybe something good was going to come for them.

Morris and Sarah talked for a while, and for the rest of their visit, Frank kept his hand in Sarah's, his eyes on hers.

When she hugged him goodbye, he gave her the semblance of a smile.

The nurses were stringing tinsel along the nurses' station as Morris and Sarah left. Christmas was creeping up on them, Sarah realized. She hadn't been paying attention to the season.

One nurse called out a greeting and Sarah waved back, her heart lighter than when she had arrived at the hospital.

"Your dad seemed interested in your basketball team," Morris said as he held the door of the ward open for Sarah.

"I'm surprised. But the team is doing well. I just

wish Billy would get his head in the game. It's almost like he's blowing this big chance."

"Billy has other fish to fry, I'm afraid." Morris sighed. "Billy's marks haven't been stellar."

Sarah rubbed her temple with her forefinger. "So you're saying his place on the team might be in jeopardy?"

"Emphasis on *might*. He still has time. I don't want Billy to be cut, but he needs to focus…" Morris let the sentence trail off as the elevator arrived.

Sarah stepped inside, and stood beside an intern frowning at his clipboard. "I need that boy on the team."

"I'm surprised you stick up for him. Logan has been pushing me to get you replaced."

The elevator stopped and the intern got out and they were alone again. "Doesn't matter. I can't let Billy go." She couldn't help remembering the blaze of conviction in Logan's eyes when he had spoken of his desire to get Billy out of Riverbend.

"Well, we're not sure how to proceed."

The elevator felt suddenly claustrophobic as Sarah sifted through her options. She had to find a way to make Billy realize what he was giving up by his thoughtless rebelliousness.

"I could talk to him," Sarah said.

"That would help."

Sarah wasn't sure it would. Billy seemed to have his own secrets. But she didn't want him to miss out on a good opportunity because he was distracted by them.

She thought of Logan and his campaign to get rid of her. She wished he would realize they were on the same side in this matter.

Chapter Five

"Block out. Block out," Sarah called, and bodies realigned themselves on the basketball court, shoes squeaking out a protest on the wooden floor at the sudden shifts and spins as the team members maneuvered to get into position.

The final game of the tournament was only five minutes away from being won by a team with less experience, shorter players, and, even more important, a male coach.

Sarah knew she should be watching the boys as they fought back. But, as if of their own will, her eyes veered right and found *him*.

Logan sat leaning forward, his clasped hands pressed against a stubbled chin. He must have come straight to the game after work.

Then, as if he sensed her scrutiny, he stared directly at her. The animosity in his eyes was a direct reflection of his brother Billy's.

She jerked her glance away in time to see a shot from the opposing team bounce off the rim. Billy Carleton hooked the ball out of the air and charged down the court.

She had to block out the noise of the home-team spectators, stop thinking of the aunts and uncles and cousins who were probably in attendance tonight, stop thinking of Logan hovering on the sidelines.

"Pop Tart! Pop Tart!" she called out, reminding Billy of the play they had gone over again and again. Now was the time for his hook shot.

Then, inexplicably, he stopped, dribbling, his eyes grazing over the court. Was he daydreaming?

"Cut your head in," Sarah shouted out her frustration.

But in the split second Billy had taken to judge the play, an opponent had stripped the ball from him and run down the court to score on the Voyageurs' sleeping defense.

When Billy mouthed an obscenity, Sarah signaled the referee for a time-out.

Sarah shut out the jeers of the visiting spectators, ignored the groans and complaints of the home-team boosters, blocked Logan's frustrated glare and directed her complete focus on the very upset high school boys gathered around her.

Sarah wasn't short, but most of these boys topped her height by almost a head. "We practice plays for a reason," she said, quietly but intently, looking around the circle. "We had these boys at the beginning of the game and then we lost momentum." She tried to think of all the things her own coach would tell them when her team was down, which words would make the connection, make the difference. She wished she could tell the team that she had more to prove tonight than they did.

Not only were her friends and relatives in the stands, watching the girl who they still thought of as Little Sarah, but Logan Carleton also watched her every move. Even now, with minipanic swirling in her mind, she sensed his eyes on her, felt his displeasure.

"You've given up already. You need to practice winning. Don, you've got to hustle." She hesitated and then plowed on. "Billy, don't pull back on your team. Be a leader."

Billy's gaze rested on her for a split second, then flicked away. Sarah felt the hostile force of his glare and tried to brush it off.

The shrill blast of the whistle indicated the end of the time-out.

"You guys can beat this team. They're getting cocky and lazy. Watch their center. They're depending on him way too much."

She stepped away as the boys nodded and jogged off to take up their positions on the court.

Five minutes later the buzzer sounded.

The Voyageurs had lost.

"Too bad about the game," Uncle Morris called out as he left the gym.

Sarah gave her uncle a quick nod as she picked up the game stats. She had just returned from talking with the boys, feeling some of her momentum lost from having to wait until they finished in the locker room.

She had hoped the gym would be empty by the time she came back to the bench to gather her things. A few parents stood in a huddle at one end of the gym, discussing intently, Sarah was sure, her lack as a coach.

Don't be paranoid, she warned herself, shuffling the papers she would be poring over. *It was your first major game. You can't blame yourself.*

As she slipped the papers and the videotape of the game into her gym bag, she sensed a presence beside her.

"Close game." Logan's voice was a low rumble.

Even after all these years, even after a couple of meetings, the sound of his voice could still affect her. She clenched her fists to delete the older memories, then turned to face him. Logan stood with his hands in the pockets of a grease-stained down-filled jacket. He still wore heavy work boots and from his clothes Sarah caught the familiar scent of diesel and dirt, underlining her initial impression that he had just come straight here from his work.

His eyes could still mesmerize her.

If she let them.

"It would have been a 'won' game if the so-called

star captain would suck up his petty squabble with his female coach."

"Young men don't take directions from women very easily." Logan's dark eyes challenged her as strongly as his words.

His anger roused her own. He had no right to hover over her, criticizing what she was doing when his own brother was part of the problem.

"So if I were to tell you to take a hike, you'd just stand where you are," she snapped, irritation and weariness making her forget her manners.

"Well, now, it seems that Kitten has claws."

"Don't call me that," she said with more anger than she intended. Kitten was Uncle Morris and Aunt Dot's pet name for her. One day, while she was walking down the school hallway, he'd called her that. Logan had been right behind.

At that time, Logan Carleton was simply an angry young man, two grades above her, who would lurk in the doorway of the gymnasium watching her practice, watching her play, his dark eyes enigmatic.

He had started calling Sarah *Kitten,* as well. Only his voice hadn't held the gentle endearment that Uncle Morris's had. His contained the faintest sneer of contempt.

This had gone on for an entire year.

He finished high school and Sarah thought she was free of him. Then he started attending her games and hanging around afterward. Though Sarah was afraid of him, she was curiously drawn, as well.

And then, one day he caught some boys teasing her unmercifully. She was crying and he came to her rescue.

Had put his hand on her shoulder. Had turned her around to face him. Had told her of all those years he'd secretly admired her, secretly wondered if he'd be able to bridge the social gap between them…and bent over and kissed her. Everything between them changed.

Even after all these years Sarah could feel the touch of those memories and a little jump in her heart.

Every young girl falls in love with at least one bad boy, she thought, yanking on the gym door.

The door was locked.

So much for a dramatic exit. Without sparing him another glance, she turned on her heel and strode toward the back door and Logan had no choice but to follow.

The sound of his booted feet on the wooden floor echoed eerily in the silence of the gym, and Sarah was glad when she finally reached the opposite door. She reached to open it, but Logan's hand landed there first, pushing it open, letting in a cloud of cold air from outside. "Ladies first," he said with an edge of irony in his voice.

She moved past him into the dark night, catching again the scent of dirt and diesel—smells she had always associated with her father and uncle's construction company. Smells of her childhood.

Her step faltered as memories flooded into her mind—stealing illegal rides with her cousin Doug on a dirt mover, riding along with her uncle when he would go the job site to check on the operations. An entire web of happy memories woven from those scents.

Logan caught her by the arm, steadying her. She wrenched her arm out of his grip.

"Sorry," he said, "I thought you were going to fall."

Against her will, her gaze found his.

And there it came again. A frisson of awareness overlaid with danger and anticipation that surrounded Logan every time they were together. In the thin glow cast by the streetlights, his face lay in shadow, but Sarah caught the glint of his dark eyes and she couldn't look away.

"That's okay. I'm just tired," she said softly, disappointed at how easily he had unearthed the old feelings.

She'd dated other men since Logan. She'd been away for six years now. A grown-up girl.

So why did one look from those dark eyes still create a tug of attraction?

"What do you actually want, Logan?" she asked, fighting the memories with the only weapon she had available: anger.

"I'm just waiting for Billy." He pushed his hands into his pockets.

"And I hear you've followed through on your

threats and have been talking to my uncle. About my suitability as a coach."

"Yeah. No surprises there. He said he was willing to give you a chance. Nice that the Westervelds take care of their own."

"Nice that someone is willing to give me a chance." She gave him a level glance, as if to remind him that she wasn't going anywhere.

"Like you gave me a chance?"

Sarah knew he alluded to the phone call she had made in the presence of her father, breaking up with Logan.

The heavy tone in Logan's voice surprised her as if, in spite of all these years, that still mattered to him. His reference to the past tugged out older emotions and regrets. Was this going to happen every time she saw him?

"What were you talking to my father about?" Her question was a direct attack, a way of pushing those emotions to the past where they belonged.

Logan pulled back and it wasn't just the winter air that made Sarah shiver. "When I caused his stroke?"

"That's not what I said."

"You don't need to. You made it pretty clear that I was the cause of that in church the other day."

"Well, you made him so upset. And shortly after that he collapsed. What else was I supposed to think?" She stopped there, immediately regretting her outburst. She wanted to lay blame somewhere, but she had no right to lay that on Logan's shoulders.

"That your father has a lousy temper. That your father is carrying a burden of guilt."

Sarah had her own experiences with her father's temper. As for his guilt, Logan's enigmatic comment raised more questions.

"If you must know," Logan continued, "I was telling your father that I'm buying out the contract he took from my father eight years ago."

"And you've been planning this for all those years?"

Logan's eyes zeroed in on hers. "No. Just the past few months."

Sarah felt a shiver at the emotions roiling around them. Old emotions. Old anger. Logan was no different than her father after all.

"Okay, I get that you don't care for my father. I get that maybe he might have done something that you perceive as wrong. But really, isn't that making my father more of an enemy than he actually is?"

Logan narrowed his eyes. "You have no idea what kind of enemy your father really is." He spoke quietly, but with an edge of anger sharper than a yell. He lifted one clenched hand toward himself as if trying to hold back anything else he might divulge. Then he shook his head and gave her another mocking smile. "No idea at all."

"What are you talking about?"

"I'm talking about a man who hated my father for his own twisted reasons." Logan locked eyes with her a moment longer, then spun around and strode across the parking lot, his tall figure dark against the snow, his shadow pushing ahead of him, anger and mysteries trailing in his wake.

Chapter Six

"Don't tell me you can't find someone else to coach these boys, Morris," Logan barked into the phone as he shoved his office chair ahead. The chair hit his father's old oak desk and bounced back toward him as if mocking his anger. "Well, my own brother is on that team and it's not working for him." He ran his hand through his hair and tried not to yank. His misgivings about Sarah's effectiveness had only increased after this past game. "I don't care how many awards she's won. The guys don't respect her." Logan clenched the phone's handset as he turned around and looked out the window at the spruce trees surrounding the house, their branches heavy with snow. When his father built this house, he had wanted it secluded. Too bad their lives weren't offered the same protection as this house.

"I've spoken to Billy about it, Morris," he continued, resuming the agitated pacing of his small office. "But the reality is Sarah has to create respect for herself and if she can't, then I go back to my original complaint. Those boys need a firm hand. You know what this can mean to a lot of them."

He heard a light knock on the door and his mother put her head into the office. "Supper time," she whispered.

He held up a hand to ask for five more minutes then turned away hoping she would get the hint and leave. But she came in and sat down in the easy chair in one corner of the office. Her chair. Whenever his father had worked in this office, she would sit here and knit or drink her tea, content to simply be with her husband.

"The boys lost their game last night against a team they should have easily beat, Morris. They respect the junior coach, Ronnie. Why not put him in charge and let Sarah be the assistant? Well, that's my solution…okay…let me know." He lowered the phone, then hit the End button, breaking the connection.

"He still won't listen to you?"

Logan shook his head and dropped the phone onto the desk.

"That family takes care of each other, you know that." Donna's voice held the same anger his had, but hers was overlaid with bitterness.

Logan wondered if she knew what he did about Frank Westerveld. Wondered if he should tell her.

And what would it do? Just create more problems.

"They sure seem to." Logan sighed and picked up one of the papers the bank had sent him to sign for the loan he needed to take out. If he signed, he would extend himself into the danger zone of financing, all to secure a contract that had made Frank Westerveld so infuriatingly angry.

Could that have caused his stroke?

Don't go there, he reminded himself. Frank Westerveld had a lot of things to answer for.

But he needed that contract if his business was going to survive. And his business had to survive so he could continue to support his mother and his brother.

He had too many things on his mind right now. Too many people depending on him.

"You're a hard worker, Logan," his mother said quietly. "And I appreciate all you do for us. I don't think I tell you that enough." She smiled at him. "I just wish you would take some time for yourself. I do eventually hope to have grandchildren, you know."

And why did his mind immediately jump to Sarah? Sarah with her soft blue eyes that had at one time looked at him with longing—something that had created an answering lifting of his heart—instead of the cool contempt she had shown this afternoon.

Now she was back and, in spite of his campaign against her, she still evoked those reluctant feelings of surprising joy and anger. Joy at the sight of her beauty, and anger that he felt this way about Frank Westerveld's daughter, a girl who had chosen her daddy over him.

"I've got a lot of years ahead of me for that, Mom."

"But you've also spent a lot of years trying to be more than you should. A father to Billy, a support for me. You've hardly had a chance to be carefree and in love." Donna lowered her hands to his and caught them between hers. "You're a good man, Logan Carleton. I know you'll find someone special someday. I just don't think you should wait too long."

"I'll pencil that in my Day-Timer." He glanced over at the agenda on his desk, lying open to this week's tasks, then winked at his mother. "I think I'll have an hour next Friday."

"No you won't. Billy has a tournament." Donna laughed lightly, then left the room.

He pushed his hand through his hair. He had to focus. For now his priority was Billy. And if Morris wouldn't listen to him, he would take it to the school superintendent. Logan intended to do whatever he possibly could for his younger brother. And if Sarah Westerveld became a casualty, so be it.

More than a couple of times during the game, she had to remind herself to focus on the team. If Logan's intention was to get rid of her by intimidation, it wasn't going to work.

Well, at least not right away.

"Billy, watch your man. Move with him," she called out, fighting down her usual frustration with her supposedly star player. He'd been dragging his feet all game. If he was trying to prove something, it wasn't working. She'd bench him for the next game if she had to.

A quick glance at the clock gave her hope. At least the Voyageurs were ahead. They were only in the first minutes of the last quarter, but if the boys did what she told them to, they could win.

Billy caught the ball on the rebound and charged down the lane. Sarah watched him, willing him to do what they had covered again and again in practice. But he didn't see his open man, was blocked and threw his arms up in frustration at the referee. Sarah benched him, ignoring his fuming, ignoring Logan's dark look. She stopped biting her nails when the final whistle blew and the Voyageurs won.

The boys celebrated, Billy sulked and, as the fans stormed the court, Sarah saw Logan walking directly toward them.

She ignored Billy's cryptic comment as he went to join his friends but she couldn't ignore Logan as he loomed beside her. She caught the whiff of soap and the faintest hint of aftershave. Logan had never been a cologne kind of guy.

"I'm guessing you've come to ask me why I benched your brother," she said, focusing on the papers with the plays they had run, wishing her hands wouldn't tremble.

"Yeah. Did sort of make me wonder, considering he made about a third of the points tonight."

"He could have made more."

"You've got to be kidding." Logan's deep voice

held a mocking note of skepticism, which immediately got Sarah's back up.

"We should have dominated this team, not just beat them by a handy score. We could have wiped the gym floor with this team if your brother would listen to me and follow the plays I laid out. Plays we practiced and went over until he should be able to do them blindfolded and in his sleep." She took a breath, controlling her frustration.

The past three weeks had been spent visiting her father, whose recovery seemed to inch along, reconnecting with her extended family, trying to settle back into a community she had left so long ago. On top of that she had spent a lot of time setting up the basketball roster, organizing practices and trying to pull together a cohesive team of boys who didn't seem to want her as a coach. Then yesterday she had gotten a phone call from her friends. They had called to say goodbye from the airport.

She was supposed to be on that plane, winging her way to fun and sun and a break after years of hard work and studying and pushing herself again and again, trying to prove to herself that she was good. That she was worthy.

Instead, she stood on the sidelines of a high school gym getting hassled by the brother of a surly player who seemed to deliberately be ruining his own game, before checking in on her sick father, who was finally acknowledging her presence but couldn't actually say the words she knew he strove so hard to articulate, all while trying to ignore a man who was far too attractive a mystery for his own good.

To say she was feeling frustrated was vastly understating her emotional state.

"Your precious little brother is not playing to his potential. You may think he's the greatest thing since carbonated beverages, but right now he's a royal pain and he's holding this team back."

Sarah glared up at Logan and to her dismay she felt the faint prick of tears. No. Not now. Not in front of this man.

"He complains that you ride him a lot. He thinks you have it in for him. I hope that the old Westerveld/Carleton issues aren't clouding your judgment."

Sarah just stared. "You honestly think I'm so petty as to let old personal feelings interfere with how I coach this team?"

"What old personal feelings, Sarah?" His question was short, but it carried a longer world of history.

Sarah chose to ignore the underlying comment. "Billy is an exceptional player and I'm doing what any coach would do when confronted with someone who isn't using their natural talent." She was determined not to let him see how he affected her. "If you think someone needs to be confronted, then I would suggest you talk to your little brother and ask what he's trying to prove. Because I can tell you right now, I'm not going anywhere."

Sarah's heart kicked up a notch when Logan took

a step closer but she held her ground, determined not to allow Logan Carleton to bully her. He may have held her heart in the past, but she wasn't going to let him affect the present. She had come to Riverbend to dump some old emotional baggage. He had featured too long in her dreams and been too long a part of her emotions. Time to cut that off.

Logan sucked in a long, slow breath, the emotion in his deep brown eyes shifting. Changing. Relief slipped through her when he looked away.

"I just might do that," he said quietly.

Sarah was saved from a scathing rejoinder when the boys surged back to the bench, coming between her and Logan.

She got a few halfhearted slaps on the back, a couple of quick smiles. She took what she got, thankful for the small acknowledgment.

Billy didn't even glance at her as he swung his bag over his shoulder and joined his brother.

When Logan looked directly at Sarah, she managed to give him a curt nod of her head, dismissing him, wishing she could get him out of her mind as easily as it was to get him out of her gym.

"Sarah Westerveld?" The woman's voice broke in over the sound of the piped-in Christmas carols in Janie's coffee shop.

Sarah looked up from her tea into the bright eyes of an older woman.

"Hello. How are you?" Sarah's mind raced as she

tried to place the woman. She looked familiar. Did she know her?

"I'm Trix Setterfeld. My son plays basketball."

"Yes. Derek's mother." Sarah gestured to the empty chair across the table. "Please. Sit down."

Trix sat, or rather perched on the edge of her seat. Her fight-or-flight stance made Sarah uneasy.

"I just want to tell you how glad I am you're willing to step up for now. The boys need to have some kind of guidance." Trix gave Sarah a tight smile. "So do you know when they're going to get a coach?"

Sarah's smile tightened. "I *am* their coach."

Trix's nervous laugh made Sarah uptight. "Well, yes. For now, but really. The boys need a male… well…role model. You know…they listen better…" She stopped, flipping her hand to one side as if dismissing Sarah, her MVP awards, her five years of college basketball, six years of junior and senior high school basketball, summer camps, training sessions and coaching clinics with one wave of her manicured fingers. "You know what I mean, don't you?"

"Unfortunately, I don't." Sarah kept her smile pasted on her face and her eyes fixed on Trix.

"Well, Logan was saying that he would like, I mean, we think it would be better if Morris could get a male coach."

"Do you know of one?"

Trix's expression grew hard. "I'm sure he could find one."

Sarah's ire rose. Silly girl. Logan's campaign had

expanded to the other parents. "Coaches aren't something you can pick up at the local store. And basketball coaches this time of the year, are, as a rule, otherwise employed."

Trix's frown deepened. "You don't need to act as if I'm simple. I'm just saying there has to be an alternative."

"Mr. DeHaan is recuperating from a heart attack. I am the alternative."

"Does that mean you aren't going to step aside?" Trix ejected herself from the chair, her hands working the handle of her purse. "You're going to keep coaching my boy?"

"Unless my uncle as principal tells me he wants to replace me with someone who can do the job better, yes." Sarah made the comment with a confidence that came from the knowledge that in a town the size of Riverbend, one didn't simply go out and find a new coach. Her job, until that happened, was fairly secure.

"I heard that Alton Berube, the biology teacher, used to coach basketball. Why isn't he doing it now?"

"I don't know." This was the first Sarah had heard of Mr. Berube. She was surprised Uncle Morris hadn't mentioned him or considered him.

Trix nodded, as if settling this information into her mind. "I guess we'll have to see how things go." She paused, then granted Sarah a condescending smile. "I'm sure you're a really good player. In fact, I know you are. When your sister, Marilee, was dating my oldest son, she was always going on about how many points you scored and how the team depended on you."

Sarah was surprised at the dull press of pain Marilee's name resurrected.

"…but you know, it's different with boys. They don't respect a woman the same."

"They had better," Sarah said, picking up her cup, hoping Trix would get the hint, "or I'll have them on the floor doing fifty push-ups."

"Of course." Trix waited a moment, as if to say more then, with another awkward flutter of her hand that Sarah presumed was a farewell wave, she left.

As the door shut behind her, Sarah slammed her mug back on the table, tea slopping over the edge of the mug.

What was Logan doing? Trying to undermine what precious little authority she had managed to garner the past few practices?

Was he crazy, or just plain vindictive?

"You look ticked," Janie said, pulling out the chair across from Sarah with a screech.

"I just got some kind of weird little lecture from Trix Setterfeld."

"Her boy plays basketball, doesn't he?"

"Oh, yes, but you know he would play much better if he had a male coach, you know." Sarah yanked a handful of napkins from the dispenser and wiped up the warm tea. "She and Logan must have been discussing my various shortcomings during the last game." She swiped the rest of the tea, then folded the soggy napkins and pushed them aside. "Which makes me wonder how many other parents he's been pulling over onto his side."

"Oh, don't listen to them. Uncle Morris knew what he was doing when he asked you to coach."

"Of course, you're going to stand up for me. You're a Westerveld after all."

"Oh brother, did she say that?"

"Actually, Logan implied it, and I'm sure she thought it, too." Sarah took a sip of tea, but the pleasure she usually found in her early morning stopover at Janie's was ruined. "This is a great start to a great day."

"What else is happening today?"

Nervousness replaced her anger at the thought of what faced her. "I get to have a case conference with the physiotherapist and the doctor and the speech pathologist and a host of others to talk about my father's long-term care."

"I thought they were going to move him to the hospital here in Riverbend."

"They are. But we need to talk about his program and what I can expect and his long-term prognosis."

"At least having him here will make visiting him easier."

"That's true." Sarah gave her tea an extra swirl with her spoon. She'd spent most of yesterday with her father in the city, helping him with his physio, hurting for the struggle every small movement had become for him.

The nurses had praised his determination and told Sarah that, all things considered, he was doing well.

She wished she shared their optimism. It was hard to watch a man once brimming with self-confidence, a man who pushed his way through life, unable to walk or even feed himself.

With every restricted movement he made, every slurred word he forced through uncooperative lips, she could feel his exasperation grow.

When the doctor said long, slow recovery, he had not been exaggerating.

Sarah put her spoon beside her teacup, wondering what shape her life was going to take over the next few months.

At least she had her coaching. The one bright spot in her life where she felt as if she had some modicum of control.

And Logan was trying to take even that away from her.

"So how is the team doing?"

"I just need to get Billy on board. He's the leader and the boys look up to and follow him. If he would listen to me and do what I tell him, then things would flow a lot easier."

The door opened, letting in a rush of cold air.

And Logan Carleton.

Sarah didn't want to look at him right now. The sight of him made her blood boil. And race. Their last enigmatic conversation still spiraled and spun through her mind. What had he been trying to imply about her poor father?

Unfortunately he wasn't having the same reaction to her that she had to him. Out of the corner of her eye she saw him approach her table.

And stop.

She glanced up at him, disliking the advantage he had over her with his imposing height. "Good morning, Logan. What can I do for you?"

"Just thought I would say hi." His puzzled tone gave Sarah pause.

"Well. Hi." She wasn't in any mood to engage in chitchat with him right now.

He waited a moment, as if to give her a chance to say something else. She simply looked up at him, her gaze unwavering.

But as he was about to turn away, she changed her mind about the chitchat. "I just had a little talk with Trix Setterfeld," she said with an airy tone, as if that particular conversation hadn't grated like sand on an open wound. "She seems to agree with you."

Logan frowned.

"About my coaching," Sarah prompted.

Then, to her dismay, Logan sat down. "What did she say?"

I should have said nothing, Sarah thought. She didn't want to be sitting at a tiny table, knees almost touching, with Logan Carleton. He created too many odd feelings that she resented yet couldn't extinguish.

"She also seemed to think the boys would do better under a male coach."

"She's entitled to her opinion."

"Is it her opinion or did you happen to plant the idea in her head?"

Logan sighed and rested his folded hands on the little table. His fingernails were short. The hairs on the back of his hands darker than she remembered. A faint scar curved from his thumb across the back of his hand. He had cut himself while he was carving a wooden duck when he was thirteen.

Sarah pulled herself up short, making a detour away from memory lane.

"Trix just happens to agree with me, Sarah." His dark eyes and deep voice combined to ignite an old stirring in her heart.

"Well, you're both wrong. And I'm fairly sure this Berube character isn't going to get better performance from these boys."

"They lost their previous game against a team they have always beaten."

"That was a different team, Logan. I checked the stats. Half of that team is new boys and one third of our team is new boys. It's a completely different dynamic and you can't compare."

"But the boys do and they're getting disheartened."

That much Logan didn't have to tell her. Sarah

was responsible for part of that disheartened feeling. After the last game, she'd put them on double drills, extended the practice. Brought them back to the basics, something they were all lacking in, rookies and seasoned players.

Mr. DeHaan may have been a good coach, but he hadn't gotten these boys working to their potential.

"And I'm sure Billy and his friends expend more energy complaining about the boring drills than actually doing the boring drills." Sarah gave him a quick smile as if to say, *See, I have a sense of humor.*

But the effort was lost on Logan. "You know I'm not the only parent concerned."

"Maybe not, but it seems you're the one spearheading the 'get rid of Sarah Westerveld' movement."

Logan shrugged. "My priority is my brother."

"It may come as a huge shock to you, Logan Carleton, but so is mine. I have as much riding on this team winning as they do. My reputation, my standing in this community. The fact that the man who asked me to coach happens to share my last name. And the fact that I didn't even get to finish my senior year of basketball, thanks to a lousy, ill-timed injury just before Christmas."

Just before my father made me break up with you. Just before Marilee…

She stopped her thoughts right there.

Logan sighed and ran his hand through his hair, rearranging the thick waves. "Well, I guess time will tell what happens, won't it?" he said, giving her a rueful grin.

"I might surprise you, Logan Carleton." She wasn't going to be taken in by that smile. She'd seen him use it whenever he needed something. Extra service from a waitress (which always made her jealous), a favor from a friend, a few minutes to goof around between classes and basketball practice when he was in town picking up parts for his father.

It still gave her that silly flutter. But, thankfully, she wasn't the same young and impressionable girl.

He pushed himself away from the table, paused a moment as if he wanted to say something more, but left.

Sarah waited until he had ordered his coffee, left the shop and climbed back in his old, dented pickup truck angle-parked in front of the store. His father's old truck. The same one he had driven when they were going out.

Only when she saw the plume of exhaust trailing in the wake of the truck, did she let herself relax.

Too many conflicting emotions, she thought. She had to get herself under control. Logan wasn't going to take this away from her.

Chapter Seven

"We need to talk about your playing." Sarah rested one foot on the bench beside her supposed star player. Practice was over for the day, but she had made Billy stay behind.

"I scored twenty-six points this game."

"You could have scored more. More important, you could have made your *teammates* score more, play better. I know you're not playing up to your potential, and your big brother seems to think it's because of me, because you can't respect me. But I suspect there's more to the equation than simple male chauvinism."

For the moment, with him sitting on the bench and her standing over him, she had the height advantage. "So what is it going to take to motivate you?"

Billy concentrated on the basketball he bounced between his feet.

Sarah bit back a sigh of frustration. This last practice had been a dismal affair, with Billy just going through the motions. She wanted to shake him.

Instead, she chose a worse weapon. A player-to-coach chat after practice. And she had chatted. Oh, how she had chatted.

But, finally, after all her talk about his potential, his talents, his gifts, she saw her words had all fallen on deaf ears. She had tried to appeal to his innate sense of sportsmanship, his youth and opportunities.

She had nothing left.

Billy fidgeted, still turning the ball over in his hands. Sarah could hear the tick of the clock on the gym wall, the muted cries of kids in the hallway. She had at least another hour before she was going to visit her father. Now that her father was in the Riverbend hospital, she had time.

Acres of time.

"I'm not going anywhere, Billy. I'm not going anywhere until you tell me what is happening in your head. Because until you do, I will ride you and I will phone your brother and tell on you and I think we both know that he can make your life even more unpleasant than I can."

She waited as her threat sank in.

Billy bounced the ball once. Then again. "Why should I tell you anything?" He threw the words out like a challenge.

"You don't have to. But then, I don't have to play you."

Billy's eyes flipped up to her. "Why would you do that?"

"If you're just going to sleepwalk out there, I'd sooner give the chance to someone who's hungry and eager to play."

Billy turned the ball around in his hands but still wouldn't look at her.

"Hey, Billy. You coming?"

Sarah looked up to see a young girl hovering in the doorway of the gym. Long brown hair, soft brown eyes and a secretive smile—all directed toward the young man on the bench.

As Billy's attention flitted from the girl with her clingy jeans and cropped jacket, to Sarah, guilt splashed all over his red face.

And suddenly things fell into place.

"He'll be with you in a moment, okay?" Sarah flashed the girl a quick smile.

Billy nodded, and the girl waggled her fingers at him, then left.

Sarah waited until she presumed she was out of earshot. "So. Is she part of the problem?"

"We're just friends."

"That line doesn't work for movie stars, and it's not playing too well with me, either."

Billy didn't confirm or deny. Instead, his desperate gaze locked on hers. "Don't tell Logan, okay? He'll throw a fit." Billy's pleading look, the surprising note of vulnerability in his voice, gave Sarah pause.

And it hearkened back to another high school student pleading with another adult about another relationship.

Only then it had been her, pleading with her uncle Morris after he came upon her and Logan kissing in the gym after a practice. Logan had just issued her an ultimatum. He was getting tired of hiding and skulking. He wanted everyone to know they were dating, that they were serious.

They had fought and Sarah had pleaded with him to stick to their plan. To keep things quiet until they were both attending college. She wasn't strong enough to brave her father's anger if he found out about them. Then, away from Riverbend and her father, they could do what they wanted. But Uncle Morris had found them and, out of respect for her father, told Frank.

Sarah took her foot off the bench and sat down beside Billy. She had learned the hard way that secrets will come out and the longer they were held down, the more potent they became. "Why does this matter so much? Why can't you tell him?"

Billy shook his head. "I can't tell him. I've got my reasons."

Sarah leaned her elbows on her knees, staring at the opposite wall. Banners denoting various championship teams hung in tidy rows. Her name was on a number of them. Three zone championships and a number of regional championships. Basketball was supposed to have been her ticket out of Riverbend, but the day of the game when the scouts were to be there, she had sprained her ankle and hadn't played. So she didn't get a scholarship for that first year of college.

And she remembered too well, the feeling of powerlessness as her father opportunistically made *his* ultimatum—break up with Logan or he wasn't going to pay for her first year of college—and she had absolutely no choice but to fall in with it.

His father's plot only worked because of Sarah's injury. But Sarah had her own plans. She was going to lay low, follow the curfew he imposed as a result, let her father think he won, then, as soon as her father thought all was well, she was going to see Logan and explain what had happened. Tell him that she loved him. Only him. Surely he would understand. He would know that she did what she did only to fool her father into thinking she was, in fact, an obedient daughter. She could have sent him a message but she was afraid of any misunderstanding. She wanted to explain to him face-to-face.

But they never had the chance to meet him face-to-face.

Because Marilee, who had always gotten everything she ever wanted, plus many of the things that Sarah desired, had left a note on Sarah's bed taunting her with the information that she was meeting up with Logan.

And that night, Marilee had died.

"You're a big boy, Billy. If Logan doesn't want you to have a girlfriend, that's his problem. Not yours."

"He thinks if I get a girlfriend here I won't focus on college." Billy bounced the ball again. "I'm not so sure I want to go to school."

"What else could you do?"

Billy shrugged. "My friend Derek knows a guy who's a welder. He needs an apprentice."

"That's your decision, then. But you also need to tell Logan that you want to make your own decisions about your life. I know we didn't have that chance."

"What do you mean *we?*"

Sarah shot him a puzzled glance.

"You said *we* didn't have that chance."

"I meant, *he*. He didn't have that chance."

"But you said *we*. I know what I heard." Billy leaned back against the wall, tossing the basketball from hand to hand, watching her. "You and my brother used to go out, didn't you?"

Though she wasn't going to answer him, Sarah couldn't stop the flush of self-consciousness migrating up her neck.

"Whoa. Look at Miss Westerveld," Billy crowed, jumping to the right conclusion.

"We were talking about you …"

"I used to sneak downstairs to listen to him talking to you on the phone. His voice always got all mushy when he did."

Sarah ignored him, trying to hold her ground emotionally. In Halifax it had been much easier to distill the grand emotions she felt with Logan to a simple high school crush. A sentimental memory. Her first serious, head-over-heels love, the one you always remember but always get over.

But since coming back here, since seeing Logan again, it was as if the six years away hadn't even happened.

She didn't want to remember a time when his voice on the phone had stolen her breath completely.

"So who broke it up?"

"I did. Just before Christmas. Six years ago."

"Aha." Billy drew out the two syllables, as if something finally clicked for him. "That's why he was such a grouch."

Curiosity trumped privacy. "What do you mean?"

"All of January that year he was miserable and snapping at us. I thought it was because Dad was sick, but thinking back I suspect it was thanks to you."

She didn't dare believe him. Logan had gone out with Marilee only days after she had broken up with him. "There were other things going on at the time. And he wasn't dating me. He was dating my sister."

Billy frowned at her. "What was her name?"

"Marilee."

He shook his head. "Don't remember him talking to her on the phone. Ever."

Sarah waited a beat. Waited to extinguish the faint flicker of hope that she had read Marilee's note wrong.

Marilee had been so clear. She was going to be with Logan.

Could she have gotten it wrong?

Sarah picked up her clipboard and fussed with the papers attached to it, trying to regain her equilibrium. "I want to get back to you. Your choices. Do you want to quit the team?"

"Are you kidding? Logan would shoot me."

"In that case, you are still my responsibility. And this is the deal. You want to play? Then play. If you do your best and give your team and yourself the chance to play—and play to your full potential—in front of those college scouts, you will have one more choice, one more opportunity. So while you're out there, I want you to give your full attention and energy to the game. If you don't, you're off the team." Sarah let this settle, bracing herself for his response.

Billy pushed himself off the bench and tossed the ball into the ball bag ten feet away. "I gotta get my gym bag. If Logan comes, I'll be in the locker room."

Billy stuffed his shirt into his gym bag, followed by his shorts. But he wouldn't look at his brother. "I'm going to stay at Derek's house."

Logan wondered what was going on. "I'd like you to come home with me, Billy."

Billy slung his bag over his shoulder, then finally glanced at Logan. "Why?"

"Because I drove all the way here to pick you up and I would hate to think the trip was for nothing."

What was the big deal with this? Teenagers. Everything became a huge drama.

"I left a message on your cell phone," Billy said.

"I didn't get it."

"Your problem. Not mine."

Billy was about to turn away when Logan caught him by the shoulder. Billy glared at him but Logan didn't let go.

"What is your problem?"

"Nothing." Billy's scowl deepened.

"What's with the anger? Someone steal your lunch?"

"Where does *your* anger come from?"

"What you talking about?" Logan lowered his hand, puzzled at his brother's question.

"For years I've had to listen to you and Mom go on and on about how awful Riverbend is. All the hypocrites here. What a rotten deal Dad got. Well, he did get a rotten deal. And maybe this ain't the greatest place to live, but I like it here. My friends are here and I don't care what happened in the past. I'm not as mad about it as you and Mom are. I like it here."

Where did this tirade come from? "Of course you do. It's home. But I think there are better places for you to live. Better opportunities elsewhere."

"Meaning goin' to college."

"Yes."

"So what's the big deal about that?" Billy continued. "You didn't go to college. You're doin' okay."

"I wanted to go. In fact, I'd worked and saved up

for two years. Six years ago I was applying to various colleges. But then, things happened. Dad got sick, and I didn't get the chance you have sitting in front of you right now. If you get a scholarship and you go to college, your world will open up. You will have opportunities to get a job that doesn't require you getting your back broken daily. One that doesn't require you going begging to a bank so that you can keep operating." Logan wished he could get this clear with his brother. Billy didn't know what he was choosing. Riverbend was no friend to the Carletons.

Billy held Logan's gaze and then he sighed. "Well, I want the chance to make my own decisions."

"You're too young to make your own decisions. You don't know what I know about this town. It can suck you dry."

"Miss Westerveld told me that there comes a point when I have to stand up for myself. When I have to know what I want. I think I came to that point."

"Miss Westerveld? As in *Sarah Westerveld?*"

"Yeah. My coach. And I think she's right."

The same anger that Billy had just spoken of reappeared in Logan. What right did Sarah think she had interfering in their lives? And since when did she know what was right for his younger brother?

"I guess I'll just have to have a talk with Miss Westerveld then."

Billy shook his head. "No. Don't. I wasn't supposed to tell you that she had talked to me. Don't tell her I told you."

"Why is this such a big secret?"

Billy squirmed. "She…well…she told me that you don't like her much. And that…well…you'd be ticked if you found out that she's been telling me what to do."

Sarah was right on the money there.

"That doesn't matter. She has no right to interfere."

Billy just nodded, then walked away. "Anyway, I'm going to Derek's. I'll see you tomorrow night."

Sarah dropped down on the bench and massaged the back of her neck, gaining a new appreciation for all her own coach had had to deal with. She remembered girls crying on the bench, and Mr. DeHaan sitting beside them patting them, awkwardly on the shoulder. Did all coaches deal with this kind of stuff?

She heard the squeak of the door and looked up, wondering what Billy had forgotten.

Her heart jumped as she saw Logan's tall figure coming toward them across the empty gym. He wore a heavy canvas jacket today, still grimy from whatever he'd been working on. His work boots were undone, the tips of the laces ticking on the floor as he walked toward her, his hands in his pockets.

When she and Logan were dating, he had always been clean shaven. His clothes had always been neat and clean.

This Logan looked like he didn't care what anyone thought of him. He hadn't shaved and the whiskers shadowing his lean jaw gave him a vaguely menacing air. He reminded her of the Logan who used to intimidate her. He stopped in front of her, his hands on his hips. Saying nothing.

She looked away, gathering her belongings, giving him a heavy hint that she was just leaving. "What can I do for you?" she asked, trying to keep her voice nonchalant. Logan didn't need to know about her chat with Billy.

Though she kept her eyes averted, it was as if every nerve was aware of him in her peripheral vision. Aware of what Billy had told her only moments before... Logan angry after she left... Logan never phoning Marilee.

Could she have gotten it all wrong?

But how? The contents of Marilee's hastily scribbled note had been painfully clear. Or at least as clear as Marilee could make it: U may nt wnt Logan. I do. Im seeing him 2 nite.

"How is Billy doing? Really?"

Sarah shrugged as she chose her words. "He's applying himself. Trying. That's all I want from him."

"That's all?" Logan shifted his weight, putting his booted feet directly in Sarah's line of vision.

"Yeah. For now, I think it's important that Billy at least recognize my authority."

"And how is that going to get him a scholarship?"

The angry tone of his voice pulled Sarah's head up. "Every journey begins with a small step. Getting Billy to listen and respect me is the first step.

It will actually enable him to learn more in the long run. Perfection and being all that he can be will just have to wait for a little later."

Logan's dark eyes held her gaze and Sarah forced herself not to look away. She wasn't going to let him intimidate her because, if that happened, she was pretty sure she was going to let Billy's secret spill.

"So the next game, he's going to be playing up to his game?"

Sarah nodded. "I think we've come to an agreement."

"Really? Is that why he was talking about choices?"

"What do you mean?"

"I was just talking to him in the locker room. He was spouting some nonsense about choices. Nonsense he says you put in his head." Logan shook his head, as if in disbelief.

Sarah had hoped that she would have at least had a few days before Billy spilled and Logan came after her for interfering. "It's not nonsense—"

"You realize, of course, that choice is a luxury he doesn't have," Logan interrupted. "Not all of us have a daddy who is willing and able to pay for our education."

"That's a cheap shot, even coming from you, Logan Carleton."

"It's true."

"You don't know anything about my life."

"Oh, c'mon, Sarah. Don't tell me that Daddy didn't cover his darling Sarah's education expenses?"

"I wasn't his darling Sarah and, yes, my dad paid for my *first* year, but when I got my first basketball scholarship, I paid my own way every year after that. Every penny of my education came from my own hard work. I washed dishes, I waited tables, I supersized and downsized. I did it all myself. Without one cent coming from Frank Westerveld. One cent." She pressed her lips together, damming the true confessions spilling out.

Logan's expression shifted, then he frowned. "Are you kidding me?"

"And why would I do that?" She held his gaze, her eyes steady and unwavering.

Logan's frown mirrored his doubt. "But I thought…"

"You thought wrong."

He rubbed his hand over his chin, making a rasping sound. "I'm sorry. I didn't mean to imply…"

"There was no implication in what you said, Logan. It was pretty much a bald statement. Sarah Westerveld needs her daddy. Well, I didn't. And I don't."

Logan let a slow smile creep across his well-shaped mouth. "You have changed, Sarah. I don't think you would have called me out on that before."

"And you've changed, too. The Logan I knew shaved more regularly and cared what he wore in public."

"The Logan you knew didn't have to work for a living."

"You worked for your father for two years after high school."

"Yeah—to save up for college."

"And why didn't you go?"

"My dad needed my help," he said. "That lousy trial took a lot out of him. When your father cancelled his contract, that kind of finished him off."

And they were back to square one. The evil that the Westerveld family had visited upon the Carleton family. "So. There you have it," she said. "We've both changed."

"Is that a good thing?" He had lowered his voice and for a heart-stopping moment, Sarah felt as if she had plunged back in time. Had returned to furtive meetings and stolen kisses in this self-same gymnasium.

"I hope so. I'm not the naive and innocent girl I once was."

Logan gave a short laugh. "Too bad. I was very fond of that girl."

"Obviously not fond enough." She meant for the statement to come out as a light, humorous comment, breaking the heavy mood that had fallen over them. But in spite of the six years that had passed, her emotions leached into her voice.

"What do you mean?"

She forced a smile and fluttered her hand at him. "Nothing. Just trying to make a joke."

Logan took another step nearer. "That didn't sound like a joke, Sarah. What did you mean?"

He was close enough that she could smell the scent of oil on his coat and under that, the faintest whiff of cologne. He may not have shaved before he came here, but he had washed up and he had splashed on a bit of scent.

For her?

"What did you mean, Sarah?" The deep timbre of his voice, pitched just low enough to create a sense of intimacy, drew out old memories and the words she had tried to cover up.

She tried to lighten the atmosphere with a laugh, but it came out forced. "I was just talking about Marilee. You know."

"No. I don't."

"She was with you…"

Sarah pressed her lips together, frustrated with the break in her voice. She had been doing so well up until then, skating the fine line of the understanding ex-girlfriend. Trying to put the past in the past.

For, to talk about Logan and Marilee together meant talking about the night Marilee died. And to cry in front of Logan was to invite an intimacy she couldn't allow to happen.

She had to keep her distance. Keep her focus. She wasn't staying here.

"With me when?"

Just breathe. Slowly. You'll be okay.

"That night…that night…" Why couldn't she finish the sentence? Why was her voice choking up like that?

"The night she died?" Logan finally asked.

Sarah took a steadying breath and nodded, her focus on the clipboard she clung to like a shield.

He took a step closer, closing the sentence between them. "She wasn't with me, Sarah."

Chapter Eight

Sarah frowned and looked up at him as his words settled into her mind, one syllable at a time. "What do you mean?"

Then, to her utter surprise, Logan laid his hand on her shoulder. "She wasn't with me."

"But, I thought…" Sarah's breath left her.

Logan tightened his hand, his fingers warm on her shoulder. "And I never had a chance to tell you how sorry I was," he continued. "About Marilee."

Sarah shook her head, trying to arrange the confusion of thoughts ricocheting around her mind.

"But you weren't hanging out with her that night?"

"No. Why do you keep asking me that?"

Sarah kept her lips pressed tight, willing the tears that pricked her eyes to stay back, willing her own silly heart not to waver at the warmth of Logan's hand.

He could always raise such a mixture of emotions

in her, she thought. Fear and anticipation. Tranquility and anxiety.

Now she struggled between the memory of her sister's death and what Logan was telling her. Had she had everything wrong all this time?

"She wrote a note. The night of the accident. She said if I didn't want you, she did. She said she was going to see you." Sarah's throat felt thick with suppressed tears and her eyes were hot. Logan's face shimmered, but she was afraid to move her head. Afraid the tears hovering in her eyes would spill over and then more would come. She didn't want Logan to see her vulnerable.

"Sarah, I have no clue what she told you, or wrote you. We weren't together. I wasn't even at the party she went to. Was supposed to be, but decided not to go at the last minute."

Sarah pressed her hands against her face, her cheeks hot with confusing emotions old and new.

Marilee hadn't been with Logan. All these years and she'd had it all wrong. How could she have made such a huge mistake? What had Marilee meant by the note then? Petty one-upmanship?

She took in a slow, trembling breath, struggling with her confusion and her emotions and as she closed her eyes, she felt the warm slide of tears down her cheek.

Then she felt Logan's thumb gently wiping them away.

"I'm sorry, Sarah."

He rested his hand on her shoulder again, his fingers gently stroking her neck, his calluses catching on the hair at the nape.

She leaned toward him, yearning for the comfort she used to find in Logan's arms.

She'd borne the pain of her sister's death intertwined with what she saw as her sister and Logan's disloyalty. She had never had a pure moment of grief for Marilee.

Right now she wanted Logan to help her through this. She wanted him to hold her. Like he used to. Wanted to feel his arms around her.

Just in time she caught herself.

Logan was merely feeling sorry for her. Simple pity for the loss of a girl they'd both known. Too much time had elapsed between then and now. She and Logan were two different people. She couldn't go back and neither could he.

With a sigh, she palmed away the rest of the tears, drawing back.

"I'm glad you told me," she said, turning away from him to dig through her purse. She was pretty sure she had a tissue. When she found it, she blew her nose and wiped away the rest of the tears. "I'm glad that's cleared up."

Though Logan said nothing, she was fully aware of him standing behind her.

But she couldn't deal with him right now. Logan was a part of her past. She had come here to find out what her father wanted and, if her father's reaction to

Logan was anything to go by, she had best keep him and her father separate entities. Best excise Logan right out of her life.

"Glad to have helped." The cold note in his voice settled her wavering emotions. "And if you want to help me, I would appreciate it if you would stop messing with Billy's mind. I'm his brother and I think I know better what's best for him than someone who doesn't even live here anymore. He's going to college. He's getting out of this town."

The next thing she heard was the sound of his boots walking away from her, each thump of his heels driving another wedge between them.

It was better this way, she thought, taking in a long, slow breath. Better for her.

I wasn't with her.

She couldn't think about that now.

The words created a peculiar hope she didn't dare nurture. That was all stuff from the past. She was here to clear up her and her father's relationship. She was finally making progress and she was thankful for that.

Everything else from the past was best left there.

"The team is doing a bit better." Sarah held her father's hand. "I promised the boys if we won the next tournament I would take them out for pizza. I thought we could go to that new place in town. The one that Cal Chernowsky started up. You remember Cal? He used to work at the car dealership. I think he sold you that blue car you always hated. You always called it Cal's Car."

Sarah gently massaged her father's veined hand lying lifelessly in her own. The therapist told her it was important to try to stimulate the right side of his body as much as possible and that casual conversation was the best way to maintain a connection with her father. Though the question "Why did you want me to come?" burned to be asked, she banked the urge. These moments gave her something that Marilee usually had with her father... sharing the ordinary moments of her life as her father listened.

"I'm hoping they do well." She was hoping especially that Billy would do well. She knew Logan would be watching.

The entire time she spoke, her father looked intently at her. She couldn't tell if he was smiling or not, but she liked to think he was.

She had been spending more time with him lately and, between visits to him and time she spent figuring out new plays for her team and going over stats and videos, her days were full.

She enjoyed coaching more than she thought she would. It was a challenge she felt she was rising to quite well. And knowing that Logan and a few other parents didn't think she could do it made her even more determined to prove them wrong.

"Sarah...Marilee..." The words came out as more

of a sigh, but Sarah understood them to be her and her sister's names.

"Sarah and Marilee," she repeated, to show that she understood. Just in time she stopped herself from praising him, like one would a small child. Mentally he was as sharp as ever, the physiotherapist had said. He had warned her and the rest of the family not to patronize Frank and treat him as if his thought processes had been affected.

"I talked to Brent," she said. "He runs the sound system and makes CDs for people who can't come to church. He said he would make some up for you. If you want."

He nodded. "Good…I like…good…"

Sarah squeezed his hand in encouragement. Her Uncle Sam had told her that for the past half a year her father had stopped going to church. He hadn't said anything to his brothers about the reasons. This had confused her as much as her father's unexpected note had.

In all the years she lived at home, rain or shine, sleet or hail, snowstorm or sickness, Sunday morning at nine-thirty he would call them down from their rooms and off to church they would go. Sometimes Marilee had been whooping it up a bit too much and she would plead illness and stay home. But Sarah, always trying to emulate her father, would go with him. Even those times when she was genuinely ill herself.

Trying too hard, Sarah thought. Always trying too hard.

"Do you want me to read to you, Dad?" Sarah asked as she gently placed his hand back on his lap.

"Please," he said, followed by a little nod.

Sarah glanced around the room, but today the only book on her father's bedside stand was the Bible. Her father had Bibles scattered through the house. One in his bedroom, one in his study. This edition was the one he always read from after supper, the one Uncle Sam had picked up and brought to her father a couple of days after his stroke.

Sarah opened it up, the soft crackling of the light paper drawing out memories of her father bent over the book, reading aloud, his voice filled with conviction and authority.

As she leafed through the Bible, she found a monthly devotional put out by their church. The theme for this month, in keeping with the coming Christmas season, was Waiting with Patience.

Not her strongest point these days. It seemed everywhere she turned, her patience was tried. By Billy, by her father's illness.

By Logan.

She opened the booklet to the reading for the day and turned to Isaiah 40—a reading often used during the time of Advent. She cleared her throat and started reading. "'Comfort, comfort my people, says your God. Speak tenderly to Jerusalem, and proclaim to her that her hard service has been completed, that her sin has been paid for.'" The passage resonated deep within her, teasing out memories of Christmases past. She had heard these words so often but now, reading them aloud to her father who had called her back home, it was as if she heard them for the first time. As she read on, she let the words wash over her.

"'…He tends his flock like a shepherd…carries them close to his heart… He brings princes to naught and reduces the rulers of the world to nothing… He gives strength to the weary and increases the power of the weak…they will run and not grow weary, they will walk and not faint.'"

The phrases settled into Sarah's mind and, like water, they gently seeped between the cracks of the brittle facade she had sculpted over her memories. Behind that facade lay pain and sorrow that she hadn't wanted to drag into this new phase of her life.

And yet…comfort…peace…strength to the weary…your sins are paid for. The words resonated and she traced her finger over the passage as if to absorb it through her skin.

She would have to read it again when she was at home. Try to find where to put them in the life she was living now. She had tried to keep God at a distance and had managed to do that away from home.

But now that she was in Riverbend, God seemed determined to find her. If not at church, then here, in this hospital room. Only thing was, she didn't know if she was ready to face Him yet.

Sarah looked up at her father, who appeared to be

smiling at her. He reached out with his good hand and Sarah caught it, sharing this moment with her earthly father.

"Sarah…I…forgive…"

Sarah's heart quickened. Had the passage she just read worked a miracle in him? Had God touched him in some way?

"Yes, Dad. What are you saying?"

He squeezed her hand, his grip surprisingly strong. His eyes were intent on hers and she sensed that he wanted to say something important.

"I forgive you." His words, punctuated by sighs, came out more clearly than before.

He was saying he forgave her? For what?

"Are you saying you forgive me for staying away?" She squeezed back, wondering where this was going. Was this why he had summoned her home?

He shook his head, looking agitated.

"I…forgive…for Marilee…" He leaned forward; sweat beading on his forehead with the effort of his speech. "I forgive you for Marilee…for Marilee dying…I forgive you…"

He looked deep into her eyes.

"You're saying you forgive me for what happened to Marilee?"

He squeezed her hand and nodded, his relief evident as he fell back in his chair.

Ice slipped through Sarah's veins as the impact of his words settled.

"What did I do that needs to be forgiven?" she asked.

"You…not…stop her."

Sarah let go of his hand and sat back, wrapping her arms around her waist, struggling to reconcile what he was saying with what had happened to her sister. "How was I supposed to stop her? What could I have done?"

"I forgive…" he repeated, looking genuinely puzzled.

"Was this what you wanted to tell me?" she said as realization dawned. "Did you send me that note because you wanted me to come back here to Riverbend so that you could grant me forgiveness for something I couldn't help?"

"I forgive…for Marilee," he repeated, looking agitated.

As Sarah looked into her father's eyes, she felt as if, once again, her world had fallen down around her. As if the life she thought she was rebuilding by coming here at the behest of her father was a sham, built on sand now washed away by the words her father had struggled to say. Words of forgiveness for a death she already harbored so much guilt over. Even though she intellectually knew she wasn't to blame, her self-recriminations and second thoughts whispered otherwise to her. For days, weeks after Marilee died, Sarah had gone over that evening again and again, wishing she could turn back time. The phone ringing at two o'clock in the morning. Marilee asking Sarah to come and get her.

But Sarah was going to be the good little daughter and not break curfew. So she told Marilee she wasn't going to pick her up.

If she had disobeyed her father, if she had listened to those other voices telling her to help her sister...

If she had simply stood up to her father and chosen her sister over pleasing him...

Sarah gathered her tattered emotions around her, wishing she knew what to say. Yes, to some degree it was her fault, but to have her father voice her own self-reproach and to add fuel to its fire by *forgiving* her?

She couldn't breathe. She got to her feet and pulled her coat off the back of the chair she had been sitting on. "I did what you wanted me to that night, Dad. I stayed home because you told me to. I didn't do anything wrong."

"Marilee..."

Her heart grew cold. "Yes. Marilee. *Do you know where she was going that night?*"

Don't do this, a tiny voice called out, drowned out by the swirl of anger filling Sarah's mind.

But she couldn't stop now. She was like a train hurtling toward its destination, carried on by the momentum of anger and hurt and disappointment.

"Do you know where your precious Marilee was? She was at a party. She was going to meet Logan

Carleton there. Only Logan didn't come. He wasn't there."

Logan wasn't there.

Her focus shifted momentarily, but she carried on, her emotions beyond reasoning. "I couldn't have stopped her from going and if I had gone to pick her up when she called I would have been disobeying you. I lost a sister that night. Someone I loved. And now you're going to tell me that you forgive me? As if I haven't felt guilty enough? As if I haven't lived through any pain, any sorrow, any tragedy myself?" She yanked her coat off the chair and stabbed her arms into the sleeves, her heart thudding like a jackhammer in her chest. She held the fronts of her coat in her fists, her knuckles white as a new sorrow coursed through her body.

Her father stared at her.

He didn't get it. He really had thought that he was extending her a gift, and, maybe in his mind, he had.

But for Sarah, she felt as if the burden she already carried had only gotten heavier. He didn't care about her. Even after all this time, it was still all about Marilee. It was as if she were a footnote to his life that he should attend to.

Snatching her purse off the floor, Sarah ran out of the room.

Sarah shifted back and forth in the foyer of the church, glancing over the congregation, trying to find a place as close to the back as possible. She was late and it didn't look like there were any seats in the back, or anywhere else for that matter.

She could have stayed home, and almost did, but something indefinable called her out of bed this morning. She needed to center herself again and hoped that maybe the faith of her childhood could give her something her father couldn't.

She wasn't sure what she would find here, but staying home wasn't going to fill the booming hollowness that her father's words had created inside her very being.

I forgive…

The organist moved into the chorus and Sarah realized that if she wanted to sit down, she had to hustle. Her black knee-high boots weren't made for speed, but she managed to slip into an empty space before the song was finished.

She glanced sidelong as she sat, and her already low spirits shifted lower. She was looking directly at Donna Carleton's profile.

She looked ahead, thankful, however, for small miracles. At least Logan wasn't here.

Then a shadow blocked the sun coming in through the high windows and Sarah looked up with a feeling of inevitability.

Logan stood, one hand resting on the pew in front of them, waiting to catch her attention so he could slip in past her.

Of course.

Sarah folded her arms, as if to contain her very

presence beside Logan. It didn't take much to resurrect the feeling of his hand on her face, the roughness of his callused fingertips.

You're in church, you ninny, she reprimanded herself. Focus.

The minister stood up, grasping the edges of the pulpit with his hands as he looked over the congregation. Sarah was reminded of her Uncle Sam, standing by his fence, looking over his herd of sheep.

"This morning we are looking at forgiveness. How God forgives us and how, during this Advent season, we realize that the greatest gift we receive at Christmas is forgiveness."

Wrong choice of words, thought Sarah, her father's voice still ringing in her ears and in her thoughts.

She pushed down the beat of anger she knew could consume her if she let it.

"Let us turn to Colossians 3, verses 12 to 14."

Sarah instinctively reached for the Bible in the pew ahead of her at the same time Logan did.

As her fingers brushed his, she jerked her hand back as if shocked. Logan simply opened the Bible to the passage, then held it out so both of them could read.

Sarah's concentration was distracted by Logan's thumb, pressed against the pages of the Bible, a dark spot on his thumbnail. He'd probably banged it with something, a hammer most likely. Sarah remembered he always had a spot on one fingernail or another from helping his father with his equipment. He'd always told Sarah that the first thing he was going to do when he started college was get a manicure.

"'...bear with each other and forgive whatever grievances you may have against one another. Forgive as the Lord forgave you....'"

Sarah shut everything off right there.

Forgive. For the past two days, she couldn't dislodge the word from her mind.

I forgive you.

That wasn't what she had prayed and yearned for, had falsely hoped for the first year with every envelope that came with his handwriting on the front. She had given up so much for him. Too much. And for what?

I forgive you.

Marilee again. Marilee still. Her father could not get Marilee out of his mind even after six years.

Logan closed the Bible and in her peripheral vision she saw his hand drop the Bible into the slot, return to his jacket and pull something out. A roll of candies. He held them out to her and, without looking, she took one. Or tried to. It wouldn't dislodge itself and he reached over with his other hand and peeled back the paper.

All the while she kept her attention on his hands.

She remembered how his hands were always warm. How he would tuck her hands between his to warm them as they sat in his truck, the radio playing, the dashboard lights the only illumination. He used to take her to the lookout point. One evening they almost got stuck in Steenbergen's field, which would have been embarrassing and difficult to explain. They'd had their first fight that night over the incident. Logan had asked her when they were going to stop sneaking around. Sarah pleaded for understanding. She didn't dare buck her father. Not yet.

"…forgiveness grants us freedom," the minister was saying. With a guilty start, Sarah pulled her attention to the service, forced herself to ignore Logan's arm brushing hers, his legs stretched out in front of him. "And freedom for the captives is one of the strongest messages of Christmas. It is what Isaiah proclaims to us and it is this message that we cling to…"

Freedom. Sarah leaned back in the pew. The word seemed to taunt her. She had hoped that by coming here, by confronting her past, she would be free from the memories that clung and tangled. Memories of her father, of the guilt that stained her memories of her sister.

Memories of Logan.

But with each day, with each experience and interaction, she felt herself more and more enmeshed. She had spent her whole life trying to please her father and to what end? To be told that he forgave her for the death of a sister that she still grieved? After all he had done in her life? All she had allowed him to do, she amended, thinking of the man beside her and their relationship.

She'd had everything planned. Her own little rebellion. She was going to do what her father wanted, then find a way to work around it. She and Logan were going to go to the same college and they would be together away from the shadows and history of Riverbend.

And then Marilee died.

Sarah chanced a quick sidelong glance only to be ensnared by Logan's dark countenance.

His expression didn't change and Sarah couldn't look away. Couldn't tear her eyes from his. He moved his hand. Just a little. Then, just past Logan, she saw Donna looking at both of them with displeasure in her face.

She and Logan never really had a chance and probably never would.

With a sigh, Sarah looked away and turned her attention back to the minister, who had begun the familiar refrain about God's eternal and unfailing love.

Billy was playing the worst game of his life. She had to concentrate. Focus.

The blast of the whistle pulled her back into the game, and with a guilty start she glanced at the ref, relieved to see him make a call against the other team.

Her next glance, of its own volition, shot to Logan sitting off to one side, elbows on his knees, chin resting on his clasped hands, alternately watching the game and her.

She couldn't help but think of that almost moment in church a few days ago. She forced herself to look away, memories and old yearnings crowding over her battered defenses.

Concentrate. Concentrate.

The game proceeded and this time Sarah kept her attention on Billy. She had warned him once, earlier on in the game, to either play smart, and with the team, or be benched.

If Logan hadn't been here she would have pulled Billy four plays ago.

Maybe she should quit. Let Alton Berube take over. Maybe he would do a better job.

And then what? Hang around that booming, empty house? Leave Riverbend and make it look as if she was the most heartless daughter on the face of the earth?

Bad enough that she hadn't visited her father since that horrible day. She didn't want to face him.

Basketball had been her life, her salvation when she left here. It was all she had then and, it seemed, all she had once again. She didn't want this taken away from her and it wasn't going to be. Not without a fight.

Unfortunately, in this case she was relying on this team to help her win that fight and so far things were not looking good.

She looked at the scoreboard; the team was down. She chanced another glance at the bleachers and saw a few other parents talking among themselves.

Probably thinking the same thing Logan and Trix Setterfeld were: she wasn't doing her job.

Stop. Stop right there. You can do this. You can help these boys win. You can help them work to their potential. You've already seen so much improvement.

Billy had the ball again and Sarah saw him checking to see where his other teammates were. Okay. Maybe this time…

An opponent swung around him, deked him out, stripped the ball away, charged down the lane and made an easy layup.

Sixty-four to fifty.

Sarah signaled a substitution and then crooked a finger at Adam, who bounded to his feet.

When she called Billy's number he stopped, frowning at her when he realized what was going on, and slammed his fist against his thigh. He came charging across the court toward her, but she looked down at her playbook and ignored the angry young man who stormed past her.

She felt like throwing the ball at him herself. He had promised he would do what he could and he had failed. From here on in the ball was, literally, in his court. If he didn't want to play, then he should quit.

And wouldn't *that* make his brother happy.

Sarah didn't dare look at Logan for the remainder of the game. She had to remove herself from what she might read in his face. She had to remove herself from the opinions of the people around her.

She made a few more lineup changes on the fly,

mixing it up, subbing in players, using plays they'd only touched on in practice. She cajoled and urged and used every trick ever used on her by her own coach, trying to read the opposing team and get her players to respond. Slowly they inched ahead, gaining ground point by point. And the whole time they did, Billy sat on the bench, glowering at her.

Five minutes to go and the game was tied.

The other team called a time-out and Sarah took the opportunity to give her boys a last-minute pep talk.

"Great work, guys, good hustle. Stay on top of these guys. Box out. Use your feet and hands, but don't lose sight of the guy you're guarding. You guys are doing great."

The whole time she spoke, Billy's anger and frustration seethed from him. Then, seconds before the time-out ended, he pushed himself in front of her. "Put me in, Coach."

Sarah shook her head. She was not going to be intimidated by this young man.

The referee lifted his hand to signal the end of the time-out.

"Please, Coach. My brother and mom are here," Billy said. "I promise, I'll put in a hundred ten percent."

As if her eyes had a will of their own, they drifted to where Logan sat hunched on the bleachers, his face set in hard lines, his mother sitting beside him.

She remembered again the faint stirring of attraction between them, so fragile that a breath could put it out. Logan caught her gaze and for a sharp moment it was as if he was the only person in the gym.

She closed her mind to those tantalizing possibilities. Closed her mind to all the things peripheral to what she had to deal with right now.

"You better brush up on your math, Carleton," she said, turning her attention back to the game. "I expect one hundred percent every minute of every game, no matter who is or isn't in the stands. Sorry."

Chapter Nine

Sarah bounced the basketball a couple of times and looked around the empty gym. Only moments ago it had been ringing with the sound of parents and friends and classmates, shouting themselves hoarse with encouragement.

I made the right call. I made the right call. Sarah repeated the words to herself even as she considered that losing this game would come back to haunt them. But for now she had to concentrate on the next game and figure out what to do about Billy Carleton. This half-effort business wasn't doing them any good—and it was giving more ammunition to Logan's "get rid of the Westerveld coach" campaign.

The angry buzz of departing fans slowly had faded away, the crowd taking their disappointment with them. But her neck still felt warm from Logan's blazing glare. Sarah wished she could tell them all she felt the failure more keenly than they did.

Even when she could no longer play the great game, she would always remember charging down the court, the thrill of the game singing through her blood—ducking, spinning, guarding, blocking and making those glorious shots, the sight of the ball arcing through the air and, in spite of the countless practices, the thrilling uncertainty of her aim.

And that moment of perfection when the ball would fall through the net without touching the rim.

She remembered Marilee standing up, waving her scarf and getting her friends going.

Sarah tested the memory of her sister, explored it like touching an old wound that had scabbed over.

It hurt to think of her, but below that a deeper, harder ache throbbed.

"I forgive you." His words resounded so clearly in her mind, it was as if they had just been spoken.

Sarah bounced the ball once. Then again.

"I forgive you."

She grabbed the ball, took two steps and launched it high into the air. It bounced off the backboard, her shot wild.

Playing with the wrong emotion, she could hear Mr. DeHaan's voice remind her. He was always helping her channel her hidden frustration with her father and turn the burning in her belly into focused energy.

She grabbed the ball again, other memories blending, layering over the most recent, painful one.

Logan watching her, cheering her on. The sight of his dark head, leaning forward, his elbows on his knees, just as he watched Billy play, always gave her heart a hitch.

Logan. Marilee. Her father.

Too intertwined. Thinking of one brought up memories of the others. She dribbled the ball again, focused on the net, ran to the side, pivoted, jumped and sent the ball out and up.

Retrieving the ball, she ran across the gym to the other side. Back and forth she went, scoring, running, purging her father's skewed confession from her thoughts and her heart.

She didn't need him. She had her purpose here. She could prove herself worthy here on this court, with these boys.

Forgiveness grants us freedom. The words from last Sunday's worship service rang in her ears. Did her father feel free? She didn't.

She ran to the other side of the court, her hand working the ball furiously, her feet darting, dodging imaginary opponents. She was in charge. This was her court. No one was going to take this away from her.

She would finish what she had started. At the end of the season she was going to get these boys to the provincial tournament. If only for them, somehow she was going to make this work, by force of will if she had to.

There was going to be a happy ending. It was

going to be like those sports movies where the team comes from behind and wins, and then everyone appreciates all the hard work the coach put into the team, and the parents say they're horribly sorry and everyone is happy and the soundtrack swells.

Panting now, Sarah paused, then took a long shot from a third of the way down the court. The ball soared through the air, seemed to hover over the net, then dropped through, creating a perfect, whispering swish.

The ball bounced off the floor a few times and rolled away.

"Good shot."

The deep voice sent her heart into her throat and she spun around to see Logan loitering in the doorway. Just as he used to when she was in high school.

His dark eyes were on her and she couldn't look away.

Sarah snatched herself back from the brink of memories and turned away, breaking the fragile connection.

"Billy should be done," she said, walking over to retrieve the ball.

"He said he was going to a friend's place."

His little girlfriend? Sarah wondered.

"So did you come to talk to me about quitting again?" Catching her breath, she bent over, scooped up the ball, walked toward the basketball cart beside the player's bench and tossed it in. "Because I'm not."

Logan pushed himself away from the doorway

and once again was walking toward her. Only this time he stopped at the player's bench and sat down.

"I'm just wondering why you pulled Billy." He straightened the books, aligning them, then pushed them a few feet over.

Sarah lifted her shoulder to her cheek and wiped away a trickle of perspiration. "I should have done it earlier in the game."

Logan sat back, his long legs stretched out in front of him, his feet crossed at the ankles. "So what's the problem? He was doing okay."

"Okay isn't good enough. Not if he wants to get to college like you want him to. He's holding back, and I think you know it."

"Why would he do that?"

Sarah thought of the little brunette that made Billy smile. Unfortunately, that wasn't her secret to tell. Billy had to make up his mind what he wanted, just as Sarah had told him that same afternoon. She wasn't going to tell tales. "Have you asked him?"

"He's been avoiding me."

Sarah sat down on her end of the bench, keeping her distance from Logan. The past few days he'd been on her mind and she preferred not to think about him.

"Something tells me you know a bit more than you're letting on," Logan said.

"If Billy doesn't want to tell you, I can't."

"But something is going on, isn't it?"

"Well, for one thing, he's having trouble keeping his marks up."

"Billy's marks are okay." Logan's tone was defensive.

"Not according to Uncle Morris."

"That stinker."

"Uncle Morris, or Billy?" Wow. She had just made a joke.

Logan even laughed. "I mean Billy."

Sarah relaxed, pleased that she had sent Logan off on another scent. She leaned back against the wall as the weariness she'd been fighting off slowly made itself known. She wished she were home now, relaxing, perhaps reading a magazine that regaled her with the antics of people with whom she had zero emotional connection.

Logan laid his head back against the wall. He seemed tired, as well. "You looked upset when you came in for the game. Everything okay with your dad?"

For a split second she wanted to lay her head on his shoulder and tell him everything. To put it all on someone else.

As she used to when she was young.

She looked away. Six years had elapsed since she had been that girl. How does one go back? So much had changed. They had each created their own lives.

And yet…

"No," she finally whispered.

"So what happened?" he pressed on.

Sarah sighed, fully aware of him sitting at the end of the bench, similar to when they had sat side by side in church. The soft note of caring in his voice hearkened back to another time….

The moment lengthened and, as they sat in the quiet, separated by three feet of bench, Sarah felt a gentle peace suffuse her.

"I've had some personal trouble with him…" she said finally.

"What kind of trouble?"

Sarah turned her attention back to the basketball she still held. "When I left, he wrote me…he wrote me a note saying that he needed to talk to me." She stopped there and bounced the basketball once. "Every month he sent me a check and that was all. No note, no letter. Nothing."

"Did he at least phone?"

"On my birthday. It was often short and awkward. But he did his duty by me."

Logan shook his head. "Your dad has a perverse sense of duty and a twisted sense of right and wrong."

Sarah chose to ignore the harsh note in Logan's voice. "And he saw his duty as that monthly check. Even though after the first year I always ripped up the check, I would still open the envelope with some small piece of hope that this time he would send something personal. I got letters from the rest of the family, but never him. Then my aunts started telling me how he had stopped going to church. How he seemed so distraught. Of course he wouldn't tell them or confide in them. He has his pride."

Sarah shook her head. "Then, one day, I got a note with my check. And all he had written on there was, 'Come home. I need to talk to you.' This was such a radical thing for my dad, after six years of simply sending money, that I added it to my aunts' and uncles' concern and packed up and came here."

"So that's what brought you back?"

"Yeah. That tiny piece of paper with those few words." She gave the ball another bounce. "It was the first time since I was young that I ever got the sense that he needed me."

"And…"

"And then I came home and the last and only things I hear him say are angry words directed at you." She couldn't talk about her father's misplaced forgiveness.

"I'm not surprised." His eyes searched hers. "Nor should you be. Your father has never liked me or my family."

"I know. I wish I knew why not," Sarah said softly.

Awareness arced between them, as tangible as a touch.

"Do *you* know?" she asked. "Do you know why my dad has harbored this strong anger toward your family?"

Logan didn't reply, but a gentle sigh sifted out of him as he reached across the bench, spanning the distance to touch her hand. His fingers lingered for just a few seconds. Then abruptly, he pushed himself away from the bench. "I gotta go."

Sarah experienced a moment of confusion at his unexpected departure.

And as he left the gym she felt as if a part of her left with him.

She waited a moment, trying to sort out her feelings, unsure of what to put where. Then, shaking the emotions loose from her fuzzy mind, she got up and walked over to the end of the bench where Logan had been sitting.

Someone's books were there on the ground. She picked them up and flipped open the cover.

Well, big surprise, they were Billy's.

As the Carletons' driveway came closer, Sarah's foot eased off the accelerator. What was she doing here? She should have just given Logan the books at church.

But she hadn't gone to church this morning. She'd spent most of her time looking over the game tapes, checking the stats and reminding herself again and again that she had done the right thing. Even if she had kept Billy on the court, they probably would not have won that game.

But it was the niggling question of the "probably" that kept her here, waiting at the end of the Carletons' driveway. She knew Billy was upset with her. Donna had made her feelings quite clear both of the Sundays she was at church. Neither of them would be killing the fatted calf for her if she showed up unexpectedly at their home.

As for Logan…

She let her mind slip back to that moment of quiet connection they had shared in the gym.

And what do you hope to do about that? Build on it? Rekindle old feelings and old emotions?

She shook her head free of the entanglements she was creating. She had simply come to bring Billy his books. She didn't need to turn it into a soap-opera moment.

With a decisive motion, she stopped on the accelerator, but was distracted by the marks she saw in the snow coming out of the Carletons' driveway.

Were those the tracks of a *sleigh?*

Sarah slowed down as she came nearer, trying to get a better look at the parallel lines punctuated with what looked like hoof marks of horses breaking the fresh snow.

Intrigued, she turned up the driveway and faced a captivating sight, straight out of a Currier and Ives painting. She was looking at red wooden sleigh being pulled by a team of perfectly matched bay horses, heads bobbing as their trotting feet kicked up snow behind them. Entranced by the sight, she followed them all the way to the Carleton house and stopped when they stopped.

The driver tied down the reins and jumped down from the curve-sided sleigh. Logan.

As she put her car into Park and got out, he turned.

"Well, well. Sarah Westerveld has decided to stop in at the Carletons'," he said, his mouth tipping up into a smile that could be construed as either mocking or teasing. "What brings you here?"

"I've brought Billy his books. He left them at practice."

"You could have brought them to church this morning."

Sarah shrugged. "I could have, but I didn't go."

Logan let that slide as she walked over to the horse closest to her. Sarah stroked his large neck, surprised at how quiet he stood. "They're beautiful." The horse she was petting slowly turned his head, then nudged her lightly.

"They're a perfectly matched team. They run very well together."

"I didn't know you had a sleigh." She stroked the horse again. "Must be fun sitting behind them when they're pulling."

"You'll have to try it sometime."

"Thank you for the invitation" was her response. "Did you train these yourself?"

"My father raised them from colts. He trained them."

"You've got more horses than these…"

"You never did come riding when we were…"

They spoke at the same time, but Sarah noticed that Logan's voice dropped just before his pause, as if unsure of how to identify their previous relationship.

"No I didn't," Sarah said, remembering precisely the day Logan had extended the invitation to her.

It was early fall when he'd asked her to come riding with him and she'd imagined any number of romantic scenarios, usually involving a quiet place overlooking the river and a picnic blanket, with horses grazing contentedly in the background while leaves fluttered down from the trees above.

And Logan. Looking at her the way she remembered best. Smiling the secretive smile that only she saw, his eyes glowing with unspoken promises.

But basketball season was in full swing and Sarah wouldn't have time until the new term in January. So they had made plans for later.

And later never came.

"Life got in the way."

"You left pretty quick. After."

"After Marilee, you mean."

"Yeah. I do. It must be hard being in the house after all this time. Being reminded of what you lost."

A familiar pain lanced her heart. "I lost a lot more than a sister that Christmas," she said, the words spilling out from a place she had kept hidden for so long.

But as soon as the words left her lips, she wished she had kept them in. It was as if each time she and Logan were together, threads of the past kept getting tangled in the present.

Logan tipped his head to one side, seemingly

digging deeper into her memories. "What do you mean?"

She lifted her hand, as if dismissing the question. "I'll give you Billy's books and then be gone."

"I have to put the horses away. Just take them up to the house."

Sarah wasn't so sure she wanted to face Donna Carleton again, but it seemed rude to simply hand Logan the books and leave. He had other things to do.

"Okay. Well, I'll see you around."

"Oh, I'm sure you will."

She wondered what he meant by that, but then left it.

She got back in her car and drove it the rest of the way to the house.

Donna answered the door after Sarah rang the doorbell. She had a flour-sprinkled apron on, and Sarah caught the scent of baking rolling out of the house like a wave of comfort. Woven through the scent was the relaxing sound of Christmas carols playing over the stereo.

This was a home, Sarah thought, nostalgia and yearning drawing her in.

"Hello, Sarah," Donna said, wiping her hands with a cloth. "What can I do for you?"

Sarah held up the books. "Billy left these behind after the game."

Donna stepped aside. "Just set them on the empty chair there. I'll tell him you stopped by."

As soon as Sarah stepped inside, she was enveloped by warmth. "Smells good in here," she said, trying to make some semblance of conversation.

"Christmas baking." Donna closed the door behind Sarah, but not all the way, as if anticipating her quick departure.

Sarah set the books on the chair but felt awkward just leaving immediately. She didn't know Donna well, but, living in the same small town, had seen her from time to time. Though after Jack's trial, Donna had disappeared from town life.

Her father thought as little of Donna as he did of her husband, often speaking of her with as much contempt as he assigned to Jack. Sarah never knew why. It was simply one of those things relegated to the adult world. As a teenager she had tried as much as possible to keep her and her father's worlds from intersecting.

Until she started dating Logan.

"I…I was sorry to hear about your husband," Sarah said, slipping her hands into her coat pocket. This would be the time to say something appropriate about his character, but the truth was the only things Sarah knew about Jack Carleton had come from her father. "I'm sure you miss him."

"He was a good man." Donna looked down at the cloth she was twisting in her hand.

An awkward pause followed her statement and then Sarah took a step toward the door. "I've taken up enough of your time. Thanks for making sure Billy gets his books."

"I'll do that. I'm sure he'll be very glad to get them."

Sarah threw Donna a questioning glance, then caught a surprising glint of humor in her eyes.

"I know how much Billy hates studying," Donna said with a wry smile.

"If he's going to go to college, he'll have to get used to it."

Donna shrugged. "We'll tackle Billy's life one step at a time, I think. For now I just want him to finish high school."

Sarah frowned. "So the college dream…"

"That's Logan's plan. Sure I'd like Billy to get out of Riverbend as well, but I'm not as fanatical about it as Logan."

"And he sees basketball as Billy's ticket out."

"That he does." Donna gave Sarah an apologetic smile. "Don't take it personally. I know what you meant to him…"

Sarah's breath caught in her chest. Donna knew as well?

"Well, that was a while ago."

"Yes. Things are a lot different now."

Sarah didn't want to know how different. Logan's life was none of her business.

But as she said goodbye and drove past the barn where Logan was unharnessing his horses, she thought of the few moments of connection they had shared in the past few days.

And she surely didn't know why those thoughts gave her heart a peculiar lift, and why she didn't want to examine them too closely.

Chapter Ten

"Yes. I agree, Trix. The boys haven't been winning like they used to." Logan tucked the phone under his ear while he ran the figures from his bank account through the calculator. He frowned at the total and started again. "Have you talked to Mr. Berube? And he's willing?"

As Logan spoke, an image of Sarah tearing up the gym came to mind. The intensity on her face, the way she handled the ball. She had skill. No one could argue with that.

And behind that, the image of Billy, dawdling his way through that last game, a complete contrast to Sarah's playing on her own. Logan had watched Billy play enough times that he knew when his brother was putting forth effort and when he was simply putting in time. Much as he hated to admit it, Sarah was right.

"You've got a parent meeting with Morris set up

already?" He punched in the numbers again, then scowled at the figure. Exactly the same as last time. "Isn't that a bit drastic?" He wrote the figure in his company checkbook, as Trix continued her tirade against Sarah, then scrawled the date Trix had given him on another scrap of paper.

"Okay. I guess I'll be there."

He dropped the phone in the cradle, then sat back in his chair, tapping his pen on the ink blotter on the desk. Business cards and scraps of paper with phone numbers were tucked into every corner. He really had to get a bulletin board.

And a loan.

Too many things on his mind. Now he was getting roped into a parent meeting to deal with Sarah's coaching. He wished he hadn't even started with that.

His emotions weren't entirely stable when it came to Sarah Westerveld. One moment she made him angry, the next frustrated and the next…well, if he were honest with himself, she still held the same fascination for him that she used to.

And then he had to go and invite her to come on a sleigh ride. Thank goodness she had treated it like a bit of a polite joke.

Logan blew out a sigh, then put thoughts of Sarah aside as he hunched back over his bookkeeping. He had to focus on the here and now. And here and now his business wasn't as healthy as he had hoped it would be. Once he finalized the deal on the contract that Crane held with Westerveld Contracting, the bottom line would look worse in the short term but actually be much better over the long run.

Which reminded him. He reached for the phone again and dialed Crane. They were supposed to get together to work out a final deal on how the contract was going to be transferred.

"Hey, Crane. How's it going?" he said when the phone was answered on the other end. He nodded, making himself smile as he listened to Crane's usual litany of complaints. He'd read somewhere that if you smiled while talking on the phone you sounded happier. And when it came to Crane, he needed a full-time grin.

After a long, roundabout conversation they finally got down to the reason for Logan's call.

And the more Crane spoke, the harder time Logan had keeping his smile intact. "We agreed on the price. What is happening in the oil patch shouldn't make it worth more," Logan insisted.

Logan spun his chair around, glaring at his reflection in the darkened window of his office. "I've got the financing in place, I'm in the process of buying another truck to put under that crusher. I can't squeeze out more for that contract."

There was no way he could pull any extra money from his operating plan and he was pretty sure the bank wasn't going to let him stretch any further. But Crane kept talking, and soon Logan couldn't even pretend to smile.

"I need to talk to my banker." Logan dragged his

hand over his face. "Give me a couple of days. I'll call you back." Logan hit End and tossed the phone onto his desk.

He grabbed a calculator, punched in the numbers and then the calculator followed the phone. At one time he'd had it all figured out. He'd had a plan. And now that plan was falling apart.

He heaved a sigh and leaned his elbows on his desk. He'd been too eager to grab the contract. Too eager to prove a point to Frank Westerveld. Too eager to be in his face. To eager to pay Frank Westerveld back for *his* past actions.

A light knock on the door pulled his attention away from his immediate problems. His mother came into the office and sat in the chair in the corner. "You look troubled," she said.

"It's nothing. Just a blip in my plans."

"Well, you know the saying. Men make plans and God laughs." Donna laced her fingers around her knee and leaned back.

"Then I seem to be giving God a lot to chuckle about lately. It seems like all my plans are getting tossed around. I just finished talking to Crane."

"Not having any luck getting your father's contract back?"

Logan rocked in his chair, looking past his mother. On the wall behind her hung an aerial photo of the farm taken ten years ago. Before his father's life fell apart. Jack Carleton had inherited the farm from his father but had never made a living from it. Up until the trial, the family's main income came from working as a contractor for various road construction crews. The farm had always been rented out. Logan preferred farming to running equipment, but the reality for him was they needed that off-farm income to help pay the farm mortgage.

"I thought I had it, but Crane upped the price on me."

"But I thought you were doing okay without it?" Donna's voice had gotten quiet. Wistful almost. "Ever since you started dealing with Crane you've been stressed and uptight. Do you really need it?"

Unfortunately, it wasn't simply dealing with Crane that was getting him tied up in knots lately. He banished the faint thought of Sarah teasing the back of his mind. "Frank should never have taken that contract away. I am going to get it back."

"But at what cost?"

"What do you mean?" Logan frowned at his mother, surprised at the change in her tone. "You've always wanted justice for Dad. I'm trying to get it."

"Maybe I was wrong."

"What?" Logan sat up, leaned his elbows on his desk and stared at his mother. "Where did that come from?"

"The minister said something this morning that caught my attention. And the same thing came to mind when Sarah came to the house after church."

Logan waited, surprised that his mother would even say Sarah's name. When he and Sarah were going out those many years ago, he had never told his parents. His father wasn't doing very well and he knew his mother would simply get too upset about him consorting with the enemy, so to speak.

But keeping the relationship quiet had seemed juvenile and petty. So after a few months he had told his mother. She had said that as long as he was happy, she would be happy for him. But he knew that she was waiting, hoping, he would break up with Sarah.

When she found out that, at the behest of her father, Sarah had broken up with him—over the phone—she was furious. Furious with Frank but also with Sarah for not standing up to her father.

Donna pulled her legs up, hugging her knees. "The minister was talking about anger and how it can eat at you, do you remember?"

He nodded. How quickly he had forgotten though.

"He said that anger can be so satisfying, at first. Gorging on injustices done and pain felt. But that in the end, the carcass at the feast is yourself." She bounced her chin on her knees in a curiously child-like gesture. "I can't get that idea out of my head. I've been angry so long and it has taken up so much of my energy...."

"What do you mean?"

Donna laid her cheek on her knee, looking away from Logan. "I started going to church because I heard Frank wasn't going anymore. I don't know if you knew, but I just couldn't face him. I was glad when you started coming with me. But when I saw that young girl walking toward us, I didn't want to talk to her. Didn't want to have anything to do with her. I was angry with her for your sake and I was angry with her because of what her father did to Jack. I knew it was childish and I knew it was wrong, but there it was."

She shook her head, then laughed a humorless laugh. "Then, a couple of days ago I went to your father's grave. That cold day? Anyway, I walked through the graveyard and I passed that young Westerveld girl's grave. Marilee. I stopped and read the headstone. She was only sixteen. And for some reason, for the first time since that accident, I realized that Frank Westerveld had buried a child."

She stopped, shaking her head again. "No parent should have to bury a child. No sister should have to stand by her own sister's grave. Then when Sarah came by today and I talked to her..."

"So what are you saying, Mom?"

Donna looked over at Logan, her eyes troubled. "I'm tired of being angry all the time. And I don't want to be angry with that young girl, that's for certain."

Logan should have felt happy about that. But he wasn't sure himself anymore how he felt about Sarah. She confused and puzzled him.

"I'm glad, Mom. I'm glad that you're finding some measure of peace."

Donna got up, walked to his side and stroked his

hair. "I want the same thing for you, Logan. You know that."

"I don't know, Mom. The peace you want for me seems as elusive as a win for Billy's basketball team. I know things…"

Donna frowned. "Tell me."

"You've just found peace, Mom. I can't tell you."

"If it's keeping you from finding that same peace, I want you to tell me Logan. I want you to trust me."

Logan sighed. "I overheard Frank saying that he should have testified for Dad. Should have been his character witness."

Donna turned to lean back against the desk. She looked away from Logan, frowning. "That doesn't surprise me."

Was that all she could say? "He's a prominent member of the community, Mom. He could have made a difference for Dad. How can you act so casual about that? Think of the trouble he could have saved us!"

"Frank Westerveld's coming forward as a character witness might have helped, but he never would have done it then, no matter what he says now."

"Why not?"

Donna crossed her arms over her chest and, as she leveled him a steady look, Logan sensed another secret looming. "Frank was punishing me through Jack. Because I wouldn't accept Frank's money. Or his gifts or his attention."

* * *

Pete Kolasa stood up, his hands on his hips, his plaid shirt straining at the buttons. "How many more games do the boys need to lose? They're almost at the bottom of their league now!"

"If they don't pull up, they're going to be matched against those boys from Beaverlodge again. Toughest team in the league," seconded Beth Sawchuk, her corkscrew curls bobbing as she glanced around the other parents in the classroom.

The only surprising thing about this parents' meeting was how quickly it had been organized. Sarah knew something was afoot when she saw a group of people clustered around Trix Setterfeld in one corner of the gym after the game on Saturday.

Sarah knew all the parents by name and had spoken to many of them after practices and games. But the only person in the group who would meet her eye was the tall man standing against the wall at the back of the room. Logan Carlton.

"All last year Mr. DeHaan kept saying that this team was going to be the best team he's ever seen," Pete said. "By this time last year, the boys had won twice as many games as they lost. This year, it's the other way around."

"How do you suppose replacing Sarah as a coach will resolve that?" Morris added a faint laugh, as if he thought the idea not even worth getting serious about. He crossed his arms, as he rested one hip on the metal teacher's desk. "This isn't the NBA. It's just high school basketball."

Trix Setterfeld stood up, her arms crossed over her corduroy blazer. "Morris, this is not *just* high school basketball. This represents an opportunity for our boys to get in front of scouts from colleges." Her gaze slid to Sarah then she focused on Morris. "*Some* of us can't afford to pay the full cost of our boys' education."

And there it was again. The fabulously wealthy Westerveld family just didn't understand the plight of the common Riverbend resident.

"Sarah, do you have anything to say about this?" Morris asked.

Sarah had lots to say, but knew that she had to tread a fine line between diplomacy and hard facts. She was very aware of Logan standing in the back of the room, watching.

She knew he had spearheaded this movement and, though it made her clench her teeth in anger, it also hurt that he seemed to have no qualms about taking the coaching position away from her. She should never have let him know what it meant to her. She had given him an edge that he could use.

"You parents are wrong about these boys," she said, looking around the room, gauging the effect of her little drama statement. Concerned frowns. Agitated whispers.

She nodded, acknowledging their protest. "This

is not a good team, this is a *great* team. They have tremendous potential—"

"So why are they losing?" Beth interrupted her.

"Short answer? Leadership."

"Is that why you pulled Billy Carleton?" Pete called out. "'Cause my boy said that's why they lost. 'Cause you pulled Billy."

Sarah glanced at Logan, who had straightened and was watching her with those intensely dark eyes. She looked away, took a breath and continued. "The boys have been depending on their captain, on Billy, too much. If Billy is off his game, then the team falters. And Billy…well, he's been letting them down. I've been addressing this problem by getting the boys to play without him. I want the team to develop their many individual talents and skills."

"But Billy has always been their leader.…"

"Which is precisely why this is a problem. Yes it's important to have a strong leader as captain, but it's even more important to play as a team. As a unit, utilizing individual strengths. Being able to cover for a player when they're down on their game, when they're injured or unable to play." Sarah stopped herself right there. She had an entire spiel memorized and had gone over it and over it while doing drills with the boys this week, while jogging in the treadmill at home, while watching the plays on her father's television. But every time she'd recited it, her anger and frustration had taken over as it did now.

"But couldn't Berube get more out of those boys?"

Trix spoke up. "Derek says that it's hard to respect a woman coach."

"That's odd, since Derek doesn't seem to have that problem once he's at practice," Sarah shot back.

"Couldn't we just try this Berube guy for a while? I mean things couldn't get much worse."

Oh yes they could, thought Sarah. Switching coaches midstream seldom worked, even in professional sports. She glanced at her uncle Morris for support, but he seemed to be keeping a low profile. Of course, as her uncle, what could he say that wouldn't seem biased?

The parents murmured among themselves, planning, talking. Each glance sent her way, each a frown, and Sarah felt the one thing that gave her even a glimmer of happiness being taken away from her.

It shouldn't matter. It was just a volunteer position.

But basketball had always been her catharsis. Had always given her a focus. Basketball was the one thing she did better than Marilee, better than anyone else she knew. It was the one place in her life where she felt in control.

Now, more than ever, she needed this. Needed the way it sucked up her time. Coaching gave her a built-in excuse to stay away from the hospital and her father and his unwelcome proclamations of forgiveness.

"And if we get Mr. Berube to come and coach, how do we know the boys will respect him?" Logan's deep voice carried through the room, over top of the murmuring voices.

Trix Setterfeld looked back, her frown clearly showing what she thought of his intrusion.

"I think Sarah has a rapport with these boys," Logan continued, "and if you look at the stats, you'll see the boys are moving up each game."

Sarah hardly dared look at him, hardly dared believe that Logan, who had been so adamant that she couldn't do the job, was suddenly confident of her skills. And no one could accuse him of patronage.

"But they're still losing."

Logan shrugged, walking to the front of the room, and came to stand beside Sarah. "It's still early enough in the season, the boys could probably absorb another loss."

Well, maybe not completely confident of her skills. The boys wouldn't lose their next game, of that Sarah was certain.

"And I don't know if Mr. Berube has enough skill and experience to coach this team," Logan continued.

"What's happening, Logan?" Trix glanced from him to Sarah as if trying to find a connection between the two. "A few weeks ago you were actively campaigning to get rid of Miss Westerveld. What made you change your mind?"

"Billy has been, as she said, dogging it on the court." He shrugged. "I see that now, and I think she has a strategy to address it. Let's see how it plays out."

Sarah could hardly believe what she was hearing. Logan defending her in a public forum. From the corner of her eye she caught him glance her way, but she didn't dare make eye contact. She was too aware of the question in Uncle Morris's eyes as he watched her, Logan standing beside her, the two of them aligned against the parents.

Some more murmuring among the parents followed Logan's suggestion. Sarah tried to gauge the tone of the looks, their words. Logan didn't join them but instead stayed beside her, his hands pushed in the pockets of his coat.

She knew she was making the situation bigger than she should. Whether she coached or not wasn't earth-shattering. But now she needed some purpose, some reason for staying here. And in spite of the grief she got from some of the boys, she knew she was getting somewhere with them.

After a few more moments of what seemed to be intense discussion, Pete got up. He scratched his head but avoided looking at Sarah. "We gotta think of our kids. I hope we have some say." He glanced at Morris. "And since we didn't have any say in Sarah taking on the position. So I want to give Mr. Berube a kick at the can. They're our kids and it's their opportunity we might be tossing out."

Sarah didn't even know she was holding her breath until it rushed out of her.

"Don't do this, Pete," Logan said. "Give her another chance."

She waited for one of the other parents to side with Logan, but the uncomfortable silence in the room excluded her.

Morris swung his foot back and forth, his arms folded over his chest as he looked at the parent group. "You realize that coaching the team is a voluntary position, but also that we need to choose based on skill and knowledge. I'm not aware of what Mr. Berube knows or how much experience he has."

"He's at least coached before," Beth said. "That's more than Sarah has done."

Morris sighed and ran his hand over his thinning hair. "I'm not so sure about this. I don't like it."

"We don't like seeing our boys lose," Trix said.

Her uncle Morris was caught in a difficult position and Sarah felt sorry for him. There was an easier way. She took a breath and made a decision.

"I'm sensing I'm not going to have a lot of support from you as parents," Sarah said quietly. "And without that, my effectiveness as a coach is pretty much nil."

Sarah slipped her bag over her shoulder and stood. "I'll quit."

Chapter Eleven

As the heavy door fell closed behind her, her knees felt suddenly rubbery. Sarah leaned against the lockers lining the hallway, staring at the gleaming floor. What had she just done?

Made a decision. Made a choice.

The door creaked open again, and Sarah jumped.

Logan joined her in the hallway.

"Hey there," he said, coming to stand in front of her. "I really thought they would give you another chance."

"They care about their boys." She clutched the strap of her backpack, clinging to it with both hands as if for support. "But thanks for the vote of confidence." She gave him a careful smile. "I appreciated that."

Logan shifted closer then, to her surprise, he laid his hand on her shoulder. "When I watched you in the gym the other night, you were tearing around that floor like it was yours. Like you owned it. I remember watching you play the same way. I'm pretty sure that this Berube guy doesn't play with the same passion—wouldn't be able to instill that same passion in those boys."

Sarah smiled at his assessment and affirmation.

"So, now that you have all this time on your hands," he said, "I was wondering if you might… come on that sleigh ride I promised you the other day."

Sarah looked up at him, surprised at the invitation.

He was looking at her, a faint smile teasing the corner of his mouth. The tension that seemed to personify their previous encounters had shifted with his defense of her.

"Was that a promise?" she asked. "I thought you were just being polite."

Had she really injected that flirty tone in her voice? Added a teasing smile?

"Yeah. It was."

Then his hand came up and touched her hair, so lightly she might have imagined it. Her heart thrummed with expectation even as one practical part of her mind warned to keep her distance.

Maybe it was the location, their old school, maybe it was the timing—she was feeling vulnerable and he was here. Maybe it was all the kisses they had shared in the past, the many times she had reached for the phone to call him, the unfulfilled anticipations of young love. Maybe it was all that, that made her lean toward him…

The door beside them swung open.

Sarah jumped back and Logan moved aside.

"…here's hoping things turn around," she heard as Pete stepped out of the room, followed by the rest of the parents.

Pete paused when he saw Sarah and Logan, then he ducked his head, as if ashamed to meet her eyes, and the rest of the people filed past them, suddenly quiet.

Morris followed them out and, as he glanced from Logan to Sarah, she felt as if she had plunged backward in time.

"You going to be okay, Sarah?" Morris asked, his tone gentle and understanding. "You don't have to quit."

Sarah laughed lightly. "Yes. I do. If the parents don't support me, I lose my effectiveness with the team." She gave her uncle what she hoped was a reassuring smile. "I'll be fine. It's not like I just lost a well-paying job."

"So you'll have time on your hands." He waited a beat. "Are you going to be visiting your dad tomorrow?" he asked.

"Maybe." She should say more. Uncle Morris deserved more than that pithy reply. But other thoughts and feelings were shouting out for attention.

But Logan, who had brushed her tears away, who had, with just a few words, erased most of her reasons for cutting him out of her life—Logan, who had once held her heart, stood beside her. Waiting.

"I have something in the car for you," her uncle said. "From your aunt."

Sarah felt suddenly awkward, torn between family obligations and the promise of what might be. She turned to Logan, unsure of what to say.

"I'll see you around," Logan said, taking a step backward and giving her an out.

"I'll call you tomorrow," she said, suddenly not caring about her uncle Morris or what he might think. "About that sleigh ride."

Logan nodded, a wry smile teasing one corner of his mouth. "You do that."

Then he turned and left.

Sarah sat in her car, the windows of the Carleton house throwing out oblique rectangles of golden light on the snow.

What was she doing here?

Collecting on a years' old promise. Getting away from that empty house and the loneliness that echoed through it.

She'd avoided coming here by phoning Janie, but Janie was headed out to do some Christmas shopping for her girls. Sarah politely turned down the invitation to come along. The Westerveld relatives had eschewed buying gifts for some years now, preferring instead to simply get together for a nice dinner and pool together whatever money they might have spent and send it to the missionary family their church supported.

The only person on her gift list was her father, and at the moment she couldn't wrap her head around buying him anything. So she worked her way down her unofficial visiting list, but her aunts were off to choir practice and Dodie had a hot date.

All obstacles for coming here had been neatly removed and here she was. Sitting in a car that was slowly getting colder, trying to work up the nerve to actually walk up to Logan's house.

Sarah slowly got out of the car, the butterflies in her stomach growing more agitated with each step she took.

Was she being wise?

A sleigh ride with Logan? With a moon hanging fat and full in the sky above her?

The moment of awareness that had trembled between them had stayed with her every waking moment. She and Logan had a history, an unfinished history. Surely they had a right to finish that off properly before she moved on.

They could excise the old ghosts, laugh about it and go on with their lives, unencumbered by the burden of history and unfinished conversations.

Yes. That was a good idea. Finish this off. Closure.

She knocked sharply on the door, then clasped her hands in front of her, shivering a moment with a combination of cold and anticipation.

But Logan wasn't the one to come to the door. Donna opened it, releasing once again the scents of home. She gave Sarah a cautious smile, then stood aside. "Logan is just finishing supper."

"I'm sorry...I..." She glanced at her watch, double-checking the time. "He told me to come at seven-thirty."

"That's okay. He came home late. Come join us."

Sarah waved away the invitation. "No. I don't want to be a bother. I can just wait outside."

"Mom made apple pie." Logan came up behind his mother, smiling. "She would be insulted if you sat outside while we ate."

"Please, do come in," Donna said, gesturing toward the dining room. "I'd like you to join us."

"Okay." Sarah slowly removed her coat, savoring the smell of dinner. Ham, she thought, and maybe potatoes. And that same cinnamon smell interlaced through the comforting aromas of food prepared for a family.

She thought of the slice of cold pizza she had eaten while watching television. College food in her father's house.

She followed Donna into the kitchen and was immediately enveloped by delicious warmth. She heard a snap and a pop and noticed the woodstove, a fire glowing through its glass doors.

"Have a seat." Donna pulled out a chair for her. "I'll get you a plate."

"Hey, Miss Westerveld." Billy threw her a quick

glance, then dove back into the book he was reading while he ate.

"How is the basketball coach working out for you guys?" she asked

"He's okay." Billy kept his eyes on his book.

"You've got a pretty big game coming up this weekend."

He only nodded.

"You playing?"

Another nod.

"You'll have to excuse Billy," Logan said, his voice holding a harsh note as he set a pie plate on the table. "He's suffering from the pangs of Older Brother Lecture."

Billy curled his lip at that very same older brother, then went back to his reading.

Sarah just nodded, hoping that was enough acknowledgment of what looked to be a controversial subject.

"I found out about Nelli and about the welding and about the plans he had made without talking to me," Logan continued as he scooped out pieces of pie and set them on plates. "And we had a talk about hiding behind his playing and using his coach as an excuse for his poor behavior."

Logan gave Sarah a look rife with apology as he handed her a piece of pie. "He's not liking the repercussions."

Billy just rolled his eyes, slapped his book shut

and dropped it on the table. "May I be excused?" he asked his mother.

"Not yet," Donna said. "We're having dessert and then we're going to have devotions. You can stay for that."

A sigh, worthy of any teenage girl, blasted out from Billy as he slouched down in his chair, the picture of put-upon adolescence.

They ate their pie in silence and Sarah wondered what the conversation would have been about had she not been there. But the pie was delicious and the silence not uncomfortable.

"Billy, why don't you get the Bible?" Donna asked, after Sarah declined seconds. "We can have devotions and then Logan can get the horses ready."

Billy leaned his chair back, pulled open a drawer and handed the heavy book to Donna. Donna leafed through the Bible, the pages rustling in the quiet that descended. "I'm reading from Psalm one hundred three," Donna said.

As she read the words, Sarah reached back into the past. Every evening, without fail her father would pull out the Bible, as well. When Sarah left Riverbend she'd packed her Bible out of duty and custom. But she hardly read it.

Now Donna's quiet voice reading words so familiar to her drew out memories of those nights around the table.

"'…For as high as the heavens are above the earth, so great is His love for those who fear Him. As far as the east is from the west, so far has He removed our transgressions from us. As a father has compassion on his children, so the Lord has compassion on those who hear Him.'"

As a father has compassion on his children...
Sarah felt a touch of melancholy. Her father was not known for his compassion. She didn't like to think that God was like Frank Westerveld.

You're starting with the wrong father.

She hung on to those words.

God. A father to the fatherless.

God. The perfect father.

Peace settled through her, soothing away the tension and frustration of the past few days, creating a calm that both puzzled and comforted her.

"'...but from everlasting to everlasting the Lord's love is with those who fear Him, and his righteousness with their children's children...'"

God's love. Everlasting.

You've been trying to please the wrong father.

Logan's words seeped up from her subconscious.

She tested those words, trying to fit them into her life. She didn't need Frank Westerveld. She just needed God.

"Logan, will you pray?" Donna's voice broke into Sarah's thoughts and with a start she looked up. Logan was watching her and as his eyes held hers his nod acknowledged his mother's request.

Logan bowed his head and began.

And once again, Sarah's preconceived notions

floundered and dissipated. The Logan she had dated had struggled with the whole notion of faith and church. He had told Sarah, often and loudly, that he didn't believe in a God that could have allowed his father to be so vilified, to be falsely accused and then to have to deal with the health problems he had. Indeed, Logan's vocal anger with God had been one of the unspoken reasons she thought her father might be right when he told Sarah to break up with Logan.

But now in Logan's quiet voice Sarah sensed a conviction she had never heard as a young girl of eighteen. It shifted her perception of him.

When Logan finished, he looked up at her and smiled, and for a moment they shared connection on another level.

"You'd better head out right away, while the moon is still up," Donna said.

"I should help with the dishes," Sarah protested.

"It's Billy's turn."

"What? Since when?" Billy dropped his teetering chair with a thud. "Why can't Logan help?"

"Because I love him the best."

Sarah felt a jolt of surprise at Donna's bold-faced comment. Her attention flew to Billy to see his reaction.

"Well, as if we didn't know that by now," Billy grumbled.

"Learn to live with it, little brother," Logan said with a laugh. "Let's go, Sarah. We can leave poor Cinder-fella to do all the cleaning and tidying."

Sarah threw a puzzled look over her shoulder.

"Sarah?" Logan prompted.

"Sorry. I'm coming." She followed him to the porch, taking her coat from him, still perplexed by the exchange. "Your mom doesn't really…"

"Love me the best? Well, yeah. Billy knows and accepts this." Logan's smile softened when he looked at her. He must have seen the confusion on her face. "My mom was *kidding*."

"I see."

"She would never mean anything like that."

"Well, some parents would." She spoke without thinking.

"Parents like your dad?"

She looked him and nodded. "Yeah. Parents like my dad." It hurt to admit, but at the same time speaking the truth was a freeing moment.

"I'm sorry," Logan said. "I shouldn't have said what I did."

"Its okay." Sarah took a step away and slipped her boots on. "It's the truth."

He followed her out the door and into the cold, the snow squeaking under their feet. She got her toque and mitts from the car then walked with him to the barn. The moon's reflected light created a pale twilight, casting shadows ahead of them. The awkward moment in the porch lessened in the eerie beauty of the snow-covered fields lit by the reflected light of the moon.

"You ever been on a sleigh before?" Logan asked.

She shook her head, pulling her mittens on.

"So you've never seen a horse get harnessed."

"Even if I had witnessed such an auspicious event, I doubt I would be much help."

"So it's all up to me," Logan said with an exaggerated sigh.

"I'm sure you'll do just fine," Sarah said, thankful for the lightening of the atmosphere.

They came to the barn and Logan slid the large door open and flicked a switch. Soft, incandescent light flooded the barn. From a stall at the back, Sarah heard a welcoming whinny.

Logan filled a pail with oats and dumped them out into the feed bins at the head of the stalls, then led the same horses Sarah had seen before into two separate stalls and tied their halters to the wall. While the horses ate, he slipped a padded collar over the horse's heads. Then he returned to the wall, holding the tack, and pulled down what looked like a tangled armful of straps and buckles and rings.

While Sarah watched, fascinated by the procedure, he draped the harness over the first horse's back, pulling and shifting, buckling and attaching, then repeating the same steps with the second horse.

"You might want to stand aside," Logan warned as he gathered up the reins. He clucked to the horses and started backing up and, to Sarah's surprise, the horses slowly backed out, as well.

"Good trick," she said, full of admiration for what he had just done.

"Good training," he said. The horses stopped, turned. "Now we need to get them to the sleigh. It's just outside. Could you grab the blanket that's lying on the shelf behind you?"

Sarah did as she was told, then followed Logan out, watching as he hitched the horses to the sleigh.

"Done here." Logan wound the reins around a bar and turned to Sarah and helped her in. He climbed in behind her then took two blankets, wrapped one around each of their legs. "It's kinda cold once we get going. No in-sleigh heater."

Sarah pulled her blanket a bit closer. Logan clucked to the horses and with a light jerk of the sleigh they were off.

The moon had risen higher, throwing out a spectral light—enough to make out the shape of the driveway and the trees beyond it. The muffled thud of the horses' hooves, the jingle of the bells on their traces and the hiss of the runners over the white snow created a gentle resonance to the pale shadows cast by the moon.

"I feel like we're the only people out here," Sarah whispered, as if the very act of speaking would break the mood.

"I love being out in the full moon. Just us and the coyotes." Logan slanted her a smile, his teeth bright white against his face.

There it was again, the flash of awareness that sprang up so easily between them. Logan watched her, his smile fading, as if he sensed it, as well.

"Thanks for taking me," Sarah said primly, determined to enjoy the sleigh ride and equally determined not to let foolish emotions intrude on the moment. He was just an old friend taking her for a ride.

"You are most welcome, madam."

Sarah pulled her blanket closer, leaning back against the padded seat, looking everywhere but at Logan.

The trees, their branches laden with caps of snow, slipped silently past them as they turned onto the road. The horses' heads bobbed as their snow-muffled hoofbeats pounded out a lulling rhythm, counterpointed to the jingling of the bells.

"This is amazing," she said quietly. "Do you do this often?"

"Never as often as I'd like," Logan admitted. "My work keeps me busier than I want to, but I try to find the time when I can. Working with the horses is relaxing and rewarding."

Logan steered the horses onto a trail and, as the horses plowed through the unbroken snow, Sarah was overcome by a sense of wonder. "We're the first people on the trail this winter."

"It ends up at the back of our property, so it doesn't really go anywhere people on snow machines would even want to venture. Most people around here know that."

"And maybe most people around here don't want

to face the wrath of Logan Carleton when they trespass."

"I can be pretty fierce," he admitted.

"I remember the time you caught those boys throwing eggs at your truck. I feared for their bones."

Logan's sidelong glance held a suggestion of hurt. "I hope you have better memories than ones of me losing it."

Sarah smiled. "I have lots of good memories of you, Logan."

He jerked his gaze away, his jaw suddenly set. "Name me one."

Sarah heard the faint challenge in his voice, underlaid with a hint of anger that often simmered just below the surface with Logan.

"I remember going for a walk. Your truck had broken down."

"That's not a best moment."

"There's more." She ignored his anger, recognizing where it had come from. "It was October and the sun was setting. The northern lights came out that night, brighter and more colorful than anything I'd ever seen before. They were dancing and shimmering, a curtain of blue and green and pink."

"You got a sore neck, watching them," Logan said.

"You remember, too?"

Logan kept his eyes on his horses, but she sensed his attention. "I kissed you for the first time that night."

A tremor of remembered connection crept through

Sarah. She swallowed as the memory grew, filling up the space between them. She forced a laugh, trying to lighten the mood. "Do real men remember first kisses?"

This time he looked at her. "I do."

Sarah's interest tipped slowly toward a headier, deeper emotion. She looked away, pulling the blanket closer as she watched the trees slip silently past the sleigh. Her mind skated back through time, resurrecting memories she thought she'd abandoned long ago.

She'd been so filled with love and all its attendant emotions. Logan was a young girl's ideal first love. Taciturn, aloof, dark and mysterious. Toss in the whole puzzling but complex Westerveld/Carleton feud, and it suddenly became very Montague and Capulet. An irresistible combination for any young girl on the cusp of womanhood.

When Logan had noticed her, started talking to her, she had felt as if she trembled on the verge of something else. Something exciting and serious. He was her first, serious love. They'd dated, kissed, made naïve, whispered plans for their future. They were in love and the rest of the world hadn't mattered. Until it intruded on them.

Sarah huddled deeper in the blanket. Since she had come back to Riverbend she had other information to work with, other experiences. She still wasn't sure what to do with this all, how to fit it into her life.

The horses sped up, just a bit, then turned onto

another trail. The trees hung low, shedding showers of snow as they passed.

"Where are we going?" Sarah finally asked, breaking the silence.

"You'll see."

No sooner had he spoken than the trees suddenly gave way to an open field. Logan turned the horses toward the edge of the field and when they stopped, Sarah felt perched on the edge of an unknown and dangerous world.

They stood on the edge of a sheer cliff dropping over a hundred feet then sloping away to the deep, wide valley. The river that had cut the valley spooled out below them, a wide band of white broken by a few tree-dotted islands.

Sarah had grown up with the river just a short drive away, had crossed over the bridge spanning it a thousand times, had walked along its edge as a young girl, throwing sticks into it to watch them being carried away downstream. But she had never experienced the immense depth and width of the valley the river had carved over the centuries.

"This is amazing," she whispered, hardly daring to speak, hardly daring to break the peace that had descended as soon as the horses stopped.

Logan wound the reins around a post and sat back, his dark eyes sweeping over the valley, lit by the ghostly light of the moon. "I come here whenever I need to think," he said, his voice growing quiet, almost reverent. "I've spent a lot of time sitting here. Dreaming."

"What dreams did you have, Logan?"

"You've heard them all."

"Things have changed in our lives. Surely your dreams have, as well."

"Yeah. A lot of my dreams are for my brother now, I guess." Logan lifted his foot, resting it on the front of the sleigh. "Who knows what he'll do with them."

"He may have his own plans, but at the same time he should be thankful that you have wishes for him. I think that kind of involvement in your brother's life speaks well of you."

"Yeah, well, he doesn't seem to want the same things I do," he said, sighing lightly. "I'm working myself to nothing trying to make sure this kid gets all the breaks I didn't get, and he doesn't even want to take advantage of them and the natural talent he has that could get him out of here."

Sarah knew he was speaking from his own youth. "Was it hard for you? Growing up a Carleton?"

"Only when I was around your father. Or when I would hear stories from my father about your father." Logan leaned forward, his elbows on his knees, his clasped hands hanging between them. "Sorry, Kitten, but our family has a complicated history."

He gave her a rueful glance. "And I don't want to talk about that now. I don't want your father to interfere again. With us."

Us. The single word created a storm of feelings in Sarah. "I didn't know there was an us."

"At one time there was."

Sarah wasn't sure she wanted to follow Logan's lead—to head in the direction his conversation was going. Instead she sat back, letting the silence surround them like a gentle blanket of forgiving. When no words were spoken, no mistakes could be made.

The horses shifted and blew as the moment drew out. One glanced back as if to ask Logan what was happening. But Logan didn't move. Didn't speak.

Normally Sarah felt uncomfortable in silence, experiencing a need to fill it with words, to create a connection with communication.

Though she was fully aware of Logan sitting beside her, a gentle peace surrounded them. As she settled in the sleigh, the blanket around her shoulder slipped off. She reached to straighten it at the same time Logan caught it.

She glanced sidelong at him and caught him watching her.

And the wide-open spaces suddenly narrowed down to his hand on her shoulder, their gazes melding, their frozen breath combining in an ethereal mist.

"Sarah..." Logan whispered.

She was going to be smart. She wasn't going to give in to the feelings of uncertainty that tantalized her. That hovered on the edge of emotions that threatened to pull her in.

But she couldn't look away and didn't want to. For the first time since she had returned to Riverbend, they were in a place of solitude, with no fear of people nearby watching, judging. Sarah had no other eyes through which she could see her and Logan.

Just hers.

And then his hand slipped behind her head as if to anchor it, and his face drew near, his breath warm on her lips. He waited, giving her an opportunity to pull back or to stop him.

An onslaught of inevitability rushed over her. A feeling that everything she had done, every decision she had made had brought her to this place with Logan. If she bridged the gap, completed the circle, everything would change. She could stop this now.

But even as those thoughts spun and wove their faint warning, Sarah felt something inside of her shift, and she knew this was right.

She moved those last few inches and, as their lips met, cool at first, then warming, Sarah felt she hovered on the threshold of a new and yet familiar happiness.

Chapter Twelve

Logan drew back and rested his forehead against hers, his eyes a dark blur against his face.

"It's been a long time, Sarah," he whispered.

Sarah pulled her mittens off and cradled his face with her hands. In spite of the chill of the air his cheeks felt warm to the touch. She traced the shape of his mouth, as if learning him by Braille.

"Lots has happened since we were together." She let her fingers drift down to his chin, then touched the new lines at the corner of his mouth.

"Did you miss me?" he asked.

Her harsh laugh was the barest glimpse into the six lonely years she had spent away from him. "I thought of you every day."

Logan leaned back against the seat, taking her with him, tucking her head under his chin, holding her close. "You never phoned. Wrote."

His voice rumbled under her cheek as she settled

against him her hand on his heart. Through the material of his denim jacket she felt the beat—steady, strong and sure. "It was because of Marilee," she replied. "She made it sound as if she was going to meet you. As if she was going out with you."

Logan brushed a strand of hair away from her forehead. "I wish you would have asked me right away. I could have told you."

"When? How? Marilee's death was like a huge boulder dropped into a pond. The resulting waves completely swamped my life." Sarah curled her fingers, catching them on a button flap of his jacket as her mind unconsciously went back to that evening. "When the police came to tell me that she had died…" Sarah stopped. Caught her breath.

Logan's arms tightened, granting her a safe harbor. "I'm so sorry you had to go through that." He stroked the top of her head with his chin, slowly, slowly.

"You lost someone you loved, too," she whispered, clutching his shirt with her hand. "You lost your father."

"But I had my mother and my brother and friends to help me through that. You were all alone in a strange place." He sighed. "I wanted to see you. Wanted to talk to you. In fact I even went to one of your games."

This made Sarah pull back, surprised. "When?"

"About two years ago. You were playing in Calgary. I drove down."

"But you never talked to me…you didn't come…"

He shrugged and tucked her hair behind her ears, his eyes intent on his hand. "Your uncle and cousins were there. I didn't want to interfere. And I wasn't sure where I stood with you. So I slunk back home."

He smiled, his teeth white in the semidarkness. "But it was great watching you play."

What-ifs and maybes hung between them. If he had come to her, if he had talked to her. If she had picked up the phone…

Maybe things would have been different. Maybe they would each be in a different place now.

And what place would that have been?

Sarah leaned forward, caught his face in her hands, pulled him close and kissed him as if erasing those questions.

Logan looked momentarily startled, then a smile lit up his face. "You continue to surprise me," he said with a chuckle.

She gave him an answering smile. "What did you expect? You had this all planned."

"Well, I wanted to talk where nobody would see and report back to your dad. I'm sure he would have something to say about this."

"I'm sure he would, if he knew." Sarah drew back, her eyes on the horses standing quietly now. "Or as much as he could say, given his disability."

"So what has he been saying?"

Sarah unfolded the mittens, folded them again, wondering what to tell him, how much she wanted to open up to him. But when she looked up and saw the concern in his face, her self-control wavered. "He said he forgave me," she said.

"*Forgave* you? For what? Leaving?"

"For Marilee. He said he forgave me for what happened to Marilee."

"What was to forgive?"

"Marilee had called me. From the party. Asked me to pick her up. I didn't go because I was being the good girl. Obeying the curfew that Dad hit me with after he found out about you. I didn't get her, and she got into the accident," she said.

"How is that your fault?"

Sarah shrugged. "If I had picked her up, she might not have been in that car with those boys."

Logan caught her by her shoulders. "How can you possibly take that on? How can you possibly think it's your responsibility that she lived or died?"

His eyes blazed into hers and for a moment Sarah feared what she had unleashed. Then she realized his anger was not directed toward her, but toward the guilt she carried. Guilt that no one had ever addressed because how Marilee died was never talked about.

"She had other options. I know who was at that party, and not everyone left drunk. She could have gotten a ride with many other people, but she chose those boys because Marilee always, always lived on the edge," Logan continued. "She didn't have to go to that party. She could have stayed home like you did."

"I had no choice."

"But *she* did. That's what I'm trying to tell you. She was just being typical Marilee when she called you, knowing that she could count on you to pick her up and then cover for her when you got home or, even better, take the heat for both of you being out at night past your curfew. Marilee always took very good care of Marilee. And in your heart you know that."

As he spoke, Sarah clung to his words, hardly daring to take the comfort he was offering with them: the assurance that she had done nothing wrong by doing nothing for her sister that night. That she was simply a bystander and that Marilee's tragedy was of her own doing.

And yet, in spite of what he was telling her, she couldn't extinguish the small spark of disloyalty she felt in putting aside the guilt she had carried so long.

"You know I'm right, Sarah. You do. Marilee was spoiled and selfish and your father had a lot to do with that…."

"She was a fun-loving person," Sarah said, defending her beloved sister.

"She was," Logan said. "And I don't want to talk ill of someone who can't defend themselves, but I'm laying out the reality of Marilee's life for your sake, not to take away from who she was. She was too big a part of your and Frank's life. She took over that house."

Sarah thought of Marilee's room. "She still does. Her room hasn't changed."

"What do you mean?"

"My dad left everything the same in that room. Her shirt is still hanging over the back of the chair, just as she left it the night she died. He put a lock on the door just before Christmas."

"You should clean that up."

"But my dad—"

"Is in the hospital and has controlled enough of your life." Logan shook his head and emitted an exasperated sigh. "You've spent enough time pleasing him. He doesn't deserve your devotion."

"Pleasing the wrong father…"

"What?"

"I've had this phrase going through my mind. That I've spent a lot of my life pleasing the wrong father."

"Instead of pleasing God?"

"I used to care about my relationship with God, but if I look back, I think my relationship with my earthly father took the upper hand."

"My dad always used to tell me that we put God and Jesus first in our lives, but that never made much sense to me," Logan said quietly. "My dad was here on earth, so I could directly talk to him. God was much harder. I always had a hard time concentrating when I was praying."

Sarah smiled at his honesty. "What was your relationship with your father like?"

Logan smiled, looking off into the middle distance. "We had fun together. He was honest. Whenever I got into trouble in school he stood up for me. He was a good man who didn't deserve what happened to him."

"The trial?"

Logan's features tightened. "The trial absolutely drained him and my mom—and what made it worse was how he was treated in the community even after he was found innocent. It was like the false accusations had stained him for life."

"I remember how my dad used to talk about it," Sarah said quietly.

"Your father has a lot to answer for, a lot that—" Logan bit off the last word as if he was going to say more.

"Are you talking about the contract you said you're trying to get back?"

"Yeah. Except there have been a few glitches with that, as well. But I'm working on it."

"How?"

"I'm trying to buy it from the guy your father gave it to. Crane Overstreet."

"But if my father gave it to Crane, why is he trying to sell it to you?" Sarah had been somewhat aware of her father's construction company's operations, but didn't always understand the intricacies of the business end.

"Because Crane claims it has a value. And he's right. A contract with Westerveld Construction is not only lucrative, it's stable. Or can be."

"But if my dad took it away once, couldn't he do it again?"

"My dad could have legally fought what your father did. That contract was binding, but after the trial my father didn't have the energy or the resources."

"And you do?"

"I have the energy. I would never let your father push me around like he did my dad. Deceive me like he did my dad. Ever."

The steel in his voice made Sarah uncomfortable and her instinctive need to stand up for her father came to the fore. "I know my dad isn't perfect. I know he's made mistakes…"

"I'm sorry. I know he's still your father and all, but Sarah, he's a complicated man and he's got a lot to answer for. Not only with my father, but with you, as well. What he said about forgiving you for Marilee, what he said about the wrong daughter dying… A *father* cares about his children more than he cares about himself." Logan's earnest voice pushed at her fragile defenses. "My father always put us first. Always took our side. When I came home from school with a bloody nose or a black eye because I got into a fight with someone over what they said about him, the only thing he would say was a gentle reminder to love my enemies. Something I'm not that good at, I'll have to admit."

"He sounds so different from the trial images that got stuck on him…. You really loved your father, didn't you?" Sarah asked.

"Dearly. Deeply. I miss him. He had a good perspective on life. He had a strong faith. When he died…" Logan stopped there.

The sleigh moved ahead a bit and Logan gently pulled on the reins, talking to his horses. The horses his father had trained.

"I'm so sorry, Logan."

He shrugged. "I am, too. I'm sorry that people believed he did what he had been falsely accused of. That was hard on my father's pride and hard on my family. I'm glad his name was cleared, but that was a long, hard road that he shouldn't have had to travel. He was a good man."

Even though Logan's father was dead, Sarah still felt a touch of jealousy, owing to the love and conviction in Logan's voice.

Logan toyed with the ends of the reins, then turned to her. "Have you ever wondered why your father disliked my family so much?"

"Often. I even asked my father once and he got angry enough that I didn't bother asking again. I always wondered why, though."

"I think it was guilt."

"Over the contract?"

Logan looked down at his hands as if weighing his words. After a long silence, he spoke. "My father asked Frank to be a character witness for him during the trial. My father always got along with his partner. To think that he would have killed him was ludicrous. Frank knew all this, knew how they got along, but when my father asked, Frank refused."

"Why?"

"My mother told me it was because Frank has harbored an attraction to my mother which she rebuffed. She claims that Frank was jealous of my father and was punishing her through him."

As he spoke, lights flicked on in Sarah's mind. Her father's unreasoning anger toward the Carletons, how his face would tighten up whenever anyone mentioned Donna's name. An old, forgotten conversation meandered into her mind…. Marilee commenting on a dress Donna had worn to church and how pretty she thought it was. This triggered a long lecture about the evils of putting our looks before our service to God that had always puzzled Sarah. Until now.

She suddenly felt as if she had lived a life of well-guarded innocence and misplaced trust. How could her father have done this?

"I'm sorry, Sarah," Logan said. "I shouldn't have told you. It's just, I've had such struggles with your father."

"Father. Such that he is. This evening, when your mom read out loud that Bible passage about a father having compassion on his children…" Sarah laughed out, but without humor. "I wonder if a lot of my struggles with God were because I pictured him as my father was. And as I mulled this over, I realized all along I've been trying to please the wrong father."

"And now?"

"Now, I want to get myself right with God. My father? I don't know about him anymore. Not after what he did. Not after what you just told me."

"He hasn't been much of a father to you, has he?"

She shook her head. "Not really. Of course, once I'm gone, I won't have to worry about him being a father at all. Won't have to see him regularly."

Logan's frown deepened and Sarah realized what she had just said. The implication that she was leaving.

Well, she was, wasn't she? Did she really want to stay here with a bitter man who couldn't even see her as his own daughter? A man who would harbor such jealousy and anger toward innocent people?

The horses stamped, jerking the sleigh forward a few inches.

"Something brought you back here, though, Sarah. Something made you return."

"That something was a note from my father." She turned to Logan. "Do you have any idea how hard it was for me growing up, wondering if I was ever going to be good enough for him? Wondering what I could possibly do to please him? I broke up with you because of him, Logan."

His expression was veiled. "I know… I guess I was hoping to hear that part of the reason you came back was that unfinished business with us."

Sarah held his gaze, her breath quickening. Her feelings for Logan were becoming stronger.

Stronger even than when she was a fresh-faced teenage girl.

Sure, Logan was on her mind when she made her plans. And now that she had found out the truth about him and Marilee, so much between them had shifted and changed.

But what was she supposed to do with it? She hadn't planned on reuniting with him. Yet, here she was, in his sleigh. She had kissed him and enjoyed it.

"I missed you."

"And now?"

She still had plans, didn't she? Could she change them? Because being with Logan meant she wouldn't be free of her father at all.

"I don't know, Logan. Can we just take things as they come? I think the horses are getting restless," Sarah said, trying to lighten the mood that had fallen over them.

"Yeah. I suppose." Logan gathered up the reins and clucked to the horses, and with a light jerk they were off. The steel runners of the sleigh hissed over the crisp snow, the moon shadow chasing Logan, Sarah and the horses down the trail toward Logan's home.

They pulled up to the barn, but before Sarah could get out of the sleigh, Logan stopped her. "Billy's team is playing this weekend here in town. Do you want to go?"

Sarah tested the thought, wondered how she would feel about watching the team and, even more important, what her family would say if she showed up with Logan.

"I'm thinking this could fall under the umbrella of taking things as they come," Logan said quietly. "And aren't you even a little bit curious about how the boys are doing?"

"I am actually. I'd love to go." The thought of spending time with Logan in public held a certain appeal.

"I'll pick you up on Saturday."

"And I'll be waiting."

Chapter Thirteen

The ringing of the phone cut off Logan's meandering thoughts. His heart jumped when he saw Westerveld on the call display, but by the time he answered he realized it was Dan Westerveld's name, not Frank's.

"Is this Logan Carleton?" the woman's voice on the other end of the phone asked.

"That's right." What would Dan's wife want with him?

"This is Tilly Westerveld. I may as well get to the point. I need to talk to you about Sarah and I'd prefer to do it face-to-face. Are you coming into town later this afternoon?"

Tilly sounded reasonable. Pleasant in fact. But Logan had no intention of discussing his relationship with Sarah, such that it was, with any Westerveld. "I'm busy all day. I can't."

"Can't or won't?"

She was astute; he'd give her that. "I'm sorry, Tilly. I really don't know what we'd have to talk about."

"It's important."

Logan hooked his foot around his chair and pulled it toward him. The serious tone of Tilly's voice told him this would be a sitting-down kind of conversation. He tried not to let a sense of déjà vu settle in. This was just Sarah's aunt.

"What do you need to say?" he said, prompting her.

"This is a bit hard, given your history, but Logan, I would like you to let Sarah go."

Logan's heart pushed against his chest. Not again.

"See, this is where we're already having a problem, Mrs. Westerveld," Logan said, aiming for a casual tone. "I don't have any kind of hold on Sarah. She's free to do as she pleases. As she always has been."

A momentary pause hung between them. It ended with a light sigh that sent a riffle of foreboding over his surface calm.

"Sarah has never been free to do as she pleases. Sarah has spent a large portion of her life trying to do as her father pleases. You know as well as I do that Sarah's relationship with her father is complicated. For the first time in her life, Frank is truly acknowledging Sarah as his daughter. You know how important this is to her. You know how she has longed for Frank to be a true father to her."

Logan thought of Frank's bizarre absolution of Sarah. Frank's twisted devotion to Logan's mother.

"Sarah has her own difficulties with her father that have nothing to do with me. I'm not keeping her away. She is choosing to stay away."

"Why would she do that?"

"Maybe you better ask her."

"Well, I'm talking to you now and all I'm asking is that you give her some space and time."

"I would think that the six years we spent apart is enough space and time."

"I know you care for Sarah," Tilly said, ignoring his outburst. "I know you cared for her six years ago and I'm sure you care for her now. Sarah hasn't been to see her father for some time. I hear you and Sarah have been spending time together. Maybe you could speak to her about her father. Encourage her to visit him again. Give her space so that she can establish her relationship with him. I know it would be good for her."

"I care for her too, Tilly. A lot. I always have. I will always do what is best for Sarah."

"I know, Logan. All we're asking is that you give her some time, and now I see I've taken up enough of yours. Give my greetings to your mother."

Logan ended the conversation and dropped the phone on the desk. He laced his fingers behind his head as he struggled to contain his own frustrated anger. With that last line, did Tilly know something about Frank's feelings toward his mother? Did any of the town know?

Logan leaned back in his chair, his thoughts slipping back to the conversation he'd overheard between Dan and Frank.

From the moment Logan had heard what Frank had done, or rather hadn't done, his anger had burned hard and hot. Buying the contract from Crane became more than a business decision: it became a way of getting in Frank Westerveld's face.

Now it seemed other emotions had worked themselves into the mix and were growing more important than his original reason.

Sarah.

Each time he saw her it was as if pieces of the six years that had separated them fell away. Old assumptions that had created such strong barriers had been brushed aside. Some of his overall anger had subsided.

He thought of the vague comment she had made the other day in the sleigh. She wasn't going to stay, of that he felt certain.

Was this worth it? Was she worth it? Surely he could find another girl who had a less complicated past, who would cause fewer problems for him.

Tilly's call underlined the fact that Sarah and her father had unfinished business. Whether Sarah wanted to admit it or not, Frank Westerveld was not going away.

And for Logan that meant if he got involved with Sarah, Frank came with.

Sarah dropped her bags of groceries on the kitchen table, the welcome warmth of the house easing away the chill from outside.

The bags held enough food for a week, as far ahead as Sarah had been planning lately. Inside one of the bags was a package of large trash bags to hold the stuff from Marilee's room.

She had talked herself carefully around the decision, weighing, considering. Logan's words kept resounding through her head.

He was right. The room was like a shrine to a person long gone. And today she was going to do something about it.

She pulled the package of trash bags out, holding it in her hand, a few second thoughts teasing the back of her mind. Should she? Did she have the right?

The doorbell broke into the moment. Logan? Already? She ran to the door, expectation hurrying her feet, and opened it, only to have her expectations doused.

Uncle Dan.

"Sarah, how are you doing?" he asked, his voice booming as he stepped into the house. "I haven't talked to you for a while."

Sarah closed the door behind him and held her hand out for his coat. "Do you want some coffee?"

"No, honey. I'm on my way home. I just came

back from the hospital though." He pulled his boots off and walked inside with the ease of someone familiar with the place. He glanced around and Sarah felt as if she should scurry through the house, tidying the magazines and books she had been reading. He gave her a wide smile. "Place looks lived in, Sarah. That's good. All you need now is some Christmas decorations. I think your dad has some in the attic."

Sarah hadn't considered decorations. That had always been Marilee's department.

Her uncle crossed his arms over his chest, tapping his index finger against his upper arm, as if considering what to say.

"So, you're not coaching basketball anymore? I was sorry to hear that."

Well, that was classic Uncle Dan. Get right down to the nitty-gritty. "That's okay, I've been keeping myself busy," she said carefully.

"Not busy visiting your father."

His blunt words plowed up the guilt Sarah had tried to bury. The past few days it had been pushing itself more and more to the surface and she knew she had to face it sometime. "Do you want to know why?" she said, taking an offensive tack, crossing her arms herself.

"I stopped by to find out."

"We had a fight." Those four concise words could not begin to cover the magnitude of what had happened to her, but she didn't know how else to proceed.

"What about?" His frown wrinkled his forehead, making him look more intimidating than he was.

"He said…he said he *forgave me*. For Marilee. As if it was all my fault." Sarah stopped there, before her voice faltered.

Dan's sigh echoed Sarah's own hurt and frustration. "Oh, honey. Tact has never been a Westerveld's strong point."

Then, to her surprise, he crossed the distance between them and pulled her into an awkward hug, his bulky coat pushing up against her check. He patted her on the head, then released her as if his duty was now done.

Sarah suppressed a sigh at her uncle's expression of the very thing he just said. "This is more than an untactful comment, Uncle Dan."

She paused, gathering her thoughts, trying to put them into a semicoherent sentence. "It's no secret to this family that Marilee was Dad's favorite. I'm not going to whine about that. But for my dad to make it sound as if I had anything to do with her death… something that he needed to forgive me for…" She lifted her hands in a gesture of surrender. "Not only hard to take, but hard to believe that still, after she's been gone six years, Marilee is still more important than me."

Dan's eyes held hers and the slow, disbelieving shake of his head made her feel less petty. Made her feel justified in staying away.

He walked into the living room and sank down on

a chair. Sarah followed him, sensing that she might be getting some answers.

"I wish you had told me this sooner, Sarah girl."

"What was I supposed to do? Phone up all my relatives and tell them what Dad had just told me? It was hard enough to take as it was."

"I'm sure it was." Dan pulled in a breath and pushed it out on a heavy sigh. "If it's any help, I think I know where this is coming from. We had a talk a while back, Frank and me. About you. About being a father. About some of the things he had done in his past. He was struggling in his faith life. In fact, he had been staying away from church. So when I asked him what the problem was, he said that he felt as if he had to atone for his sins and he didn't know where to start." Dan leaned forward, his eyes gentle with understanding. "I think, in some convoluted way, he thought that you were waiting to be forgiven."

As Sarah sorted through what her uncle was saying, she realized that if her father was feeling contrite, this might be exactly the kind of thing he would think. And maybe, just maybe, his misdirected forgiveness for Marilee was something she needed to hear, as well.

"I know he's not been the best father," Dan continued, "And I'm not excusing what he said. I'm sure that was hard for you to deal with, but Frank is a complicated man. And I think he has a few more secrets hiding behind that paralyzed face. He's not one to open up much, but I do know he's been struggling with what to say to you."

Sarah sat back in the chair, letting the words settle over her hurt and anger with her father.

"I know he's not been the best father, he's still your father. And you're still his daughter. And he misses you. More than you realize."

Sarah felt the gentle tug of his words, his unspoken expectations mix with the reality of Sarah's lifelong desire to be close to her father. "Okay. I'll go see him. But I won't do it alone." She thought of Logan and the hurt her father had caused him. "I want to take Logan Carleton with me."

"This Logan, you've been spending time with him again?"

"Yes. I have."

Dan nodded. "He means a lot to you?"

"Even more than he used to."

Dan nodded again.

"And you've got this great big 'however' waiting to come out," Sarah said.

Dan gave her a casual shrug. "We know that Logan doesn't have much love for Frank. So Tilly and I were thinking that maybe he was the reason you weren't visiting your father."

"If Logan doesn't have much love for my father, that's my dad's fault, not Logan's. He should never have done what he did to Logan's father."

"What happened to Jack Carleton during his trial

was wrong and I am sure that Frank has much to atone for."

"Like Dad canceling his contract?"

"I'm hoping to fix the contract." Dan gave Sarah a cautious smile. "Logan will be getting a contract with us. But I don't want you to tell him. That will be my job."

"He shouldn't have to buy it, Uncle Dan. Logan said that was the same contract that my dad took away from Logan's father."

"He won't have to buy it. Crane is going to be very disappointed to find out that we were thinking of canceling his contract anyway on grounds of misperformance."

Though Sarah knew enough to advocate for Logan, she didn't know what her uncle was talking about. But she suspected he and Logan did. And that was good enough for her.

"I'm glad."

Dan smiled. "Me, too. Logan has had a rough time the past few years. He was one miserable young pup when you left."

Sarah felt a curious stab of joy at the thought, and on its heels came her own misguided notion of what she thought Logan had done. With Marilee.

And right behind that came a flash of realization.

She had made mistakes, too. Just like her father had.

In the midst of these musings, Dan glanced at his watch, then pushed himself off the chair. "I gotta go. I promised Tilly that I'd be home on time. She wants to do some shopping before the game. Are you going to come?"

Sarah pulled herself back into the moment.

"Yeah, I hope to."

"It's really too bad you're not coaching the team," Dan grumbled, a heavy frown creasing his forehead.

"How are they doing?" Sarah couldn't help asking.

"Okay, but this Berube guy doesn't seem to know what he's doing."

Sarah laughed at her uncle's grumpy defense of her as she followed him to the foyer. Family. She did miss it. "I hear the boys have been winning, so that's good."

"Not because of him, that's for sure. That Billy kid is finally doing his job and turning into a leader."

Then the ringing of the phone broke into the question she was about to ask. She gave her uncle a quick hug as he put his boots on, nearly throwing him off balance. "I've got to answer the phone. Thanks for coming."

"I'm glad I did." Dan gave her another avuncular pat on her cheek, then left.

Sarah ran to the kitchen, grabbed the phone and hit Talk. She didn't have a chance to check who was calling and assumed it was another concerned relative, determined to reunite father and daughter.

"Sarah, how are you?" Logan's voice drifted into her ear.

Sarah leaned back against the kitchen counter with a sigh of contentment. "Hey, Logan. I'm doing okay."

"What are you up to?"

She smiled at the very ordinariness of his question. The kind of slow introduction to conversation between couples.

"Just puttering in the house. I'm probably going to clean up Marilee's room."

"By yourself? Why don't you get Janie or Dodie or someone else to help you?"

"They're busy."

"I was going to pick you up at three-thirty, but I can come earlier."

"That would be nice." She had steeled herself for doing the job alone, but at the same time she knew that sitting in the middle of all of Marilee's things would bring on loneliness and grief.

"I'll be by as soon as I can. I've gotta run now, but I'll see you later, right?"

"See you then." Her heart lifted up in her chest at the thought. They said goodbye and, as Sarah put the phone back on the cradle, she glanced over at her father's study, thought of the Bible he had lying on the desk.

She pushed the door open to her father's study, pausing a moment.

This room had always been his sanctuary even when her mother was still alive. His books were here, his computer. If she let go of the picture of her father in the hospital, she could easily picture him here, sitting at his desk, frowning as he worked on his computer. He didn't like computers, but he put up with them, recognizing what they were able to do for his business.

The book-lined room held a chill and Sarah shivered as she sat on the cool leather of the chair. Her father's Bible lay on the desk and with a sense of expectation, she pulled it toward her.

At one time daily readings of the Bible were as much a part of her life as breathing was. She had pushed that aside with the rest of her past, when she left, disillusioned and heartsick.

Since coming back, her perception of the past had shifted. She had been freed from the guilt that had kept her and God apart.

It had taken coming back to realize that Marilee's death was not her fault. And it had taken talking to Logan to put Marilee's actions of that night in the right light.

She had been wrong about Logan. So wrong.

Sarah flipped open the Bible and paged through it. Books, word, phrases, all as familiar to her as the lines on her hand, flowed through her fingers.

She skipped past Numbers, Deuteronomy—books her father resolutely plowed through with his usual Westerveld stubbornness and thoroughness. Her eyes skimmed familiar passages and then she stopped.

Psalm 103. The same Psalm Donna had read. And now, she read it again.

"'Praise the Lord, O my soul; all my inmost being praise His holy name. Praise the Lord O my soul and forget not all His benefits....'" she paused, letting the memory of the words sink in. This Psalm was often read after communion and it brought Sarah back to a time when they were Sarah and her mother, Frank and Marilee. A complete family. She read on. "'He does not treat us as our sins deserve... as far as the east is from the west, so far has He removed our transgressions from us. As a father has compassion on his children, so the Lord has compassion on those who fear Him.'"

He doesn't deserve you.

Logan's words sifted through her thoughts. Maybe not, Sarah thought as the words from the Psalm settled in her soul, but *I have not been a faithful daughter to God, either. I don't deserve God's love. God loves me like a father, a perfect father and I am not worthy of that love. I have come to wrong conclusions, judged and assumed. I have put many things ahead of God—my father, basketball, my career. And, at one time, Logan. When have I ever put God first?*

She felt a stirring in her soul as the reality of her thoughts came home.

"'...but from everlasting to everlasting the Lord's love is with those who fear Him...'"

Sarah read on to the next Psalm, her soul thirsting for the solace and comfort she found in words extolling God's creation.

This world was God's and she'd been walking through it so focused on so many other things and neglecting her perfect, heavenly Father who wanted to give what she needed most.

She ran her fingers over the Bible passage again as two words rose up as a whisper in her mind, circling, waiting for expression.

"Forgive me," she said aloud. "Father, forgive."

She laid her head in her hands and let her heavenly Father's perfect love and perfect forgiveness wash over her.

Then she read on, drawing nourishment, strength, forgiveness and love from the Father she'd neglected so long.

A while later, she set the Bible aside, pushed herself away from the desk and walked upstairs.

She stopped in front of the door to Marilee's room.

The wrong daughter died.

I forgive you for Marilee.

Her father had it wrong, but hadn't she also made big mistakes? Hadn't she also judged Logan wrongly? Who didn't err in this world?

The past was too much a part of the present. She needed to narrow its hold. Sarah slowly opened the door to Marilee's room, stepped inside and flicked on the light. She walked to the chair where Marilee's shirt hung like a beacon and gently drew it off the back. She held it a moment, catching the vaguest scent of Marilee.

She smiled, and then she began.

The time passed in a blur as she bagged clothes and memories. The dress from Marilee's eighth-grade Christmas pageant, her neat and respectable school clothes and, as Sarah dug further back into the cupboard, the alternate ones that Marilee would change into at school. Each outfit brought a flood of recollections and tears. But she kept on, sometimes wiping her eyes with the very clothes Marilee had once worn. Now and again she would pause over an item, allowing herself time for a memory. Then she would put it in its rightful place on one of the piles.

She pulled a pair of pants that lay haphazardly on the bottom of the closet and pain clutched at her again. Sarah had bought these pants and Marilee had borrowed them, later telling her they'd been lost. Sarah remembered being angry with Marilee as much because she hadn't returned the pants as the fact that there had been twenty dollars in one of the pockets.

Sisters, Sarah thought, allowing herself a smile. Just out of curiosity, Sarah dug her hands in the pockets. Nope. No twenty. *Sisters.*

The chimes of the doorbell rolled into the room and Sarah's heart jumped. Logan was here.

She dropped the blue jeans and ran downstairs.

Since Uncle Dan had left, it had started to snow, dusting the shoulders of Logan's coat, glistening in his hair and glinting off his thick eyelashes. He looked healthy, alive and real. She wanted to hug him but restrained herself.

"Come in," she said, standing aside as he stepped into the foyer. "I got started already."

"You didn't want to wait?"

"I couldn't anymore." She bit her lip to stop the faint tremble in her voice then quickly took his coat.

He either didn't notice her wobbly emotions or was kind enough to disregard them. Instead he looked around, a frown pinching his eyebrows together.

"Where's your Christmas decorations?"

"Not you, too." She hung his coat in the hallway closet, right beside one of her father's.

"What do you mean?"

"My uncle Dan stopped by. Said the same thing."

Logan shook his head as he glanced around the house. "You don't have one twinkly light or piece of tinsel up." He toed his boots off then took a few steps, looking into the living room. "Not even a tree?"

"I'm out of practice." Sarah shrugged. "Haven't been much for Christmas in the past few years."

"Fair enough." He gave her a concerned look. "Well, I came to help you. Lead the way."

As Logan followed Sarah up the carpeted stairs, her mind returned to a time when having him in her house seemed an improbable dream. Yet, here he was.

He followed her into the room, his presence immediately banishing the ghosts, the memories and the emptiness. "Where do I start?"

"You can put those clothes in bags while I finish up in the closet."

As they worked, his practical attitude reduced the memories to items that needed to be dealt with, which helped keep her from feeling overwhelmed.

Half an hour later, five green garbage bags perched in the center of the room. Four held clothes destined for the thrift store in town and the fifth was stuffed with old papers and other trash. Sarah had arranged some mementos of her sister on a now-tidy desk. A few pictures of Marilee and Sarah, a figurine their father had given each of the girls, an award, and an assortment of the precious few books Marilee liked reading.

In spite of Marilee's constant mocking of people who kept diaries, Sarah had hoped she might stumble upon a book with some of Marilee's recorded thoughts. But other than the obligatory journals for school that Sarah had saved, nothing.

"I'll take these downstairs," Logan said, picking up the bags.

As Logan hauled out the bags Sarah went through her sister's desk. She found a cardboard box holding some jewelry. Inside, nestled in the tangle of necklaces, earrings and paper clips lay a friendship bracelet. Alicia Mays, Marilee's best friend, had been teaching Marilee how to make them. Sarah tucked it in her pocket. Maybe Alicia would appreciate getting it back.

She experienced a momentary letdown as the last

drawer revealed only a stash of forbidden teen style magazines. She put these in another bag.

Sarah pushed herself to her feet, turning a slow circle, letting the change settle. Stripped of Marilee's essence, the room suddenly looked sterile. Cold. A sliver of regret lanced her as she wondered about her father's reaction to this. Would he even be coming home to see what she had done?

Sarah pushed that thought aside. She couldn't dwell on the idea that her father might not improve enough to live on his own. Because if he didn't, she would have to stay around long enough to make a decision about his care. To make plans that meant staying here.

Could she? Should she?

Logan came back upstairs and together they finished cleaning out the desk. When they were done, Sarah gave the room one last look, then felt the living warmth of Logan's hand on her shoulder.

"Goodbye, Marilee," she whispered, closing the door. She paused a moment, as if waiting for an echo of farewell.

Then she and Logan left.

Chapter Fourteen

He shouldn't feel this nervous. Coming to the basketball game had been his idea. But now that they were here, he thought of her aunt Tilly, and cousin Ethan, and Aunt Dot, and Uncle Morris and who-knows-what other Westervelds that might want to attend the game and maybe have negative thoughts about them being together.

He glanced over at Sarah, surprised when she took his hand. Her smile gave him the encouragement he needed.

"So you still okay with this?" he asked.

"It will be interesting to watch the game from a spectator's point of view. And to wonder if he can manage those boys better than me."

The boys were warming up, basketballs bouncing, flying, shouts of support echoing in the gym as Logan and Sarah walked, hand in hand along the bleachers. Logan clutched her hand just a bit tighter as they passed the players bench. Alton Berube glanced up at Sarah and Logan as they passed by. His smile grew huge.

"Hey, Sarah. Did you get my message?" he called out.

"No." Sarah glanced at Logan who shrugged. He had no idea what that was all about.

"I need to talk to you. The boys said they wanted to try some play called Pop-Tart? I can't find it in the playbook."

"I made it up and didn't write it down, I guess."

"Could you go over it with me?"

"Now?"

"Or when you have time." Alton shifted his weight, looking uncomfortable. "Unless it's confidential. I mean, I understand."

"I'll go over it with you after the game."

"Good. Good." He smiled at her, relief etched all over his face. "From what they told me it sounds like it could be effective."

Logan glanced around as Sarah talked with Alton. His eyes ticked over the Westerveld family, taking over the bleachers in one corner of the gym. To a person they were watching him and Sarah.

He felt a flicker of despair. They weren't going away. They were as much a part of Riverbend as the land and the river that bent it. Did he really think he and Sarah stood a chance?

One day at a time, he reminded himself. He and Sarah were simply finishing what they had started all those years ago. Yet as he glanced over at her, he knew, for himself, that she had become even more important to him now than she had been back then.

She comes with so much stuff. Their history. Her family.

Her father.

Logan's resolve faltered.

Tilly's phone call was a vivid reminder that Sarah's relationship with her father would still affect their own relationship.

He wasn't sure where things were going, wasn't even sure what Sarah had planned. Though he had fought it initially, lately it seemed he and Sarah had effortlessly slid into a newer, better place. But what he had created in his head had been a momentary bubble of refuge.

Sooner or later life was going to intrude. Her father. His father.

"Maybe I'll stop by practice on Tuesday," Sarah said to Alton. She glanced Logan's way and gave him a radiant smile as she took his hand. "Sorry. Alton just needed some advice."

"Of course he did." He smiled as he squeezed her hand, then glanced around the gym, affecting a nonchalant air. "Where should we sit?"

"How about your usual spot? Close enough to the players bench that the coach can see you glowering at her, I mean him, yet far enough away that she, I mean he, can't throw a basketball at you."

Her teasing smile lifted his heart, and he lifted one eyebrow in response. "Very funny."

They settled on the bench and a few minutes later the boys lined up to play. As the game started, Sarah leaned forward, her hands on her knees, her eyes darting from their team to the opposition, as if delving for weaknesses.

But this evening, Logan's entire attention was on the beautiful woman beside him, her blue eyes bright, her cheeks flushed, her hands alternately clenched into fists or thrown into the air in disgust as the referee made what she thought were bad calls.

Now and again he glanced at Alton Berube, but he never saw on that man's face the love of the game that he saw in Sarah even in the bleachers.

What had he been thinking to take this away from her? How could he have been so selfish? Sure he had been thinking of his brother and what Billy needed and sure Sarah had survived this loss. But as he watched her now he realized that he had come between her and this job.

He recalled Tilly Westerveld's conversation with him. He wasn't coming between her and her father now, but he wasn't encouraging her to maintain that relationship.

But he couldn't bring her father into his life. Not yet. Not now. He and Sarah were just beginning to breathe new energy into a relationship that had haunted him ever since they met.

"Oh c'mon. Get going, guys," Sarah called out,

pulling him back to the game. She jumped to her feet, cheering as the Voyageurs scored another basket.

She turned to him and grabbed his hands, oblivious to the fact that her family was watching. "They're doing great, aren't they?" she exclaimed, her face flushed, her eyes bright.

Maybe it was her compelling exuberance, maybe it was how her eyes sparkled with infectious glee, maybe it was simply sheer fear of losing the moment—Logan bent over and kissed her.

In public, in front of a large portion of the population of Riverbend. And to his immense surprise and joy, Sarah threw her arms around him and kissed him back.

"Okay, much as I hate to admit it, that was a great game," Sarah said, slipping her jacket back on. Somehow in the heat of the game she had tossed it off. "Didn't you think it was good?" she asked Logan, who had been strangely quiet the last part of the game.

Sure, it had turned into a bit of a nail-biter and Alton had made some calls she wouldn't have, but they had won.

"I think, if you were coaching, they would have done better," Logan said quietly.

His words were a gentle gift that boosted her self-confidence just enough that she dared to joke about it. "Well, we *know* that."

He caught her hands and, as the warmth of his

fingers enveloped hers, a tingle of awareness flickered up her spine. Logan Carleton was holding her hands in a public place. In the very gym where they had first met.

On top of his kiss, this felt so right. So sure.

Did she dare let her wishes take her further? Did she dare dream that more of a relationship might come of this? She looked up into his dark eyes so intent on her and felt her pulse beating against her temples as possibilities danced around them, insulating them from the noise of the people leaving the gym.

"Hey, Sarah."

Sarah dragged her attention away from Logan but didn't let go of his hand and, with a sense of inevitability, turned to see who wanted her. But the person calling her was not a relative. It was Alicia, Marilee's good friend.

Almost as bad, Sarah thought.

"I want to go congratulate Billy," Logan murmured.

Sarah didn't blame his defection. Alicia was a sweet person, but once captured, it was hard to release oneself from the inevitable avalanche of words that would pour from her.

"I've been meaning to call you and talk. It's been ages and you haven't been around much, not that I blame you, but hey, this is your hometown and you know, you gotta come back once in a while if only to see what you haven't been missing. Of course—" while she talked, Alicia threw a meaningful glance

Logan's way "—I'm surprised, for that one's sake, you didn't come home more often."

As she chatted, Sarah slipped her hands in her pockets and then found a way to take control of the conversation.

She waited for an infinitesimal pause on Alicia's part and dove in. "I found this in Marilee's dresser when I cleaned out her room," she said, pulling out the friendship bracelet. "I think you must have made it for her."

Alicia took the bracelet and for a moment her eyes glistened. "I helped her make it."

She handed it back as she gave Sarah a slow, sad smile. "Actually she had plans to give it to Logan, to give to you. The night she died."

"What?"

"Yeah. I remember her saying that one way or another she was going to figure out how to get you two together again, so she was going to meet Logan at that party."

Sarah heard the words but couldn't seem to string them in any coherent order. "She wrote me a note that night. Something about if I didn't want Logan…" She stopped, trying to remember.

"I remember her writing that note. She was in a hurry because that Setterfeld boy was coming to pick her up to go to that party."

"You were over that night? I don't remember."

Alicia's eyes held a glimmer of sorrow. "Yeah. Last time I saw her alive. We snuck out of the house.

Marilee didn't want your dad to know what she was up to. Said he'd be fuming mad if he found out she was trying to get you two together again. She wrote that note out so fast, I said I'd be surprised if it was readable, but, you know Marilee, she said you would know what it was about. I just wished she wouldn't have decided to get hammered at that party. Things would have turned out so different."

Sarah fingered the friendship bracelet, clinging to the reality of it as she sorted through what Alicia was saying.

Marilee had tried to get her and Logan together. How could she have misread that note so completely?

Misconception upon misconception.

What had she done? She glanced over at Logan and she felt the relentless onslaught of misunderstandings that had been created by her perception of her sister, her lack of trust in Logan, her lack of self-confidence and her overwhelming desire to please her father.

She clutched the bracelet and pressed her lips against the flutter of sorrow working its way up her throat. "Thanks, Alicia. I really appreciate you telling me this."

And before Alicia could say another word, Sarah left. She had much to think about. Much to rediscover.

Her sister had tried to get her and Logan together. Sarah almost stumbled as another wave of sorrow and regret washed over her. She had ruthlessly cleaned out her sister's room, had tried to purge her life of memories.

But now, she had a new one, a good one to take their place.

Logan was still talking to Billy by the time she joined them. Billy gave her a curt nod. "Hey, Miss Westerveld. You coming back to help Mr. Berube?"

Still bemused by what she had just discovered, Sarah could only shake her head.

"'Cause he said you were coming to practice." Billy sighed. "You should come. I mean, Mr. B's okay, but—" Billy lifted one shoulder in an exaggerated shrug "—he doesn't know the game like you do."

His words settled past her confused emotions. "Really?"

"Yeah. The plays he wants us to do are so basic the other teams can anticipate every move we make. Makes it brutal to try and score on them."

"And this matters to you because..." she couldn't help add, grabbing onto the very orneriness of Billy to ground her back in reality.

Billy just rolled his eyes. "C'mon, Miss Westerveld. I know I was a jerk, but hey, I want to win, too. Logan kind of made things clear to me and Nelli is cool with me going to college. So yeah, I want to win." He leaned forward, as if his sheer height and size would intimidate her into agreeing. "Whaddya say? You gonna help him? I know the other guys would like you to come back."

"Even though I'm *only* a girl?" Sarah couldn't resist the gibe.

Billy had the grace to look sheepish. "Yeah, well. You're still better than Berube."

"It depends on what the parents say."

"Derek was plenty ticked at his mom for what she pulled off." Billy slid Logan a quick glance as if including his brother in this censure.

Oh, the fickleness of youth.

"We'll see." She gave Billy a polite smile, then tucked her arm inside his brother's and gave Logan a proprietary tug. "And now, we have to go." They didn't, but she had much to think about and she wanted to have Logan to herself. She wanted to tell him what Alicia had just told him. Wanted to fix what had been broken between them all these years.

Billy's eyebrows lifted a fraction, then his mouth curved in a smirk. "Well, ain't that a picture." And with that eloquent comment, he left to join his teammates.

Logan looked down at her, covering his hand with hers. His eyes smoldered. "So, where is it we have to go?"

"Sarah. There you are."

She suppressed a groan as her relatives descended on her en masse. She felt suddenly torn. Most of her wanted to be with Logan, to discover where this relationship, if she dared call it that, might be going. Things were still so uncertain between them and she wasn't sure herself.

And yet, this was her family. The people she loved.

"You coming with us?" Janie touched Sarah's arm, as if laying a small claim on her. "We're going to celebrate at Cal's."

Sarah glanced at Logan, hoping he would say he would come with them, hoping she wouldn't have to choose between him and her family.

And yet, circling that thought was another hope that he would want to be alone with her.

"Actually, Logan and I have other plans," Sarah said, making her choice.

Janie sent Sarah a frown but Sarah just smiled. "Some other time maybe," she said, letting Logan pull her away from her relatives.

Ten minutes later they were driving down a country road and Sarah had no idea where they were going but only knew that she and Logan were alone again, this time in a place that held no old memories and regrets.

He pulled off the road into a narrow lane, his truck fishtailing in the snow, his headlights stabbing the darkness ahead of them. Snow flew up, sparkling in the headlights and then they came to a stop.

"Aha," Sarah said, recognizing the place. "The lookout point. I *love* the view from this place."

Logan's face glowed a faint green in the reflected light of the dashboard of his truck. The serious expression on his face made her heart beat just a little faster.

She looked at him again, studying the planes of his face, cast into sharp relief in the half-light. His deep-set eyes glowed and she felt herself falling in love with this man all over again.

He traced a gentle circle with his finger on the backs of her hands, then looked up at her with those deep, secretive eyes. Eyes that had haunted her dreams. Eyes that she had yearned for and hurt for. All because of a mistake.

She wanted to tell him about Marilee, but she waited.

A quiet, insistent voice pushed at the back of her mind as, in spite of the moment, she thought of her father. She had to say it and sooner or later they had to deal with it. Uncle Dan was right. She couldn't ignore her father forever. In spite of all the things he had done wrong, he was still a part of her life.

In the past few days she had learned some valuable lessons about who and what to put first in her life. Her priorities had shifted and been rearranged.

And she realized that she wanted Logan in her life.

But she also wanted her father.

Logan remained quiet, so she took a chance to move into this new place in her life. With Logan.

"I was wondering if you would come with me. To visit my dad."

"What about what he said to you. About Marilee?" he said, continuing to trace a circle on the back of her hand.

"I know what he did was wrong, and he hurt me badly, but we all sin. We all make mistakes that have repercussions. Like I did thinking you were with Marilee, when you weren't."

"Sarah, that wasn't your fault…"

"No, but in a way I was involved. You know what Alicia told me? That Marilee had snuck out to see you so she could convince you that we should be together." Her mind slipped back to Marilee's room and the myriad of memories she had pushed into bags and boxes. "I had misjudged her, too. Misjudged you. I'm just as sinful. Just as stubborn. Had just as much unforgiving anger. I could have phoned you, asked you, but I didn't. I'm sure my dad was hurting, too."

"And now you're making excuses for him again?" Logan's question came out as more of a growl than a query. His anger set her back.

"Logan, please don't think that I'm falling back into the same patterns. I've changed. My dad doesn't have power over me anymore. But I can't change the fact that he is still my father. I know what he did to your family was wrong and I'm sure you still have a lot to deal with. But he's not going away and he is still in my life. That's why I want you to come with me. I want to start over. And I want to start over right. I want to face him with you at my side."

"I'm sorry, Sarah. I can't go with you." His voice held a note of finality that Sarah sensed was futile to argue with.

"Ever?"

He shrugged. "Someday, maybe, but not yet." She looked at Logan, trying to put herself in his place, trying to understand. Her father had hurt Logan's family and even though she might think Logan should forgive her father, the only forgiveness that was hers to grant was hers to her father. Logan had to come to that place on his own.

Now she had to make a decision. But this time, this time she was going to follow her heart, instead of expectations from her father and her family.

"Okay. I understand," Sarah said, her voice quiet. "He hurt your family badly and that will take some time to get over."

"Sarah, I need you to understand…"

She held her hand up, forestalling him. "Logan, I do understand. And I know that what he did was wrong. So I want you to know that I'm standing beside you in this." She took a deep breath and sent up a prayer for wisdom. "I know that my father needs me, but I sense that you need me, too. And until you're ready to see him, I want you to know that I choose you. I choose you over my father. You are more important to me than he is right now." She banished all the pleas that her family, her uncles and aunts and cousins with their expectations, would make. She had made up her mind.

Logan sighed, raised her hands to his mouth and brushed a kiss over her knuckles. "Thank you." His voice was quiet, almost reverential.

"I know he caused a lot of pain…" She stopped

there. Enough. They didn't need to talk about Frank. And though in her heart she had hoped that she and Logan could go together, she wanted him to know that she was willing to wait.

"I don't think you should avoid him completely," Logan said. He stroked the back of her hand with his thumb. "But I can't come with you."

She shook her head. "Not until you're ready to come with me."

Though it seemed they were caught in the same tensions when they dated the first time, she knew they had actually come to a different place. It would simply take time.

She cut off the thread of despair that started to wind itself around her heart. Time. She had to give him the time he needed.

And how long would that be?

"Could you take me home, please?" she asked.

They drove in silence and, when he stopped in front of the house, he turned to her. "Sarah, I'm sorry."

She paused, just a moment, wishing she had the right words to bridge this shadowy gap between them. "I am, too. But I am serious, Logan. You come first in my life."

He kissed her again, but, even as he drew away, she sensed the specter of her father still hovered between them.

Chapter Fifteen

Logan sat back in his office chair, staring sightlessly out the window, rehashing what he and Sarah had talked about, going over and over in his head what he should have said, what he should have done, but each time he came back to this same point: he should be rejoicing. She had chosen him over her father.

When she had spoken the words that, he was sure, came at a cost to her, he had felt a surge of happiness that had overwhelmed his practical self.

When he had come back down, the reality of what she had done struck him. She had sacrificed, or at least put on hold, a relationship with her father.

A light knock on the door pulled him out of his thoughts. His mother poked her head inside.

"You ready to go?"

Logan shook his head and sat forward, looking down at the checkbook he'd had open for the past hour but done nothing with.

"I don't think I'll come to church with you this morning. I've got some bookkeeping to catch up on."

"And *that's* your excuse?" Donna asked, stepping a little farther into the office.

He just nodded.

"Wouldn't have anything to do with why you came roaring into the yard last night and slammed the door hard enough that you shook the house?"

"Sorry. The wind must have caught it."

"A whole pile of hot air must have caught it. Did you and Sarah have a fight?"

He shrugged her question aside. They hadn't exactly had a fight, but it hadn't been the romantic moment he had anticipated it would be.

"I'm not dumb," she continued, accurately reading his stunned expression. "You leave to get Sarah, all smiley and happy. Billy says you leave the gym after the game all smiley and happy. With Sarah. You come home all grumpy. Don't have to be brilliant to figure out that something went wrong."

Logan ran his hands through his hair and clutched the back of his neck in frustration. "She asked me to come with her to visit Frank."

"Well, that would be difficult. But not impossible."

Logan thought of another conversation he'd had with his mother in this same room when she told him the reason for Frank's ongoing animosity. How she was tired of being angry herself.

"Can you forgive Frank for what happened?"

Donna leaned back against the door. "It's hard. But what I have been struggling to do is separate the man from the actions. Frank did not kill your father. Frank made a bad judgment call that had long-lasting repercussions. On top of that he was a lonely man struggling with some misdirected anger. But I don't think his life has been easy, either. He buried a wife. And, like I told you, burying a child has got to be one of the most heartrending things a father has to handle. And then to have his other daughter move across the country... I feel sorry for him. And though pity is maybe not the best reason to forgive someone, I think it's a good place to start. For my sake as well as his."

"So you can say you forgive him?"

Donna looked off into the distance, then smiled. "Yes. I think I can. And knowing that makes me really free." She directed her attention to Logan. "By forgiving him I feel like I've stopped letting him have control over me and over my emotions. Holding a grudge, being angry at what he did gives him power over me. I was tired of that, as well."

"He told Sarah, when Marilee died, that the wrong daughter died. How can a father say that? How could he possibly even think that?"

"A grieving man might conceivably say the wrong thing...."

"If it was just that." He rocked in his chair, his agitation growing. "He wanted her to come back so he could tell her that he forgave her. For what happened to Marilee. As if it was her fault. What kind of father is he?"

Donna said nothing.

"What kind of father does that, Mom?"

Donna held his gaze, an enigmatic smile teasing her mouth. "You've spent a lot of time and energy trying to imagine restitution for what Frank did to your father, haven't you?"

Logan nodded at his mother's comment, wondering where she was going.

"Lately, I'm surprised how quickly that anger has been superceded by what you see as injustice for Sarah."

"She wants to go to forgive him. But he doesn't deserve her."

"Do you feel she's going back to the person she was?"

"No. She told me that she felt she had spent too much time trying to please the wrong father."

"So she's found her way through this mess of history and brokenness then."

Logan nodded his head. "When she asked me to come with her to see him and I said no, she told me that she chose me over him. That until I was ready to see him, she wasn't going to see him." His smile held an edge of melancholy.

"You love her, don't you?"

Logan sank back in his chair, a long, slow sigh drifting out of him. "Yes, Mom. I do."

"Does she know?"

"How am I supposed to tell her with her father still hovering between us?"

"Then maybe you better do something about *that,* Logan. She asked you to come with her and you chose not to. She chose you over her father. Now I'm going to say that if you really care about her, you'll put her needs first."

"I am. I have, but I don't trust her dad. I don't trust him to care for her and love her the way she should be loved. I don't trust him to not break her heart repeatedly." He felt he had a strong foundation on which to build that lack of trust.

Donna smiled. "You are a good man, Logan Carleton. And if that's how you feel, then maybe it's even more important to let this man into your life. So you can keep an eye on him."

Logan let her words settle over his agitation, seeing the practical sense in it.

"I'm not sure she is going to stay."

"Well, I've seen the way she looks at you and, from what you've said, I'm pretty sure that even if she does decide she doesn't want to stay I'm sure you're not going to let her go as easily as you did the first time." Donna's eyed probed his as if driving home the truth of what she had just said.

She walked over to his desk, picked up his Bible and started flipping through it. She seemed to find what she was looking for, and turned the book back to him, open.

"You might want to read this and then decide

whether you can forgive Frank or not." Donna gave her son another smile. "You're a good man, Logan. And I'm sure you'll do the right thing."

After he heard the outside door close, he leaned over the Bible and started reading what she had pointed out.

"Then Peter came to Jesus and asked, 'Lord, how many times shall I forgive my brother when he sins against me? Up to seven times?' Jesus answered, 'I tell you, not seven times, but seventy-seven times.'"

Logan continued to read the story of a king who wanted to settle accounts with his servants and of the large debt that one owed him. The servant pleaded for mercy and the king forgave him. But then the servant went out and found a man who owed him far less than what the servant had owed the king. But he had no mercy. When the king found out he was furious and punished the servant.

"'This is how my heavenly Father will treat each of you unless you forgive your brother from your heart.'"

Logan knew the story. Had heard it often growing up. He had never thought it applied to him personally.

Until now. How much hadn't God forgiven him? All the anger and bitterness he had stored up and still held. All the sins he had committed against other people and, worse, against God Himself.

How could he possibly presume to withhold forgiveness from anyone else?

And yet could he really let go that easily?

If he wanted Sarah, if he wanted peace with a God who had forgiven him, he had to. Simple as that.

Logan closed his eyes, fought his second thoughts and let his prayer ascend, hoping that the emotion would follow the action. "Forgive me, Lord. Forgive my lack of forgiveness."

He prayed for strength and wisdom. And he prayed for courage. He kept praying until he felt he was as close to ready as he was going to get.

He picked up the phone and called Sarah's cell phone. She answered it on the second ring.

"Hey there," she said, sounding breathless. "I missed you in church."

Logan glanced at the Bible still lying open on the desk beside him. "I had some thinking to do. And some praying." He paused, sent up a prayer for strength, then said, "I'd like to come with you. To see your dad."

"When?"

"Today?"

Silence. Had he misread her last night?

"Are you sure you want to do this?"

"I need to do this. I'll meet you at three o'clock inside, by the reception desk."

Sarah pulled her jacket closer as she hurried down the snow-covered sidewalk to the hospital entrance. A chilly wind had sprung up, snatching away what precious warmth she had soaked up in her car. The snow squeaked under her feet, underlining how cold it was.

But she didn't care. Nothing mattered. She and Logan were going to finish this chapter in their life and then move on. Where to, she wasn't sure yet. But one thing she knew, right now Logan was the most important person in her life.

A few more steps and she was out of the wind. She stamped her feet, getting rid of the snow that stuck to her boots, then scooted inside the warmth of the hospital. The foyer was a jumble of boots of every size and melting snow and Sarah had to do some fancy footwork to get her boots off and shoes on without getting her feet wet.

The woman at the reception desk greeted her with a smile. Sarah wasn't even aware that she was smiling, as well.

She glanced around the room. No dark head, no tall figure slouching in a chair. A quick peek at her watch showed her that she was only five minutes late.

She walked toward the doors, glanced out over the parking lot beside the hospital, then back to the reception area. None of the magazines held her interest, but she picked one up anyway and flipped through it, the picture of nonchalance.

Ten minutes later still no Logan.

Had she missed him? Impossible. Every time the door opened, sending in a rush of cold air, she had looked up. She had walked to the door any number of times; there was no way he could have walked past her.

So where was he? Had he changed his mind? Had second thoughts?

The questions spun and danced, teasing and taunting.

Should she worry?

Well, she was at the hospital. Surely if something had happened, she would be one of the first to know.

She dug in her purse for her cell phone, then realized she had left it at home, so she called from a pay phone but Logan wasn't answering.

She pushed herself up from her chair, the reality of the situation hitting her like a slap. Logan wasn't coming. She didn't know if she should be sad or angry or disheartened or a mixture of all three.

She glanced down the hallway toward her father's ward. She had made a promise to Logan, but she figured that the circumstances had changed. She was here now; she should go see her father.

But the closer she got to his room, however, the slower her steps became. Could she do this after what she had promised to Logan? Were her father and family's wishes still controlling her?

She became aware of music coming from a room beside her father's. A Christmas carol.

"O come, O come Emmanuel, and ransom captive Israel, that mourns in lonely exile here, until the Son of God appear."

She stopped, letting the song flow over her questions and doubts. If she didn't forgive her father and find atonement with him, she was just like the Israelites. Captive. And in this Christmas season she was reminded that Christ came to give freedom to the captives. Just as she had experienced that day in her father's room when she read to him from Isaiah.

Freedom.

She had been in bondage to her father and her feelings about him for too long. She needed to move on to a different relationship with him.

And while she had desperately hoped Logan would be with her to give her moral support, to stand beside her, maybe it was better to do this on her own.

Her step faltered when she thought of Logan.

Please help me, Lord, she prayed. *Help me to care for Logan in the right way. As first of all your child and second of all....* She didn't know what to put there.

She knew she had come to a place of forgiveness for what her father had done to her. What he had done to Logan's father and Logan's family was not hers to forgive.

A lab tech pushed a rattling cart past her. A nurse hurried in the other direction. Another carol played from the other room. *Joy to the World.*

She pressed her hand to her stomach to still her shaking nerves. *Help me, Lord,* she prayed. *Help me to say the right thing. Help me not to be weak, but help me to love him. And thank You for Your love for me. Thank You that You are my perfect Father.*

One more long, slow breath and she was ready.

But as she came nearer his room, she heard a voice coming from inside. A deep voice. She stopped just outside the room, puzzled as to who it would be.

"…that she still cares about you in spite of what you said to her is a miracle."

Her heart thundered in her chest.

Logan? Here?

Her feet wouldn't move. Her legs seized up.

Had he slipped past her?

Then her heart sang. Logan was here. Talking to her father. On his own.

"…I want you to know that I don't deserve her," he was saying, his voice ringing with conviction. "But you know, you don't deserve her, either. She has a deep and pure love that I don't understand. I'm trying because I know that you are not going out of her life. But I want you to know that I'm not going out of her life, either. I'm here. For as long as she needs me, or wants me, I'm here. I love her, Frank. I love her with all my heart."

Sarah's breath trembled in her throat. She was running out of air. Was he really saying those precious words? To her father?

"…I need to forgive you, because for now, this is the only way I'm going to be able to be a part of Sarah's life. You've hurt a lot of people and I'm still learning to forgive you for my father and my mother. I have to confess I still struggle with bitterness over that, but I can't presume to withhold forgiveness when God has forgiven me so much himself."

As he spoke his words of absolution, the sorrow and hurt she had been carrying all night slipped away.

"But I may as well be honest," Logan continued. "I'm struggling even harder with forgiving you for what you did to Sarah. What you said to her. You hurt someone I love dearly."

"I...love her, too," Sarah heard her father say.

Go inside, a voice urged her. Move.

But she felt frozen and unsure she should intrude on this moment.

"Then show her. For her sake. And mine."

Sarah finally felt her legs. Finally could force her paralyzed feet to move. She pushed herself away from the wall and walked into the room.

Her father sat in a wheelchair beside his bed, Logan in an armchair facing him. Logan leaned forward, his elbows resting on his knees, his hands clasped between them.

He hadn't shaved. His tumbled hair looked as if he had been running his fingers through it.

And as he turned to see who was coming into the room, his dark eyes looked as if he hadn't slept in days.

And he looked fantastic.

He loves me, Sarah thought, the words singing through her with all the promise of a Christmas carol.

"Sarah." Her name burst from him as he got to his

feet. Logan glanced from her to his father, a frown creasing his forehead. "What did you…"

"I love you, too," she said quietly. It was all she could say. It was all she needed to say.

Logan swallowed the distance between them with two strides and dragged her into his arms. His one hand held her head, his other arm wrapped all the way around her, holding her tight, close. Safe and secure.

"Sarah, oh, Sarah," he murmured into her hair. "I tried to call you to tell you that I needed to talk to your father on my own, but you weren't answering."

He pulled back just enough to look into her eyes, his own scanning her features as if seeing them for the first time.

"I love you," he whispered, then, in front of her father, he bent over and kissed her mouth, her cheeks, each eyelid, her hair.

Then he hugged her again.

Chapter Sixteen

Logan stood back as Sarah walked over to her father, leaned over and gave him a careful hug.

Frank's one hand came up and he caught her around her neck, his awkward response.

When Logan had first walked into this room the change in Frank Westerveld had set him back on his heels. The once proud face hung slack on one side. One eyelid drooped, masking the bright intensity blazing out of his other eye. When he saw Logan, his one eye widened and then he looked away, as if ashamed.

Or so Logan preferred to interpret it.

All the things he had rehearsed on the way here, all the things he was going to say, fled in the sight of Frank's incapacitated state. This man was not an enemy to be subdued.

But he had come to talk to Frank and talk he did, going where his thoughts and heart led him. He wondered how much Sarah had overheard. Wondered what she thought.

"I'm going to get a coffee," he said to Sarah as she settled into the chair beside her father. He wanted to give her some time with him alone.

"No. Please. Don't go," she said, catching his hand. Her eyes, eyes that shone with love, caught and held his and he couldn't say no.

"Okay." He gave her a smile as he knelt down beside her, his one hand on her back for support, his other holding hers.

Sarah turned back to her father.

"Do you know why I haven't visited you?"

He nodded. "Dan told," he said.

"When you told me you forgave me for Marilee, I didn't know what to think, Dad," she said. "I may as well be honest, I was angry. And I was hurt. I didn't think I had done anything that needed forgiving."

"No…I…was wrong."

Watching Frank struggle to formulate even these simple words created pity for this man. He had so little now.

"I know I can't judge you, Dad," Sarah was saying, "but I was so hurt by what you said. That's why I stayed away." She glanced at Logan over her shoulder, gave him a tremulous smile, then turned back to her father.

"I was going to tell you that I forgive you for what you did to me, but that I couldn't pardon what you did to Logan's family until I heard him forgiving you.

And I know I've been wrong in staying away, but I needed to figure out who I was apart from you." She turned to Logan, granting him a gentle smile. "And Logan and I spent time together, finding out where we fit in each other's lives. And I think I know that now."

Logan squeezed her hand, returning her smile.

She turned back to her father who was watching them with a look of futility. "But I want you to know that I forgive you, Dad. I forgive you for what you did to me then and what you did to me now." She squeezed Logan's hand. Hard. "I was young and I cared too much what you thought those many years ago when you told me to break up with Logan. I should have had the courage to stand up to you, but I didn't. Thank goodness Logan and I found each other again."

Frank's good hand opened and closed. "Sorry," he whispered. "I'm sorry."

Then he looked at Logan. "Thought lots. Nothing else to do." The time it took Frank to work his mouth around these words lent a weight to them. "Please. For your father. Forgive. For Sarah. Forgive."

Logan looked into Frank's eyes, held his gaze, his own unwavering. But all he could see in Frank's expression was brokenness and sorrow.

And suddenly, the feeling of forgiveness he didn't think he could muster flowed through him like a refreshing stream, washing away the residue of anger and resentment.

Logan was realistic enough to know that when he was away from Frank, away from the brokenness on his face and the sorrow in his expression some of his feelings might return.

Logan had much to be forgiven for, as well.

And Sarah, dear, precious, loving Sarah had forgiven her father for what he had done to her. Surely he could do no less himself. God required no less.

"I forgive you, Frank." He spoke the words slowly and quietly, giving them weight. "I forgive you because Christ has forgiven me."

And as he repeated those precious and, yes, holy words, which he knew would help release Frank from his pain, Logan felt as if God's hand of grace and mercy brushed over him.

Sarah sniffed lightly and as she pulled a tissue from a box beside the bed, her father's Bible fell down.

Logan bent over and picked it up.

"Shall I read a piece?" he asked as he opened it.

Sarah and Frank nodded.

Logan found a Psalm of praise and thanksgiving. And as he read the words, he once again felt God's presence in this room.

When he was done, Sarah wiped her eyes, then slowly got to her feet. She stood in front of her father, hovering. Then she reached out, gently wrapped her arms around her father's shoulders and held him for a few, precious seconds. Frank pressed his good hand against Sarah's back and Logan caught the shimmer of tears tracking down his cheeks.

Poor, poor man, he thought as Sarah drew away. What you have missed out on in this precious woman's life.

He pulled himself back from a moment of pity for himself and Sarah. For what they had missed of each other's last years.

They were together now, he thought. Maybe they had needed this time apart to complete whatever journey God had in mind for them. But God had brought them together now.

And now was all that mattered.

Logan stood, as well, and cleared his throat, suddenly nervous. "Frank, I have something to ask you." He waited, then amended that. "No, actually, I have something to tell you."

He took Sarah's hand, lifted it to his mouth and brushed a kiss over her knuckles, smiling down into his beloved Sarah's eyes. "I want to marry your daughter. If she'll have me."

Frank looked from Sarah to Logan and what looked to Logan like resignation flitted across his face. But then he nodded and raised his hand as if in blessing.

Sarah turned to Logan, flung her arms around his neck and pulled him close.

"My answer is yes," she said, hope, peace and triumph ringing in her voice. "My answer, Logan Carleton, is yes."

* * *

"You know, this is the first time in six years I've looked forward to Christmas," Sarah said quietly as she let herself into the house.

Logan thought of the gift he had in his pocket. A gift that had sat in a corner of his dresser for six years. Taking it today had put him through agonies of indecision. He didn't want to presume on a relationship that had uncertainty hovering around the edges. But he wanted to show her that she mattered to him.

He'd bought it when he was so sure that he had found his soul mate and that they would be together forever. He was now older and wiser about love, but he still held remnants of that old hope in his heart.

Sarah turned to him. "So do you want some coffee? Or hot chocolate?"

"Just you," he said, with a contented smile.

Then he turned serious and drew her close. "How are you doing?"

Sarah melted into his arms, leaning into his embrace. She sighed as if she was releasing all the tension of the day.

"It was hard, but it was good. I feel like I've turned a page in my life again." She pulled back. "How about you? You've had a lot to deal with, too."

"I'll admit it's been a rough day. But what my mother made me read helped. I have no right to withhold forgiveness when I've been forgiven for so much more." He looked down at her, his dark eyes glimmering with intensity. "But what bugged me the most, what had me running absolutely scared was the thought that we weren't an 'us' anymore. Now that I know that's not true, everything else seems pretty inconsequential."

His deep voice rang with a conviction that created an answering tremble in Sarah's heart.

"I'm glad we're still 'us,' too," she said quietly.

He kissed her again, then pulled back. "So, still no Christmas decorations in this place?"

Sarah shook her head. "No energy and no desire to put them up."

"Do you have any of that stuff?" Logan asked.

"In the attic, though Marilee was always the one to do the decorating." Another little hitch to her heart, though a gentle one this time. "She had a better eye for that."

"I'll help you put some up."

"But it's late and you have to work tomorrow," Sarah protested. He couldn't be serious.

"Hey, I have a guaranteed contract with Westerveld Construction, so I'm on easy street." He gave her hand a gentle tug. "I'm kidding, but I want to bring some Yuletide cheer into this home."

"In the attic. But I'm not kidding—it's not worth it. It's only me in the house."

Logan caught her by the arms and gave her a little shake of reprimand. "You're worth a bit of Christmas cheer. It depresses me to think of you coming home to this place and there's not one single candle or twinkly thing."

"That's not very guyish of you to admit."

He held up a warning hand. "Don't tell my brother. Now, let's get that Christmas stuff up and plugged in."

An hour later the lights in the artificial Christmas tree twinkled from one corner of the living room. The Christmas village was set up and Logan was haphazardly weaving garland up the banister of the staircase.

Marilee would have laughed, Sarah thought, watching Logan struggling with the fake garland. Every now and then he would sigh, looking down at Sarah following him, weaving lights through the boughs. Whenever she offered to help, he turned her down. "This is not rocket science," he grumbled, unkinking the strands that had sat twisted too long in the attic.

Finally they were done, and in spite of her initial protests, Sarah had to admit that the lights, the decorations and the tree all heightened a sense of anticipation and nostalgia that were the hallmarks of any Yuletide season.

She could enjoy coming home to this, she thought with a smile as she swept up the bits of garland that had come loose.

Logan took the broom from her and set it aside. "Come over here," Logan said, pulling Sarah out of the foyer into the living room.

"Why?"

Logan pointed up at the mistletoe he had pinned above the entrance.

"That's rather cheesy, don't you think?" Sarah said.

Logan shrugged. "But traditional." He drew her into his arms and his chest lifted in a sigh. "And here we are. In your house. And I've got you in my arms. I think I like this setup."

"I think I like it, too." She slipped her arms around him, holding him tight.

He looked down into her eyes, his expression growing serious. "You know I love you."

"I'm getting that." She gave him a joyful smile. "I love you too."

"Sarah…will you marry me?"

Her breath slipped out of her so that all she could do was nod her acceptance.

Logan reached into his pocket and pulled out a small box. "I took a chance and picked this out myself." He flicked the box open and in the overhead lights, the single diamond winked back at her like the most glorious promise.

"It's beautiful, Logan."

He slipped the ring on her finger and held her hand up, a smile teasing the corners of his mouth. "Fits just right," he said, turning her hand this way and that, the ring shooting out sparkles of light.

"Feels just right." As Sarah looked down at the ring, a sense of wonderment flooded her. "Is this real, Logan? Is this really happening to us?"

"Better be," he said. "We've waited long enough."

"Too long," she agreed.

"We'll have to make some decisions. About where we're going to live."

"Later," she whispered, unwilling to let thoughts of this house, her father, his mother and the myriad of people involved in their lives intrude on the moment. "We'll talk about that later."

He smiled his agreement and pulled her close.

Then when he bent to kiss her, the empty years slipped away into memory and forgetting.

She was here. With Logan.

And for the first time in months she felt as if she had finally come home.

* * * * *

Dear Reader,

Our relationship with our parents is our first and, probably, most defining one. I've been thankful to have loving parents who have nurtured me in my faith. In this story, however, I wanted to examine this relationship from the point of view of a woman who didn't have the same relationship I had.

Sarah has tried most of her life to please the wrong father. In the end she learns, thanks to a man who has always loved her, to see her father through other eyes.

Her discoveries lead her to reexamine her relationship with Frank Westerveld and learn, first of all, that God is her perfect Father, who cares for her more than any earthly father can. And then, she has to learn an even harder lesson: how to forgive this imperfect man, just as God has forgiven imperfect us.

I think there are many people who don't have good relationships with their fathers, many people whose fathers have disappointed them. I just want to assure you that God's love is perfect and unfailing. May you find comfort in Him.

I like to hear from my readers. Send me a letter at caarsen@xplornet.com. Or check out my website at www.carolyneaarsen.com.

Carolyne Aarsen

QUESTIONS FOR DISCUSSION

1. What do you think were some of the factors contributing to Sarah's estrangement from her father?

2. What lesson did she learn that enabled her to deal with this estrangement? How did her distance from her father hinder her growth as a person and as a Christian?

3. What is your opinion on Sarah's reasons for staying away from her hometown and her father? Were they legitimate?

4. Could she have done things differently? How could her attitude have been different?

5. Sarah's sister, Marilee, was a favorite child. Do you think parents who favor certain children over others even recognize they're doing so? Why would a parent favor one child over another?

6. In the book Sarah is faced with the idea that all her life she has been trying to please the wrong father (i.e. her earthly father as opposed to her heavenly Father). What is your opinion of this statement? Do you find yourself trying to please

other people first? How does this affect your relationship with God?

7. What part of Sarah's life could you most identify with?

8. Logan had dreams for his brother. How did Logan's dreams and plans for Billy affect his relationship with the people of Riverbend? How did they affect his relationship with Billy himself?

9. What did it take for Logan to switch his attitude toward Riverbend and toward Sarah's father? Why did this change occur when it did?

10. Forgiveness is a strong theme in this book. Think of a person you are having difficulty forgiving. What are some of the things from the past that prevent your forgiveness? Can we forgive before we are asked to forgive by the person who has hurt us? Why or why not?

Linda Goodnight

brings you a tale of a cowboy you can trust.

Rancher Austin Blackwell sees Annalisa Keller as a wounded person with too many secrets. This town is the perfect place for her to start over—just as it was for him. Trying to keep his own past hidden, Austin finds himself falling for Annalisa, whose warmth and love of life works its way into his heart…and promises never to leave.

Rancher's Refuge

Where every prayer is answered….

Available December 2012, wherever books are sold.

www.LoveInspiredBooks.com

LI87787

REQUEST YOUR FREE BOOKS!

2 FREE INSPIRATIONAL NOVELS
PLUS 2
FREE
MYSTERY GIFTS

Love Inspired®
SUSPENSE
RIVETING INSPIRATIONAL ROMANCE

Police detective Austin Black assures desperate single mother Eva Billows that he'll find her son, who went missing from his bedroom in the middle of the night. With his search-and-rescue bloodhound, Justice, Austin searches every inch of Sagebrush, Texas. And when Eva insists on helping, Austin can't turn her away. Eva trusts no one, especially police, but this time, Austin—and Justice—won't let her down.

TEXAS K-9 UNIT

TRACKING JUSTICE

by

SHIRLEE MCCOY

Available January 2013 wherever books are sold.

www.LoveInspiredBooks.com

LIS44520

Brave police officers tackle crime with the help of their canine partners in TEXAS K-9 UNIT, *an exciting new series from Love Inspired® Suspense.*

Read on for a preview of the first book,
TRACKING JUSTICE by Shirlee McCoy.

Police detective Austin Black glanced at his dashboard clock as he raced up Oak Drive. Two in the morning. Not a good time to get a call about a missing child.

Then again, there was never a good time for that; never a good time to look in the worried eyes of a parent or to follow a scent trail and know that it might lead to a joyful reunion or a sorrowful goodbye.

If it led anywhere.

Sometimes trails went cold, scents were lost and the missing were never found. Austin wanted to bring them all home safe. Hopefully, this time, he would.

He pulled into the driveway of a small house.

Justice whined. A three-year-old bloodhound, he was trained in search and rescue and knew when it was time to work.

Austin jumped out of the vehicle when a woman darted out the front door. "You called about a missing child?"

"Yes. My son. I heard Brady call for me, and when I walked into his room, he was gone." She ran back up the porch stairs.

Austin jogged in after her. She waved from a doorway. "This is my son's room."

Austin followed her into the room. "How old is your son, Ms….?"

"Billows. Eva. He's seven."

"Did you argue?"

"We didn't argue about anything, Officer…"

"Detective Austin Black. I'm with Sagebrush Police Department's Special Operation K-9 Unit."

"You have a search dog with you?" Her face brightened. "I can give you something of his. A shirt or—"

"Hold on. I need to get a little more information first."

"How about you start out there?" She gestured to the window.

"Was it open when you came in the room?"

"Yes. It looks like someone carried Brady out the window. But I don't know how anyone could have gotten into his room when all the doors and windows were locked."

"You're sure?"

"Of course." She frowned. "I always double-check. I have ever since…"

"What?"

"Nothing that matters. I just need to find my son."

Hiding something?

"Everything matters when a child is missing, Eva."

To see Justice the bloodhound in action, pick up
TRACKING JUSTICE by Shirlee McCoy.
Available January 2013 from Love Inspired® Suspense.

SHLISEXP1212

Love Inspired®
SUSPENSE
RIVETING INSPIRATIONAL ROMANCE

TEXAS K-9 UNIT

Lawmen that solve the toughest cases with the help of their brave canine partners.

Follow Lone Star State police officers and their canine partners in action each month as they get closer to not only uncovering a mastermind criminal but also finding love.

TRACKING JUSTICE by Shirlee McCoy
January 2013

DETECTION MISSION by Margaret Daley
February 2013

GUARD DUTY by Sharon Dunn
March 2013

EXPLOSIVE SECRETS by Valerie Hansen
April 2013

SCENT OF DANGER by Terri Reed
May 2013

LONE STAR PROTECTOR by Lenora Worth
June 2013

Available wherever books are sold.

www.LoveInspiredBooks.com

LISCONT13